"LIEUTENANT BAK! COME QUICKLY! A MAN'S BEEN FOUND DEAD!"

"Baket-Amon." Bak stared, dismayed at the body stuffed into a storage area under the stairway that led to the roof. He had not yet seen the face, but no one could mistake that large, heavy form for anyone other than the prince.

"I fear so, sir." Psuro, a thickset Medjay with a face scarred by childhood disease, looked stricken. He had been in charge of the men guarding the house through the night. Bak would not have been surprised if the Inspector of the Fortresses of Wawat had been slain, but Baket-Amon? He had asked the prince to speak with Amonked and he had refused. Now here he was in Amonked's house and he was dead.

Had that plea for help brought about his death?

Other Mysteries of Ancient Egypt by
Lauren Haney
from Avon Books

THE RIGHT HAND OF AMON
A FACE TURNED BACKWARD
A VILE JUSTICE

LAUREN HANEY

A CURSE OF SILENCE

A MYSTERY OF ANCIENT EGYPT

AVON BOOKS
An Imprint of HarperCollinsPublishers

This is a work of fiction. Names, characters, places, and incidents are products of the author's imagination or are used fictitiously and are not to be construed as real. Any resemblance to actual events, locales, organizations, or persons, living or dead, is entirely coincidental.

AVON BOOKS
An Imprint of HarperCollins*Publishers*
10 East 53rd Street
New York, New York 10022-5299

Copyright © 2000 by Betty J. Winkelman
ISBN: 0-380-81285-1
www.avonbooks.com

First Avon Books paperback printing: October 2000

Avon Trademark Reg. U.S. Pat. Off. and in Other Countries, Marca Registrada, Hecho en U.S.A.
HarperCollins® is a trademark of HarperCollins Publishers Inc.

Printed in the U.S.A.

WCD   10 9 8 7 6 5 4 3 2 1

Acknowledgments

First and foremost, I wish to thank Dennis Forbes, whose generosity with his time, knowledge, and library knows no bounds. I also thank Tavo Serina for critiquing the manuscript and for making suggestions in his usual common-sense manner.

I also wish to thank those Egyptologists who've documented their work in sufficient detail to help me recreate ancient Egypt on the pages of this novel. Not a day went by that I didn't search for information, and I usually found what I sought. Though too numerous to name, they all have my gratitude.

Last, but certainly not least, I wish to thank my agent, Nancy Yost, and my editor, Lyssa Keusch, for all the effort they've made on my behalf.

CAST OF CHARACTERS

At the Fortress of Buhen

Lieutenant Bak	Egyptian officer in charge of a company of Medjay police
Sergeant Imsiba	Bak's second-in-command, a Medjay
Sergeant Pashenuro	Another Medjay, next in line after Imsiba
Commandant Thuty	Officer in charge of the garrison of Buhen
Troop Captain Nebwa	Thuty's second-in-command
Sergeant Dedu	Pashenuro's counterpart in the army
Hori	Youthful police scribe
Nofery	Proprietress of a house of pleasure in Buhen, serves as Bak's spy

Those who have come from the capital city of Waset

Amonked	Storekeeper of Amon, inspector of the fortresses of Wawat, the queen's cousin

Nefret	Amonked's lovely young concubine
Lieutenant Horhotep	Amonked's military adviser
Sennefer	Amonked's wife's brother, a wealthy nobleman
Captain Minkheper	High-ranking naval officer on special assignment for the queen
Lieutenant Merymose	Officer in charge of Amonked's guards
Sergeant Roy	Merymose's second-in-command
Thaneny	Amonked's scribe
Pawah	Amonked's youthful herald
Mesutu	Nefret's maid

Others of greater or lesser importance to the journey up-river

Baket-Amon	A prince of Wawat
Seshu	The caravan master
Hor-pen-Deshret	A powerful leader of desert tribesmen
Menu	A wealthy playboy in Waset
Thutnofer	Proprietor of a house of pleasure in Waset
Meretre	A lovely young girl in Waset
Commander Woser	Commander of the garrison of Iken
Lieutenant Ahmose	Commander of the garrison of Askut
Rona	A village headman near Askut

Plus various and sundry soldiers, guards, farmers, and townspeople.

Those who walk the corridors of power of Kemet

Maatkare Hatshepsut	Sovereign of the land of Kemet
Menkheperre Thutmose	The queen's nephew and stepson, ostensibly shares the throne with his aunt

The Gods and Goddesses

Amon	The primary god during much of ancient Egyptian history, especially the early 18th Dynasty, the time of this story; takes the form of a human being
Horus of Buhen	A local version of the falcon god Horus
Maat	Goddess of truth and order, represented by a feather
Hathor	Goddess of love, often represented as a cow
Hapi	Personification of the Nile
Osiris	God of the netherworld, depicted as a man swathed in bandages like a mummy
Re	The sun god
Khepre	The rising sun
Set	An ambivalent god generally representing violence, a mythical creature usually shown with the body of a man and a dog-like head
Thoth	Patron god of scribes
Khonsu	The moon god
Dedun	A god of Kush

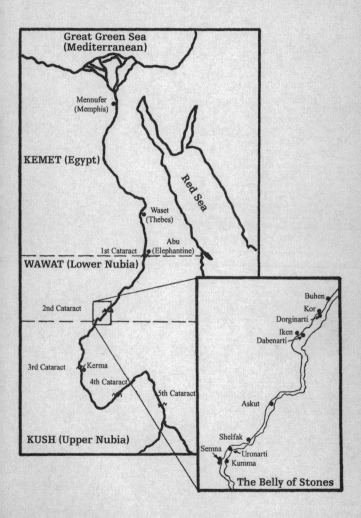

Great Green Sea
(Mediterranean)

Mennufer
(Memphis)

KEMET (Egypt)

Red Sea

Waset
(Thebes)

Abu
(Elephantine)

1st Cataract

WAWAT (Lower Nubia)

2nd Cataract

Buhen
Kor
Dorginarti
Iken
Dabenarti

3rd Cataract   Kerma

4th Cataract

5th Cataract

Askut

KUSH (Upper Nubia)

Shelfak

Semna   Uronarti
Kumma

The Belly of Stones

Chapter One

"The next one's yours, my friend." Sergeant Imsiba ducked around a pair of dressed geese hanging by their feet from the frame of a spindly lean-to. "Less than half the morning gone and already I've seen enough men dancing around the truth for one day."

Lieutenant Bak, officer in charge of the Medjay police at the fortress of Buhen, grinned at the tall, dark, heavy-muscled man walking by his side, his stride smooth, leonine. "You're much too generous, Sergeant."

"I doubt that wretch thinks so." Imsiba pointed toward a short, wiry man being hustled along a sandy path by two spearmen, one on each arm, heading toward the citadel gate. "Did you see the way he added weight to the balance each time he rested his hand on the upright?" The big Medjay shook his head in disbelief. "You'd think we'd have seen everything by this time, but the trick was new to me."

"Another lesson learned, another triumph for the lady Maat." Maat was the goddess of right and order.

Imsiba smiled at the pomposity, a mimicking of a scribe neither man especially liked.

Bak stepped aside, letting two young women pass by. They giggled, flustered at the small courtesy paid by this man who was slightly taller than average, with broad shoulders and strong limbs, carrying a baton of office. Running his fingers through his short-cropped dark hair, unaware of

1

the stir he had caused in their breasts, he said, "Commandant Thuty will see he cheats no one else for many years to come."

A grim smile played across Imsiba's face. The commandant of Buhen was not a man to be toyed with. His judgments were firm, the punishments he meted out seldom forgotten by those who erred.

The two men strolled on, following a casual path between lean-tos set up in irregular rows to shade sellers, buyers, and trade goods offered in the twice-weekly market located on an empty stretch of sand between Buhen's outer wall and the citadel. They veered around men, women, children, and animals; stepped over discarded garbage and manure piles, and tried not to bump the slender posts that supported the frail shelters. All the while, their eyes darted hither and yon, searching for a furtive look or action that hinted at a dishonest trading practice. A nod here, a good-humored smile there, a wave and a shout of greeting accompanied them along the way, easing a task thankless but necessary, one they performed periodically.

Though this was the coolest time of the year, the day was unseasonably warm. The sun beat down, wrapping them in heat, sealing them in a thin layer of sweat. A light, sporadic northerly breeze sent dust devils racing along the paths. The smells of commerce rose around them: spices, fish, livestock, fresh-cut wood, braised meat, manure, onions, unwashed bodies, perfume. Voices ebbed and flowed, donkeys brayed in distant paddocks, and dogs barked constantly.

"Lieutenant Bak!" Raising his weapon, waving the bronze point above his head to catch the sun and attract attention, a husky spearman wove a hurried path toward them. "Sir!"

Bak and Imsiba quickened their pace to meet him. "What's the problem?" Bak demanded. He recognized the man as a member of the ten-man company of soldiers assigned to maintain peace in the market.

"A rumor, sir. At least I hope that's all it is." They were probably of a like age—twenty-five years—but the spearman responded to the officer with the respect he would show an older, senior man. "A tale sweeping through the market even now. One I pray you can put to rest."

Rumors flew up and down the river faster than the swiftest wind, growing in detail as a sandstorm builds while sweeping across the desert. Bak would have smiled, but the worry he saw on the soldier's face warned him not to take this tale too lightly. "Tell me what you've heard."

"They say the army is going to be torn from Buhen, from all the fortresses along the southern frontier. They say we'll have to return to Kemet. That those who wish to stay in this land of Wawat—and there are many of us—will be men alone, abandoned by our sovereign and our homeland." The spearman's voice shook with emotion. "Sir, I took as my wife a woman of this land. How can I tear her and our children from their home, their many relatives, their village? I can't! I just can't!"

"We've heard no such rumor." Imsiba, Bak noticed, looked as concerned by the tale as he was—and as skeptical. The very idea was unthinkable.

Commandant Thuty would have been the first to hear and pass on news of such import. Thuty had said nothing; therefore, the rumor must be just that: a rumor. A tale that must be laid to rest before everyone along the river, military and civilian, grew worried and afraid. The army consumed not only grain shipped from Kemet, but large quantities of produce grown and supplied by farmers who dwelt along the river. Without the army, the farmers would not only be vulnerable to raiding desert tribesmen, but they would have no ready market for their crops. Their farms would decline, the land would die.

But oft times even the most outrageous of rumors carried a grain of truth. "I doubt the tale is true," Bak reassured, "but I'll look into the matter before nightfall."

*   *   *

"He's trying to cheat me, sir!" The thin, dark man, whose knee-length kilt made of soft cowhide, dyed red and worn shiny from use, identified him as a man of the southern desert, glared at the pudgy trader seated on the sand in front of him.

The trader sniffed his indignation. "He errs, Lieutenant. Have you ever known me not to give fair measure?"

Bak, who had never before seen the trader, walked among a dozen or so long-haired white goats milling around the tribesman. A yellow dog held them close, nipping the flank of any who dared stray. Ignoring the fine, soft hair brushing his bare legs, Bak placed his hands on his hips and eyed the objects spread out in front of the trader: a basket filled with stone beads and amulets, a dozen sacks open at the top to show the grain inside, fifteen or so baked clay jars of beer and honey and oil, and a stack of hides stinking of the acrid solution in which they had been tanned. Beads of all colors, strung to make them more desirable and coiled for maximum effect, and seven stone amulets on braided cords lay on a strip of white cloth. Nothing out of the ordinary; an indifferent offering at best.

"I can count as well as the next man," the tribesman said, "and I know what's right and what's not."

"You people are all alike." The trader raised his chin high and looked scornfully at his accuser. "You come off the desert, bringing the most pathetic of your animals, and expect to get in exchange half the wealth of the land of Kemet."

The tribesman's eyes flashed anger. "He tried to give me five jars of oil, lieutenant, not the six he promised. The rock crystal amulet is cracked, and none of the bead necklaces look as long as he claims they are. I'd bet my only daughter that the wheat has been weighted with stones."

The trader scooped the bright necklaces off the cloth, flung them into the basket of beads, and sprang to his feet. "Look at those creatures!" he said, sweeping his arm in an arc over the goats. "They're as poor and lean as the ears of grain in a dessicated field, unfit for slaughter for at least two months."

The abrupt removal of the strung beads told Bak they would not stand up to close examination. Nor, he suspected, would the trader's other wares. Smothering a sigh, he glanced up at the lord Re, a yellow orb in a pallid sky. Barely midday with at least an hour before buyers and sellers began to drift away. He prayed to the lord Amon for sufficient patience. He wanted very much to speak with Commandant Thuty, to set his heart at rest about the rumor he had heard time and time again since talking to the spearman.

Wiping the sweat from his brow, rubbing his hand on his damp kilt, he knelt among the goats. He caught the nearest, whose alarmed bleat frightened the rest and set them to flight. With short, sharp barks, the dog turned them back. Bak ran his hands over the captive animal's back, stomach, legs. The hair was as soft and curly as that of a nobleman's pampered concubine. Freeing the animal, he went on to the next and a third.

"They could use some fattening," he said, "but are otherwise in good condition."

"You see!" The trader swung toward the tribesman, his expression gleeful. "They're not worth full price. As I told you."

The tribesman flashed Bak a look of frustration and disillusionment. He obviously believed that, as so often happened, a man of authority had here again taken the side of the man with the smoother tongue.

Muttering an oath at the nomad's unfounded fear, Bak rose to his feet. With a quick step forward, he lifted the strings of beads from the basket. The trader sucked in his breath, reached out to grab, pulled back at the last moment. Bak held up the bright lengths of color and measured them against his arm. No two strings were the same length and all were shorter than they should be. Picking up the amulets suspended from cords, he examined each in turn. The rock crystal was cracked, as the tribesman had said. The others were poorly carved and inferior, the stones more often than not faulted.

Flinging beads and amulets into the basket, Bak knelt before a bag of wheat. The trader muttered an obscenity. Bak dug his fingers deep into the bag and fished out a pebble the size of a radish. Exploring further, he retrieved a half-dozen similar stones and two roughly the size of duck eggs. A goat came close, nudging his elbow, inching toward the open bag and the grain inside. The trader stood tight-lipped, plainly aware that no excuse would serve. The tribesman looked torn, his satisfaction at being proven right mingled with mistrust of the outcome.

Bak stood up, having seen enough, and motioned the nomad to remove his goat before it could eat any of the wheat, altering the weight and thus destroying the evidence. He waved an arm to catch the eye of the sergeant in charge of the ten-man patrol. The soldier came running, two spearmen close on his heels.

"Take this man and his trade goods to the guardhouse. Have my scribe Hori inventory everything, making special note of the weighted bags of grain, inconsistent lengths of beads, and whatever else he finds amiss. I'd not be surprised if the beer is diluted, and he'll probably find pebbles in the honey and oil."

"Lieutenant." The trader sidled close to Bak and lowered his voice. "I enjoy my freedom, sir, as you enjoy yours. There must be something I can do for you, or some object I can give you that you'd not ordinarily get for yourself. Something of value, something worthy of a man of good taste, a man willing to overlook one small mistake."

The tribesman edged closer, suspicious, trying to eavesdrop.

"Small mistake?" Bak asked, accenting the word *small*.

The trader failed to notice the dangerous glint in the officer's eye. "I've a servant, a pretty thing of fourteen years.

She's no longer pure and chaste, but the better for it. A gift well worth accepting."

"Are you offering me a bribe, sir?"

The trader paled. "No! No, sir. You misunderstand me, sir."

"Take him away," Bak said.

With the indifference of a man who had repeated the task many times, the sergeant ordered his men to collect the objects spread out on the sand while he clamped his prisoner's arms together with wooden manacles and led him away.

The tribesman watched, dumbfounded.

Bak laid a hand on his shoulder. "He'll not cheat you or any other man for many months to come—if ever again."

The man, made shy by the kindness, stared at the animals milling around his legs. "I could not sacrifice my goats for items so shoddy. They're like children to me and my woman, brothers and sisters to our boy and girl."

"Most men who trade at this market are honest, many of them farmers who give value for value." Bak knelt among the goats and scratched several eager heads. "Has no one ever told you that the value of these animals is in their fine hair, not their meat?"

"I sometimes trade the yarn my wife spins from their hair, and I know its worth. But to live, we must eat their flesh as well as take their milk and their warm coats."

Bak rose to his feet. The goats pressed close against his legs, trusting, innocent. As tame and gentle as household pets. He glanced around the market, his eyes darting from one lean-to to another, seeking a farmer who often came to sell his produce. At last he found, seated in the shade beneath a woven reed roof, surrounded by fruits and vegetables, the large sturdy body of Netermose, a warm-hearted and considerate man who loved his land and animals above all things.

"I know a man, a farmer who'd value these goats more alive than dead. Let me take you to him."

*   *   *

"Hor-pen-Deshret." The caravan master Seshu made the name sound like a curse. "They say the swine has come back."

Troop Captain Nebwa scowled. "He wouldn't dare."

"Who?" Bak, standing at the edge of the market, tore his eyes from the fluctuating stream of people walking toward the citadel gate, hastening home with produce, live animals, and innumerable other necessities of life.

"Hor-pen-Deshret." Nebwa spat on the ground in a show of contempt. "Self-styled Horus of the Desert."

The tall, bulky officer, a coarse-featured man in his early thirties with unruly hair that always needed cutting, was Commandant Thuty's second-in-command. Having come from the practice field outside the walls of Buhen, where he had been overseeing the training of new recruits, he was covered with dust streaked and mottled by sweat.

"The wiliest and most ferocious of all tribesmen," Seshu said. "A man who knows no fear."

Nebwa's scorn was evident. "For years he dreamed of ruling this segment of the river, making himself rich by collecting tolls from all who pass through."

The caravan master nodded. "A dream he's never lost, so they say."

Seshu was of medium height with the rangy muscles and sun-darkened skin of one who had spent many of his forty years marching beneath the sun. His eyes were sharp and quick, his cheekbones prominent, his nose aquiline, testifying to ancestors who trod the sands of the eastern desert.

Bak, who vaguely recalled hearing of Hor-pen-Deshret, stepped into the thinning stream of people. With Nebwa and Seshu on either side, he strode toward the citadel gate and the commandant's residence. Compared to the rumor that the army might be leaving the frontier, the return of a desert bandit seemed of minor significance.

"He and his followers raided caravans, farms, villages, even small units of troops when he deemed the risk worth the gain," Nebwa explained. "They made off with food, animals, women, weapons—anything they could lay their hands on. All who dwelt along the river feared him. Finally, five or six years ago—long before you came to Buhen, Bak—Thuty's predecessor, Commandant Nakht, had all he could take of the miserable snake. He took out a company of troops to destroy him, personally leading the column, with me at his side. We never managed to lay hands on the wretch, but we slew many of his followers and chased him far into the desert. I've not heard of him for several years and thought never to see him again."

"I dared hope he'd died." Seshu, his face rueful, stopped at an intersecting path that would take him to the animal paddocks. "It seems the gods have chosen not to bless us."

"I don't believe it!" Nebwa's voice was hard, his expression resolute, the troop captain at his most stubborn. "He wouldn't have the nerve to come back."

Flinging a skeptical look Bak's way, Seshu turned around and walked up the path.

A spate of laughter drew Bak's eyes to a party of soldiers cleaning windblown sand out of the sunken road which abutted the terrace that ran along the base of the citadel wall. He did not envy them. The sun beat full-force on the tall towered wall, which rose stark white above the desert sand, catching the heat and holding it close, turning the deep-set road into an oven. High above, a sentry patrolling the battlements walked out onto a projecting tower to look down upon the rapidly emptying market.

"Whether true or not," he said, "we must tell Commandant Thuty of the rumor, along with the tale that the army's to be torn from Wawat. And we must go now, before he hears from another source."

"He won't thank us for passing on such nonsense."

"Nor will he thank us if we tell him nothing and the rumor gets out of hand."

"Lieutenant Bak! Sir!"

Bak's eyes darted forward to where his scribe Hori was

trotting toward them along the path, dodging men and women laden with trade goods and a couple panting dogs too tired and hot to bark.

The pudgy youth of fifteen or so years swung in beside his superior officer. "Commandant Thuty has summoned you, sir. You and Troop Captain Nebwa."

"What now, I wonder?"

"The scribe who brought word to the guardhouse said a courier came from Ma'am, bringing a message from the viceroy." Hori licked beads of sweat off his upper lip. "Soon after, he heard the commandant yelling at mistresses Tiya and Meryet, ordering them to silence the children and keep them out of his way." Tiya was Thuty's wife and Meryet his concubine. The many small children of the household were always underfoot, usually ignored by their unabashedly tolerant father.

"Oh-oh," Nebwa murmured.

Bak muttered an oath. Thuty could be erratic at times, but he was basically a fair man. What could the viceroy's message have contained that would make him strike out at those closest to him?

"He's a mid-level bureaucrat! Storekeeper of Amon!" Commandant Thuty's voice pulsed with fury. "What can our sovereign be thinking? A man like that. One who doesn't know a thing about the army, probably doesn't know how to heft a spear or even march in step, and he's supposed to inspect the fortresses of Wawat!" Thuty raised a fist and smashed it down hard on the arm of his chair. "By the beard of Amon! What malign spirit has possessed her?"

Bak exchanged a quick look with Nebwa, standing beside him before the commandant. Normally lacking in tact, too honest and straightforward to exercise patience, Nebwa had for once been silenced, as unwilling to break in on the tirade as Bak was. Neither had seen fit to pass on the rumors they had heard in the market.

"Not even Inebny, the viceroy, the most powerful man in Wawat and Kush, can stop that wretched inspection. Do you know why?"

"No, sir," Bak and Nebwa chorused. The fact that Thuty had not thought to offer them seats or beer to quench their thirst was a measure of his anger.

Thuty bounded onto his feet and stalked across his private reception room to the open door. He was a short, powerful man, with thick dark brows and a strong chin thrust forward under a tight, angry mouth. The courtyard outside was as still as a tomb sealed for eternity. To attain such rare peace, Tiya and Meryet must have removed their children from the building.

"He's our sovereign's cousin!" Thuty spat out. "Cousin to Maatkare Hatshepsut herself. One who crawled the corridors of power as a babe and who's walked them ever since. One well-practiced in pleasing the most lofty of the land."

"I don't see the point, sir." Bak ran his thumb under the waistband of his kilt, trying to displace some of the grit collected there. He felt as dirty as Nebwa looked. "The viceroy inspects the fortresses on a regular basis. Why would she send another man to tread in his footsteps?"

"Doesn't she trust Inebny?" Nebwa asked.

Thuty gave the pair a surprised look, as if it had never occurred to him that in all his ranting and raving he might not have made himself clear. "Why aren't you two seated? Where's the beer I ordered for us?" He walked out into the courtyard and yelled for a servant to bring the beverage.

Nebwa winked at Bak, who returned a quick smile and glanced around the room in search of something to sit on. Weapons were stacked against the wall. Toys were scattered across the floor and on every chest, table, and stool. Beside Thuty's armchair, a basket overflowed with scrolls. He brushed the playing pieces for a game of senet into the drawer of a game table and set several child-sized bowls on top, freeing a stool for its proper use. Nebwa grabbed a portable camp stool in one hand and with the other scooped up from the floor a rag doll, a wooden pull toy, and several balls, and threw them into a basket. Practicing, Bak assumed, for the time when his baby son would reach an age to clutter.

Marching back to his chair, Thuty adjusted the thick, colorful pillow and dropped onto it. While the two younger men settled themselves before him, he rubbed his forehead, his eyes, the stubble on his chin. Not until the servant had come and gone and each man had sampled the thick, acrid brew in his jar did he begin to speak. He sounded tired, worn down by his outburst.

"Amonked, storekeeper of Amon, is this very instant on his way upriver, inspecting the fortresses of Wawat. According to Inebny—warned by several dependable sources in the royal house—our sovereign has dismissed as of no consequence our military actions against raiding tribesmen who covet what by right is ours. She wants to shut down most of the fortresses along the Belly of Stones and turn the rest into storehouses for trade goods traveling up and down the river. The army would be pared down to a few men. The bureaucrats would reign supreme."

So the rumor is true, Bak thought, appalled. No wonder Thuty is so upset.

As commandant of Buhen, the largest fully manned fortified city on the frontier, Thuty loosely administered the chain of ten fortresses strung farther south along the segment of river known as the Belly of Stones. This was a most rugged, desolate, and arid land, and the river was filled with rapids and small islands, making navigation impossible except at the highest flood stage. Even then, ships could only make the voyage with extreme difficulty and at great peril. Much of the year, trade goods were carried past the Belly of Stones on donkey caravans traveling the desert trail alongside the river. Troops were garrisoned in the area to protect and control traffic through this natural corridor, collect tribute and tolls, and conduct punitive military expeditions. None of these tasks was of sufficient importance to earn a man the gold of valor, but Bak had no doubt of their necessity.

"We've blinded the woman with our success," Nebwa growled. "If we'd ever lost a gold caravan or if one of her precious envoys had been carried off to the desert to stand as a hostage in exchange for riches, she'd not be so quick to dismiss us as useless."

"Does Menkheperre Thutmose know of this?" Bak asked. The young man of whom he spoke was Maatkare Hatshepsut's stepson and nephew, co-ruler in name only, the individual many people believed to be the sole rightful heir to the throne. While she resided in Waset surrounded by loyal advisers, the youth lived in the northern capital of Mennufer, where he had begun to rebuild an army that had languished from years of royal neglect.

"What difference would it make? You know how she is when she sets her heart on a goal." Thuty took a deep drink of beer, wiped his mouth with the back of his hand. "Amonked's well into his mission. He should reach Buhen in about a week."

"What can we do?" Bak asked in a grim voice.

"I plan to go upriver with the inspection party." Thuty formed a calculating smile. "I'll tell him how important the army is to this land and its people, and how important they are to us. How they thrive because we're here to protect them as well as the gold and ebony and precious stones so desired by the royal house. I'll . . ." He caught himself, gave a cynical snort. "I want each of you to assign a man to go with me. Both should be trustworthy and dependable, sergeants who can stand up for themselves should the need arise and not let a flock of self-important scribes browbeat them into submission."

"Sergeant Pashenuro," Bak said. "Other than Imsiba, he's the best Medjay I have."

Nebwa scratched his head, thinking. "Sergeant Dedu. He's been training new recruits and can use a break."

"I know them both and approve." Thuty threw an annoyed glance at the courtyard, beyond which could be heard the loud whispers of two women. "I've sent a courier up the Belly of Stones, warning the fortress commanders of Amonked's mission. I hated to give them the bad news so soon, but thought they should be prepared."

"Better now than after they hear the rumor going round," Bak said, and went on to explain, adding for good measure Seshu's tale of Hor-pen-Deshret's return.

Thuty was irritated, yet relieved his message had gone out when it had. The anger and resentment the courier would leave in his wake would in no way equal the resentment a rumor would rouse. As for Hor-pen-Deshret, Thuty paid small heed. He shared Bak's feeling: with potential disaster so near at hand, the news of one tribesman's return seemed of small import.

"You'll need more than two sergeants to guard Amonked's back," Nebwa said, stretching his legs in front of him and wiggling his filthy toes. "Maybe I'd better send along a company of spearmen."

Thuty scowled at a jest too close to the truth.

"How long will he remain in Buhen," Bak asked, "and what kind of protection will he need?"

"Not for long, I hope." Thuty tapped the arm of his chair, thinking. "While he's here, we'll quarter him and his party in the house Lieutenant Neferperet occupied before he and his family returned to Kemet. It's close enough to this residence that he can't complain and far enough away that they'll not be underfoot."

"The building's run-down," Nebwa said.

Thuty waved his hand, dismissing the objection. "I'll have it repaired, repainted, and refurnished. That should suffice. They can't expect the same luxury they have in the capital."

"Protection?" Bak reminded him.

"I want that house well-guarded, Lieutenant. By Medjays, not soldiers whose futures might lay in Amonked's hands." Thuty's voice turned as hard as granite. "I don't want him harmed while he's here by someone angered at his mission. Nor do I want any of his minions in trouble or causing trouble."

"Yes, sir." A new thought intruded. "Has he been told the river's too low to sail south beyond Kor? That he'll have to travel by donkey caravan between Kor and Semna?"

The old fortification of Kor was an hour's march upriver from Buhen. Located at the mouth of the Belly of Stones, it was used as a staging post, where trade goods were transferred from ships to donkey caravans for the long journey south around the rapids, and from donkeys to ships after the return trip.

"If he hasn't heard it from the men who sail these waters, the viceroy will see he knows." A burst of laughter, quickly stifled, drew Thuty's eyes toward the door. "He'll need a caravan master, troop captain. A man you'd trust with your life. As much as we dislike what he's come to do, his journey must go well, giving him no reason for complaint."

"Seshu," Nebwa said without hesitation. He glanced toward the door and the lengthening shadows visible in the courtyard. "He's in Buhen now. Shall I go get him, sir?"

"Yes, and quickly." Thuty's voice turned as dry as a field long untouched by floodwaters. "With luck, I can coerce him into taking on Amonked's caravan."

"I fed that boy Hori," Nofery grumbled. "Now I suppose you'll want me to fill your belly, too."

"A jar of beer will do." Bak followed the obese old woman out to the courtyard, where a slender dusky-skinned youth was lighting a torch to stave off the dark of night. "I ate at the barracks with my Medjays. Stewed fish—as usual."

"You heard him, Amonaya," she said to the boy. "Bring some beer, then get out your writing implements. Hori awaits you."

The youth made a face behind her back, letting Bak

know he did not appreciate the lessons the police scribe had agreed to give him. Lessons Nofery had insisted he take so he could, in the future, help her run her place of business, the largest house of pleasure in Buhen.

A loud curse drew Bak's eyes to an open doorway and the good-sized front room of the house. Inside, four men sat on the floor playing knucklebones, while a dozen more and two scantily clad young women stood in clusters around the room, beer jars in hand, talking in low, agitated voices. Wagers were made, the bones clattered across the floor, the winner raised his hands high and shouted his pleasure. Bak feared for his safety. Tempers had shortened as word of Amonked's mission spread.

Nofery shuffled across the court to an armless wooden chair positioned so she could see into the front room and her customers could see her. With a self-satisfied smile, she settled herself like royalty on the thick pillows padding the seat. The chair, which she had had shipped all the way from Waset, was new, a symbol of her prosperity.

Turning away to hide a fond smile, Bak sat on a mud-brick bench built against the wall. The cool breeze he had first noticed while bathing in the river at sunset had stiffened, rattling the dry palm fronds atop the lean-to that covered half the courtyard and making the leaves of a potted sycamore dance and rustle. A half-dozen large jars leaning against the rear wall gave off a strong odor of beer.

"The commandant's expecting a lofty visitor. Have you heard?"

"Who hasn't? Word spread through Buhen like chaff in the wind." She shifted her massive buttocks, grimaced. "A nobleman's coming to the Belly of Stones, they say, to conduct an inspection. To write the fortresses all off as useless, and us with them."

The tale had not yet lost touch with reality, Bak noted, but within a few days it would be exaggerated beyond recognition. By the time the inspection party arrived, Amonked would be the most despised man on the frontier. "You long ago dwelt in the capital, old woman. Did you know the one who's coming, this storekeeper of Amon?"

A young, almost grown lion padded out of the shadows to lay at her feet. As she reached down to scratch the creature's neck, Bak glimpsed a familiar look of calculation on her face. "If I'm to tell you anything of value, I must know his name."

"You haven't heard?" Bak asked, with exaggerated amazement. "What am I to do? Seek out a new spy, one whose business isn't so prosperous it distracts her from walking through this city, eyes and ears wide open?"

She clasped her hands before her breast and raised her eyes to the stars. "How many times have I prayed to the gods to free me from your attentions?" Her voice was as exaggerated as his had been.

He patted her fat knee, covered by the long white shift she wore. "Now admit it, old woman. You'd miss me and the tasks I set you."

"Like I'd miss a thorn in the sole of my foot." Her voice was gruff, but her eyes twinkled.

Laughing softly, Bak stretched out his legs and crossed them at the ankles. "The inspector is named Amonked. Cousin to our sovereign."

She stared at him, thinking thoughts he found impossible to read but suspected would cost him dearly. Suddenly she began to chuckle. "Storekeeper of Amon. Not much of a task, if you ask me. I'd have thought his unquestioning devotion worth far more than that to our sovereign."

"You never cease to amaze me," Bak admitted, laughing. "Did you know every man in the capital?"

"I knew *of* Amonked, that's all." She glanced at Amonaya coming through the door, carrying a basket filled with beer jars. The youth drew a low table close, set his burden on top, and hurried away. "He never came to the place of business where I toiled, nor did I ever see him when I was summoned elsewhere to entertain men of status or worth."

Bak reached for a jar, broke the dried mud plug that

sealed it, and handed the drink to her. She had once been young and beautiful, a courtesan who had counted princes among her customers, so he had been told by a man who had known her long ago. The years had stolen her good looks but not her memories, unpleasant for her but good fortune for him. Prying those memories from her oft times took more patience than the lord Amon himself possessed, but the knowledge she passed on was well worth the effort.

The knucklebones clattered, a man moaned, and Nebwa burst through the door. He grabbed a jar from the basket, broke the plug, and swung around to hand it to Seshu, close behind. Both men's hair was damp, betraying a recent dip in the river, and both wore spotless white thigh-length kilts similar to the garment Bak wore.

"Look at the two of them," Nebwa said, eyes darting from Bak to Nofery and back again. "As somber as a priest and a god's chantress."

Seshu walked up to Nofery, smiled, patted her cheek. "Nice chair, my dear. As the most delightful woman on the southern frontier, it befits you."

Bak choked on a laugh, and Nebwa looked uncertain how to react. To treat the old woman in so impudent a manner required either a strong friendship or uncommon courage. She guffawed, laughing so hard the tears flowed, and Seshu with her. The two officers joined in.

When the laughter died away, Bak asked Seshu, "Did you agree to lead Amonked's caravan?"

"I did." The caravan master found two stools and drew them close, offering one to Nebwa. "I can't say I like the swine's purpose. Without the army manning the garrisons along the Belly of Stones, the land of Kemet may as well surrender the whole of Wawat. But . . . well, I couldn't refuse the task. I know better than most the marauding tribes who make sporadic raids along the Belly of Stones—and there's the rumor about Hor-pen-Deshret."

"A tale as false as a ceremonial wig," Nebwa stated with conviction.

Ignoring a certitude he obviously did not share, Seshu said, "I'd never rest easy if I turned my back and let this caravan walk into trouble. Not only Amonked could be injured or slain, but many drovers as well."

"I've heard of no recent raids," Nofery said.

"There've been none." Seshu rested both hands on his knees, his beer jar between them. "The tribesmen have been quiet this year, staying well clear of the river, because water has been plentiful on the desert and food has been available for animals and men. From what I hear, none of the waterholes has dried up, and most of the oases are lush. But that doesn't mean they'll ignore temptation." He paused, drank from his jar, added, "I can't see a man of Amonked's status traveling with as few amenities as you and I would."

The four looked at one another, sobered by his words. They, like all who lived on the frontier, knew how fierce tribesmen could be when tempted by sufficient bounty. All three men had firsthand experience, having personally faced desert raiders in combat, while Nofery had seen caravans straggle into the fortress with most of the donkeys strayed or stolen and more men dead than alive.

Rather than belabor the point, Bak took a fresh beer for himself and passed replacements to the others. "Nofery was about to reveal her deepest, darkest secrets."

"Aha!" Seshu's brow cleared, his voice grew husky with false emotion. "Have you been holding out on me, my love?"

A smile flitted across her face. "We were speaking of Amonked as a youth. As I told Bak, I didn't know him. He was younger than I, and not one to spend time in houses of pleasure. Still, the world of the nobility is small, and I knew of him."

She reached down to pet the great tawny cat, making him purr. "Amonked was reputed to be a nice, good-natured boy, a favorite of Hatshepsut, then a princess. The king's first and most favored daughter, spoiled by both mother and father. He was her shadow, a child she could always depend upon to do her bidding." Nofery's expression darkened, her voice turned grim. "Unless he's changed, he'll see she gets her way even if he firmly believes the army should retain control of the Belly of Stones."

Chapter Two

"He surely doesn't expect to travel upriver with so many people! So many belongings!" Seshu stared, appalled, at the seven ships standing off Buhen, preparing to moor at two of the three stone quays reaching into the river. "Look at those decks!" he exclaimed, pointing down from the tall fortified wall on which he stood with Bak and Imsiba. "Each and every one piled high. Baskets and chests. Carrying chairs. Jars of all sizes . . ."

"Filled with fine wines and oils, no doubt," Imsiba said, wrinkling his nose in disapproval.

"He's brought along at least two women." Bak shaded his eyes with a hand, lessening the sun's glare on the water. "Do you see them? They're seated in the pavilion set against the deckhouse of the foremost traveling ship. The one with the red and white banners flying from the masthead."

"Commandant Thuty must stop this madness," Seshu said. "We haven't enough donkeys in the whole of Wawat to carry everything I see on those decks."

The caravan master was exaggerating, at least in part. The ships' crews would remain behind, and their nonperishable rations were undoubtedly a good portion of the cargo.

More than a week had passed since the commandant had first announced Amonked's inspection. Now Bak and his companions awaited their first look at the storekeeper of Amon and his inspection party. A cool northerly breeze blew across the battlements, alleviating the heat of the midmorning sun, bright and intense in a brilliant blue sky. A dog stood at the river's edge, barking at a turtle secure within its shell.

Except for three little boys tormenting a small brownish snake, the two stone terraces overlooking the harbor were empty of life. The residents of Buhen, men, women, and children who rarely missed the opportunity to watch the arrival of visiting dignitaries, had failed to appear. Instead of crowding the terraces and chattering with excitement, instead of raising their voices in greeting, they had refused to welcome the man they feared would destroy their way of life.

"Careful!" Bak murmured half to himself as a broad-beamed cargo ship swung across the strong midstream current, heading toward the upriver side of the southern quay.

The vessel rode low under a heavy load. The oarsmen toiled to the beat of a drum, rowing with an urgency visible from a distance. The helmsman yelled orders impossible to distinguish so far away, but the stridence of his voice betrayed a concern at docking so large a ship in unfamiliar waters. A large group of men, soldiers armed with spears and shields, stood on the deck, poised to abandon ship if need be.

The vessel neared the quay. The helmsman shouted new orders, the drummer altered the beat, and the oarsmen's pattern changed. The ship hit the pier with a solid thud and skidded alongside, fenders grinding between hull and stone. At least half the spearmen were flung to the deck. Sailors threw hawsers over mooring posts, pulling the vessel up short. The soldiers scrambled to their feet.

The lead vessel and another, both sleek traveling ships with bright-painted deckhouses and fore- and aftercastles, swung one after the other into the space between the southern and central quays, where oarsmen eased them close to their mooring posts. Another pair of ships fell in behind to moor at the sterns of the first two. Colorful banners high on the mastheads snapped in the breeze. The remaining vessels, one a well-appointed traveling ship and the second a sturdier boat that served as a kitchen, docked along the downstream side of the central quay.

A loud, heartfelt curse drew Bak's glance toward the northern quay, against which was moored a smaller cargo ship. A broad-shouldered man stood on the stern, glaring at a long line of workmen, each with a heavy sack of grain on his shoulder, that snaked from the forward hold, down the gangplank, and up the quay to Buhen's northern water-side gate. Duty forgotten, the men stood tight-lipped and silent, watching the incoming ships and their unwelcome passengers. The overseer leaped from the deck to the quay and strode up the line, slapping a short baton of office against his thigh. The workmen plodded on with obvious reluctance toward the gate and the storage granaries inside the citadel.

The ship, the largest to make Buhen its home port, belonged to Imsiba's new wife, Sitamon. At present it occupied its usual mooring place, but the other vessels that plied local waters were not so fortunate. Two trading ships, scarred from hard use and needing paint, lay on the opposite side of the quay from Sitamon's craft. Three other trading vessels were moored north of the harbor, close to the muddy riverbank. Dozens of small boats and skiffs had been pulled out of the water and lay along the shore. All had been forced out of time-honored mooring places to make space for the visiting flotilla.

"I'll wager my new kilt that those seven vessels will remain in Buhen throughout the time Amonked travels up-river," Imsiba said in a sour voice.

Bak knew what his friend was thinking: Sitamon's ship and all those that sailed nearby waters would have to wait in line to load and unload cargo at the single quay available to them. "Where else can they moor this far south? Kor has no space for them."

Imsiba muttered an oath in his own tongue. He had no desire to captain his wife's vessel or tend to her business, but anything contrary to her well-being distressed him.

The three small boys scrambled to their feet and ran to the massive pylon gate that stood before the mansion of the lord Horus of Buhen. The snake slithered quickly into a hole in the mudbrick wall. Commandant Thuty, Nebwa, a white-clad priest, and several local princes, each wearing the bright garb of his own people, filed through the portal and walked down the southern quay.

A rather plump man of medium height crossed the gangplank of the lead traveling ship and strode forward to greet them. He wore the calf-length kilt of a scribe, a broad multicolored bead collar, and wide matching bracelets. An unimpressive costume for a man who trod the corridors of power. A younger man followed, carrying a spear, a shield, and a baton of office; an army officer, Bak guessed. Not far behind walked two more men, both tall and slim, one with hair so light it caught the sun. The women remained on board.

The two parties met and words were spoken. Thuty and his party swung around to escort the newcomers up the quay. A crow flying overhead called to two of its mates perched on the battlements. Their loud, harsh voices shattered the silence, emphasizing the absence of people and their failure to welcome this man who had come to steal away the fragile prosperity along the Belly of Stones.

Bak prayed to the lord Amon that Amonked would come and go without incident. He did not know the man and he abhorred the task he had traveled south to perform, but he could well imagine the wrath of their sovereign should her cousin suffer hurt or humiliation while traveling at her behest.

*   *   *

Bak raised his baton of office, saluting the guard standing in the entry hall of the commandant's residence, and hurried down the corridor beyond. Coming toward him were the priest of the lord Horus of Buhen and the local princes who had accompanied Thuty to the harbor. Greeting them with a smile, he stepped aside to let them pass, then hastened on to the audience hall.

Bright shafts of light reached through windows near the high ceiling and fell into a forest of red octagonal columns. Across this largest room in the building, he heard voices softened to murmurs beyond the open portals of several rooms in which scribes and officers toiled. The hall itself was empty, the public scribe gone, his place by the entrance unoccupied. No craftsmen or soldiers or traders sat on the long bench built against the opposite wall, awaiting their turn to speak of a record gone awry, a reprimand made, short rations, long hours, or any other of the innumerable complaints arising from life in a frontier garrison. The empty space, the near silence, and unfamiliar voices in the room Thuty used as an office told him Amonked and his companions had not yet gone.

The commandant had summoned Bak, the reason unspecified. Not sure if he should make himself known or wait until the lofty visitors left, he peeked into a good-sized room with four red pillars supporting a high ceiling. Thuty occupied an armchair that held pride of place on a low dais against the far wall. He sat stiff and straight, feet planted flat on the floor, hands flat on the arms of his chair, his demeanor stern. Bak smiled at the stance. Thuty giving the visitors from Waset a taste of frontier formality.

Nebwa, standing at the commandant's right hand, noticed Bak and beckoned. Crossing the room, he took his place at Thuty's left hand, where he studied the newcomers with interest. Amonked stood immediately in front of the dais. He was probably in his mid-thirties but looked older. Wearing no wig over his thinning hair and jewelry that could only be described as modest, he was no more impressive at short range than at a distance. To his left stood the man with golden hair. On his right, a tall refined-looking individual, groomed to perfection, also in his mid-thirties. A nobleman without doubt.

"This is Lieutenant Bak," Thuty said. "He's the officer in charge of the Medjay police in Buhen. His men will guard your quarters while you're here."

"I have my own guards," Amonked said. "I need no additional men."

Bak queried Nebwa with a raised eyebrow. The only guard he had seen anywhere near the commandant's residence was the man in the entry hall, long assigned to the garrison. Certainly not a member of Amonked's entourage.

"Our worthy guest has brought fifty men," Nebwa said. "Spearmen." Only one who knew the troop captain as well as Bak did would have noticed the covert cynicism. "They'll accompany him upriver."

The soldiers on the cargo ship, Bak assumed. A guard of honor probably. But would they be alert, competent defenders of Amonked's person? Directing a smile at the lofty visitor from Waset, he said in a smooth voice, "You're a man of substance, sir. One who shoulders the weighty tasks of the storekeeper of Amon. My Medjays may not be needed, but their presence will add to your status in the eyes of those who reside in this city." He dared not look at Nebwa, fearing his friend would laugh aloud at so shameless a ploy.

"Oh, very well." Amonked's face was blank, revealing nothing, but Bak had the uncomfortable feeling that he not only knew he had been manipulated but had allowed it to happen.

A twitch at the corners of the light-haired man's mouth drew Bak's attention. Pale hair and greenish eyes betrayed an ancestry far to the north of Kemet, from Keftiu perhaps or from the mainland north of that island kingdom. Burnished skin indicated a life spent outdoors. Muscles rippled each time he moved his arms and legs, speaking of an active life. He looked older than his companions, around forty years of age.

Amonked's glance shifted to Thuty. "I've served as storekeeper of Amon for a number of years, sir, and I'm proud to hold the title. However, our sovereign, Maatkare Hatshepsut, has deemed me worthy of a new title, one more fitting to my present task. I'm now inspector of the fortresses of Wawat."

Bak caught his breath, startled. Nebwa muttered a few quick words, impossible to understand but the meaning easy to guess. Thuty sat quite still, as if unable to move. The title was ominous, indicating an uncommon power over the fortresses for which the commandant and the viceroy were responsible. A power to make decisions no man without military experience should ever be allowed to make.

Amonked seemed not to notice how shocked they were. The light-haired man shifted his feet, looking uncomfortable with the disclosure. The nobleman watched closely the officers on the dais, his face expressing interest but no involvement.

Thuty cleared his throat, pulling himself together. He should have praised the queen for her discernment in appointing so talented a man to so responsible a position. Instead, avoiding the issue altogether, he let his eyes settle on the light-haired man in an uncompromising stare. "Captain Minkheper. You know, I assume, that no ships can journey through the Belly of Stones when the river's as low as it is at present."

Minkheper smiled, letting the commandant know he took no offense. "I've sailed the waters of Kemet for many years, sir, and I've vast experience on the Great Green Sea. I'd never dare challenge the lord Hapi or any other god great or small without first learning of the many hazards I'm likely to face."

"We're fully aware," Amonked said, "that we'll have to transfer to donkey caravan and march through the desert along the Belly of Stones. A long, tedious journey, I've been told, with none of the comforts of sailing, but we'll manage."

Thuty stared hard at Amonked for some moments, as if measuring the man. Suddenly his eyes leaped toward Minkheper. "Our harbor here is small, as you've seen. The fortress of Kor has only one quay, always in full use. Where do you intend to moor the vessels under your command while the inspection party travels upstream?" He left no room for doubt: so many ships would not be welcome for an extended period of time.

"The presence of our vessels may cause some inconvenience," Amonked stated before the captain could respond, "but they must remain here. Here in Buhen where their crews can be maintained in a reasonably comfortable manner."

"Let me get this straight," Thuty said, acting his most obtuse. "Not only will your vessels take up much-needed space at the harbor, but your sailors must be provided with perishable foodstuffs and furnished with supplies, most of which have been shipped from afar specifically for the use of the troops in this garrison."

"Those men will need close supervision, sir," Bak said, aiding and abetting his superior. "Idleness will breed boredom, causing them to drink too much and to carouse and fight. I can see no end to the trouble they'll cause."

Nebwa opened his mouth to offer additional support, but Amonked cut in, "We'll be away no more than a month and a half. If you can't manage so few men for so short a time, what would you do if the whole army of Kemet came marching through, heading south to do battle with the kings of Kush?"

Thuty's face flamed. Bak feared for his health.

The tall nobleman stepped forward. "I sailed south from Kemet in my personal traveling ship. I'd have no objection to mooring the vessel against the riverbank, preferably across the water from Buhen. The oasis there appears to be large and fertile, a place where my crew could exchange their labor for fruit, vegetables, and fresh meat."

Amonked scowled. "That won't be necessary, Sennefer."

"I insist." The nobleman's smile grew self-deprecating. "I've come to Wawat not as an official member of Amonked's inspection party, but as his friend and brother-in-law. For much of my life, I've divided my time between our southern capital of Waset and my estate in the province of Sheresy. I'm here on sufferance, satisfying a yearning to travel beyond the borders of Kemet. If my ship must be moved, so be it."

"Excellent!" Anger sharpened Thuty's voice; a need to regain the upper hand drew his eyes from Sennefer to Amonked. "Sir? Any other suggestions as to how our load can be lightened?"

Amonked stiffened but otherwise remained unruffled. "I'll talk the matter over with Captain Minkheper. You'll have my answer before we march south from Kor."

Minkheper stared straight ahead, looking none too happy. "Must I go with you, sir? I'd be of more value if I remained behind. After resolving this problem of too many ships in too small a harbor, I could hire a local man with a skiff and experience close-up the obstacles that currently prevent trading vessels traveling through the Belly of Stones. By doing so, I could make a more knowledgeable recommendation to our sovereign as to how we can ease their passage."

"Recommendation?" Bak asked, the word slipping out unbidden. Did Maatkare Hatshepsut hope to tame the Belly of Stones? Only a god could influence the rise and fall of the water, the shifting of boulders along the riverbed, the changing and hazardous currents.

"You'll come with us as she commanded." Amonked's voice was firm, the look he gave Minkheper allowing no argument. "As a candidate for admiral of her fleet, you've no choice but to obey." His eyes darted toward the dais and Thuty. "Maatkare Hatshepsut has ordered the captain to assess the possibility of cutting a canal through the rapids, enhancing the movement of trade goods between here and the fortress of Semna."

Thuty frowned. "The task would be formidable."

"Impossible," Bak said, shaking his head. "Too many men would lose their lives in the effort."

Nebwa barked out a humorless laugh. "A canal in such troubled waters could never be kept open and navigable. The channel through the rapids above Abu is constantly clogged with boulders. The river here is much faster, more powerful by far."

"We'll see." The words hung heavy in the air, a dismissal of objections. Amonked's voice grew curt. "I plan to inspect Buhen tomorrow. The following day, we'll sail to Kor, and I'd like to begin our march south the next morning."

"I shall accompany your inspection party upriver." Thuty's expression was hard, his tone at its most autocratic.

"No!" Evidently recalling the commandant's status, Amonked formed a stiff smile, tempering the rudeness. "As much as I'd enjoy your company, sir, you cannot travel with us. Maatkare Hatshepsut has ordered that no man be allowed to influence my final decision. That command I mean to obey."

Color flooded Thuty's face. His mouth snapped shut, suppressing fury. He took a deep breath, controlling himself, and leaned forward toward Amonked to accent his words. "Our sovereign knows nothing about the frontier, sir, nor do you. With luck, you and all who came with you from Waset will survive your journey unscathed."

"Did you see the look on Amonked's face?" Nebwa wiped tears of laughter from his eyes. "He didn't know if Thuty was joking or putting some kind of spell on him."

Bak smiled. "I guess he intended a subtle threat, but it came out all wrong."

"I wanted to laugh so bad I thought I'd burst. If Seshu hadn't come along when he did, giving us an excuse to leave, I'd've made a grand spectacle of myself."

"Concern for Thuty kept my laughter in check. He's toiled long and hard to attain his exalted position, and I feared he'd lose everything in an instant of reckless speech."

Bak leaned a hip against the wall surrounding the animal paddock. The enclosure was filled to capacity with donkeys. About half the sturdy creatures surrounded broken sheaves of half-dried clover, eating a portion and spreading the rest over the sand on which they stood. A few animals dozed on their feet, the rest milled around, too fretful to settle down. The fine dust stirred up by their hooves, the stench of fresh manure, and the harsh odor of the fodder made Bak sneeze.

"What now, I wonder?" he asked, not expecting an answer. "With no one to watch over Amonked, no one to provide the knowledge he'll need to see the fortresses in a true light, how can he make a rational decision?"

"We must see that Dedu and Pashenuro go, with or without Thuty."

"Amonked won't listen to two sergeants, or anyone else for that matter. He made that clear." Bak waved off a fly buzzing around his head. "They could go as drovers, I suppose, keeping their true task a secret. Seshu can certainly use their help. And they could report by courier each time they reach a fortress."

"Good idea." Nebwa planted his backside against the wall, picked up a length of yellow straw, and stuck it in the corner of his mouth. "Amonked brought an officer with him, a military adviser he calls him. A lieutenant named Horhotep. The lord Amon only knows how competent a warrior he is."

"One who's fought all his battles in the corridors of power, I'd wager."

Bak hoisted himself onto the wall. Legs dangling, he eyed the dozen or so paddocks that filled the northwest corner of the outer fortress. Many contained donkeys, vital to the movement of trade goods, supplies and foodstuffs for the army, and ores and valuable stones taken from the desert mines and quarries. Without these sturdy beasts of burden, nothing could cross the southern frontier during the long months when the Belly of Stones could not be navigated. Their drovers were squatting together in the shade of the corner tower, playing a game of chance, awaiting Seshu for word as to how many men and animals he would need on the long, slow trek to Semna.

Sheep and goats occupied a few of the remaining enclosures, awaiting slaughter or shipment downriver. A small but fine herd of tan short-horned cattle, soon to travel to the royal house in Waset as tribute for Maatkare Hatshepsut, stood in a pen near the fortress wall.

Seshu came hurrying down a path between two paddocks. He stopped before the two officers and wiped the sweat from his brow. He appeared to be in a state of shock.

Bak dropped to the ground, his feet sending up a thin puff of dust, and laid a sympathetic hand on the caravan master's shoulder. "What is it, Seshu? Amonked again?"

"That man's a menace to himself and everyone around him." Seshu's brow wrinkled with worry. "He refuses to leave behind any of the luxuries he brought from Waset. He insists his concubine come along and . . ." He let out a harsh, cynical laugh. ". . . and he wishes her to travel with every amenity."

"How many servants does she have?" Nebwa asked.

"Only one. I thank the lord Amon. Her personal maid." Seshu shook his head in disgust. "Altogether there are nine people in his party. Plus fifty spearmen, guards he calls them, and their sergeant, and twelve porters."

"Porters?" Nebwa demanded.

"For the carrying chairs. Three of them. One for Amonked. One for his noble brother-in-law. And one for the concubine. You didn't think they'd walk, did you?"

Nebwa muttered an oath in the local dialect spoken by his wife. "Seventy-two people who have to be provided with food and drink. I don't envy you your task."

"Plus the many drovers necessary to handle the donkeys," Bak said.

Seshu heaved a deep, dejected sigh. "The caravan will not only be large and hard to manage, but he's bringing along a portable pavilion, furniture, any number of items that will make it a target for bandits. I've led bigger and richer caravans from the desert mines, but they were well-guarded, peopled with soldiers and officers who knew the desert—and knew how to stand up to the enemy."

"Thuty should send along a company of spearmen," Nebwa said.

"He suggested as much, but Amonked refused, saying his own guards could manage."

"Fifty men? If they know what they're doing, and if their officer has, at most, a modest amount of experience, you should be all right." Bak prayed such was the case.

Seshu, looking dubious, straightened his spine and pulled back his shoulders. "I must go speak with the drovers, warn them what they'll face, then convince them to risk life and limb and donkeys on this witless adventure."

Bak, his face grim, watched him walk away. "I care nothing for Amonked the man, Nebwa, and I wholeheartedly resent the inspector of the fortresses of Wawat, but I fear for our sovereign's cousin. Should he not survive this mission of his, every man along the Belly of Stones will have to pay for his poor judgment."

Chapter Three

"Other than stay behind and hazard guesses as to what may be happening upriver, what can we do?" Nebwa ran his fingers through his hair, making unruly locks go in all directions. "We're as helpless as a couple of speared fish."

Bak looked the length of the street, but barely saw the blocks of interconnected buildings that hugged the thoroughfare, their walls a brilliant white in the early afternoon sun, or the tall towered gate straddling the far end. Nor was he fully aware of four comely young women standing in an intersecting lane, talking, or a brown goose waddling up the pavement, leading her brood of seven downy goslings.

"Amonked looks as plain and straightforward as my father." He scooped a cast-off beer jar from a low drift of sand that had formed against the closed and sealed door of a storehouse. "Would that such would prove to be the case."

Nebwa snorted. "I always thought you a man of common sense, not one who dreams while awake." The young women must have thought the accompanying frown directed at them, for they ducked into the side lane.

The two men stepped apart, letting the goose lead her brood up the street between them, and continued on to the guardhouse, the back half of which was unoccupied, badly in need of repair. With Nebwa a pace or two behind, Bak strode through the door. He paused just inside, halted by the silence. For the first time since the Medjay police had occupied the building, the clatter of knucklebones had ceased. Instead of sitting on the floor, playing a game that continued through day and night, never ending, the two guards on duty stood at attention on either side of the rear door leading to the sleeping quarters and the prison. Something was decidedly wrong.

One of the guards took a quick step forward. "Lieutenant Bak. Sir . . ." His eyes flitted past Bak's shoulder, his mouth snapped shut.

A man's curt voice from behind: "I caught those two neglecting their duty, Lieutenant, playing a game of chance."

Bak pivoted. Standing in the door of the room he used as an office was a swarthy man of thirty or so years, medium of height and sturdily built, wearing an impressive multicolored broad collar, bracelets, anklets, and armlets. A sheathed dagger hung from his belt and he carried the baton of office of an army officer. A stranger to Buhen. Amonked's military adviser, without doubt.

"I admonished them thoroughly, but as they report to you, you must decide their punishment." The officer flung a censorious look at the pair. "If I were you, I'd spare them not at all. They're a disgrace to the military."

The man's words, his imperious tone rankled. As far as Bak was concerned, only he had the right to reprimand his Medjays.

"You are . . . ?" He pushed his way past the man, reclaiming his office. Another stranger stood inside, another officer from the look of him.

The swarthy man gave Bak a haughty stare. "Lieutenant Horhotep. Military adviser to Amonked, inspector of the fortresses of Wawat."

Nebwa leaned a shoulder against the doorjamb, blocking the exit, and examined the adviser as he would an interesting but rather distasteful specimen dug from a muddy riverbank. As usual, he carried no baton of office. Unless

Horhotep remembered him at Thuty's side on the quay, he had no way of knowing Nebwa was a senior officer.

"Who are you?" Bak demanded of the second stranger.

"Lieutenant Merymose." The tall, gangly young man flushed at the sudden attention. "I stand at the head of the company of guards assigned to escort the inspector upriver." He had a long face and prominent nose and ears. Bak doubted he was more than eighteen years of age.

Tossing the empty beer jar into a half-full basket of refuse, Bak brushed his hands together to clear them of grit. As usual, his office was cluttered with objects left for the moment and forgotten by his men and Hori. Writing implements and an unrolled scroll were spread over the mud-brick bench built against the rear wall. Weapons, shields, and leather armor were stacked along a side wall. A white man-shaped coffin stood on end in the corner. A basket half full of scrolls stood between two low three-legged stools. The rich, tangy aroma of cumin was strong, the odor wafting from a small basket confiscated from a man who had claimed to be a physician.

"Why have you come to me?" he asked.

Merymose opened his mouth to answer, but Horhotep raised his voice, overriding the younger officer. "I'm fully aware, Lieutenant, that Amonked gave you permission to post your Medjays around the house we're to occupy here in Buhen. The offer was well-intended, I've no doubt, but their presence is unnecessary."

His chill tone and smug attitude demanded a comeuppance, and the dangerous glint in Nebwa's eyes indicated that he, like Bak, wanted very much to give him his due. Unfortunately, this was neither the time nor the place.

Bak pulled close a three-legged stool and planted a foot on it, displaying, he hoped, a casual indifference to the adviser's sharp tone. "My men are there not to protect Amonked's inspection party, but to impress upon the people of this city that the responsibility for your well-being resides in the hands of our commandant."

Nebwa spoke up, curt and to the point. "In case you haven't noticed, Lieutenant, you and your precious inspection party aren't exactly welcome in Buhen."

"The guards under my command have fought no battles, sir," Lieutenant Merymose said, "but I've been assured that they're good and brave men, trained especially for duty on the royal estates. A singular honor that should commend them to the most critical of men."

Horhotep silenced his young companion with an irritated scowl. "Commandant Thuty may hold the reins of power in this godforsaken garrison, but our authority comes from Maatkare Hatshepsut herself."

"Thuty is here," Bak pointed out. "Our sovereign resides far away. By the time she could send men to punish those who would harm you, your dessicated and wrapped bodies would be awaiting burial at the capital."

Horhotep raked Bak with his eyes, his expression scathing. "You people, every one from the lowliest camp follower to officers of the highest rank, have been here far too long. You've settled in, formed a tight little kingdom of your own. You've made yourselves aloof from all authority except when it serves your purpose to obey."

He turned on his heel and stalked to the door. Nebwa, his expression stormy, stepped aside to let him pass. Face aflame, Lieutenant Merymose fled behind his superior.

Bak whistled. "There goes a man who's already made his decision. One that doesn't bode well for anyone living along the Belly of Stones."

"A man yearning for a smile from on high, I'd say." Nebwa spat contemptuously into a bowl of sand near the street door. "And a substantial promotion, as well."

"As you can see, my friend, any man posted here can look the length of the street from the water-side gate to the west wall." Imsiba made a quarter turn to peer down into the intersecting lane. Much narrower than the street, it ran arrow-straight between the two-story structure on which he

stood with Bak and the single-level building block where
Amonked and his party were housed. "Like the street, he
can see into this lane the entire width of the citadel, in this
case from north to south."

"And he can look down upon the rooftops across the
lane," Bak said, eyeing the white-plastered expanse that
covered the interconnected dwellings. "Perfect."

"I've posted two men on the roof of Amonked's quarters,
and I've assigned two more to patrol the streets surrounding
the block. I believe a day watch and a night watch of five
men each more than adequate."

"How many people dwell in the adjoining houses?"

"Four officers, their families and servants. I thought to
move them away, but for three days at most? No."

"You've done well, Imsiba." Bak walked with the sergeant across the stark white rooftop to a small open court
that allowed light into the building and, nearby, an enclosed
stairwell. As they descended to ground level, he asked,
"Amonked's guards are quartered in this building?"

"In the old storage rooms on the second floor." The big
Medjay chuckled. "Their sergeant, Roy by name, was none
too happy, but when I told him the alternatives—tents in
the outer city or return to the cargo ship—he agreed."

"Would they prefer the eastern barracks and have the
roof fall down around their ears?"

The thought gave reason for worry. Several generations
had passed since the warrior-king Ahmose Nebpehtire had
marched victorious against the armies of Kush to retake the
land of Wawat. Through the intervening years, most of the
old buildings had been repaired; the dwellings reoccupied
by the families of officers, senior scribes, and merchants;
and the barracks and storehouses either used for their orig-
inal purpose or converted for a multitude of uses. With a
smaller occupying force and no need for haste, a few struc-
tures—like the eastern barracks—remained untouched. Bak
prayed Amonked would see them as a promise for the future, not an indication of neglect.

*   *   *

Nofery's lion padded across the courtyard and stretched out on a woven palm mat outside her bedchamber. A strong scent of perfume wafted through a rear door, competing with the reek of beer emanating from the front room. Knucklebones rattled across the floor. A shout of triumph was drowned by a spate of yells and catcalls. No matter how unhappy or worried the people of Buhen, nothing less than a major catastrophe could arrest their desire to wager. A cool breeze dipped into the courtyard, making the torch sputter. The chill sneaked beneath the linen shift Bak had donned at nightfall, when the lord Re had vanished into the netherworld, stealing the day's warmth. Nofery, seated on her chair, keeping an eye on the gamblers, had thrown a fringed shawl over her shoulders.

"I didn't see you among the princes who welcomed Amonked to Buhen." Bak handed a fresh beer jar to the tall, dark, heavy man who occupied a stool facing Nofery and settled himself on the mudbrick bench against the wall. "And you an envoy to the royal house, too."

With a broad smile, the big man, Baket-Amon by name, raised his jar in salute. His oiled body glistened in the light of the torch, as did a gold pendant of the ram-headed Amon that hung from a heavy gold chain around his neck. "As a man who shares my name, one I'm pleased to call a friend, I pray the lord Dedun will give you a long and happy life— and many sons."

Dedun was the primary god of the land of Kush, a deity worshipped by many of the people who lived along the Belly of Stones. Bak suspected the lord Amon held pride of place in Baket-Amon's heart when he sat side-by-side with men of Kemet and the local god when he dwelt among his people in Wawat.

He returned the salute. He knew he could never be close to this man—as a tribal prince of Wawat, Baket-Amon fol-lowed a very different path—but to be counted among his friends was more than satisfactory.

"Five or six princes met Amonked's ship, they tell me." Nofery's brows drew together in disapproval. "Too many, considering he's come to rape the Belly of Stones."

As Bak had expected, Amonked's mission had soared on the wings of idle speculation, exaggerating an inspection with ominous possibilities to tales of Kemet's total abandonment of the frontier. Nothing less than the inspector's immediate return to Waset would halt the rumors.

"Prince Baket-Amon." A pretty young woman with a long braid hanging to her buttocks fell on her knees before the prince and offered him a bowl of honeyed dates. Around her hips she wore a bronze chain with pendants that tinkled as she moved.

He popped a date into his mouth and savored it with closed eyes. "My ship hit a sandbar south of Abu and we snagged the prow on a fallen tree. By the time my crew repaired the damage, we were far behind Amonked's flotilla."

"Would that you had caught him," Bak said. "Since you both grew to manhood in the royal house, he might listen to you."

"Do you imagine us as playmates?" Baket-Amon's fleshy body shook with laughter. "I was a hostage prince, one among many. Son of a minor king with no army to fear and small tribute to give. His blood ran in royal veins, and his closest playmate was the pampered daughter of the most powerful ruler in the world." He rubbed the sleek back of the girl sitting before him. "I doubt he knew I existed until I returned to Waset, a man representing my people to the royal house."

A young woman with freckles and fuzzy red hair strolled into the courtyard. She wore a girdle similar to that of the seated girl and carried a lute. She walked up behind the prince, kissed him under the ear, and slumped down beside his right leg.

"You know what he's come for," Nofery grumbled.

"Of course. It's important that I know of every act or

deed that could have any impact on the farms and villages for which I'm responsible." Baket-Amon placed a date between his lips, leaned forward, and kissed the girl with the lute, passing the sweet fruit into her mouth. "Let me assure you, I feel strong resentment for the woman who sent him here. My well-being and that of my people depends upon the army of Kemet occupying the fortresses along the Belly of Stones."

"Will you plead our case to him?" Bak rubbed his arms, trying to warm them. "Commandant Thuty can say nothing more. He's too angry to speak with patience and guile. But a word or two from you, a man Amonked knows and no doubt respects, might convince him of a truth he would otherwise fail to see."

Baket-Amon's expression changed, not in any definable way but in a new stillness of his body and a dimming of the light in his smile. "I fear I can do nothing. Amonked and I . . ." His eyes darted toward a rear door, where two naked young women clung together in a seductive pose, beckoning him. He stood up, looking like a man saved from a charging hippopotamus. "I wish I could help. Indeed I do. For my sake as well as yours. But I cannot, I will not get down on my knees before him and touch my forehead to the floor."

He rushed out of the courtyard. The women seated on the floor exchanged a startled look, scrambled up, and hurried after him.

Bak snapped out an oath. "How can he be so stubborn? Can he not swallow his pride? Would it not be more rational to approach a man he knows and convince him of the truth rather than turn his back on his allies and his people?"

"He's unpredictable, Bak. You know he is." Nofery handed him a fresh jar of beer. "He may yet speak with Amonked. He may think over your plea and realize he must."

"I'll offer a prayer to the lord Amon before I go to my

sleeping pallet, and another to the lord Horus of Buhen."
Bak stretched out his legs, crossed his ankles, and eyed the
door through which the prince had disappeared. "I've never
seen a man so popular with your women. The appeal can't
be his lofty title. No other local prince who patronizes this
place of business receives so much attention."

She gave him a wry smile. "I've seen none of my girls
turn you down when you've seen fit to lie with them."

"They don't come to me in vast numbers, as they do
him." Bak paused, grinned. "I thank the lord Amon."

She laughed, but quickly sobered as the sweet, melodious
sounds of harp, lute, and oboe filled the air, coming from
the rear of the house where Baket-Amon had fled. "They
tell me he's a brilliant lover, and never rough like some
men are."

Bak barely heard. His thoughts had returned to the
prince's refusal to speak with Amonked. Something had
happened between them. Something unpleasant, without
doubt. Still, how could Baket-Amon allow pride to jeopardize the well-being of every man, woman, and child who
dwelt along the Belly of Stones?

Chapter Four

"Amonked wants you to accompany him when he inspects Buhen?" Nebwa gave a cynical laugh. "May the gods be blessed!"

"Isn't he afraid you'll unduly influence him?" Bak asked.

"I'm to guide, not instruct. So he said." Thuty curled his lip in disgust. "He suggested I bring along a couple of senior officers. You two must come, and I'll select two or three others, as well."

Bak exchanged a quick glance with Nebwa. They both understood that by taking along more men than specified, Thuty meant to see how far he could push Amonked.

"How many troops occupy this garrison when it's fully manned?" Amonked asked.

"The optimum number would be about a thousand." Thuty paused outside the door of a two-story structure so large it filled the building block, a building that housed troops, the company offices, and services. The members of the inspection party—Lieutenant Horhotep, Sennefer, Nebwa, Bak, and three additional officers of Buhen—closed ranks around him and Amonked. All five men selected by the commandant had been accepted with no word of complaint from the inspector. "I've heard that several hundred more were posted here when first the fortress was built, but those days are long past. Now we have around four hundred."

"Would that number be sufficient should the fortress be attacked or besieged?"

A good question, Bak thought. Interesting. Especially coming from the storekeeper of Amon, a man who knows nothing of the needs of war.

"We'd have to fall back from the outer wall, abandoning the outer city and animal paddocks, but I believe we could hold the citadel as long as our supplies lasted." Thuty added, the words grudging but honest, "We'd like to believe we've tamed this wild land to a point where we won't be attacked."

Lest Amonked take the final statement at face value and use it for his own purposes, Bak added quickly, "It's easy enough to draw together sufficient men to fall upon a caravan spread across the desert or to raid vulnerable farms and hamlets, but quite another to muster a large enough force to attack a fully manned walled city."

The inspector's eyes rested on Bak for an instant, his thoughts hidden behind an expressionless mask. A mask carefully molded, Bak suspected, by a lifetime of tiptoeing among those who held the reins of power.

Thuty led the party into the building.

They walked corridor after corridor, passing room after room. Amonked paused now and again to ask a question, which Thuty answered, or simply to watch a man at work. Many of the soldiers were on the practice field outside the walls of the fortress. Those who remained went on with their tasks, studiously ignoring the intruders. As far as Bak could tell, the inspector missed nothing, yet his expression throughout was noncommittal, registering neither approval nor disapproval. Nor did he react in any way to the men's silence, their excessive concentration on their tasks.

Back on the street, the inspector asked, "How many men have taken local women as wives and now call Wawat their home?"

Thuty looked as surprised by the question as Bak was. What difference would numbers make if the army was torn from the Belly of Stones? Or was Amonked in fact concerned about all those who had made this land their home?

"A hundred and fifty, maybe more, dwell in the oasis across the river. More than two thousand live along the river between here and Semna."

"I see." Amonked raised his head, sniffing the air. The odor of baking bread wafted from a doorway brightly lit by the sun. "Ah, the cooking area. If that bread tastes as good as it smells, we must share a loaf."

Obediently, Thuty headed toward the kitchen. Amonked stopped outside the door to look back at the barracks building.

"Impressive," he said. "The structure is in excellent condition, Commandant, and the space inside could not be better arranged for more efficient use." He nodded, smiled. "Yes, it could be converted to a warehouse quite easily."

"On the final day of every week, each commander of the fortresses along the Belly of Stones selects the most important information from his daybook and compiles a report." Thuty, his stance stiff and remote, removed a scroll at random from a wooden shelf built against the wall. He broke the seal, untied the cord that bound it, unrolled a segment half the length of his arm, and held it out for Amonked to see. "He sends this compilation to me by courier." His voice was as cold and distant as his manner.

Bak recognized the loose, flowing scrawl of the commander of the fortress of Semna. The report was at least a month old and probably three times the length of the visible segment. Amonked and Horhotep moved in close to get a better look.

Before they could possibly read the few visible entries, Thuty rolled the document into a tight cylinder and handed it to a scribe for refiling. "After I've read them all and passed them by my senior staff, I give them to the chief scribe, Kha."

He walked the length of the long, narrow room, followed by his retinue. Two rows of ten scribes each sat cross-legged on the floor, facing Kha. Their heads were bowed over open scrolls, their reed pens scratching across the papyrus in a pretense of work, a slim excuse for ignoring their exalted visitor.

The commandant stopped before the chief scribe, an aging, bald man who sat on a thick linen pad facing his minions. "Kha excerpts major occurrences from the various garrison reports and compiles them in a new document. We send that to the viceroy, who forwards it on to the vizier in Waset." The elderly man handed over a slender roll of papyrus, which Thuty unrolled. The scroll was less than a cubit in length, the report two narrow columns filling half the available space. "As you can see, it's short and concise, containing only items of major import."

Horhotep caught hold of the corner of the scroll. "May I?" His voice was sharp, more a demand than a question.

Anger darkened Thuty's face. Bak, fearing the commandant's tight control would snap, slapped hard at the back of his neck and at the same time took a quick step forward and pivoted, striking Horhotep's head with his elbow.

The adviser loosed his grip on the scroll and swung around. "How dare you strike me!"

Bak rubbed his neck, forced a rueful smile. "Something bit me. An insect. I meant no harm."

Nebwa, quick to understand, flicked a spot from his kilt. "Fleas. They're vicious this time of year."

"I've noticed a good number of the pests in the dwelling in which we're staying," Amonked said. "I assumed the former inhabitants had pets, but perhaps all of Buhen is infested." With a distasteful grimace, he took the scroll from Thuty. "Shall we get on with our task?" and he began to read.

Horhotep gave Bak a mean glare, then turned his attention to the document. Seeing the pair distracted, Nebwa pretended to wipe his brow. Thuty, very much aware of how close he had come to losing his temper, threw Bak a quick look of gratitude. A scribe near the back of the room scratched his thigh, setting off a rustling of kilts and a subdued stir that sounded suspiciously like muffled laughter.

Amonked's eyes darted toward the seated men and back to the scroll, a bland look masking his thoughts.

"This report contains the barest of details." Horhotep tapped the scroll with a finger and sniffed his disdain. "If the scrolls of each of the ten garrison commanders include as much information as their length indicates, most of what occurs is omitted here. No wonder officials in Waset know so little of the activities along the Belly of Stones."

"Perhaps nothing of significance occurs," Amonked said, "as our sovereign believes."

Bak muttered an oath. Their very efficiency was speaking against them.

"This building serves as our treasury. Many of the items stored here are products of the land of Kush, but the majority have traveled from farther south, from strange and exotic lands few men from Kemet have seen."

Thuty paused in the anteroom, waiting for the two guards to light torches so the inspection party could see into the darkest corners. He and his entourage filled the small space, crowding the two scribes, who feigned indifference to their lofty visitors. "About half what you see was obtained through trade. Roughly a quarter was given as tribute to our sovereign, offered by tribal princes and kings who wish to acknowledge her friendship with gifts. The remaining quarter . . ."

"Commandant Thuty." Amonked's voice held an edge of irritation. "I've been storekeeper of Amon for almost ten years. I'm fully aware of the source of all the valuable and exotic items that pass through the land of Wawat."

Thuty crossed the threshold and followed a guard into a

large room. If the reproach troubled him, he gave no sign. "The items you see here will remain until suitable transportation and security can be guaranteed. They're reasonably safe within the walls of Buhen, but we must take many additional precautions to protect them during the long voyage north."

The remainder of the party followed, with the second guard bringing up the rear, keeping a close eye on the visitors. Flickering torchlight fell on baskets and jars and sacks and woven reed chests stacked in rows, sometimes precariously high. The contents of each jar was scrawled across its shoulder or scratched into its dried mud plug, while baked clay tags identified the products inside the less solid containers. The air was heavy with the odors of herbs and spices, rare woods, aromatic oils, dust, and a musty smell Bak suspected was a long-dead mouse.

"In addition to trade goods and tribute," Thuty droned on, "we also keep here the more valuable items paid as tolls by individuals crossing the frontier on legitimate business and items of worth confiscated from smugglers and other wrongdoers."

Amonked walked along the narrow aisles, peering at tags, poking and prodding lumpy sacks, sniffing packets wrapped in linen or papyrus or leaves. Horhotep tried to emulate his superior, but could not shut out the wearisome lecture. He glanced often at Thuty, obviously suspicious the commandant was mocking them. Sennefer remained near the entry, taking in everything, saying nothing, wearing a good-humored smile that might or might not have been sincere.

When the inspector indicated he was ready to move on, Thuty signaled a guard to precede them to the next room. Larger than the first, it had a ceiling supported on two columns. Light was admitted through high, narrow windows secured by stone grills. This was the safest room in the treasury, its contents the most valuable. Jars containing precious oils, myrrh, and incense. Baskets laden with chunks of stone destined to be worked into royal jewelry. Piles of skins taken from lions and leopards and long-haired monkeys. Ostrich eggs and feathers.

Amonked, his hands clasped behind his back, wandered along the aisles with the same relish as before. At the far end of the room, he stopped before six elephant tusks leaning pointed-end-up in a corner. "Magnificent." He glanced at Bak. "Were you not the man who laid hands on the vile criminals who were smuggling tusks downriver?"

"Yes, sir." Bak was surprised by the question, and by the fact that Amonked would have heard of his exploit.

Horhotep's head snapped around.

"Lieutenant Bak is a fine officer," Thuty said, forgetting for a moment the monotone. "We're fortunate to have him at Buhen."

"Indeed." Amonked walked to a small wooden enclosure built into the corner of the room. The solid wood door was closed. A dried-mud seal affixed to the latch verified its integrity. "What have we here?"

Irritated by the quick dismissal, Thuty signaled the guard, who broke the seal, released the latch, and swung the door wide. Gold glittered in the torchlight. Small rectangular bars stacked in rows. Thick bracelet-sized rings collected on stout wooden rods. Rough kernels, formed when molten gold was slowly poured into water, mounded in baskets. Pottery cones filled with gold dust.

A smile spread across Amonked's face. "Most impressive. Would that Maatkare Hatshepsut could be here to see so magnificent a display in its native land. No doubt one day, when I can assure her she'll suffer no harm . . ."

"One day soon, I'll wager." Horhotep flashed the officers from Buhen a look of satisfaction that reminded Bak of a jackal watching a poor family place a deceased relative's body in a too-shallow grave in the soft desert sand.

"How did the inspection go?" Baket-Amon asked.

Bak gave him a bleak look. "Let me put it this way:

Throughout the day I could imagine Amonked rubbing his hands with delight at so comfortable a place to rest and relax in a land flowing with the bounties of trade."

The prince, who had been examining a newly repaired rudder on his traveling ship, turned his back to the stern to study Bak's face. "That bad. I see."

Noting the objects on deck, baskets and bundles securely tied down and five stalls spread with fresh hay, Bak asked, "You're preparing to leave Buhen?"

"Tomorrow at first light we sail north to Ma'am. My firstborn son, my heir, will celebrate his eighth year in four days' time. I wish to be there." Baket-Amon flung a perfunctory smile at the two sailors who had repaired the rudder. "Well done. You're free to go into the city, but take care how much beer you drink. You must bring the cows from the paddocks at daybreak."

The men hurried away, arguing about the merits of the several houses of pleasure in Buhen. Nofery's apparently ranked high in their esteem.

"I'm taking ten cows to Ma'am," Baket-Amon explained. "My tribute to Maatkare Hatshepsut. Another ship will carry them north from there." As a native prince, he was obliged to send gifts to the sovereign of Kemet and to pay court to her as would any subject of note.

Bak walked to the rail and stared out across the water. Specks of gold and orange and red danced on the swells, a shattered reflection of a sky painted bright by the setting sun. "I've come again to ask if you'll speak with Amonked."

"Would that I could, Bak, but I can't." Baket-Amon crossed the deck to stand beside him. He looked sincerely distressed, but adamant. "Now more than ever . . ." He paused, frowned at the water splashing against the hull. "Now that I've seen . . ." A sharp laugh. "Now that my past has come back to taunt me." He shook his head. "No, I will not, I cannot speak with Amonked."

"But, sir . . ." Bak said, planning to beg if necessary.

"I'd leave Buhen today if I could," the prince said, cutting him short, "but the hour is late and neither my men nor I are so foolhardy as to sail through the night."

Looking closer at the man beside him, Bak saw that his face was drawn, his manner distracted. He clasped tightly the pendant of the ram-headed Amon, as if holding the golden image would give him strength. Whatever had occurred between him and Amonked must be serious indeed. As much as Bak hated to give up, he saw that to continue his plea would be fruitless.

Baket-Amon stiffened his spine, pulled his head back, and forced a smile. "I feel greatly in need of diversion. Will I see you at Nofery's place of business this evening?"

Bak shook his head. "Like you, Amonked sails tomorrow, though in a different direction. So far, the people of this garrison have behaved themselves, pretending to ignore him and his party when in fact they're seething with anger. Neither my men nor I dare rest easy until they're gone."

"There they go, my friend, and good riddance."

"My feeling exactly, Imsiba." Leaning against the parapet that edged the terrace running along the base of the fortress wall, Bak watched the distant flotilla sailing upriver toward the fortress of Kor. With the hulls too low to see, the rectangular sails, swollen by the northerly breeze, looked like birds skimming the water's surface in the blue morning haze. "I'd be happier if they were sailing north to Kemet."

Imsiba broke a chunk of hard bread from the loaf he and Bak were sharing and dunked it into a bowl of goat's milk. "If only Amonked had taken the commandant with him. At least we'd have some reassurance that all might go well."

"After the inspection, he had nothing but praise for all he saw here. For a short while, I dared hope he was so impressed he'd think Thuty's presence necessary." Bak, dipping his bread to soften it, added in a bitter voice, "How wrong I was."

"This fortress *is* well-run, the best I've ever seen."

Bak took a bite, testing for hardness. "Lieutenant Horhotep, oozing honeyed words, reminded Amonked that the warrior kings whose blood he and our sovereign share rebuilt the fortress after centuries of neglect and established the rules by which it's run." He popped the soggy chunk into his mouth, ate, and licked the milk from his fingers. "He made it sound as if anything accomplished since that long ago time is of minor significance."

"Amonked allowed a glib tongue to influence him?"

Bak shrugged. "I spent the whole day trying to understand what sways that man. I failed utterly."

Tearing another piece of bread from the loaf, he scanned the harbor. The central and southern quays stood empty, awaiting the return of Amonked's flotilla. No surprise there. But he was surprised at seeing Baket-Amon's traveling ship still moored at the northern quay. A small herd of tan short-horned cows filled the stalls. The ship's master stood on deck near the gangplank, looking toward the fortress gate; the helmsman sat on the edge of the forecastle; and the crew meandered around the deck, trying to look busy. The vessel was ready to sail, the crew clearly awaiting the prince. Perhaps he was detained, Bak thought, by a bevy of young women at Nofery's house of pleasure.

"Lieutenant Horhotep sounds a complete fool." Imsiba glanced at a crow landing on the parapet a dozen paces away, eyeing the bread, squawking. "Does he not know of the commandant's close friendship with Viceroy Inebny?"

Bak soaked more bread, pulled it from the milk, and ducked backward, saving his kilt from the dripping white liquid. "I doubt he believes anyone posted outside the capital is of any consequence. Including the viceroy."

The Medjay stared dolefully at the departing vessels. "Where do you think we'll go, my friend, if go we must?"

He had asked the question Bak had asked himself time and time again. "Back to Waset? To Mennufer? To a remote post on the northeastern frontier?" His gloom matched that of the sergeant's. "I wish I could guess with authority, but I'm as much at a loss as you are."

"I suppose we'll all be sent our separate ways." The words were spoken with the reluctance of one who fears the answer.

"Who'd think to keep us together? That's not the army way."

They ate in unhappy silence, watching the flotilla's sails merge into the haze. The sunny terrace was warm after a cool night. The river was calm, its surface a sheet of brownish water broken at times by a leaping fish. Ducks and geese swam around the empty quays, seeking food thrown overboard by the departed sailors. Sitamon's cargo ship had sailed north to Abu and a traveling ship had taken its space. The sailors on board shouted across the quay at the men on Baket-Amon's ship, their jokes vulgar, their laughter raucous.

"Do you remember the plans Commandant Nakht had for Buhen and Wawat?" Bak asked, recalling his first day within the fortress and his first conversation with the man who had preceded Thuty.

Imsiba gave his friend a surprised look. Bak seldom mentioned their earliest days on the frontier, when friendships had been forged, love had come and gone, and they had begun to feel the fortress their home. "He wished to make Buhen into a thriving city, in which soldiers and craftsmen and traders could live in safety and contentment with their families. He wished the people of this land to live in peace and to prosper."

"If Amonked deems the army useless, all Nakht hoped for will die."

Regret filled the ensuing silence. Bak's eyes strayed toward the northern quay, and the prince's troubled mien came back to him. Maybe all was not as it should be. "Baket-Amon was determined to leave at first light. Let's see what's keeping him." He threw the last of the bread at the crow, which hopped along the wall, head cocked, wary of the generosity.

Walking north along the terrace, Bak gave his friend a rueful look. "The thought of losing all Nakht hoped for bothers me exceedingly. The thought of leaving this place and the people I've come to love is almost more than I can bear."

"I know, my friend. I, too, feel closer to Buhen than any other place, and closer to all those I've come to know."

Hori burst through the northern gate, spotted them, and raced up the terrace to meet them. The chubby scribe's face was flushed, his eyes alight with excitement. "Lieutenant Bak! Come quickly! A man's been found dead. Stabbed. In the house where Amonked and his party were quartered."

Chapter Five

"Baket-Amon." Bak stared, dismayed, at the body stuffed into a storage area under the mudbrick stairway that led to the roof. He had not yet seen the face, but no one could mistake that large, heavy form for anyone other than the prince.

"I fear so, sir." Psuro, a thickset Medjay with a face scarred by some childhood disease, looked stricken. He had been in charge of the men guarding the house through the night.

Bak would not have been surprised if the inspector of the fortresses of Wawat had been slain, but Baket-Amon? He had asked the prince to speak with Amonked and he had refused. Now here he was in Amonked's house and he was dead. Had that plea for help brought about his death?

Imsiba cursed in his own tongue. "The gods have surely turned their backs to us. The prince's power was slight, with Commandant Thuty sitting in the seat of authority, but he was beloved of his people. What manner of trouble this will cause, I can't begin to guess."

"Go tell Thuty of this murder," Bak said, shaking off the guilt that stood in the way of clear thinking. "Warn him. And then bring two men with a litter so they can carry the body to the house of death."

As the big Medjay slipped out the door, Bak knelt for a closer look at the dead man. The floor-level closet in which the prince had been hidden was almost square, about two cubits to a side, and scarcely deep enough for his broad shoulders. Psuro had rolled up and tied the woven mat that had covered the opening when he found the body. Baket-Amon was seated, arms hanging down, legs drawn close, cheek resting on his knees, face turned away. He might have been sleeping—except for the blood that had drained onto the rush floormat beneath him, coloring a goodly portion a dull reddish brown. Bending low, Bak glimpsed between the legs the bronze hilt of a dagger entangled by the chain of the gold pendant of the ram-headed Amon.

Back on his feet, he eyed the room, empty except for the mats that had been spread over the floor in preparation for Amonked's arrival. The chamber shared a wall with a room the concubine had occupied; the vague scent of perfume hung in the air, not quite masking the metallic odor of blood. The room opened onto the main hallway near the street door. Not directly connected to any other room, this chamber had not appealed to Amonked, who had left it unfurnished and empty. Thus the men who had carried off Amonked's belongings had not found the prince hidden in the storage space. Anyone could have entered from outside without passing through any other portion of the house, just as anyone from inside could have slipped into the room unseen.

He studied the encrustation of blood on the mat beneath the dead man and stains that spilled over two edges. Certain the prince, too heavy to move far, had been slain close by, he raised the mat nearest the body. A tiny splash of rusty brown led him to the next mat to the right. Psuro, drawing in a long, unhappy breath, lifted another mat and another, revealing a large, irregular oval discolored by blood, marked in the weave pattern of the mats that had covered it.

Bak looked again at the body. He pictured Baket-Amon as he had last seen him, with two pretty young women seated at his feet and two more awaiting him, offering music and joy. A man who had lived life at its fullest, mowed down in his prime. Shoving away the sadness, the regret, he said, "Let's pull him out of there, Psuro."

The mat slid with relative ease across the plastered floor, soon freeing the body from the space in which it had been confined. For some inexplicable reason, it remained upright in its seated position. Bak placed a hand under the chin and turned the head to reveal the face. Baket-Amon, as expected. The body was cool, but not yet clammy, nor had it had time to grow rigid. He could not be sure, but he guessed death had occurred sometime around daybreak.

Bak gently laid the prince on the floor. Psuro straightened out the legs without being asked, a measure of the distress he felt at having failed in his duty. The dagger protruded from the dead man's lower chest. It angled upward, piercing the heart with the single thrust. The broad collar, bracelets, anklets, and especially the pendant were finely crafted and of sufficient value to proclaim theft as an unlikely reason for the slaying.

Faced with a task he abhorred, Bak swallowed hard, took hold of the dagger, and pulled it free. The bronze blade was narrow and pointed, about the length of a man's hand. The hilt, also of bronze, had been slightly roughened to provide a secure grip. The dagger was simple and unadorned, not of military issue but as easily come by. He had seen many similar weapons offered in the markets of Mennufer and Waset and Abu.

He laid the dagger beside the body, stood erect, and focused on Psuro. The Medjay, one of his best and most dependable men, stood stiff and straight, tense, awaiting an interrogation he obviously dreaded.

Bak eyed the stocky policeman, his demeanor stern. "How long ago did Baket-Amon come to this house?"

"I can't say for a fact," Psuro admitted, shame-faced. "None of us saw him enter."

"If each and every guard was at his assigned post, how could he possibly have escaped notice?"

The Medjay stared straight ahead. "We were obliged to leave our posts, sir."

Bak gave him an incredulous look. "All of you?"

"Yes, sir."

"I assume you have an explanation. A good one." Bak's grim expression, his severe tone promised dire consequences if no suitable reason was offered.

"I believe so, sir."

"Let's hear it."

Psuro licked his lips, shifted his weight from foot to foot. "At break of day, Amonked's sailors began to carry away the furnishings in this house, taking what was his back to his ship. Eight or ten youths—apprentices, they were, on the way to their masters' workshops—came upon them a block down the street. They began pelting them with stones. The sailors were laden with objects of value they had no choice but to protect. Rather than allow a fight to break out, giving both Amonked and the people of this garrison additional reason for anger, we went to their aid." The Medjay paused, cleared his throat. "It was then, I believe, that the prince entered the house."

And soon after, he was slain, Bak thought. "How long were you away from your posts?"

"A few moments at most." Psuro saw the doubt on Bak's face and hastened to be more exact. "I raced full-tilt down the stairs and out onto the street, where I found the others already gathering. As soon as the youths saw us coming and realized our purpose, they ran. I sent Kasaya after them to make sure they wouldn't return, and the rest of us went back to our posts."

Psuro was not a man to lie or exaggerate, so Bak knew his tale was true and unembellished. The house had indeed been unobserved for only a short while. Too short, he suspected, for Baket-Amon to enter unseen, and for someone else to follow him inside, stab him, stuff his body into the storage area, and leave the house unnoticed. A theory that did not include time for the angry words that most likely preceded the murder. Some member of the inspection party had slain the prince, he felt sure.

But why? Could the prince have entered the building for some reason other than to beseech Amonked to keep the army on the frontier? Some reason related to the past that had troubled him so?

He turned his thoughts back to Psuro. The knowledge that the Medjays had not strayed for long was no excuse. They should not have lowered their guard. "You had no idea Baket-Amon was inside?"

"None, sir."

"What of the people in Amonked's party?" Not ready to relent, he remained stern. "Were they all in the dwelling when the fight occurred up the street?"

"Yes, sir. Probably because of the early hour. The streets were fairly dark, uninviting to people who have limited knowledge of this city."

"And later?"

"It was chaos, sir, complete chaos." Psuro shook his head in wonder. "They were milling around all over the place. Going into and out of the house, following the sailors down the street to see if any precious belonging had been damaged in the fight, or to retrieve something they'd already packed and couldn't live without until they boarded their ship, or to pack something they'd forgotten to stow in a chest or basket."

Bak eyed the Medjay critically. "You did what you thought best, Psuro, and I'll not fault you for that. You clearly had no choice but to go to the sailors' aid. However, you should've left at least one man at his post to watch over the house."

Psuro, as transparent as a pool of clear water, failed to hide his shame. "I know I erred, sir. I'll never let it happen again."

"After Baket-Amon is taken away, you may go back to the barracks and get some sleep, you and the others who were posted here through the night. First, tell them what's

happened and pledge their silence. It's not up to us to add
fuel to the rumors which will all too soon spread throughout
Buhen and beyond."

"Yes, sir." Psuro swung around, openly relieved his ordeal was over, and hurried from the room.

Bak stood over the body, looking at the remains of a
man who had two days before called him a friend. He offered a silent prayer to the lady Maat that Commandant
Thuty would allow him to pursue the slayer and snare
him—no matter who or how lofty the killer proved to be.

"I don't care what Amonked says, Lieutenant." Thuty
paced the length of the courtyard outside his private reception room, swung around, stalked back in the opposite direction. Struck at an angle by the midmorning sun, the open
court lay half in shadow, half in brightness, emphasizing
the play of his powerful muscles. "He and his party must
either return to Buhen, or you must travel upriver with
them. The prince was slain in the house they occupied, and
someone inside that house took his life."

Bak, seated on the floor beside a loom on which was
stretched a length of white linen, was delighted with
Thuty's decision that he investigate the murder, although
he did not know what else the commandant could in all
good conscience do.

"He'll not come back to Buhen." Nebwa rearranged a
twig nestled in the corner of his mouth. "That'd be too
much like an admission that someone he holds close is
guilty of wrongdoing." The troop captain occupied a low
stool in the sunny space between two potted acacias.

The court, like the rest of Thuty's private quarters, was
cluttered with toys and reminders of household tasks. A
couple of spindles and the loom, a bowl filled with peas
that needed shelling, a tunic with a partly mended tear,
strips of beef drying on a line stretched overhead. Four
black puppies played around a large bowl of water on
which floated a half-dozen blue lilies. Their sweet scent

vied with the aromas of baking bread and roasting lamb, setting Bak's stomach to growling.

"Nor will he wish to delay a task ordered by our sovereign," Thuty grumbled. "A small matter of murder won't halt his wretched inspection."

"He'll claim—with good reason—that my men allowed their attention to stray." Bak raised a knee and wrapped his arm around his leg. "I'll wager he'll say someone resentful of the inspection entered the dwelling and slew the first man he came upon. A resident of Buhen or someone passing through."

Nebwa snorted. "Baket-Amon? A man known and liked throughout Wawat?"

Thuty jerked a stool away from the wall, swept three leather balls onto the floor, and sat down. "I don't care what the swine claims. I'm giving you unlimited authority to investigate, and I'll send a courier to Ma'am with a letter to the viceroy, seeking support I'm sure he'll give."

"If Amonked's as determined to do our sovereign's bidding as we think he is," Nebwa said, "he'll send a letter of his own to the royal house."

Thuty shifted his stool to escape the sun's glare. "A courier sailing a fast skiff, traveling night and day, can usually reach Ma'am in two days. The voyage to the capital is more than four times longer, with a lot more distance in which to run into difficulties. By the time fresh orders can be issued by Maatkare Hatshepsut, you . . ." Baring his teeth in a nasty grin, he pointed at Bak. ". . . will have laid hands on the slayer."

Thuty was actually enjoying himself, Bak could see, now that he had an excuse to grab the offensive. "Sixteen or more days coming and going." He scratched the neck of a fuzzy black puppy that had strayed from its siblings. Unwilling to make too rash a commitment, he said, "That might be enough time—if Amonked and his party will answer my questions with a frank and open tongue. If not . . . Well, each day that goes by lessens the chance of success."

"You've never yet failed. You won't this time." Thuty delivered the statement like a proclamation, a feat accomplished rather than a difficult task still to be performed.

Nebwa winked at Bak. This was not the first time the commandant had issued such an edict, and as always, such certainty of success troubled him. One day he might fall short of so high an expectation. What would Thuty do then?

"I'll take Imsiba along," he said. "He won't be happy, parting from his wife and her son, but he has the wit to ask the right questions and to see through misleading answers."

"No. I don't think so." Thuty spoke slowly, his brows drawn together in thought, then his expression cleared and he stated, "No, Lieutenant, you cannot take Imsiba with you."

"But, sir!" Frightened by the sudden sharpness in Bak's voice, the puppy scurried away.

"He's the best man for the task," Nebwa said.

"No." Thuty's gaze settled on the husky officer, and a wicked gleam entered his eye. "You, Troop Captain, are the best for the task. You've the rank and authority to override any man in that caravan except Amonked himself."

Bak groaned deep down inside himself. He loved Nebwa like a brother, but feared his quick temper and rash tongue.

"Sir!" Nebwa stared at the commandant, appalled. He disliked leaving his wife and child as much as Imsiba did. "I've fresh troops to train, desert patrols to inspect, repairs to the outer wall to supervise, new construction to . . ."

"The matter has been decided." Thuty glared at Nebwa, forcing him to abandon the protest, and at Bak to ensure he got no additional complaint. "You'll depart for Kor immediately. I wish you to join Amonked's party before nightfall, and to set out with the caravan at first light tomorrow when it begins the long trek south." He bounded to his feet and headed toward the stairs leading to the first floor. "While you make ready, I'll dictate a letter to Amonked, painting a vivid picture of your talents as an investigator, Bak, and of you, Nebwa, as a man of long experience with raiding tribesmen. He's taking too many valuable objects not to make himself a target, and I'll point that out."

Thuty's intentions were well meant, Bak knew, but he wanted more than a few fine words on a scroll. Plunging down the stairs at the commandant's heels, he said, "I'd like to take along a unit of archers or spearmen. They'll give us added authority and, should we need personal protection for any reason, we'll have them."

"An excellent idea." Thuty stopped abruptly at the bottom of the stairs, swung around, queried Nebwa with a glance. The troop captain knew more of the day-to-day workings of the garrison than the commandant himself, and knew which men could be removed from duty, causing the least disruption.

Nebwa pulled up short to avoid bumping into the pair below. "I've twenty archers awaiting reassignment. They can be ready within the hour."

The trio hastened on down the hall, Thuty to fetch a scribe and dictate his letters, his subordinates to prepare to join a caravan and a party of travelers who would, at best, resent their presence. Bak prayed the commandant's decision to send Nebwa would not prove a mistake. He consoled himself with the thought that Imsiba could conduct a parallel investigation in Buhen, thereby satisfying Amonked that all was being done that should be—and responding to a tiny nagging fear within himself that he might be wrong in assuming the slayer was one who had dwelt within the house.

"You and Nebwa are going upriver with Amonked?" Nofery laughed. "If I didn't know better, I'd think the commandant slew Baket-Amon just to have an excuse to send men along with the inspection party."

Bak placed a finger to his lips. "Silence, old woman. Should a rumor like that spread along the river, reaching the ears of Baket-Amon's subjects and allies, Thuty would be forced to leave Buhen."

"What of Amonked? Will the people dare threaten a man

of royal blood? One sent to Wawat by Maatkare Hatshepsut herself?"

"Suffice it to say, those twenty archers we're taking along may prove a godsend." Settling back on his stool, he raised his drinking bowl, inhaled the tangy aroma of the deep red wine it contained, and drank. "Delicious. I wish I could tarry, but I'm to meet Nebwa at the quay within the hour."

Nofery's house of pleasure was quiet, most of its occupants resting after a busy night. The old man who cleaned was wielding a rush broom in a rear room, sending dust drifting across slender shafts of light falling through the courtyard's lean-to roof. Bak had found the obese old woman seated on a low stool, examining the many objects she had received during the past few evenings in exchange for the pleasures provided. Spread out on the bench before her were jewelry of small value, items of clothing, woven reed sandals and baskets and mats, fresh and dried fruits and vegetables, pottery dishes and ornaments, several measures of grain, and a few small weapons: two daggers, a mace, and a scimitar. The lion lay in a patch of sun across the court, gnawing on a bone, growling softly at times in contentment.

Bak removed the weapons from the bench and laid them on the floor beside his stool. The troops were forbidden to trade away army issue equipment.

Nofery gave him a black look, but she knew the rules as well as he did and could not complain. She had succumbed to greed and lost.

"The prince said, when I saw him yesterday at the quay, that his past had come back to taunt him. Do you have any idea what he meant?"

"His past?" She gave an exaggerated shrug, letting him know how indifferent she was to his questions, how much she resented the loss of the weapons. "He was a mere child when I left the capital, one hostage among many who lived and studied in the royal house, rubbing shoulders with the sons of the nobility. I had no way of knowing him."

"You counted princes among those who loved you. Don't deny what I know for a fact."

Her smile was fleeting, grudgingly given. "They were young, yes, but they were men. This one was a child of six or seven years, a duckling who never strayed from the poultry yard. I never knew of his existence until I came to Buhen."

"Too bad. He grew into quite a man."

"That he did."

Bak sipped from his bowl, studying her across the rim. He always thought of Nofery as the least sensuous of women, but something in her voice made him wonder if she, like the young women who toiled in her place of business, had shared Baket-Amon's passion. Her face gave away no secrets.

"When did you last see him?"

"Two nights ago, when you were here." With a dramatic sigh, she gave the weapons a final, rueful look, turned to face the bench, and picked up a copper bangle to study it for value. "He left at daybreak, fully sated."

"He didn't come back last night? Before he was slain? He told me he meant to."

She laid down the bangle and picked up a bronze ring with a mounting of yellowish stone. "I expected him—he seldom missed a night when he was in Buhen—but no, he never returned."

"I can't believe he's dead." The captain of Baket-Amon's ship, a tall, bony man of middle years, slammed the palm of his hand against the frame of the brightly painted deckhouse, as if to punish the structure for the prince's death. "He was so much a man, so strong and virile, so well-liked by one and all."

Bak glanced across the quay, where Nebwa and the archers who would accompany them upriver were boarding the traveling ship that would transport them south to Kor. They all carried baskets and bundles containing rations, extra clothing and weapons, and whatever else they would need on the long trek south past the Belly of Stones.

"Did he have any enemies that you know of?"

"None." The captain walked forward, passing the empty stalls, and sat on the edge of the forecastle, head down, hands between his knees. The cattle had been led away to the animal paddocks, where they would remain until the ship was allowed to sail. "Could the one who took his life have erred, slaying the wrong man?"

"He was a man not easily mistaken for another," Bak reminded him. The mildness of his manner belied his impatience to be gone.

"Yes. Yes, of course." The captain looked up, a puzzled frown on his face. "He was big, bigger than most, and as strong as an ox. Was he slain from behind?"

Bak thought it best to be frank. The captain would resent anything less. "He was stabbed in the breast. By someone he knew, I'd wager, someone he trusted who caught him unaware." He leaned back against the nearest stall. The smell of fresh fodder tickled his nostrils. "Did he stay on board last night?"

"Yes, sir." The captain cleared a roughness from his throat. "Most of the night he was here, but I can't say he slept. Oh, maybe an hour or two, but he spent much of the time pacing. Sometimes here on deck, sometimes on the quay where he had more room."

"Did he tell you what troubled him?" The question was crucial and both men knew it.

"Would that he had." The captain spoke with genuine regret. "He wasn't a man to confide in anyone. Not those of us who knew him well, at any rate." He cleared his throat again, blinked hard. "I've heard he talked freely to the women he played with. Have you spoken with any of the girls at Nofery's place of business?"

"He said nothing to them." Bak glanced toward Nebwa, busy with the men stowing their gear. "He hinted, when last I saw him, of some unpleasant secret in his past. Do you know anything about his younger days?"

"I've been with him barely three years."

"Long enough to have heard many tales."

The captain managed a crooked smile. "I know he was a wild one when he was young. And even now . . ." The hint of humor vanished. "Well, his wives are fine women and his children are as good as can be, especially his first-born son. I thank the gods they seldom traveled to Waset with him—or anywhere else, for that matter—so the children were spared the knowledge that he spent his nights engaging in the diversions of the flesh."

"You disapprove."

The captain shrugged. "A man's a man, and I can find no fault with that. He was well-liked by his people and, if anything, his sexual prowess increased his popularity. But enough's enough, if you know what I mean."

"He made Ma'am his home?"

"He kept his family there, yes." A hint of a smile touched the captain's lips. "Close to the seat of power, he always said, where his sons could be brothers to the viceroy's children and at the same time learn the ways of Kemet."

"His oldest son is his heir, he told me. I assume he'll succeed him."

"He will, but Baket-Amon's chief wife will wield the power. The boy's not yet eight years of age. If he should die before he reaches his majority, she's borne other sons to take his place." Again the captain smiled, this more overtly cynical. "She's a strong woman, and a determined one. She wants no blood but her own—and that of Baket-Amon—in the line of descent."

In other words, Bak thought, the odds were good that Baket-Amon had not been slain by someone who wished to take his place as a prince of Wawat. "I pray she shares her husband's love for the land of Kemet."

The captain stared at his hands, locked between his bare knees, as if uncertain what he should say. "She's a wife and mother first and foremost. Now, with her husband dead, she'll protect her sons and their interests with all the ferocity of a lioness with her cubs."

"Could she have slain Baket-Amon, fearing he'd bring into his household a woman he preferred over her?"

"That wouldn't have been in her best interest, or that of her sons."

Chapter Six

"Is it true?" Sergeant Pashenuro called, hurrying along the riverbank toward the ship. "Has Baket-Amon been slain?"

"By the beard of Amon!" Bak stopped midway down the gangplank that spanned the space between the vessel and the bank against which the craft was moored. He stared aghast at the Medjay. "Has word spread already?"

"It's true then." Pashenuro, a short, broad man whose intelligence and bravery came close to equaling Imsiba's, shook his head in consternation. "The people of this land will not take the news lightly."

Realizing he was barring the sole path off the ship, Bak hurried on down the narrow board, leaped a patch of mud, and hustled the sergeant off to the side, out of the way. "Has Amonked heard?"

"I've seen no sign that he has."

Bak disliked surprising anyone with bad news, but perhaps it would be to his advantage to approach the inspector unaware. "How did you get word?"

"A trader came from Buhen an hour ago, setting men to whispering. Speculating. He knew nothing substantial, but with you turning up, and Nebwa and the men, they'll guess the tale is true."

Bak accepted the inevitable. What other choice did he have? "Does Amonked believe you and Dedu to be Seshu's drovers?"

"Yes, sir. If he's noticed us at all." The sergeant raised a hand in salute to Nebwa, striding down the gangplank. "The caravan is large. A man can easily get lost among its members."

The archers followed the troop captain, each man carrying his long bow, heavy leather quiver, and supplies. Their loads ill-balanced, they rushed one by one down the board, teetering, laughing with the good humor of men released from the tedium of garrison duty.

"Have you managed to befriend anyone in the inspection party?" Bak asked.

"Pawah, Amonked's herald. A boy of twelve or so years." Pashenuro smiled. "He likes animals so he comes often to see the donkeys. And as I'm a Medjay from the eastern desert and he a nomad from the western sands, he thinks of me as kin."

Waving good-bye to the ship's master, Bak and the sergeant fell in beside Nebwa and strode up a path that ran along the riverbank. The archers straggled after them. They passed two local trading ships evicted from the quay in favor of Amonked's flotilla. Few men remained on board, their crews no doubt at the harbor, gawking at the lofty arrivals. The fishing fleet could be seen far out on the river, seining.

Bak looked ahead at the mudbrick walls of Kor. Subsidiary to Buhen, the fortress was used as a staging post for caravans and as a place where military units traveling through the area could camp out and rest in safety. He came often to Kor, summoned by scribes charged with collecting tolls or soldiers who maintained order. Never before had he noticed how shabby the structure looked. The towered walls had reverted to the natural deep brown of the mudbricks, mottled by patches of white plaster in spots sheltered from the wind and blowing sand. The battlements were eroded, with time softening their once crisp, sharp edges. Several of the projecting towers had been rebuilt, but many were cracked and a few leaned at odd angles.

Kor was ideal for its purpose but what, Bak wondered, would Amonked think of it? What would a man fresh from the capital, with its well-maintained and brightly painted buildings, think of this dilapidated old fortress?

"The lord Amon must be watching from afar, made speechless by his storekeeper's excess!" This from Nebwa, looking down from the battlements, watching a long line of sailors file into the harbor-side gate, burdened with sleeping pallets, portable furniture, and innumerable woven reed chests.

Hands on the parapet, weight resting on his arms, Bak looked down upon the fortress's interior. He felt awe and disgust in equal measure. Royal envoys often traveled south with showy gifts for Kushite royalty, but nothing like this. "Could Amonked not leave anything behind?"

Nebwa crossed the walkway to stand beside him. He made no comment. The scene below spoke for itself. The space within the walled rectangle, usually quiet and scantly occupied, teemed with life. Donkeys milled around an area fenced off at the far end, braying, raising a cloud of dust. Vast piles of fodder and sacks and baskets and jars stood in and among buildings whose roofs had long ago fallen and whose walls had collapsed. Additional supplies were being piled with the rest by men unloading the last string of donkeys to arrive from Buhen.

A white linen pavilion stood in the center of an open stretch of sand normally used for the formation or disbanding of caravans, and several of Amonked's guards were erecting small tents beside the larger structure for the inspector's party. The remaining guards were setting up nearby a more casual camp for themselves, scurrying around like ants but not as well organized. Nebwa's archers, more efficient by far, had settled down near a cluster of intact buildings, their preparations for the night complete. The barracks and four houses, all remodeled over the past few years to shelter the scribes and troops posted at

Kor, provided an oasis of quiet among the bustle.

Bak eyed the pavilion, exasperated. "Did he not talk to any of our sovereign's envoys before he left the capital? They surely would've told him that less is best when traveling through this barren land."

"He didn't bring his wife or as many servants as I'd have expected." Nebwa's tone grew wry. "Maybe he thinks he's sacrificed enough in the name of common sense."

Bak spotted Amonked and Lieutenant Horhotep walking along the base of the far wall, escorted by the young lieutenant who commanded the post. "The inspection should be finished soon."

"Amonked will have heard we're here. We'd better go see him."

They walked to the towered gate, where zigzagging ladders would take them to ground level. There they stopped for one last look from on high.

"Seshu must be tearing out his hair," Nebwa said.

"Can you blame him?"

Nebwa grinned at his friend. "You grew to manhood near Waset. I'd think you'd be accustomed to the flaunting of wealth and power."

What Bak was accustomed to was Nebwa's teasing, which in this case he chose to ignore. "There's a critical difference between the frontier and the capital, a difference Amonked has failed to see. No risk is involved in the land of Kemet. No danger. No desert tribesmen who'll be tempted by what, to them, are vast riches."

Bak and Nebwa wove a path through the half-erected tents, their goal Amonked, who stood with Horhotep outside the pavilion, watching the officer in charge of Kor hurry toward the barracks like a man escaping some dire fate. Red and white pennants fluttered in the breeze from atop the center post, and a tall, leggy white dog, a breed used by the nobility for racing and hunting, lay stretched out in the sun near the entrance. Neither the inspector nor his military adviser noticed the approaching officers.

"This fortress is an abomination," they heard Horhotep say, "an insult to our sovereign. Peasants could make better use of it, crushing the bricks and spreading them across their fields as fertilizer."

"The gods made a poor choice," Bak murmured, "taking Baket-Amon's life and sparing this one."

"A large number of caravans seek shelter here each year." Amonked glanced around, as if trying to imagine the space during normal usage. "I must look at the fortresses upriver before making a firm decision, but Kor may have some value. If another quay were added, for instance . . ."

"No."

Amonked gave his military adviser a sharp look, displeased, Bak suspected, by so curt a rejection of his thought.

Unaware, Horhotep looked toward the desert-facing gate, openly disdainful. "To be fully functional, the walls would have to be rebuilt from the ground up, as would the buildings. Since Kor is used for shelter, not defense, the gain wouldn't be worth the cost." He swung around, saw Bak and Nebwa, frowned. "What're you two doing here? Did not Amonked make it clear he wants no interference from Buhen?"

Nebwa's countenance darkened, he looked about to spit out a barbed retort—at the very least.

Bak, no less angry at the affront, squeezed his friend's shoulder, curbing him, and stepped forward. He spoke to Amonked, paying no heed to the military adviser. "We've come on an urgent errand, sir." He displayed the scroll Thuty had prepared. "We must speak with you."

The inspector could not miss the gravity on Bak's face. He swung around and raised the cloth that covered the pavilion's entryway. "Very well. You may come in."

Bak gave Horhotep a pointed look. "I see no reason to trouble the lieutenant at the moment."

If Amonked noticed the flush of anger on his adviser's

face, he chose to overlook it. "Go to our ship, Horhotep. See that the vessel's been cleared of our possessions and send it back to Buhen."

Horhotep flung Bak a look of impotent fury, pivoted on his heel, and strode away. Bak could understand the adviser's anger; he would be equally upset if Thuty sent him on so menial an errand. He wasted no time on sympathy, thinking instead of the abrupt dismissal, which offered unexpected reassurance. So far, it seemed, Amonked was holding his adviser at sufficient distance that the man's influence might be contained within reasonable bounds. Or was the inspector simply retaliating for the earlier rejection of his thought?

The pavilion was a haven of comfort in the midst of frontier austerity. A gentle breeze ruffled the cloth at the entrance and filtered light seeped through the linen roof and walls. Embroidered linen hangings divided the space, allowing for privacy at the back. Thick mats covered the floor, soft linen pallets and portable stools provided seating, and small tables and woven reed chests offered surfaces for game pieces, drinking bowls, and scrolls. A god's shrine stood against one wall, draped with a cloth to give privacy to the deity inside—the lord Amon, Bak assumed. Furniture and hangings were far more abundant and elegant than any available to the officers of Buhen. Small wonder that Seshu was upset. How many donkeys would be required to transport the pavilion and its accouterments?

"Prince Baket-Amon dead." Amonked, dropping onto a stool, looked taken aback. "Slain in the house where we spent the night."

"Yes, sir." Nebwa sat down on another stool. Horhotep's demeaning errand had cheered him considerably. "He entered the building at daybreak, we believe, and was stabbed a short time after."

"I'm appalled, as any man would be," Amonked said, "but I can't help wondering why you've come to me."

Bak, standing near the entryway, thought he heard a woman quietly sobbing beyond the hangings that divided the pavilion. The concubine, he guessed. "As you know, sir, my Medjays were watching the dwelling. They saw no one enter or leave."

"If I'm not mistaken, young man, your Medjays left their posts to ward off an attack on the sailors who were carrying my furnishings to our ship."

Bak hoped the warm feeling in his cheeks was not a telltale flush. "The house stood unwatched for only a few moments."

"I appreciate the aid they gave my men—a brawl would've been most unseemly—and the uncommon speed at which they dealt with the difficulty." Amonked's voice sharpened. "But you can't ignore the fact that not a man among them remained behind to keep watch on our quarters."

"Baket-Amon had to've entered the house at that time," Bak said, steering the discussion back to the murder, away from the inescapable fact that his men had erred.

"And the slayer with him."

"No one other than a god could've gone inside with him—or followed him—and still have had the time to slay him, hide his body, and leave unseen." Bak spoke with certainty, his demeanor set, allowing for no rebuttal.

"I see. You're determined to lay blame on a member of my party." Amonked laughed, a sound flat, hard, cynical. Loud enough to stifle the sobbing behind the hanging. "How convenient, Lieutenant. For you and for Commandant Thuty."

Bak bristled. "I mean to lay hands on the guilty man, and on no one else. If he's one who came with you from the capital, so be it."

"You can't change the facts, sir," Nebwa stated. "Baket-Amon was slain in the house where you were staying, and the odds greatly favor a man inside as the slayer."

"This inspection will be difficult enough, with every

man's hand set against me merely because I'm doing my
duty. I'll not let you add an accusation of murder, giving
further excuse for failure to cooperate."

Amonked was speaking primarily of the military, Bak
suspected, giving little thought to the people of Wawat,
who might choose to be equally obstructive.

He stepped forward and handed the inspector the scroll
Thuty had prepared. Tamping down his irritation, he said,
"As you'll see when you read this document, Commandant
Thuty has no intention of interfering with your task. You
may return to Buhen if you wish. If not, Troop Captain
Nebwa and I will travel upriver with you, taking no part in
your inspection. The slayer of Prince Baket-Amon must be
snared, and this is the place to search for him."

"I'll not return to Buhen." Amonked eyed the scroll with
distaste. "It's you who should go back. You're far more
apt to find the killer among the prince's friends and ac-
quaintances—men there at the scene of the crime—than
here with us."

"My sergeant, Imsiba, who remained behind, will leave
no field unplowed. If the slayer's in Buhen, he'll find him.
In the meantime, we've come to search what I believe is
the more fertile field."

Amonked's mouth tightened, locking inside further comment. He ran a thumbnail under the seal, snapping it apart,
and untied the string around the scroll. Unrolling the document, he began to read. As his eyes traveled down the
several columns, his scowl deepened.

"This is an intrusion I greatly resent." He tossed the
scroll onto a low table, where it rolled off the edge and fell
to the ground. "I have the authority of our sovereign, Maatkare Hatshepsut, and I have her complete confidence. I can
and I should send the pair of you back to Buhen."

Bak could well imagine Thuty's anger should they return. All who stood before him would suffer, especially the
two officers who had failed to stand up to Amonked. His

thoughts raced. How could they forestall banishment from the caravan?

He said, "When a man is slain outside of Buhen and I'm called upon to seek the one who took his life, I usually travel with two Medjays. Yet this time Troop Captain Nebwa came and we brought with us a unit of archers. Have you not asked yourself why?"

"To make a show of strength, I would assume."

"For whose benefit?"

The inspector, too shrewd to walk into a verbal trap, stared hard at the officers, offering no answer.

Bak scooped Thuty's letter off the ground and laid it on the table. "Baket-Amon was a prince much liked by the people who dwell along the Belly of Stones. Whether or not he was slain by a member of your party—and I'm convinced he was—blame will be laid at your feet. Without a strong military presence from Buhen and an active investigation into the prince's death, the inspection party might well be attacked and vanish forever." He was exaggerating. At least, he thought so. Nebwa must have agreed, for he looked straight ahead, carefully avoiding Bak's glance.

Amonked, looking thoughtful, picked up Thuty's letter and read through it a second time. Unconvinced, or only partially so, he said, "All right, you may stay. Both of you. But I must warn you: the least interference in my inspection and you'll return to Buhen."

Bak breathed an imperceptible sigh of relief. "A decision you'll not regret, sir. If the local people believe you're supporting our investigation, you'll be far more apt to win their confidence."

Nebwa stood up. "Now that that's settled, I must go speak to Seshu. He'll need to know of Baket-Amon's death and of the twenty-two additional men who'll be traveling south with the caravan."

"I'll be frank with you, sir," Bak said, watching Nebwa hurry toward the animal enclosure.

Amonked knelt outside the pavilion entryway to scratch his dog's head. "More forthright than before? I find that hard to believe." His voice was as dry as dust.

Was the man teasing? Bak wondered. Could he possibly have a sense of humor? "Two days ago, I pleaded with Baket-Amon to go see you, to explain how important the presence of the army is to the land of Wawat. He refused. Then I saw him yesterday and asked him a second time. Again, he refused. I believed that to be his final word, but when I found him lifeless in the dwelling you occupied, I couldn't help but think he reversed his decision."

"And you feel responsible for his death." Amonked stood erect; a humorless smile flitted across his face. "I can assure you, you've no need. He didn't come to see me."

"How can you be sure?"

"I never left the house until we departed for the harbor. I spent much of the time in the room next to the one where he was slain. Mistress Nefret, my concubine, was unhappy, begging to return to Waset. Anyone who entered the building would've heard her—and probably me." Amonked grimaced his distaste. "Between her tantrum and a confusion among the sailors as to the order in which to take the furnishings and to which ship they should be delivered, I found it impossible to remain calm and soft-spoken."

Though Amonked seemed always to keep himself under tight control, the explanation made sense. The inspection party was not cared for as well as one would expect, with a minimum of servants and inefficiency and ineptitude on the part of sailors and guards. The latter, in fact, had not yet managed to set up camp and the lord Re was rapidly approaching the western horizon. Even now, Bak could hear them squabbling as to the best way to ward off snakes: incantation as opposed to laying a rope on the ground around each man's sleeping mat in the belief that the reptiles would not cross the low barrier.

"How well did you know Baket-Amon?" he asked.

A pack of feral dogs raced across the campsite, barking

at a cat speeding just out of harm's way. Amonked's dog shot to its feet. The inspector grabbed its collar before it, too, could give chase. The animal whined and struggled to get away, but he held on tight. "He was an envoy to the royal house. I saw him when he came to pay his respects to our sovereign or when he reported to the vizier. We were by no means friendly."

Bak thought he heard a faint harshness in the inspector's voice, a tension, but his face revealed nothing. "He spoke of his past coming back to taunt him. Do you have any idea what he might've been talking about?"

"I've never been good at guessing what lies in another man's heart, Lieutenant." Amonked swept aside the cloth covering the entryway and stepped inside, half choking the struggling dog. "I must dictate the results of our inspection of this fortress while my impressions are fresh."

Bak held his ground. "If I'm to lay hands on Baket-Amon's slayer, I'll need the cooperation of every member of your party. Will you see that they help me, sir?"

"I'll tell them of your mission, yes, and I'll suggest they cooperate. How willing they'll be, I have no idea. That, I suspect, will be up to you." Amonked dropped the cloth behind him, leaving Bak standing by himself in the sunshine.

Quashing an urge to shake the inspector until his teeth rattled, Bak strode toward the commanding officer's quarters. He had to send a message to Thuty, reporting that he and Nebwa had Amonked's reluctant permission to remain with the caravan and investigate the murder. As for the inspector himself, what could he report? The man was like a boulder, solid and difficult to move. That he and Baket-Amon had crossed paths in the past, Bak was certain, and neither man had come away content. Could their differences have been so serious that Amonked—cousin to Maatkare Hatshepsut herself—had slain the prince? Bak shuddered at the possibility.

*   *   *

"I hate this place! This wild and unruly land of Wawat!" Nefret, Amonked's concubine, blinked back angry tears. "Amonked is a good and gentle man. One who'd never knowingly hurt anyone. I can't think why he wished me to come."

Bak had trouble holding back a smile. He had a good idea why the inspector had brought the young woman along. About twenty years of age, she was one of the most sensuous creatures he had seen since coming to Wawat close on two years earlier. Her firm breasts, narrow waist, and rounded hips, covered but not concealed by a white linen sheath, vied in beauty with those of the lady Hathor. Large black eyes, long thick lashes, and wide, seductive lips adorned an oval face framed by a mass of black hair that cascaded around her shoulders. He prayed she'd stay inside the pavilion. Should the troops assigned to Kor see her, he feared a riot. Aware Amonked was sharing his evening meal with the commander of Kor, he had decided he must meet the other members of the inspector's traveling household, especially the woman. The sobbing he had heard earlier hinted at discontent, and discontent often led to a failure to guard one's tongue.

"His traveling ship is a prison. A benevolent prison, to be sure, but, oh, so confining!" She drew her legs beneath her, fluffed up the mound of pillows at her back, and reclined against them. "He equipped the vessel with every comfort, but to sail up the river day after day, with no diversions except a few ugly fortresses and a multitude of villages too small and poor and filthy to visit was an abomination. I thought, once we reached the viceroy's residence in Ma'am, that I could at least talk to a few women and maybe visit a decent market." Her laugh was bitter, close to a whimper. "How wrong I was."

"Mistress, please . . ." The maid, a girl of twelve or so years whose youthful form had just begun to blossom, hovered at Nefret's side, a mirror in one hand, an ivory comb in the other. A small wooden chest containing cosmetics and hair ornaments stood open on the mat at her feet.

"Go away, Mesutu." Nefret frowned at the girl. "Go fetch us some wine. Some honey cakes, too."

The girl threw a helpless look at the scribe seated on the floor at the opposite end of the pavilion, laid mirror and comb beside the box, and hastened through the wall of fabric that separated the sleeping quarters from the more public area.

"The viceroy's wife was not there. She'd sailed north to the fortress of Kubban to assist her daughter in childbirth." Nefret picked up the mirror, glanced at her image, and screwed up her nose in distaste. "The women who were there talked of nothing but their dreary lives in that dreary fortress." She laid the mirror on the floor mat, sniffed back tears. "As for Buhen . . . Well, it was no better. I had to remain in that dreadful house." She flashed a bitter look at the scribe. "And now, I must stay here. Where it's safe, they tell me."

The scribe stared unhappily at the scroll spread across his lap.

"After his meeting with Commandant Thuty," Nefret went on, "Amonked issued an order that we not socialize with the officers and their families while he inspects the fortresses along the Belly of Stones." Her voice rang with frustration. "I can't imagine what prompted him. Did they quarrel?"

"Mistress Nefret." The scribe, whom Bak guessed at thirty or so years, laid aside the scroll, struggled to his feet, and crossed the room, his gait heavy and off-center. Unlike most men of his profession, he wore a shorter, thigh-length kilt, probably to ease the effort of walking. A monstrous scar ran from his right ankle up his lower leg and deformed knee, to vanish beneath the garment. "You must not speak out in anger. You'll hurt no one but yourself."

"Can't you ever leave me in peace, Thaneny?" She shot

to her feet, glared. "Must you constantly repeat Amonked's words like the pale shadow you are?" Bursting into sobs, she ran from the room.

The scribe looked as if he had been slapped. "She's very upset, sir. Lonely. Afraid. She doesn't mean half of what she says." A blind man could see he doted on the young woman.

To no avail, Bak feared, if the contempt she had displayed were sincere. "Most women come to Wawat with their husbands and children, and they tolerate this life for a year, two years, sometimes three, because they must. She's fortunate she has to remain only a few weeks." He had no doubt Nefret could hear through the flimsy wall of hangings. His words would offer no comfort, but they might set her to thinking of others besides herself.

"She shouldn't get so angry with Amonked. From the day he took her into his household, he's cherished her, plied her with gifts, surrounded her with beauty and comfort." Thaneny looked away and spoke in a wistful voice. "Would that I could someday give a woman all he's given her."

"Has not the lord Amon given you far more than material objects?" Bak asked, thinking of the misshapen leg.

"My life, yes. I thank him each and every day for sparing me." Thaneny spoke as if reciting a litany, deeply felt but too often uttered. "Nefret can't find it in her heart to understand, but I never cease to thank that most benevolent of gods for allowing me to serve a kind and generous man, one who doesn't look away each time I walk into the room."

Bak was aware that Thaneny's labored gait would arouse a pity few men wished to acknowledge. Especially since the scribe was a handsome man still in his prime, with well-formed facial features, broad shoulders, narrow waist, and muscular arms. If Amonked could look at the man and not see the deformity, he had at least one redeeming quality.

"Thaneny . . ." A slender youth of about twelve years

peeked into the room. "Oh, we've a guest. I'll come back later."

"Come in," Bak commanded the already retreating figure.

From the deep ruddy skin and dark, tight curls, he guessed the boy was a child of the western desert, the herald Pashenuro had befriended, another individual who must journey across the desert sands for no good reason. A child brought along, like the concubine and her servant, not out of necessity but to satisfy Amonked's personal needs. And how was Thaneny to travel? A man whose every step was a struggle.

The boy turned back, his eyes wide with curiosity. He held four ostrich feathers, their long shafts rising far above his bony shoulder.

"You found something for her." Thaneny gave the youth a grateful smile. "I thank the lord Thoth." Thoth was the god of writing and knowledge, the patron of scribes.

"I found a merchant who's come from far-off Kush." Guilt vanquished the boy's sunny smile and he glanced around as if afraid he had been heard. "I know Amonked told us not to stray, but when I asked the drover Pashenuro where I could find something for mistress Nefret . . . Well, I had to go aboard a ship outside the walls of Kor." His eyes leaped toward Thaneny's face and an anxious smile touched his lips. "The feathers were worth it, don't you think? She'll like them, won't she?"

"How can she not?" The scribe took them from the boy, held them at a distance, nodded. "Yes, they're lovely. No woman could ask for better." The pleasure left his smile and resignation entered his voice. "Now I fear she'll wish to visit that ship."

"It's gone. The captain wanted to reach Buhen before full dark."

Thaneny gave the boy a relieved smile, then his eyes flitted toward Bak. "Pawah, this is Lieutenant Bak, officer in charge of the Medjay police. Pawah is Amonked's herald."

The boy gaped. "A police officer? Really?"

Forming a smile, Bak asked the boy, "Have you always lived in Kemet, or was Wawat the land of your birth?"

"I was born here, sir, into a tribe that roamed the desert. Five years ago, when a drought struck and many waterholes dried up, my father traded me to a merchant so my brothers and sisters wouldn't starve."

Thaneny laid his arm across the boy's shoulder as if to shelter him. "The merchant took him to Waset and traded him to the owner of a house of pleasure. Later, Sennefer bought him, saving him from unspeakable cruelties, and passed him on to our household. He's been with us ever since, a part of our family."

Bak ruffled the boy's hair, distracting him from his unpleasant past. "Are you glad to be back in Wawat?"

"It's all right." Pawah shrugged. "As long as I can serve my master, I'm happy anywhere."

Bak eyed the pair standing before him. He wondered how they would feel about Amonked a week or two hence, after spending the days marching across the hot, barren desert and the nights trying to sleep in cold, drafty tents. They'd not be so charitable, he suspected.

"What am I to do, sir?" Pashenuro asked. "Return to Buhen? Or travel upriver with you?"

"You'll remain with the caravan." Bak had been undecided as to where the sergeant would be better placed, but a brief visit to the animal enclosure and a close look at the mounds of supplies that had to be transported had given the answer. "Seshu is greatly overburdened. He needs a strong right hand, and that you must be. Say nothing of your true task to anyone in Amonked's party. As long as they believe you to be a drover, they'll speak with a far less guarded tongue when you're near."

"Yes, sir."

They sat with the archers from Buhen, who were seated around a rough mudbrick hearth to absorb the small amount of warmth the dying fuel offered. The men passed around large cooking bowls containing braised duck and vegetables, a feast to send them on their way upriver. The fire in the hearth oft times flared, making the barracks wall behind them glow, but its light was transitory, its heat negligible.

"Maintain your friendship with the youth Pawah. I doubt he's had any contact with his family since he was taken from the land of Wawat, but be watchful anyway. I don't want the child tempting his desert kin with tales of Amonked's wealth."

"I understand, sir."

Bak raised his voice, catching the attention of the men around them. "You all know Pashenuro as a policeman, but to Amonked and all who travel with him, he's a drover. The truth must never be aired."

"I'll personally geld the first man to betray him." Nebwa, closer to the hearth, scanned the circle of archers, his eyes catching the flame, burning with promise. "Do I make myself clear?"

The men murmured assent.

"What am I to do, sir?" Sergeant Dedu asked.

Nebwa reached into a bowl and tore the wing off the remains of a duck. "I've not traveled through the Belly of Stones for several years, so I've lost touch. This journey will give me a chance to perform an inspection of my own, to check on the state of repair of the fortresses, the needs of the officers and men, their morale." He tore the wing into two parts and gnawed off a bite. "I know Seshu could use you, too, but as I'll be otherwise occupied much of the time, you'll be of more use as a military man, standing at the head of these archers. You've some experience with the bow and you've spent many long weeks on desert patrol, so you know how dangerous this land and its people can be. Especially if Hor-pen-Deshret has come back. Frankly, I doubt the rumor is true, but you never know."

Hissing a sudden warning, Pashenuro shoved himself backward to vanish in the dark. Two men strode out of the gloom beyond the hearth, Lieutenants Horhotep and Merymose. How much they had overheard, Bak could not begin to guess.

"What do we have here?" Horhotep looked around the circle of men, his lips curled into a sarcastic smile. "Good food. Good company. Entertaining tales designed to bolster courage and self-worth. What good fortune for us. May we join you?"

Pashenuro's hearing was as sharp as a jackal's, Bak knew. With luck, this cursed military adviser had been so preoccupied with planning his own performance that he had heard nothing but the march of his own two feet.

Horhotep glanced at Bak and surely saw him, but his eyes came to rest on Nebwa. He looked down his nose at the more senior officer, assuming a superiority designed to chafe. "First you try to frighten Amonked with talk of imminent attack by Baket-Amon's subjects, who in truth are nothing but impoverished farmers. Now you speak of rag-tag tribesmen as an army. What do you take us for, Troop Captain? Children who'll believe any tale you throw at us?"

Lieutenant Merymose stepped back a pace, as if distancing himself from the sharp-tongued adviser.

Nebwa stood up, teeth bared in an unfriendly smile. "If we come upon an enemy during this journey, even if only one man with a pole sharpened to a point for use as a spear, I pray to the lord Horus of Buhen that you'll be the first to face him." He spat on the ground, reinforcing the contempt in his voice. "You with your proud bearing and unproven courage. How will you fare when tested?"

"You swine!" Horhotep, forgetting himself, throwing off his haughty indifference, reached for his dagger, drew it.

An archer slipped back, out of range of the flickering light cast by the fire. He took a bow and quiver from among several leaning against the barracks wall and armed the weapon. Two other men followed his example. Aware the situation could rapidly go out of control, Bak scrambled to his feet.

Nebwa, tut-tutting at the show of temper, slid his dagger from its sheath and spat again, barely missing his opponent's foot. Horhotep, his stance, his weapon ready to strike, stood as if glued to the spot.

"What's wrong, Lieutenant?" Nebwa goaded. "Have you no stomach for combat?"

"Nebwa, no!" Bak shouted. He lunged toward the adversaries, placing himself between them.

Merymose, leaping forward at the same time, caught hold of Horhotep's weapon and twisted it out of his hand.

"You cur!" Horhotep screamed at the younger officer. "I could've taken him with ease! You'd no right to touch me!"

Merymose stumbled back as if struck and stared at the dagger in his hand. He seemed surprised to find it there, appalled at what he had done.

"Lieutenant Horhotep!" Bak's voice rang out, hard and cold like the crack of a whip. "Go back to your tent and calm yourself."

"How dare you speak to me like that!"

Bak pointed toward the archers standing in the shadows, weapons at the ready. "Do you have any idea, Lieutenant, how close you stand to death?"

Even in the uncertain light, they could see the color drain from the adviser's face. He jerked his dagger from Merymose's hand and spun around to vanish in the dark. Merymose flung Bak a look of apology and hurried after his superior officer.

Nebwa muttered a string of curses, blowing off steam. The men growled vain threats. Bak bowed his head and offered a silent prayer to the lord Amon that neither he nor Nebwa nor their men would live to regret this small victory.

Chapter Seven

The double doors of the western, desert-facing gate were spread wide, admitting the soft early morning light into the tunnel-like passage through the twin-towered portal. A long train of heavily burdened donkeys plodded through, drawn by the fresh, clean air outside the walls. Walking in single file, the sturdy beasts set off along the desert trail, following the drover Seshu had assigned to lead the foremost string. A pack of feral dogs appeared out of nowhere to range alongside, a dozen or so slick-haired, medium sized animals of varying colors.

Drovers cracked their short, stout whips to keep the younger, friskier donkeys in line. Foals gamboled around their mothers. Each time a hoof struck the sand, a tiny puff of dust rose in the animal's wake. Soon a thin cloud formed above the caravan, tinting the sky a dull gold.

Bak, who had climbed up to the battlements to watch the first animals set out, eyed that golden cloud as he would a pennant held aloft above a unit of his own troops hiding in ambush. It was pleasant to look at but a dead giveaway to an enemy force—and within the hour would be visible from a long way off. A beacon inviting attack.

A shout rent the air, drawing every eye within and without the fortress. A sentry raced along the parapet atop the southern wall, heading toward the corner tower. Bak burst into a run and sped along the walkway atop the western, desert-facing wall, thinking to intercept him. He could see nothing amiss, but the sentry was responding to what was clearly an urgent problem.

Then he saw a man heave himself into a crenel near the tower and scramble through the opening. At the same time a large gray bird rose into the air. It flew a distance several times the height of a man and stopped abruptly, as if held in place by a god. Wings beating the air, crying a frantic kek-kek-kek, it struggled to free itself from what looked like a long cord binding it to the parapet.

The sentry, with the shorter distance to travel, reached the empty crenel ahead of Bak. He peered through, yelled. The bird's actions grew more frenzied. Bak dashed through the corner tower and came out beside the soldier. Looking out the next crenel, he saw a man climbing rapidly down the wall, finding easy handholds among the eroded mud-bricks.

Snarling an angry curse, the sentry thrust his spear through the crenel and flung it at the fleeing man. The spear struck the fugitive's shoulder, drawing blood, but the wound failed to slow him. He dropped the last few cubits to the sand below and swung around to face the desert, poised to flee in that direction. Spotting several men racing toward him from the caravan, he pivoted and headed full-tilt toward the river. He vanished among a stand of trees at the edge of the water.

Bak turned away to look at the bird, frantically flapping its wings and crying out for freedom. A falcon, the sacred bird of the lord Horus. A long cord had been tied to its leg and tethered to a spear planted deep within the mudbrick parapet wall. Bak knew nothing of the handling of such birds of prey, but one thing he did know: no man would get close to that frantic creature without protection and knowledge. He leaned over the parapet and called for help to the men below.

A drover from Buhen, wearing heavy leather gloves and

using the patience and gentleness of a man long accustomed to handling such birds, brought the falcon down and covered its head to quiet it. Bak stood with Nebwa, looking it over before he set it free. It was a magnificent creature, more than a cubit long from head to tail, with pale feathers below and darker gray above, a hooked beak and long curved talons. Sharp-eyed and deadly when hunting, gentle and loving when satiated. Or so the drover said.

"Why, in the name of the lord Amon, would anyone tie a bird up here?" Nebwa demanded.

"The deed was done deliberately," Bak said. "The man came, left it in the most conspicuous place he could find, and ran away. We were meant to see it now, as the caravan moves out."

"Why?" Nebwa repeated, glaring at the falcon.

Bak had had plenty of time to think while he waited for someone to rescue the bird. "The falcon is a creature of the desert, Nebwa, a creature of Horus."

His friend, quick to understand, glared. "You can't be thinking what I suspect you're thinking."

"Hor-pen-Deshret. Falcon of the desert. I think this bird was meant to announce his return."

"No. I don't believe it." Hebwa hesitated, then said more thoughtfully, "He is a man who likes to show off, to prove himself braver and more clever than others. But . . ." He shook his head. "No, it can't be true."

He spoke, Bak noticed, with less assurance than he had when first he had heard the rumors of Hor-pen-Deshret's return.

Bak thought of the many desirable objects he had seen in Amonked's pavilion, with far more hidden behind the wall hangings, he suspected. If Hor-pen-Deshret did not already know of them he soon would. And the way rumors spread along the river, their content growing faster than aphids on a flower . . . The very thought was abhorrent.

*   *   *

"I advise you to sail to the new fortress, sir." Nebwa was on his best behavior, congenial to a fault. He had refused to dwell on whatever significance the falcon might have had, preferring instead to deal with the more practical concerns. "It's not far from Kor, but it'll be a lot faster than walking up the trail with the caravan. You'd have to use a boat anyway to cross from the west bank to the island on which it's being built, so you may as well go all the way in comfort."

Thus far, Amonked had given no sign that he had heard about the previous night's confrontation with Horhotep, but neither Nebwa nor Bak had any doubt that the adviser had told him of the incident and, in the telling, had made himself look good at their expense.

"Captain Minkheper's task would certainly benefit," Bak said. "To get a true picture of the Belly of Stones, he must not only speak with men who sail these waters, but he must spend time on the river."

"I'd planned to remain with the caravan all the way to Semna, letting men and animals rest each time I go off to inspect a fortress." Amonked glanced toward Horhotep, frowned. If he wanted help in making his decision, he was out of luck. His adviser was too far away, walking along the fortress wall, spear in hand, poking and prodding the mudbricks, apparently checking their integrity.

"Oh, all right. Perhaps I should travel by skiff." Amonked gave Nebwa a cautionary look. "This time, at any rate."

They stood close to the spot where the pavilion had stood. The structure had been dismantled, its various pieces and furnishings parceled out among a small herd of donkeys. Nefret and her maid Mesutu, Pawah, Theneny, and Sennefer stood near the gate among the carrying chairs, awaiting Amonked. The scribe had Amonked's dog on a leash so it could not run loose with the strays. One chair was shaded by a canopy the porters had erected to protect Nefrets's delicate complexion.

The falcon was still fresh in Bak's thoughts, as was the

tall column of yellowish dust. "I suggest you keep the caravan moving, sir, stopping only at night."

"I've come to Wawat to inspect the fortresses, young man, not break speed records traveling between Buhen and Semna."

"Speed?" Nebwa laughed, forgetting restraint. "With a caravan as large as this?"

Amonked flung an annoyed look his way.

Bak saw Horhotep hurrying toward them. They had to settle the matter before that swine could interfere. "Troop Captain Nebwa is right, sir. Speed isn't the issue. For any caravan, large or small, forward movement is preferable to no movement. Each time you must inspect a fortress, let the caravan go on without you. Its size will hold it to a modest pace, preventing it from getting so far ahead that you can't readily catch up."

Nebwa, though he must have seen the adviser approaching, kept his voice level, his manner composed and unhurried. "The river in this area is relatively free of rapids, so you can sail on upstream after you've finished. The caravan might have to catch up with you, not the other way around."

"Will you obtain a skiff, Troop Captain, while I gather together those men who'll go with me?" Amonked seemed not to notice Horhotep, coming to a halt beside him, looking suspicious of what might have occurred while his back was turned.

Nebwa exchanged a quick, satisfied look with Bak, let his eyes skip over Horhotep, and gave the inspector his most hearty smile. "I'd be glad to, sir."

"Go on about your business," Nebwa told Bak. "I'll summon you when we're ready to sail."

"Amonked has no intention of taking us with him, Nebwa."

"He'll take us."

Nebwa glanced toward the inspector, who stood among the carrying chairs, facing Nefret. Mesutu and the three men who had been with her earlier had drifted away, allowing privacy. The concubine was clutching the inspector's arm, the look on her face intense, pleading. Amonked shook off her hand, signaled Thaneny and Pawah to go to her, and walked away.

"Just don't dawdle when I send for you," Nebwa added.

Bak was amazed at the confidence his friend could sometimes muster against all odds. "We vowed we'd not interfere in his inspection, and so did Commandant Thuty. Are we to break our pledge?"

"We'll break no oaths if he chooses to invite us along." Laughing, Nebwa swung around and strode toward the twin-towered gate that opened onto the quay.

Bak was unsure what he planned, but if the mischievous look he had glimpsed told a true tale, Amonked's insistence on privacy during his inspections was about to be reversed.

Bak found Lieutenant Merymose standing with his sergeant, Seshu, and the drover of a dozen donkeys awaiting their burdens. All were watching the guards Amonked had brought from the capital, who were scurrying around, packing their belongings. Seshu's mouth was clamped tight, his irritation plain. Merymose, face flushed, looked mortified. Their sergeant, Roy, stood, hands on hips, glaring at the men for whom he was responsible. The drover watched the guards closely, checking their effort. Bak realized as he came close that the men were not packing for the first time. They were repacking. No wonder Seshu and the drover were annoyed.

"If these are an example of the men who guard our sovereign, I fear for her well-being." Seshu did not bother to lower his voice. "Look at them. Dolts, each and every one."

"You should've seen what they intended my donkeys to carry." The drover snorted his disgust. "Loads unbalanced. So loosely tied they'd fall apart. If I hadn't taken a close look, they'd be dropping equipment and supplies all along the trail. Half the animals would drop, too, from loads too weighty for their slight backs."

"They'll learn." Seshu eyed the guards with contempt. "Even if I have to take them out into the desert one by one and lay a whip to their backsides."

The guards sneaked furtive glances his way, checking to see if the threat was sincere. They evidently decided it was, for the pace of their packing grew frantic. Sergeant Roy threw Seshu and the drover a vicious look. Merymose's color deepened.

Bak could understand men trained for duty as royal guards being innocent of the ways of living outdoors, but these men should have been taught within a night or two of leaving Waset. Merymose and Roy should be called to account for negligence.

"I've come to borrow Lieutenant Merymose," he said, trying not to smile at the guards' alarm. "Are you finished with him?"

"Take him!" Seshu glared at the young officer. "He's no good to me."

Merymose threw Bak a look of immense relief and hurried along beside him to the western gate. By the time they stopped well out of hearing distance of the sentry and the men and donkeys filing through, the younger officer looked about to burst.

"I'm sorry, sir," he blurted.

Bak stared at him, caught off-guard.

"I can't seem to do anything right, sir." The words tumbled out in a rush. "I thought myself a good officer. But now . . ." He looked crushed by failure. "Sergeant Roy treats me like a child, and he stands between me and the men. Even if he'd let me do my duty, I wouldn't know what to do."

Bak appreciated the honesty. Not many young officers would be so frank, even when desperate to speak out. "Is this the first posting you've shared with Roy?"

"Yes, sir. He was in charge of training the men for guard

duty. The unit was to be disbanded and they were to be sent to several of our sovereign's estates. Instead, when I was given this assignment, they were all turned over to me." Merymose's voice cracked. "As was he."

"You've never been posted outside of the royal house?"

"No, sir." Merymose gulped air, calming himself. "I know nothing of the desert, and I've come to realize that I know nothing of leading men, training them, guiding them. What am I to do, sir?"

Bak studied the young officer, remembering his own trial by fire at the hands of a surly sergeant. The man had come close to breaking him, stealing his confidence and self-respect before anger and resentment had taken hold. They had fought and Bak had won, ending the cruel game. "I'll speak with Troop Captain Nebwa. I'm sure he'll allow Sergeant Dedu to help you learn what you must so you can lead your men as you should. He's a man of lesser rank, true, but he has the experience and knowledge you need."

Merymose's eyes lit up. "That would be wonderful, sir! I despise looking the fool."

"He can't help you stand up to Sergeant Roy. You alone must do that. Only then will you be able to take your rightful place at the head of your company."

"Roy's not a good sergeant, I know. He's indolent at best, incompetent I'm convinced. When I learn what I'm to do, I'll know how to deal with him."

The words were a promise and Bak took them as such. "I can ask no more."

Another trial Merymose must face was Horhotep, but Bak said nothing of him. The young man had disarmed the more senior officer the previous evening, which had required both courage and conviction. With the help of the gods, he would build upon both assets, gaining the strength of character he would need to deal not only with the sergeant but with the lieutenant.

The braying of a donkey drew Bak's eyes to the gateway. A dark gray beast stood facing the passage, ears drawn back, legs stiff, teeth bared. Cursing vehemently, the drover slapped the creature's flank with the flat of a hand. It refused to budge. The sentry pointed to a spot above the passageway, where several wasps were buzzing around a nest. Muttering an oath, the drover grabbed the donkey's bridle and pulled it past the insects.

Bak glanced toward the gate on the opposite side of the fortress. No sign of Nebwa, but if he somehow managed to keep his vow that they would accompany Amonked to the island, time was pressing. "In Buhen, did you spend your nights in the barracks, or in the house where Amonked's party was quartered?"

"The house." Merymose gave a self-deprecating smile. "Do you think Sergeant Roy wanted me near my own men?"

Bak was pleased the young man could laugh at himself, an invaluable trait given the obstacles he must face. "You know Prince Baket-Amon was slain in the dwelling, I assume, and of the circumstances surrounding his death."

Merymose's face clouded over. "Amonked told us last night while we shared our evening meal."

"Did you see him the morning he died?"

"No, sir."

Bak realized he had gotten ahead of himself. "Would you have known him if you saw him?"

"Oh, yes, sir." Merymose ducked, avoiding a wasp speeding toward the nest. "I often passed him in the corridors of the royal house while I checked to be sure the guards remained at their assigned stations. I also saw him in the audience hall and in other, lesser chambers, awaiting some lofty official."

Bak well remembered his one visit to the royal house. A multitude of buildings, a maze of corridors, dozens of rooms, and too many men to count walking hither and yon, not a face among them one he recognized. "How could you be sure the man you saw was Baket-Amon?"

"Did I not tell you of my good fortune?" Merymose

blinked, surprised by the lapse. "I was assigned to accompany him on a hunting trip. To serve as his aide. Close on two years ago, it was. We went far to the north of Mennufer, seeking wild cattle in the marshes. It was a time I shall never forget." The young officer glowed with enthusiasm.

"You liked him, I see."

"Oh, yes, sir! He always made his wishes clear and he made no demands I couldn't comply with. He was easy to please and generous in showing appreciation. I was sorry when our journey ended."

A hunting expedition, Bak thought. He had never participated in a hunt arranged by and for the nobility, but he had heard tales. Accidents oft times happened during the chase, when wild animals were fleeing in panic and the men who chased them grew so excited they lost control of their wits. "Did anything out of the ordinary happen during the hunt?"

"No, sir." Merymose smiled. "We never did come upon any wild cattle, but one man speared a boar and another laid low a farmer's cow, wounding it so gravely it had to be slain. We also slew small game, mostly hares."

The death of a cow in the northern marshes could in no way have led to the murder of a prince on the southern frontier, almost a month's journey away. "Did Baket-Amon often go hunting?"

"So I understand."

"Did the men who accompanied him appear to like him?"

"Oh, yes, sir!" Merymose must have realized how enthused he sounded, for he blushed. "He was exceptionally skilled with the bow and the spear, but he often held back, allowing the other men to take as much game as he did."

Envy could be a cruel master. "Was anyone slain or injured during that trip?"

"One man sprained an ankle and we all fell into the mud at one time or another. Not a man among us came away unscratched and unbruised."

Nothing there, Bak decided. "Were any young women taken along?"

"Yes, sir. A sufficient number for each of the noblemen." As if anticipating Bak's next question, Merymose added, "No one had cause for jealousy, sir. The women made sure no man ever lay alone."

Bak studied the young officer, who made the expedition sound idyllic. Had the days and nights been as untroubled by contention as Merymose believed—or claimed to believe? "Did Amonked or any of the others who've come with him to Wawat participate in that hunting expedition?"

"No, sir."

Bak had been reaching for the stars and he knew it. A hunting expedition might lead to murder, but not necessarily. And if so, the first expedition he heard about was not likely to be the important one.

Bak stood with Nebwa on the riverbank, watching Amonked's party board the small boat that would carry them upstream to the island fortress. The inspector crossed the narrow plank with surprising agility for one who looked so much the scribe. Captain Minkheper crossed like the seasoned sailor he was, as did Sennefer. Horhotep hesitated on the bank, but Nebwa's expectant grin sent him racing on board.

The boat was broad-beamed and flat, rather like a cargo ship but a fraction of the size. Used to ferry people and animals from one side of the river to the other or from island to island, it was strictly utilitarian, unpainted, unadorned. A heavy canvas spread across spindly poles provided shade. The vessel stunk of animals and their waste, and of fish and human sweat. The hull groaned, the fittings creaked, the patched sail flapped against the mast and yards.

"How did you convince Amonked to bring us along?" Bak asked, keeping his voice low so only Nebwa would hear.

Nebwa's eyes raked the half-dozen skiffs pulled up on

the riverbank. "I meant to lie, to tell him the local men wouldn't have him on their vessels unless we came. I had no need."

Bak gave his friend a sharp look. "Reality was worse than the falsehood?"

"To a man, the fishermen wanted nothing to do with him. A couple of farmers agreed to take him, but they're so resentful of the inspection—so fearful the army will be torn from Wawat—and so angry about Baket-Amon's death that I feared an unfortunate accident."

"With you and me on board?" Bak asked, surprised.

"One man asked if we could swim."

Normally Bak would have laughed, but not now. "What of him?" He nodded toward the ferryman.

Nebwa scowled. "We're paying four times the usual rate, and I vowed he'd be the first to drown if the boat sinks."

"I'm totally out of my element in this barren and desolate land." Captain Minkheper stood with Bak on a crag, looking across the narrow channel between the island and the west bank, where the river nibbled at the edge of a blanket of golden sand blown off the western desert. "I've lived in Kemet much of my life, sailing a river that's broad and deep, looking at fields green and fertile, generous with their bounty. The sands are poised above the valley to either side, to be sure, but at a safe distance for much of the voyage."

"If you're being considered for the lofty position of admiral, you must also have sailed the Great Green Sea." Bak was referring to the huge expanse of water north of the land of Kemet.

"More often than not, especially in the past few years, but I'm a man of Kemet to the core."

"The color of your hair tells another tale."

Minkheper reached up to touch his tousled golden mane, his smile self-conscious. "My ancestors hailed from the island kingdom of Keftiu and lands farther north. Like me, they were men of the sea." Letting the smile fade, he studied the water flowing past, the rippled surface that indicated rocks below. "The river is now at a low level. How much higher will it be at its fullest?"

"Men who fish these waters and whose fathers before them have done so for many generations say it swells four times the height of a man, sometimes more. They speak of the river near Buhen, not through the Belly of Stones, but I assume the difference is slight." Bak climbed down from the crag, as did Minkheper, and they walked toward the partly constructed mudbrick wall of the new fortress. "I've never felt the need to investigate for myself. The water runs much faster when it's high and can take a life in an instant."

"It looks safe enough now."

"Appearances can be deceptive." Bak's voice was hard, incontestable. He knew of what he spoke. The water had once carried him through some of the worst rapids in the river.

The captain queried him with a glance, but the experience was no longer fresh in Bak's thoughts and he preferred not to revive the memory. "Do you spend much time in the capital?"

"I never used to, but now I must." Minkheper's voice grew wry. "How can I hope to attain the exalted position of admiral without making myself known to men who can speak on my behalf to our sovereign?"

Bak veered around a stand of wild grain, setting to flight a pair of quail. "You're very frank, sir."

"Believe me, Lieutenant, I've grown weary of the effort. That's the main reason I agreed to come south with Amonked."

That, Bak thought, and the hope of gaining Maatkare Hatshepsut's favor by looking into the feasibility of digging a canal through the Belly of Stones. "Who offered you the journey?"

"The overseer of royal shipping, a man I've come to know through the years. He took me to Amonked, and there

I met Sennefer and Horhotep." As an afterthought, Minkheper added, "The rest of the party were strangers to me until we set sail."

"Did you know Prince Baket-Amon?"

"I met him only one time. I can't say I knew him."

They circled the stub of a wall and stepped up onto a thick layer of stone fill that would one day serve as a foundation. Farther on, a long and ragged line of boys was delivering mudbricks to twenty or so masons laying level courses across an expanse of wall.

"Did you by chance see him the morning he was slain?"

"I fear I can't help you, Lieutenant."

Bak was growing weary of asking questions no one seemed able to answer. "Did you hear anything that morning out of the ordinary, anything that might've hinted trouble was in the air?"

Minkheper let out a short, cynical laugh. "I overheard parts of an argument between Nefret and Amonked. The way they spoke to each other, I'd not have been surprised to hear that she'd been slain." He paused, added, "Other than that, only the attack on our sailors, which was over before it began."

Discouraged, Bak looked across the building site, where the fortress commander was pointing out some construction or defense feature to Amonked, Horhotep, and Sennefer. Nebwa had vanished, gone off to talk to the spearmen assigned to prevent pilferage of materials and equipment. As one who had risen through the ranks, he was popular with the troops and trusted by them.

Bak led the way through a gate awaiting a lintel. Passing a field of bricks drying in the sun, they crossed an expanse of rough, rocky ground dotted with dead and dying tamarisks. Minkheper was a true outsider, Bak thought. His light hair set him apart from other men of Kemet, his occupation required that he stand alone as a leader of men. Now here he was in an alien land, traveling among strangers. His presence was fortuitous, for Bak was in need of an uninterested observer.

"Will you give me your impressions of your traveling companions?"

Minkheper eyed him thoughtfully. "Amonked would not be pleased if he thought I spoke with too loose a tongue."

"He need never know." Bak scrambled down a narrow, rocky path to the water's edge. He did not press, preferring that the captain decide for himself.

Minkheper climbed onto a boulder that reached out over the water. From there, he studied the several craggy islands and the narrow, turbulent channels between them and the east bank of the river. "I spent much of the voyage from Waset performing my duties as commander of Amonked's flotilla. With so many ships to see to, I had little opportunity to get to know anyone. I can only give you impressions based on limited contact."

"I accept that, sir."

Minkheper scanned the river, searching out its secrets, then dropped off the boulder to walk with Bak along the shore. The chatter of sparrows rose above the murmur of shallow water flowing among rocks.

"I believe Amonked to be a kind and gentle man, one who wouldn't hurt a scorpion." Minkheper paused to study a stain on a rock crag, a high-water mark. "Nefret has gone out of her way to try his patience. He's snapped back at her, argued with her, but he hasn't laid a hand on her, as some men would. I at first thought him to be weak, but now I'm not so sure."

"To me, he seems always under tight control." Or is he merely stubborn and plodding? Bak wondered.

The captain gave him an ironic smile. "I doubt you'd say that if you'd heard him argue with Nefret the morning we left Buhen."

"Could their dispute have been about Baket-Amon?"

"Not at all. She wanted to return to Kemet and he insisted she travel on to Semna." Minkheper eyed a clump of brush, torn from the ground, roots and all, by the previous year's flood. "I think she likes him and respects him, but as a beloved uncle, not the lover she should consider him to be. And she's frightened of this wild land through which we're traveling. She hasn't the wit to see how unattractive she's making herself. Frankly, if I walked in Amonked's sandals, I'd send her back to her father and have nothing more to do with her."

Bak pictured the lovely young woman he had seen in the pavilion, upset but dry-eyed. It wouldn't be easy to spurn her.

"The scribe Thaneny, a man conscientious to a fault, is her devoted slave," Minkheper continued, "and the herald Pawah, a mere boy, is equally eager to please her. Even Sennefer is beguiled by her."

Surprised, Bak said, "I had an idea nothing touched him, unless in a cynical vein."

"He appears aloof, yes, but I can see he's uneasy around the woman; he's drawn to her. I've also noticed that he's not comfortable with this expedition." Minkheper must have spotted Bak's heightened interest, for he added, "You mustn't count on him to aid your cause. He's here as Amonked's friend, so he'll do or say nothing that will influence the outcome."

"Lieutenant Horhotep is the man who troubles me," Bak said, casting a line he hoped would catch a weapon he could use against the officer. "I doubt he's competent, yet he holds the fate of hundreds upon hundreds of people in his hands. I suspect he'd sell his soul for promotion and the chance to catch our sovereign's eye."

Minkheper flashed a smile. "I know nothing of his talents as a man of arms, but he wears his ambition as men of valor wear the gold of honor, in plain sight and with pride. I believe Lieutenant Merymose to be a much better man, but unfortunately he's at Horhotep's mercy."

They reached the southern end of the island and Minkheper returned to the task he had traveled south to per-

form. Bak answered his questions about the river as best
he could and showed him all he asked to see and more. It
was the least he could do. He had learned almost nothing
from the captain, but he appreciated the fact that the man
had spoken with an open and forthright tongue. Or had he?

The ferry, its sail aloft and swollen, sped south before a
stiff breeze. The late afternoon sun was washed out, weak,
allowing the air to cool, making Bak and the others shiver.
To the west, the faint yellow cloud that marked the caravan's location had moved past the tall, conical hill that
served as a watch station south of Kor. Seshu was keeping
animals and men moving at a good speed, taking advantage
of the first day out when they had not yet grown weary and
foot-sore.

"Three fortresses so close together you can shout from
one to another." Lieutenant Horhotep stood with Amonked
under the canvas roof, taking advantage of what little shelter it gave from the breeze. "The reason is beyond my com-
prehension."

"The journey by boat was swift," Amonked said. "I
imagine the trek on foot would take over an hour."

"Buhen I can understand. It's large, reasonably strong,
and in a halfway acceptable condition. As for Kor," Horhotep scoffed, "the men who toil there are lucky to be alive.
If its walls weren't so thick, they'd long ago have fallen,
crushing those inside. And the fortress we viewed today . . ."

"The swine." Nebwa, standing a half-dozen paces forward, spat over the rail. "I'd like to throw him overboard
and let the crocodiles make a meal of him." He had the
good sense to speak softly.

Bak pointed aft, toward the man at the tiller. "You're not
the only one." The ferryman who, like everyone else on
board had heard every word, was glaring at the adviser, his
expression stormy.

Sennefer, he noticed, was also watching the ferryman.

His demeanor was serious, lacking the usual touch of irony. Captain Minkheper eyed the adviser with poorly concealed disgust.

"Why? Pray tell me why they feel the need to build a new fortress?" Horhotep ranted. "Why go to so much effort and expense? Tearing down the old ruins, rebuilding on an island that can't be reached without a boat? It'll be hard to man, more difficult to equip, and close to impossible to supply."

"The man hasn't the wits of a lump of dirt," Nebwa growled. "Doesn't he know that nearly half the fortresses along the Belly of Stones are located on islands?"

Bak, like his friend, had heard enough. Stepping under the shelter, certain he was wasting his breath, he asked, "Has it not occurred to you, Lieutenant, that the new fortress occupies a strategic position on the river? Surrounded by water and at the downstream end of the rapids, it'll be virtually indestructible."

"Buhen is bigger and stronger. Would it not serve the same purpose?"

"Buhen offers a second line of defense. Have you never heard of a fall-back position?"

"In areas of serious trouble, yes. But here?" The adviser laughed sarcastically and turned his back, a rude dismissal.

Anger swept through Bak. He hated being treated as of no significance by a man he considered unworthy. Swallowing words he knew he would regret, clenching his hands so tight they ached, he strode forward, passed Nebwa and the others without a word, and stood at the prow, thinking the breeze would cool him down. If he knew for a fact that the falcon delivered to Kor had been a message from Hor-pen-Deshret, he would have a weapon of sorts to counter Horhotep's scorn. He had no proof, however, only a feeling even Nebwa ridiculed.

The ferryman turned the vessel toward a small oasis at the end of a dry wadi. Vegetable plots and clusters of date palms spoke of fertile ground and a habitation nearby, probably farther up the wadi on land less precious than the tiny floodplain. A stand of acacias clung to a high mudbank at the southern end of the oasis, and two small skiffs lay on the shore in their shade. A good place to off-load passengers, an easy walk to the desert trail and the caravan.

A movement among the palms caught Bak's eye, a cluster of men standing in their shade, watching the approaching vessel. He counted fourteen. Men, he guessed, who had left farms or hamlets up and down the river to register their aversion to the inspector and his mission.

As the ferry neared the shore, the men walked out from among the palms and strode along the sunny southern edge of the tiny oasis, skirting the fields, heading toward the water. Each carried a hoe or sickle or staff or mallet or some other farm tool. All of which could serve as weapons.

Chapter Eight

Nebwa came up beside Bak, looking grim. "So it's begun."

The men on shore strode down a narrow cut in the mud-bank a few paces downstream from the skiffs and formed a ragged line near the river's edge. Every eye was locked on the approaching ferry. Bak recognized about half, men who farmed small plots of land along the river or on the islands above Kor. They sometimes came to Buhen to the market or to air complaints.

Sennefer hurried to the prow. "Men who till the fields in the province of Sheresy, where my country estate lies, seem never to have the leisure to gather together for no good reason. Am I to assume the same is true here?"

"Should we expect trouble?" Minkheper asked, joining them.

Nebwa looked to Bak for an answer. Though reared in Wawat and wed to a local woman, he spent most of his time in the garrison and considered himself out of touch. Untrue, but so he believed.

Bak shrugged. "I can make no promises, but I doubt they'll harm us. I suspect they've come to create unease in our hearts."

"To threaten," Amonked said, coming up behind them.

The ferryman dropped the sail, slowing the vessel, and set a course for the beached skiffs. The waiting men stood grim-faced and unmoving, silent, watchful. Unnerving.

Amonked rested his hands on the rail and scowled toward the men across the water. "Will these people continue this . . . this silent confrontation throughout our journey to Semna?"

"I'd not count on them remaining silent," Nebwa said.

"This is abominable! Demeaning to our sovereign!" Horhotep, standing behind Amonked, slapped his leg with his baton of office. "A good beating here and now would put a stop to this outrage once and for all."

Nebwa swung around, eyes smoldering. "You'll lay your baton on no man or woman in Wawat, Lieutenant. You hear me?"

"You've no right . . . !"

The ferry swung suddenly toward the waiting men and swept into the shallows, throwing muddy water to either side and splattering the men on deck. Without warning, the prow dug into the soft bottom. The vessel stopped as if it had struck a solid wall. Bak stumbled against the rail and at the same time grabbed Nebwa's arm to keep him from falling. Amonked held on tight. Horhotep, who dared not grab the inspector, was thrown off his feet and skidded across the deck. Minkheper, flung backward, grabbed an upright supporting the canvas roof, threatening to topple the shelter. Sennefer fell to his knees. The men on shore, though they must have been surprised—and delighted— maintained their stony silence.

Bak glimpsed a look of exultation on the ferryman's face. The impact had been deliberate, prompted by Horhotep's cruel threat.

"I fear you'll have to wade ashore, Troop Captain," the ferryman said. "We're too far out to use the gangplank."

Nebwa gave the man a fierce look, then noticed Horhotep lifting himself off the deck and searching for splinters. Shaken by silent laughter, he handed over the token the ferryman would present to the garrison quartermaster for payment for services. "I trust next time you'll be more careful," he said with mock severity.

The ferryman tried not to smile, failed. "Yes, sir!"

Bak was the first to drop off the vessel. He sank into the muck up to his ankles, and thick, black water swirled around his lower legs. He waded to dry ground and stopped midway along the line of men. Feeling a bit ridiculous with grime to the knees and his sandals oozing mud, he bade them a good afternoon, his expression uncritical but stern. He called those he knew by name so they would have no doubt he could identify them later if trouble arose.

The line held firm; the men clung to their silence and their grim demeanor. He stood where he was, his stance as firm as theirs, letting his eyes travel from one man to the next, settling briefly on each in turn. He heard Nebwa behind him and Amonked drop into the water with a loud splash. Three further splashes told him the remainder of the party had left the ferry.

He walked forward, displaying a confidence he did not entirely feel. The line of men parted, slowly, reluctantly, and allowed him through. Resisting the urge to look back, to make sure Nebwa and the others remained unmolested, he walked to the cut in the mudbank and climbed partway to the top. Only then did he turn around.

Nebwa stood knee-deep in the water with Amonked's small party around him. He was speaking low but with vehemence—giving orders, Bak assumed. With a hasty smile, Amonked broke away from the group and strode after Bak. Walking relaxed and easy, his expression benign, he passed through the break in the line of men. Minkheper followed close behind, talking of the coolness of the evening. Sennefer passed through with the aplomb of a wealthy landowner accustomed to dealing with the poor. Horhotep, looking furious, marched out of the water with Nebwa so close he might have been guarding him. Maybe he was.

Never missing a step, Nebwa clapped the nearest farmer on the shoulder, asked another how his eldest son was, waved to a third and called him by name. Within moments he was walking up the cut in the wake of his charges.

*   *   *

Bak wove a path through piles of equipment and supplies, listening to men's voices and the sounds of animals settling down for the night. A faint odor of burning fuel hung in the air and the scent of onions and fish clung to empty bowls and the breaths of the men he passed. The feral dogs were nosing around in their endless quest for sustenance. Peace and contentment reigned, a peace he prayed would continue.

He thought of the falcon left atop the wall at Kor. Of how easily the man had entered the fortress, breaching its defenses, and climbed undetected to the battlements. During the light of day, no man could infiltrate the caravan, but the moon was waning, each night darker than the one before.

He walked past Amonked's guards' encampment. The men, divided into two units, were seated around makeshift hearths, basking in the warmth after consuming their evening meal. Their camp had long ago been set up—thanks to Sergeant Dedu. They spoke quietly to one another, content with a task well learned, no longer argumentative as before.

Earlier, Nebwa had taken aside Sergeant Roy, telling him in no uncertain terms what he expected of him: full and unquestioning cooperation. Dedu would provide the training Roy had been unwilling or unable to give, and Merymose would take his rightful place at the head of the guards. Roy had grumbled, but the threat of having him reassigned to Horhotep had shut him up fast enough.

Bak circled Amonked's pavilion, which smelled faintly of oil lamps and Nefret's perfume. The light inside made the fabric walls glow, and vague shadows darted back and forth. Beyond, he found the row of tents occupied by the remainder of the inspection party. The one he sought was the sole shelter not yet erected, that of Thaneny, who had had to aid Amonked in preparing his report on the island fortress. Pawah, who shared the flimsy structure, had been pressed into service to run errands and serve as the inspector's personal servant. Now here they were, later than everyone else, preparing to raise their shelter.

"Do we have to sleep in a tent?" Pawah asked. "I'd much rather lie in the open—like the drovers do."

"Not another word." Thaneny bent at the waist to straighten the heavy linen. "Have you forgotten already how cold you were last night?"

"I'll sleep with my head outside," the youth said defiantly.

"Grab a pole," Thaneny commanded.

Pawah made a face for Bak's benefit, but obeyed. Thaneny proved to be surprisingly agile for one so crippled, and soon the center of the canvas was raised on waist-high poles, the sides pinned down with rocks. A simple but ideal shelter for two men—except in a high wind.

Thanks to the gods, the breeze had died and the night was clear, with pinpoints of light glittering strong and bright overhead. Such clarity meant the night would be cool. Bak shivered at the thought. He, like everyone outside of Amonked's immediate party, had to sleep beneath the stars.

Thaneny slipped into a tunic to ward off the chill and sat on the ground in front of the tent. Bak dropped down beside him. Pawah picked up a handful of sand and let it trickle down the sloping side of the shelter.

"How did you manage the trek today?" Bak asked the scribe.

"He traveled in utmost comfort," Pawah said, "like a great nobleman."

The scribe cuffed the youth on the rear. "Go away, waif."

Grinning, Pawah ducked out of his reach.

Thaneny smiled at Bak. "I must admit, the child is right. Amonked gave me leave to use his carrying chair, saying he wished me to watch over mistress Nefret while he was away inspecting the island fortress. Throughout the morning I felt presumptuous, but by day's end, I reveled in the luxury."

Bak laughed. "You'll rapidly become spoiled. Your master has another inspection tomorrow."

The scribe's good humor faded. "Will the local men show themselves again, hoping to intimidate him as they tried to do today?"

"They don't give up easily."

Pawah plopped down on the sand facing Bak. "Sennefer said you were very brave today, sir."

Bak rolled his eyes skyward. "A gross exaggeration."

"Still . . ." The boy leaned toward him, eyes wide, willing him to admit to a courage Bak felt unwarranted under the circumstances.

Mindful of the pavilion a few paces away and its flimsy linen walls, he took care how he answered. "The men who faced us today saw Nebwa and me with Amonked. They surely concluded that I, a man they know as fair and compassionate, have come to look into Prince Baket-Amon's murder. They can also be sure Nebwa, a man highly respected in Wawat for his rough honesty, his integrity, will see that no harm comes to the caravan or to any who dwell along the river. They had far more to gain by allowing us to pass than by attacking us."

"Do you and the troop captain hold so much power?" the scribe asked.

"Not power. Trust." Bak rubbed his arms, wishing he had thought to don a tunic before leaving the archers' hearth. "To retain that trust, I must lay hands on Baket-Amon's slayer and Nebwa must see that no man suffers loss of life or property."

"If you don't?"

Bak shrugged, unable to answer.

"Has it never occurred to you that the prince might've been slain by someone wishing to take his place as leader of his people?" Thaneny asked.

The question was valid, but Bak suspected it was

prompted more by hope than conviction that the slayer would be found outside of Amonked's party. "The succession has never been an issue. He had a young son, whose mother will serve as regent, and other, younger sons of the same woman."

"He was very loyal to Kemet, I've been told. Would anyone have wished him dead in order to tear this part of Wawat out of our sovereign's grasp?"

"Certainly not the kings of Kush who dwell beyond our southern frontier. Many years ago, the powerful kingdom centered in Kerma was crushed by Ahkheperkare Thutmose, and it's now fragmented into a number of smaller, weaker kingdoms. Each thrives on the trade passing between Kemet and the lands farther south. Who would jeopardize that? As for the people who dwell here in Wawat, they need us just as we need them."

Unable to offer another option, Thaneny fell silent. His expression was glum, as was Pawah's, neither wanting to believe the prince had been slain by someone close to them.

"Have you been with Amonked for long?" Bak asked.

"Four years." Thaneny, looking relieved at the change of subject, shifted position. He had trouble bending the damaged knee. "Since I was hurt in an accident at our sovereign's new memorial temple across the river from the capital. A weakened rope, a stone sliding out of control . . ." His voice tailed off, leaving the rest to the imagination.

Bak nodded his understanding. He had grown to manhood near the southern capital of Waset, where men toiled year after year on the mansions of the gods and the tombs and memorial temples of royalty. Raised by his physician father, he had grown accustomed to seeing men crippled and maimed or hearing of men killed by heavy stones falling while being lifted into place or scaffolds collapsing or mounds of sand or rocks sliding out of control. "And the lord Amon chose to smile upon you."

"The god, yes, and Amonked." Thaneny flashed a grateful look toward the pavilion. "He'd come to the temple that day to see how the work progressed. He saw the stone lifted off me and the way my leg was crushed, and he had me carried to a royal physician. Later, while I lay drugged and senseless, he took me to his home where his servants could care for me. I came close to death, they tell me, and I spent many days unable to get off my sleeping pallet."

No wonder he's so devoted to Amonked, Bak thought. Few men with so serious an injury would have survived. Only constant and dutiful care could have kept him alive—and a bright, clean house instead of a hovel.

"My debt to Amonked grew each day." The scribe glanced again toward the pavilion and the shadows flitting across the lighted walls. "I couldn't walk, but I could read and write. As soon as I could sit erect, he allowed me to read to his children and to teach them. When I learned to walk on crutches, he took me into his office."

"There you've been ever since?"

Thaneny's voice pulsed with emotion. "I can never repay him. Never. He gave me my life."

"Must you dwell on the past, Thaneny?" Amonked stood at the corner of the pavilion, baton of office in hand, mouth pursed in disapproval. "You've long since repaid me with your competence, your honesty, your loyalty. You offend me by thinking otherwise."

The scribe bowed his head. "Yes, sir."

A frustrated sigh burst from Amonked's lips. He greeted Bak with a nod and beckoned Pawah. "Come. I wish to speak with the caravan master."

The boy's eyes lit up and he leaped to his feet.

When they were well out of hearing distance, Bak returned to the purpose for which he had come. "Did you see Baket-Amon the morning he was slain?"

"No, sir." The answer came fast and firm, with no hesitation betraying doubt.

Bak gave him a sharp look. "You knew him, I see."

"I did, yes." Thaneny noticed Bak's heightened interest and his voice turned wry. "We were far from intimate,

Lieutenant. I'm a servant and he was a man of substance."

Bak doubted the scribe spent much time in the royal house. Other than errands, Amonked would have no need to send him there. He would be more useful in his master's home in Waset or on his country estate—or estates. "How did you meet him? Where?"

The scribe hesitated, his reluctance to answer apparent.

"I'll learn the truth, Thaneny, with or without your help."

The scribe took a long time answering. "Two years ago, or was it three? He took a liking to mistress Nefret. He . . . Well, I don't know if you, who dwell here in his homeland, ever heard tales of his exploits in Waset. But he was a man who loved women. Many women."

"Wawat was also his playground," Bak assured him.

"Then you know he wasn't one to give up easily."

"I've heard no tales of Baket-Amon pursuing a woman who offered no encouragement."

"Mistress Nefret gave him none. I swear she didn't." The protest was made with the intensity of a zealot. "Nonetheless, he came often to Amonked's house, thinking to attract her attention."

Nefret was lovely, Bak granted, but would beauty alone have been sufficient to draw the prince away from more fruitful pursuits? "Did he catch her eye?"

"She's a good girl, honest and loyal, and she knows she owes Amonked everything. At times she isn't happy, and now and again they quarrel, but her father—a minor nobleman with no wealth to speak of—committed her to him, and she vowed to live up to their agreement. Since she's shared his bed, many young men have paraded before her. She's looked at none of them."

A strong avowal of unwavering fidelity. Enough to make Bak weary—and arouse suspicion. "Did she ever acknowledge the prince's pursuit?"

"I doubt she even noticed him."

Bak bestowed upon the scribe a long, skeptical look. Thaneny did not so much as flinch. His admiration for the woman, his adoration, was unshakable. "Did Amonked know of Baket-Amon's interest in mistress Nefret and of his many visits?"

"No, sir!" Thaneny eyed Bak furtively, realized another answer had come too fast, and hastened to explain. "When we're in residence in Waset, he goes each day to the royal house and continues on to the warehouses of the lord Amon. He returns in the late afternoon, when he summons me to his private reception room to discuss the business of the day. The women are alone much of the time, left to their own resources."

The lord Amon spare me, Bak thought. Amonked may have been away much of the time, but the servants were there. Men and women who would keep their master informed. And a wife who might resent the lovely young concubine and wish her harm. Amonked most certainly knew the prince had come too often to the house, his intent not entirely honorable.

As Bak walked past the far side of the pavilion, retracing his earlier footsteps, he heard a woman's quiet sobbing. Nefret. Other than her servant, she was probably alone. What better time to ask her of what Thaneny had unwittingly hinted?

He walked to the entry portal, lifted the cloth, and peered inside. The maid Mesutu huddled close to a lighted brazier, hugging herself, staring at the burning fuel. She was a picture of abject misery. Listening to the sobbing woman beyond the flimsy wall would certainly not help to improve her outlook.

"I've come to see your mistress," Bak said.

The girl looked up, startled. Recognition touched her face and she scrambled to her feet. She hurried to the hangings dividing the space, patted the linen until she found a place where two edges of fabric came together, and slipped through. The sobbing stopped, replaced by soft murmurs.

Mesutu came back. "She'll see you. Please seat yourself."

After sitting outside with Thaneny, he thought the pavilion warm and cozy, the pillow on which he sat luxurious. The girl brought him a jar of beer and a stemmed bowl from which to drink the brew. She set a shallow bowl of dates and sweetcakes on a low table beside him. With a shy smile, she returned to her mistress.

Bak sipped, he nibbled, he waited. And waited. He silently cursed the woman. What could she be doing? Hiding the ravages of her unhappiness beneath a thick coat of makeup? He preferred to speak with her alone, but soon Amonked would return. The inspector would not be pleased at finding him with the concubine at such a late hour.

"Lieutenant Bak," Nefret said, holding back the fabric to either side, letting it drape gracefully around her.

He recognized a pose when he saw one. "Mistress Nefret, I know you must be tired after a long day's trek, but I fear I must speak with you."

"I knew you'd come. Perhaps not tonight, but I doubted you'd wait for long." She let the fabric fall free and walked to the brazier, followed closely by her maid. Placing an arm around the child's shoulders, she raised her voice so her words would carry to Thaneny's tent. "Mesutu heard you with Thaneny."

"He told me nothing I couldn't have learned elsewhere."

Her eyes, puffy from sobbing and heavily made up, glittered with anger. Again, she raised her voice. "Why that accursed scribe can't mind his own business I'll never understand!"

"He's fond of you."

"Fond!" Releasing Mesutu, she plopped down on a loose stack of pillows, and dropped her voice to a normal level. "If he cared so much, he'd convince Amonked to let me return to Kemet." She reached for a date, bit into it, frowned. "I hate this horrible desert, this empty land. I want to go home!"

"Would Amonked listen to a scribe's pleas?"

"He listens to him in matters of business." Nefret noticed Mesutu standing off to the side, shivering. She patted the pillow beside her, inviting the child near the heat. "You're right, though. He's too angry with me, too stubborn, to listen to Thaneny now."

Footsteps outside drew near and passed on, reminding Bak of Amonked's imminent arrival. How could he distract Nefret from herself? "You're fortunate you're not wed to a soldier, one who would bring you here to live for many long months."

She took another date, nibbled. "Thaneny could speak for me to Sennefer. Amonked would listen to his wife's brother."

"Sennefer seems easy enough to talk to. Why don't you speak with him yourself?"

"He's always so cold toward me." She bit her lip, swallowed what Bak feared would be more sobs. "I understand he must protect his sister's interests, and Amonked is her greatest interest. She adores him, shelters him from domestic troubles, prays I'll give him the son she never could." Tears spilled over and she whimpered, "I don't want his child. I want Sennef . . ."

With a sharp little groan, the child Mesutu grabbed her mistress's arm and dug her nails in, cutting short the indiscretion.

Nefret clapped a hand over her mouth. "Oh! Oh, please, Lieutenant . . ."

Startled by the disclosure, but not so badly that his thoughts were hampered, he placed a finger before his lips and pointed in the general direction of the row of tents. Speaking softly, he said, "You have my pledge. I'll say nothing."

"I'll be forever in your debt," she murmured.

"Did you see Prince Baket-Amon in Buhen?" he asked, raising his voice to a normal level, taking advantage of the need to distract both her and Thaneny—if the scribe was listening. Or anyone in that row of tents.

She threw him a quick look of gratitude. "How could I see him or anyone else? Amonked insisted I stay inside all the while we were there."

"You didn't see him the morning he came to the dwelling?"

"Of course not," she said, indignant. "Did I not just tell you I didn't see him in Buhen?"

He had to smile. She was either a superb actress or her powers of recovery were uncommonly fast. "You met him in Waset, Thaneny told me."

"Waset!" she said scornfully. "If that witless goose knew half as much as he thinks he does, he'd be toiling for Maatkare Hatshepsut herself, not her cousin." She tossed her head, making her thick dark hair swing across her shoulders. "I met him in Sheresy. My father has a farm adjoining Sennefer's estate, which is very large and teems with wild creatures. Amonked sometimes took guests there, and they hunted in the marshes or out on the desert. That's how I met him, and that's how I met the prince."

Bak eyed her sharply. "Are you saying Amonked took the prince to Sennefer's estate to hunt?"

"He might've, or perhaps someone else did." She took a sweetcake from the bowl and broke it in half. "Our sovereign may wear the trappings of a king, but she long ago gave up any pretense of performing the manly arts. Now, when she wants to impress foreign dignitaries or reward with sport the nobility of Kemet, she has Amonked and other trusted advisers invite them on her behalf to hunt or fish or partake of some other form of active diversion. As the marshes of Sheresy and the nearby desert have an abundance of wildlife, Amonked takes them to Sennefer's estate rather than to his own more modest holding near Mennufer. As do a few close friends of Sennefer."

Bak could not remember Amonked's exact words, but he had led him to believe he barely knew the prince. Yet the best way to get to know a man, other than on the field of battle, was to share the excitement and danger of a hunt. "I never would've thought Amonked a man of action."

"He does what he must."

"Did Baket-Amon desire you then, as he did later in Waset?"

She laughed derisively. "When first I met the prince, I wore the sidelock of youth. He failed to notice me." She was speaking of the braided hairstyle children of the wealthy often wore before they reached maturity. "When I became a woman, Amonked took me as his own and I left my father's dwelling in Sheresy. Not until later did I meet the prince again, in Waset."

"What did you think of him?"

"Baket-Amon?" She scowled. "He made me feel uncomfortable. Staring at me with those great cow eyes of his. I finally told Amonked I wanted him sent away."

Bak's spirits plummeted. The odds were good that Amonked had hunted with Baket-Amon. They were even better that he had confronted the prince about the concubine, warning him away from her. And he a man who claimed he barely knew the dead man.

Amonked. Maatkare Hatshepsut's cousin. The only man in the inspection party Bak had found thus far who had a reason to slay Baket-Amon. A reason but not a strong reason.

He wished he could talk to Imsiba, compare what the two of them had learned over the past two days. Had the Medjay discovered some key fact that pointed to a slayer far outside of Amonked's party? Surely not. A courier would have brought news of such import. Rumor would have spread the word.

Chapter Nine

"What in the name of the lord Amon did I do with my sandals?" Sergeant Dedu grumbled.

"Mine are missing, too," an archer said, rubbing his arms to stave off the early morning chill.

"And mine," another man said, lifting the edge of his sleeping pallet to look beneath it.

Four other archers reported a similar loss.

Nebwa planted his fists on his hips and scowled at the men, his patience made thin by the need to arise so early. "When did you last see them?" he demanded.

"I took them off last night when I lay down to sleep," Dedu said, "and I set them beside me so I'd have no trouble finding them."

The other men agreed that they, too, had kept their footwear close by.

Nebwa could no more hide his impatience to have the problem over and done with than the moon could hide in a clear night sky. "They'll turn up. They're bound to. In the meantime, go barefoot."

The lord Khepre, not yet peering over the eastern horizon, painted the sky a silvery white that rapidly turned a brilliant gold. A gentle breeze fanned the air, holding off the sun's warmth, feeding the chill. The lead donkeys of the caravan struck out along the trail, with others falling in line as soon as their loads were in place. The animals that would bring up the rear trotted in from the river, a few laden with water jars, the rest bare-backed. The feral dogs, wet and boisterous, sped past them to race alongside the donkeys already on the move.

Throughout the previous day, the caravan had traveled across the broad, gentle slope between the river and a long sandy ridge that formed a horizon off to the right, blocking their view of the open desert beyond. As the afternoon waned, the ridge had drawn closer, ending in a high, sheer precipice that overlooked a seemingly unending stretch of rapids. Seshu had halted men and animals to set up camp a short distance north of the steep drift of windblown sand that rose up the formation, near the point where the trail crossed the ridge.

Now, while the lead animals plodded up the slope and disappeared over the crest, Amonked, Minkheper, Horhotep, and Sennefer prepared to climb the promontory to inspect the watch station located on top. The post was crucial to the defense of the frontier, offering a panoramic view of river and desert in all directions. Bak prayed the inspector would recognize its value.

"Come, Lieutenant," Nebwa said. "We've another inspection to accompany."

Bak studied the coarse-featured officer with a mixture of fondness and suspicion. "What excuse will you give today?"

Nebwa's expression grew bland, overly innocent. "I saw farmers when I bathed in the river this morning and I told Amonked so. He thought it best that you and I stay close."

Bak, who had bathed in the same still pool as Nebwa and at the same time, gave his friend a wide-eyed look of exaggerated shock. "You would tell our sovereign's cousin a falsehood?"

Nebwa turned dead serious. "If you don't have time to besiege a fortress, you have two choices. You can march your army on, praying the men sheltered within its walls don't attack you from behind—or you can find a way to get inside by stealth."

"Impressive," Captain Minkheper said. "Far grander than the rapids above Abu."

Bak stood at the edge of the precipice, chilled by the breeze that ruffled his hair and the hem of his kilt. He looked down upon a tortured landscape of rock and water, a labyrinth so wild and cruel it might have been created by denizens of the netherworld. He had been here before, and each time the river had shown a different face. Low water or high made no difference; he felt the same awe each time.

"Only at the highest flood can a ship travel these rapids," he explained, "and only with the aid of men with stout ropes, pulling the vessel upstream along channels of rushing water or holding it in place as they let it down. North of Iken, when that's impossible, the ships are dragged alongside the river on a slipway built across the sand."

"Granite. A stone difficult to work in the best of conditions. And the conditions here are appalling."

"Yes, sir." Bak made no further comment. Better that Minkheper decide for himself how difficult and hazardous it would be to excavate a canal through the Belly of Stones.

Together they studied the harsh and wild river below. Water gushing smooth and fast where its course was free, foaming and eddying and cascading where interrupted, murmuring and singing and splashing. Hundreds of separate channels flowing around a multitude of black glistening islets. A few full-blown islands supporting trees and brush and rough grass and sometimes a tiny house, with fruits and vegetables growing in pockets of soil, goats nibbling wild vegetation, and waterfowl swimming in the shallows.

"How long is this stretch of rapids?" Minkheper asked.

"I've not seen it from end to end with my own eyes," Bak admitted, "but they say a four-hour journey by foot."

Minkheper whistled, thoroughly impressed.

Satisfied the captain understood the impracticality of

their sovereign's plan, Bak left him at the edge of the precipice to further mold his thoughts. He walked up the ridge
to join the inspection party.

"How many men are posted here?" Lieutenant Horhotep
asked in a sharp voice.

"Ten." The sergeant in charge of the watch station
paused—long enough to attract notice, not long enough to
earn a reprimand. "Sir."

Horhotep's mouth tightened. He slapped his leg with his
baton of office. "Ten men for ten days. Another ten for ten
more days. On and on forever. I'd think the commander of
Iken could find a better occupation for so many men."

The sergeant, a short, powerful man of twenty-five or so
years, threw a disgusted look Bak's way. They had met
before and shared a mutual regard. "Without prior warning,
how can the troops assigned to man the walls of Buhen or
Iken make the necessary final preparations to hold off the
enemy?"

"What enemy?" Horhotep swung his arm in an arc en-
compassing the boulder-strewn river and the barren, rolling
desert to the west. Other than the caravan, made small by
distance, and a flock of geese flying low over the rapids,
not a creature stirred in any direction.

"I've heard tales that an old foe of ours has come back
from off the desert. Hor-pen-Deshret by name. A man to
be reckoned with. All who remember him fear him."

"Tales!" Horhotep snorted. "Rumors designed to plant
fear in the hearts of men who know no better. Gossip created by men who wish this land to remain a ward of the
army."

Nebwa threw the adviser a look of profound disgust,
clamped his mouth tight, and stalked off along the ridge.

Amonked eyed him thoughtfully, then walked to a reed
lean-to built against a crude mudbrick hut. The shelter stood
among the ruined walls of several older buildings that
hugged the ridge not far below the summit. "You live
rough, I see."

The sergeant hurried to the inspector's side. "We need no more than a roof over our heads, sir, and the supplies brought daily by the desert patrol. We've plenty of water close to hand and each other's company to stave off boredom."

"Ah, I see!" Horhotep said, walking up behind them. "Ten men are posted here at all times, not out of necessity but so you'll always be entertained."

The sergeant, his face flushed with fury, balled his hands into fists. With a mighty effort, he restrained himself.

Sennefer leaned close to Bak and murmured, "If Horhotep survives this journey, the gods will have blundered exceedingly."

"I'd be pleased to serve as the instrument of their wrath."

Amonked, who may or may not have heard, turned to his advisor. "I understand there's a trail along the ridge, Lieutenant. I wish you to take that route to the caravan." He paused, awaiting a response. When he received none, his voice sharpened. "You've seen all you need to see here, Lieutenant. I suggest you leave at once."

Horhotep pivoted, hiding his expression, and strode away, his steps quick and stiff, his back as rigid as a tree.

Surprised by the order, Bak looked closely at Amonked. As usual, the inspector's face revealed nothing. Was he growing weary of his adviser's abrasive manner? Or, better yet, had he begun to mistrust Horhotep's continual faultfinding?

The inspection party caught up with the caravan within the hour. Amonked and his companions hastened to rejoin Nefret near the foremost donkeys, where the air was cleaner. Bak and Nebwa lagged behind, talking to the drovers. The archers were strung out along both sides of the caravan, well out of the dust and far enough away to see approaching strangers. The feral dogs roamed up and down the line or wandered off into the desert or down toward the river.

With the ridge no longer restricting their view, they could see the vast undulating plain to the west, a barren land covered with golden sand from which protruded dark, isolated islands of rock. To the east, beyond gentle mounds of windblown sand, they caught glimpses of green and spotted flashes of silver. The sparse vegetation, the gleaming water relieved the eye and reassured both men and animals that the life-giving river was close by, a place to drink one's fill, to rest, and to bathe.

The serenity was short-lived. Soon after the inspection party returned from the watch station, men appeared without warning, taking up positions at the edge of the desert, where sand met the river's verge, watching the caravan slowly trudge past. They stood at a distance, to be sure, but were ever-present, nagging reminders of how strongly the people resented Amonked's mission.

Midday came and went. At infrequent intervals the desert trail drew close to the river, giving the members of the caravan a better look at those who watched them. One man or two or three, sometimes a family, sometimes the entire population of a tiny hamlet. They stood quietly, watching, their immobility and silence more fearsome than threats.

Seshu drew Bak aside and pointed toward the distant figures. "Those people are beginning to erode the confidence of my drovers. Can you not do something to make them stay home?"

Bak gave him a regretful smile. "You've been making this journey for years, Seshu. You know what I face. They may be acting in unison, but they've no single man to lead them."

"Who is Prince Baket-Amon's heir, do you know?"

"His firstborn son, a child eight years of age."

Seshu groaned. "And the mother to serve as regent."

"Yes." Bak eyed the small vague images standing along the river. "Baket-Amon kept her in Ma'am and there she'll remain until his body is prepared for the netherworld." That groan troubled him. "I've no doubt she'll soon hear what these people are doing. The question is: Can she do anything to stop them and would she if she could?"

"She has the power, but she'll do nothing. She doted on her husband."

Bak looked hard at the caravan master. "Are you telling me she'll encourage the people to make a display against Amonked, not because she resents his mission but as a way of demanding that her husband's slayer be brought to justice?"

Seshu spread his hands wide, shrugged. "Her way of thinking is not my way. Nor yours." He saluted the drover of an approaching string of donkeys, their backs piled high with fresh hay. "Are you close to learning the name of his slayer?"

Bak sneezed and sneezed again. "I'm no further along today than I was the morning I learned his ka had fled."

Seshu muttered a curse. "Two days ago, I'd have sworn not a man along the river would raise a hand against a caravan, mine or any other. But today? Well, I'd make no wagers now."

Staving off a feeling of futility, Bak sought out Sennefer, whom he had yet to question about Baket-Amon. He spotted the tall, slender nobleman, walking alone on a parallel course to the caravan. He loped across the sand to intercept him. "What are you doing out here by yourself?" he asked, falling in beside him.

"I've grown weary of donkeys and drovers and dust, and of the constant bickering between Nefret and Amonked." Sennefer stared regretfully at the rolling sands to the west. "One would think, with so large a landscape surrounding us, that it would be easy to find a place to be alone. Unfortunately, I'm a stranger to the desert. I fear I'd get lost."

"I'd not go far without a guide," Bak admitted.

Sennefer turned to look at the river and the farmers watching the caravan. "I'd like very much to bathe. Would

I not be safe if you went down to the water with me?" He gave Bak a disarming smile. "I saw you and Nebwa returning this morning, and you came to no harm."

Bak, not sure how serious the nobleman was, returned the smile. "Seshu intends us to camp tonight inside the walls of Iken even if we must march through an hour or two of darkness. There you can bathe in safety."

"Will we not be resented at Iken as we were in Buhen?"

"You will be, yes, but Commander Woser will see that you remain unharmed." Bak was on the verge of saying "as Commandant Thuty did," but Baket-Amon's murder in the house the inspection team had occupied made the addendum questionable.

The nobleman bowed his head in reluctant acquiescence.

"I understand you knew Prince Baket-Amon," Bak said.

"I knew him and liked him. I shall miss him." Sennefer spoke with a real regret. "He came now and again to my estate in Sheresy, where we hunted and fished and played games of chance."

"At Amonked's invitation?"

"I usually invited him myself. I found him to be a most congenial man."

"You must often have seen him in Waset then."

The nobleman's soft laugh contained more than a hint of cynicism. "The older I get, Lieutenant, the less often I visit the capital. I find the life of a courtier to be demeaning." He glanced quickly at Bak, offered a wry smile. "Kowtowing to first one man and then another. Hoping not to offend anyone who has the ear of our sovereign. Always on my best behavior, with very little time to myself. I much prefer Sheresy."

Considering Sennefer's close relationship to Maatkare Hatshepsut's cousin, Bak thought it best to make no comment. "Did you see the prince while you were in Buhen?"

"If I'd known he was there, I'd have sought him out. But I had no idea until I heard of his death." Regret once again crept into Sennefer's voice. "To think he was but a few steps from my bedchamber when he was slain. I shall always wonder if he came to see me, if I was inadvertently responsible."

And so shall I always wonder, Bak thought. "If I knew more about him I might more quickly lay hands on the man who slew him. Will you help me?"

"What can I tell you?" Sennefer stared at the caravan, his thoughts far away. "He was a man with a smile on his face at all times and he had the most generous of hearts. He was so greedy for life he was exhausting to be around. I went twice with him to houses of pleasure in the capital, places he often frequented. He was a memorable carouser, believe me, and his appetite for women was insatiable."

Bak remembered the prince in Nofery's place of business, the young women at his feet and those awaiting him at the door. Were they mourning his loss or had they already begun to forget? "I've been told he was a skilled hunter, but the most accurate of bowmen sometimes strike in error. Did he ever fell a man by mistake, do you know?"

"Certainly not while at Sheresy," Sennefer said with a touch of indignation, "nor anywhere else to my knowledge."

The thickening dust roused Bak to the fact that they were nearing the column of donkeys. "He spoke to me briefly before his death, saying his past had come back to taunt him. Do you have any idea what he was talking about? Or what could have prompted someone to slay him?"

"I wish I did, but no." Sennefer's expression was puzzled. "He was such a congenial man, so skilled in every endeavor. I can't imagine anyone disliking him so."

They parted at the caravan, Sennefer hurrying forward and Bak remaining behind to think. He had learned nothing new, but the information he had gained from the nobleman had reinforced his earlier thoughts. Baket-Amon's major claims to fame were sexual prowess and hunting skills, both volatile pastimes that might lead to murder.

As for Sennefer, he had appeared at first to be aloof,

distant, but time and the discomfort of the long, dusty trek had made him more approachable, more human. Bak rather liked him but he did not delude himself. The man could as easily have slain Baket-Amon as anyone else in the inspection party. Still, he had no apparent reason for murder. Unless the friendship he claimed to have had with Baket-Amon was a complete fabrication.

Bak found Nebwa with Lieutenant Merymose farther back along the caravan. They were walking far enough away from the column to avoid the worst of the dust, keeping pace with a string of donkeys carrying sacks of grain.

"I admit I'm worried." Merymose looked off toward the river, his face gloomy. "If I had any say in the matter, I'd recommend to Amonked that we remain at Iken. I've been told the outer wall surrounds a huge area, with plenty of open space to accommodate a caravan of this size."

"We can't stay there forever." Nebwa pointed toward a small group of men standing outside a serpentine wall that held the sand back from a cluster of small houses near the river. "Those people won't give up their vigil until Amonked leaves Wawat."

Merymose turned to Bak. "We need remain only until you snare the man who took Baket-Amon's life."

"I appreciate your faith in my ability, Lieutenant, but what would we do if I never identify the slayer?" Bak shook his head. "No. We must either go on to Semna or return to Buhen. Which Amonked will never do."

"I suspect the guards under my command would be useless if they had to fight a battle."

"The people here want justice, and I can't say I blame them," Bak said, "but they'd be decimated if they aroused the wrath of our sovereign. That knowledge alone should prevent an attack."

He exchanged a glance with Nebwa. Both men knew that if the local people ever banded together with no true leader, forming a mob, they would be impossible to control. Twenty men with bows would fall before them in an instant.

"If I could just stand up to Lieutenant Horhotep!" Merymose's shoulders slumped. "I dare not. He'd destroy me, telling a tale of insubordination to the senior guard officer in the royal house."

Nebwa eyed the young officer, his face thoughtful. "Dedu and his archers are alert and ready for action, but should trouble arise, they'd need help. He taught your men to set up camp, now let him train them in the arts of war."

"Would he do that?" Merymose asked, his gloom lifting. "I can think of nothing I'd like better." His voice turned rueful. "He'd have to train me, too."

"Easily done."

"Troop Captain Nebwa!" Horhotep, who had come up behind them as silent as a stalking cat, raked his eyes across Bak and Merymose. Dismissing the lesser officers with a curled lip, he said, "Lieutenant Merymose is a promising officer, but he's young and green. You must look to me for decisions, not him."

Nebwa's expression turned stormy—as the adviser had intended, Bak felt sure. Horhotep had early on taken the troop captain's measure, he guessed, and decided he could prod and poke until the senior officer grew so angry he would perform some imprudent act. An act the adviser could use later to discredit Nebwa and use to his own advantage.

"Lieutenant Horhotep!" Bak said in the same brusque voice the adviser had used. "I've been told you knew Prince Baket-Amon." A falsehood, but a likely guess.

Horhotep gave him a caustic look. "You mean to question me about the man's death?"

"You were in the dwelling where and when he was slain." Bak surreptitiously signaled Nebwa and Merymose to slip away. "Why would I think you any less a suspect than Amonked and the others who were there?"

"Amonked?" Horhotep looked incredulous. "He's our sovereign's cousin!"

"Did you ever go hunting with Baket-Amon?" Bak asked, careful not to look at the two officers hurrying away.

"I did." Horhotep sniffed. "Why our sovereign thought he should be invited, I'll never know. A minor prince of Wawat, a tributary land of no worth."

If the land is so worthless, Bak thought, why are you here? "They say he was skilled with weapons above all others."

"Bah! A tale once told to make him seem special, and told again and again by men who never saw him with a spear in his hand or an arrow on the fly."

"I see," Bak said, and he did. The adviser reeked of envy.

Horhotep suddenly noticed that Nebwa and Merymose had gone. He glared at their backs, far up the line of donkeys.

"Were you ever with the prince when he sought sexual comfort?" Bak asked.

The adviser tore his eyes from the fleeing pair and gave Bak a scathing look. "Come now, Lieutenant. I'm far more selective than he was. I prefer refinement to the coarseness of a harbor-side house of pleasure."

Bak had had about all he could take, but stubbornness and necessity kept him going. He walked slowly toward the caravan. "I'm not talking about the young women who toil in places of business in the capital. I'm speaking of the women made available on hunting trips organized on behalf of our sovereign."

"I took no part in that," Horhotep said stiffly.

"Then you must've been invited along as some lofty official's aide."

Color flooded Horhotep's face and he sputtered, "You . . . You . . ." Taking hold of himself, he snarled, "You're wasting your time questioning me or anyone else in Amonked's party. When you return to Buhen, you'll find the slayer already caught, someone who came into our quarters to steal."

Giving Bak no time to answer, he stepped through the line of donkeys, placing the animals between them, and hastened toward the front of the column.

"Neatly done, Lieutenant," said Captain Minkheper, who had been walking behind them unseen. "He may never forgive you for seeing through his facade of self-importance."

"So be it." Bak shrugged off his irritation and smiled. "With luck, I'll discover he's the man who slew Baket-Amon."

Minkheper knelt beside a foal to scratch its muzzle. "I don't see how anyone could slay a man with so many people living in such close confines, whether he spent the night there or sneaked in from outside."

"No one sneaked in," Bak said with certainty. "The slayer was already in the house."

"For a man to take such a risk, he'd have to've had a most compelling reason."

"Agreed, but what it was I've no idea. Not yet, at any rate. Other than the lovely Nefret, none has shown itself, and looking at her is like looking at one grain of sand in a desert. From what I've heard, Baket-Amon took his pleasure at any time or any place, especially in the capital where a man of wealth can satisfy the most demanding of tastes."

Nonetheless, he must look closer at Amonked. As reluctant as he was to think of the inspector as a murderer—to face the consequences if Maatkare Hatshepsut's cousin should prove to be guilty—he could not turn his back on the possibility. As slight as it seemed at present, no other likely suspects had presented themselves.

Distant barking drew Bak's attention. An archer walking apart from the caravan stopped to look up a long, broad sandy valley that came out of the western desert between rugged clumps of craggy hills. A half-dozen feral dogs were racing down the valley, veering to left and right, nipping at the heels of a yellow cur. No, they were nipping at something dragging behind the cur.

He hurried to the archer's side and they stood together, watching the pack draw close. The nearest drovers, plodding with their donkeys past the wadi mouth, stopped to look. The yellow dog ran as if for its very life, either afraid of its burden or the dogs who chased it. Its frightened yelps were almost lost among the excited barking of the others.

The pack veered around Bak and the archer, passing so close he recognized the large, muscular yellow-gold mutt in the lead. The thing dragging along behind, bumping and bouncing over the sandy surface, was a bound package the length of his arm from elbow to closed fist. It was tied to the dog by a rope wrapped around the creature's neck.

"Stop that dog!" he yelled as the pack swerved to run alongside the caravan.

A drover, standing close to his lead donkey, grabbed a rope from a basket on its back, made a hasty loop, and swung. The luck of the gods was with him. The loop settled around the yellow cur's neck, he jerked it tight, and dropped the creature in its tracks. Snapping his short whip to scare the other dogs off, he hurried to the downed animal, which was baring its teeth and snarling.

Bak and the archer ran to his aid, as did several drovers. Nebwa sped up the line of donkeys to see what the problem was. While the newcomers chased away the rest of the pack, the drover who had caught the yellow dog quickly wrapped his rope around the animal's legs and muzzle so it could not run away or bite.

Bak knelt to study the bundle. At first glance, it looked like the wrapped body of a tiny child, but he saw right away that it was not. The linen wrapping, discolored and dirty, was all wrong. The narrow bands of fabric, ragged and torn from the hard journey across the sand, were wound around the bundle in a random fashion that in no way resembled the careful binding done in the house of death.

"In the name of the lord Amon," Nebwa said, kneeling

beside him, "I feared for a moment the dog had burrowed into a tomb."

Bak looked at the cord that bound the bundle to the cur. It was dark and worn, unlike the lighter, newer rope the drover had used. Examining the end around the struggling animal's neck, he found a knot securely tied by a man, not the casual knot formed by accident. If the rope had caught on a protruding rock, the dog would surely have been strangled.

With his dagger, he cut the rope from around the dog's neck so the drover could release the mongrel. As it raced away, Bak cut the strips of linen that held the package together and unrolled the broader piece in which the contents were wrapped. Out fell seven pairs of sandals.

Both men burst into laughter. Until they saw among the sandals a long gray feather plucked from the tail of a falcon. And grasped the fact that the footwear had been taken in the dark of night. Taken by a man who had crept into the encampment and walked undetected among the twenty sleeping archers.

Nebwa glared off in the direction of the desert, no longer able to deny that Hor-pen-Deshret had returned. "We'd best keep our suspicions to ourselves, telling no one but our own men. Let the rest enjoy our one night in Iken."

Chapter Ten

"I thank the lord Amon that we'll soon reach Iken." Pashenuro, whom Bak had just told about the sandals, glanced eastward, where a distant row of trees marked the course of the river, and toward the long escarpment that barred their view of the western desert. If any people watched the caravan, whether farmers or desert raiders, they were too far away to see. "I have no desire to march a couple of hours into the night."

"All who dwell along this segment of the river are far more afraid of the denizens of darkness than you are," Bak said. "I doubt they'll stray far from their homes on a night as black as this one promises to be, with the lord Khonsu hiding much of his face, leaving only the stars for light. As for Hor-pen-Deshret's men, I suspect we've seen—or not seen, as the case may be—the last of them until we travel on south of Iken."

Pashenuro gave his superior a good-natured smile. "I was thinking of the donkeys, sir. The pace Seshu set and the long march across the barren sands has worn them out—and me, too, if the truth be told. If we're to set out at daybreak tomorrow—and he says we are—we'll need a full night's rest."

Bak eyed the line of animals plodding ahead of them across the sandy plain north of Iken, a broad flat area lying between the rapid-strewn river and the escarpment. A dozen or so donkeys filled the space between Pashenuro's string and the three carrying chairs. Nefret occupied one chair, Thaneny another, the third was empty. Rather than ride in comfort as was their due, Amonked and Sennefer were walking with the remainder of their party. The Medjay was well positioned: close enough to see all that occurred and to rush to their aid if need be, but far enough away to remain anonymous.

"Has anything of note occurred in Amonked's party?"

"Not that I've seen. If Seshu didn't need my help each time we set up or break camp, I'd be more useful helping Dedu train those oafs who call themselves guards."

"They learned fast enough to build a proper fire and set up their camp in an orderly manner. If they're as quick to master the arts of war, you'll be of more use as a drover." Bak glanced toward the west, where the barque of Re hovered above the escarpment, streaking the sky red. "I saw Pawah walking with you an hour or so ago."

"Yes, sir. The boy's early childhood here in Wawat was one of need and hunger, yet he's curious about his homeland. He asks a multitude of questions, wishing to recall all he's forgotten."

"He said nothing about Baket-Amon?"

"Not a word."

With a resigned sigh, Bak walked on lest he draw attention to the Medjay. Spotting Captain Minkheper off to the right, examining the slipway along which ships were dragged past the most formidable of the rapids below Iken, he struck off across the sand to join him.

He knew what he was doing: procrastinating. He feared Amonked might be the man he sought, the one who slew Baket-Amon, and he dreaded the thought. He had twice drawn Maatkare Hatshepsut's attention, both times with mixed results. Once he had lost his rank of lieutenant and had been exiled to Buhen, a blessing in disguise though her intent had been to punish. He had regained his rank the second time and had been rewarded, but grudgingly. Then and three times more he had earned the gold of valor, but had never been awarded the prize. Her memory was long, her unwillingness to forgive legendary. He could well imagine her reaction should he reveal that her cousin was a slayer.

Minkheper greeted Bak with a smile. "I'm forever amazed at the ingenuity of man and the effort he'll make to get what he wants. In this case, the rare and exotic products of lands far to the south."

The slipway stretched farther than the eye could see across the sandy desert flat, a route paved with logs slightly curved to form a cradle, lying side by side along a bed of dry and cracking silt. The concave surface would support a ship's gently rounded hull, holding it steady. When moistened with water, the silt would grow slick, easing the vessel's overland journey.

"I not long ago saw the barque of Amon dragged along here," Bak said, "not the great vessel used during the festival of Opet, but one of sufficient size to impress a Kushite king. It was a sight I shall never forget."

"I've never seen a slipway used," the captain admitted. "My days have been spent on the water, not sailing the arid sands."

"It's a task not taken lightly. Nebwa set an entire company of spearmen to tow the barque. A larger vessel, even with its cargo off-loaded, would be far heavier and more difficult to manage."

"Did not our sovereign's father take a large fleet of warships up the Belly of Stones and bring them back downriver many months later?"

"During times of high water," Bak pointed out. "And he had the might of an army to tow the vessels."

Minkheper looked back along the slipway to where it vanished in the distance. "I'll make no firm decision until I've seen the rapids through the whole of the Belly of

Stones, but I've already begun to question the advisability of cutting a canal through here."

Bak offered a cautious prayer of thanks to the lord Amon that the captain was a sensible and rational man.

Turning south, they walked along the slipway, well out of the dust drifting up from the caravan. Two feral dogs trotted across the plain to join them, exploring the smells left by those who had last trod a similar path.

"As a man who wishes to be appointed admiral," Bak said, "you must've approached this expedition to Wawat with a certain amount of caution."

The captain flashed a smile. "You'd do well in the capital, Lieutenant. You're more aware than most of the hazards one must face when climbing to the airy heights of our bureaucracy."

Bak laughed. "I doubt I have the tact."

Minkheper's expression darkened. "You never know how far you'll go until you must."

Bak was not sure how to interpret the statement, the sudden gloom. Did Minkheper feel he was stooping too low in his quest for a position of status? "What did you learn of Amonked before you accepted the task?"

"An interesting question." The officer gave Bak a curious look. "Are you asking to further your investigation into Baket-Amon's death? Or are you seeking a character flaw in the hope of aiding Commandant Thuty and all those whose lives will be disrupted should Amonked tear the army from this frontier?"

"My goal is to find the man who slew the prince." Bak hated himself for sounding so righteous.

Minkheper's lips twitched with a suppressed smile. "I learned nothing about him to his discredit. He's often accused of bowing too readily to our sovereign's wishes, but is also considered a man of integrity. As I'm to give my conclusions to her rather than to him and he'll take no part in my decision, I thought this journey to be to my advantage."

"Even if you recommend she give up her plan to cut a canal through the rapids?"

"If Amonked is as honorable as he's reputed to be, he'll respect my conclusions and tell her so." Minkheper scooped up a shattered length of wood lying at the side of the slipway. He called out to the dogs and threw it hard, but they refused to chase it. No one had taught them to play as puppies. "He's neither blind nor stupid, Lieutenant. He's seen the same rapids I have and he knows the toll so difficult a task can take on human life. Should he by chance forget, he has merely to look at Thaneny to remind him of the dangers of working with hard stone."

Bak wondered if Minkheper truly believed in Amonked's integrity. Could a man of principles kowtow, in all good conscience, to Maatkare Hatshepsut's every whim? "I've been told he acts on our sovereign's behalf, taking guests to Sennefer's estate in Sheresy so they may hunt and fish and enjoy the good things of life."

"So I hear."

"You've not been invited?" Bak asked, surprised.

"I've been too much on board my ship, sailing far away from the capital." Minkheper's smile carried a touch of cynicism. "Perhaps when I'm an admiral, I'll be so rewarded."

No invitation to hunt; therefore, no opportunity to see Baket-Amon at play. At least not with an official party. "Why, I wonder, does he take them to Sennefer's estate rather than his own?"

The captain's smile broadened. "You've made a common error, I fear. Most men assume, because he's our sovereign's cousin, that he's a man of wealth. He isn't."

"He has an estate, does he not?"

"A small one, yes, near Mennufer. Too far away from the river to hunt birds in the marshes or to fish and too far from the desert. The house is modest, they tell me, not large enough to entertain exalted guests. His dwelling in Waset— where he received me—is rather grand, befitting his status as a courtier and his relationship to the royal house. That property, I believe, came to him when he wed Sennefer's sister."

"Is the marriage a good one?"

"Your questions are excellent, Lieutenant, but misguided. He adores his wife." Minkheper's quick smile faded. "Much to his dismay, the gods have forbade that she give him children."

"Thus the lovely Nefret."

Minkheper nodded.

A shadow flitted across the sand, drawing Bak's eyes toward the setting sun and a falcon soaring low over the escarpment, seeking its evening meal. He wondered if it was missing a tail feather. "How long has she been a part of his household?"

"Too long to have remained childless, and too long to act like a child when she must know by now that he wants a woman."

"Would he have slain Baket-Amon to keep her as his alone?"

Minkheper raised an eyebrow. "If he's your best suspect, Lieutenant, I fear we'll be plagued forever more by the local farmers."

So the captain believes Amonked innocent, Bak thought. He prayed fervently that such was the case. If only he could find a new reason for Baket-Amon's death, another suspect.

The sun had vanished behind the escarpment, leaving a pinkish afterglow, when Amonked displayed their traveling pass and the foremost donkey plodded through the northern gate of the fortress of Iken. Commander Woser and his senior staff greeted the inspector and Nebwa at the gate. Leaving an officer behind to guide the caravan to its camping place, they hurried off to the citadel, which stood atop the escarpment, overlooking a river dotted with islands and partly submerged rocks and offering a broad view of the western desert. Close in size to Buhen, the white towered walls loomed tall and impressive over the lower city through which the caravan marched.

Still mulling over Minkheper's words, Bak walked along the long train of donkeys, which followed a well-trod path across a stretch of barren, windblown sand. Sensing nightfall, fodder, and rest, the animals had quickened their pace. The drovers joked and laughed, secure within the fortress walls. He, too, was glad to be there, no longer menaced by the silent men and women along the water's edge or the unseen enemy in the desert.

The path narrowed to pass between blocks of ruined houses. The stone and mudbrick dwellings, many partially collapsed, some showing signs of burning, all buried in sand to varying depths, were reminders of a time when the land of Kemet had abandoned Wawat to Kushite kings and, many years later, of a war waged to retake the fortresses along the Belly of Stones. Flimsy lean-tos and mud-daubed reed mats had been tacked onto broken walls and collapsing roofs to shelter the many people who came from far upriver or out of the desert to do business. Iken was an important trading and manufacturing center, a place Bak assumed Amonked would view with favor.

The drovers' good spirits were quickly quenched. The bright-garbed men and women who dwelt among the ruins abandoned their smoky hearths and evening meals to stand along the lane, their voices mute, their backs turned as the inspection party passed by. An action that spoke more truly than words of their feeling about Amonked's mission. Bak allowed himself a secret smile. Even these people, residents of faraway lands, preferred that the army remain.

He found Thaneny and Pawah near Pashenuro's string of donkeys. The scribe was utterly devoted to Nefret and would do anything for her. He was equally devoted to Amonked, the man to whom he owed his life. Would he have slain Baket-Amon to eliminate the prince from both their lives?

"Why are you not riding in comfort?" Bak asked. "Amonked's carrying chair is empty."

"After several hours," Thaneny said, "I feel a need to walk, to give new life to my backside."

Bak laughed. Although they were valued by the nobility, he, too, found the chairs uncomfortable.

"Sometimes I fear he'll think me ungrateful," Thaneny went on, "but thus far he's offered no comment."

"Amonked's a most understanding man," Pawah assured him.

"I doubt those people would agree with you," Bak said sweeping his arm wide.

The scribe looked with regret at the many backs turned their way. "They don't know him as we do. The decision he'll make will be fair, taking their needs into consideration as well as those of the army and all others concerned."

"Will it?" Bak prodded. "From what I hear, he's a tool of our sovereign, quick to do her bidding no matter how imprudent her command."

"He's not!" Pawah glared. "He does what he thinks best, not what she or anyone else urges him to do."

Thaneny stepped to the side of the lane. A dark gray donkey brayed as if thanking him for clearing its path. "Why have you searched us out, Lieutenant? Have you concluded that your purpose would best be served if you point a finger at Amonked as the one who slew Baket-Amon? Do you think by baiting us we'll blurt out some truth that'll ease your path?"

Bak was irritated, as the scribe meant him to be. "I've no desire to accuse the wrong man, but I must lay hands on the prince's slayer." He pointed toward the people standing alongside the lane. "You can see for yourself the importance of my quest."

Pawah directed an impish grin, barely visible in the rapidly fading light, toward Thaneny. "Lieutenant Horhotep claims Commandant Thuty set those apprentices against our sailors, and he says the people who've been watching us along the way are curious, not threatening."

The scribe scowled at his young friend. "The man's every thought is addled. To quote him is to turn the truth upside down."

"Can you not prove Horhotep the slayer?" Pawah asked Bak, not altogether in jest.

"Would that I could," Bak said ruefully, "but so far I've found nothing that speaks against him except his envy of the prince." Noticing Thaneny shifting his weight, he signaled that they move on. The scribe had to be exhausted after so long a day. "What can you tell me of him?"

With his master no longer the focus of Bak's questions, the scribe answered more readily. "Horhotep never crossed Amonked's path, or ours, until two weeks before we left the capital. He'd served as an aide, one among many, with nothing to distinguish him from his fellows, to first one officer and then another in the royal house. The chancellor heard of our mission and recommended him to our sovereign."

"He's the son of a provincial governor," Pawah said, making a face.

Bak offered a silent prayer to the lord Amon that the land of Kemet would survive in spite of the many decisions made based on a man's birth rather than his competence. "Does Amonked realize he's been given an adviser who has neither ability nor knowledge?"

"He's said nothing . . ." Thaneny glanced at Pawah, who shook his head. ". . . but he's far more astute than most men believe."

They walked past a sentry holding aloft a flaming torch to light an intersecting street down which the caravan was turning. The buildings here were intact, blocks of interconnected houses inhabited by families who looked down from their rooftops, grim-faced and silent. The smells of cooking oil and fish hung in the air, along with a resentment Bak could almost touch.

He drew the pair into a side lane deeply shadowed in the twilight. "One thing I must know and I'll trouble you no more."

Thaneny stiffened. "I'll not point a finger at my master."

"You told me you doubted Nefret noticed Baket-Amon's attentions, but she told me herself she was troubled enough to voice a protest to Amonked. You must've known of her complaint, yet you failed to tell me. Now how did he react?"

"I . . . I don't know."

Bak hardened his voice. "Your lie seems a confirmation of your master's guilt."

"No."

"Must I take you to the garrison and use the cudgel?" Bak had little faith in the use of a stick, but the promise to do so more often than not produced the truth.

"Please, Thaneny!" Pawah cried.

"No."

The boy wrung his hands, agonizing over his friend's stubborn silence. At last, he blurted, "Before Amonked could act, Baket-Amon came to our house and . . ."

"Silence, child!" Thaneny commanded.

"Mesutu told me that he pushed his way into our master's private reception room," the youth said, paying no heed. "They argued over Nefret, their exact words no one could hear. The prince stormed out and later Amonked merely laughed, making light of the quarrel." He looked at Bak, his eyes large and worried. "So you see, it was nothing. Of no importance. Not worthy of a second thought."

"How long ago was this?" Bak asked.

"I don't know exactly. Almost two years ago, I think."

"Did Baket-Amon ever come again?"

"No, sir."

Bak ruffled the boy's hair. "I value the truth, Pawah, and I'll not use it to Amonked's disadvantage."

He prayed, not for their sake alone but also for his own,

that he could live up to the vow, that the inspector would prove to be the man they clearly thought he was.

"Our storage magazines are full to overflowing with trade goods, items awaiting shipment when the river floods." Commander Woser stood behind his armchair on the dais, his hands resting on one of the finest giraffe skins Bak had ever seen. The hide was draped over the back of the chair in a careful display designed to dazzle the eye. The light of the torch mounted by the door made the hairs glisten. "You'll have noticed I said nothing to Amonked. He'll see for himself tomorrow and no doubt be impressed. I fear so large a quantity will convince him that Iken is already more a storehouse than a garrison, reinforcing the idea that only a token force remain here."

"Tell him you await the flood and also that you've had reports of tribesmen lurking near the desert trail." Nebwa stood in the center of the room, resting a shoulder against the single red column that supported the deep blue ceiling. "Say you held back shipment until you could verify or disprove their presence."

"There have, in fact, been rumors that that wretched bandit Hor-pen-Deshret has returned, but our desert patrols have seen no sign of him, nor have they come upon any unexpected gatherings of men."

"The rumors may be true," Nebwa said and went on to tell of the falcon at Kor and the stolen sandals. "We've not yet told Amonked lest we err. We don't want Horhotep to turn an honest mistake against us."

Woser's mouth tightened. "Whatever we do, then, must not only convince the inspector that the army is necessary along the Belly of Stones, but we must truly protect ourselves in case Hor-pen-Deshret chooses to attack." The commander, a medium-sized man in his early forties with a slight paunch and thick, graying hair, eyed Bak. "Any suggestions, Lieutenant? I seem to recall you as a most creative man."

Bak, who had dragged a stool into the room as soon as Amonked departed, lifted his drinking bowl off the floor and sipped the wine, a heady red creation with a faint floral bouquet. He had come to know Woser several months earlier, and liked him.

"I'd post guards in conspicuous places and double the number of sentries on the outer wall. At some appropriate time, I'd say additional men have been added to discourage robbery from within and attacks from without."

Woser nodded. "Direct enough to make him think, not so forthright he'll disbelieve."

"Take care that that swine he calls his adviser can't accuse the army of stealing." Nebwa tossed down the remains of his wine and set the bowl on the dais. "It's getting late and I must go to the garrison. The desert trail to the south is long and empty, and I assured Seshu I'd talk to the patrols, learning all I can of what we might face. Are you coming, Bak?"

"I've a slayer to snare and . . ." Bak queried Woser with a glance. ". . . I've been told that Baket-Amon's chief wife grew to womanhood near here." His expectations were small—the prince and his family had dwelt in Ma'am for at least ten years—but a minute step forward was better than no progress at all.

Woser nodded. "In the lower city, where her parents still live."

Nebwa bade them good-bye and hastened away.

"She's a child of Iken?" Bak asked, surprised. "I know the prince was a man of Kemet deep down in his heart, but I'd've thought he'd wed a woman of Wawat, one who shared his noble blood."

"So she does." Woser slipped around his chair, removed the giraffe skin, and rolled it carefully. Sitting down, he laid it across his lap. "She was his cousin, the daughter of his father's brother. Her father is headman of a local tribe that long ago moved into the lower city, during the time the Kushites ruled. When the Kushite army fled, they chose to remain, and our sovereign at the time saw no reason to throw them from homes safe within the fortress walls."

Bak smiled, appreciative of the prince's political acumen. "She must've seemed an ideal match to Baket-Amon. A cousin and at the same time a woman who knew well the people of Kemet and our customs."

"So he may have believed at the beginning, but her father is an old-fashioned man, one who retains the traditions of his people. For my part, I've come to appreciate his unbending honesty, his forthrightness. But Baket-Amon could scarcely go through the motions. His heart lay in the modern world, not the past."

"I knew he kept his family in Ma'am. He preferred, I suppose, that they fall under the viceroy's influence, not that of his wife's father."

"The instant they wed, he took her away. The old man wasn't happy, but what could he do?"

What indeed? Bak sipped from his bowl, thinking of a woman torn from her family and her home, thinking of Seshu's talk of her irrationality. "What kind of woman is she?"

"On the surface, she's shy and retiring. Underneath she's as hard as granite and as unyielding." The patter of sandals drew Woser's eyes to the door, but whoever was outside walked on by. "I believe the people you've seen standing along the river, watching your caravan, are there to register disapproval of Amonked's mission. But her thoughts may travel a different path, one meant to avenge her husband's death. If so, she'll take advantage of her people's unsettling vigil, using their actions to serve her own purpose. And she'll not relent until she gets her way."

"Until Baket-Amon's slayer is snared and punished." Feeling entangled by necessity, Bak stood up and paced the length of the room. "The local people need the army. They've nothing to gain by totally alienating Amonked. How far, do you think, are they willing to go to satisfy a woman's quest for revenge?"

"I can't say." Woser lifted his drinking bowl, swirled the deep red liquid around inside. "I suggest you contact the old headman Rona, who lives in a village not far downriver from the fortress of Askut. He's a man of great good sense, one who has much influence all along the river between here and Askut."

"I'll do so." Bak returned to his stool but could not bear to sit. "Baket-Amon was known in Buhen, in Waset, and elsewhere as a man with a strong appetite for the delights of the flesh."

"The tales of his behavior have not escaped my attention," Woser said in a wry voice. "And no, he did not flaunt his desires here. His father-in-law demanded he show respect, and he did. Each time he came, he displayed unparalleled virtue. The reason he seldom blessed us with his presence, I suspect."

The torch sputtered, barely drawing Bak's glance. "Like you, others must've heard of his carousing. How were the stories received?" He could guess the answer and Woser proved him right.

"He was admired exceedingly."

"Have you heard any guesses about the reason for his death?"

"All who dwell here lay the blame at Amonked's feet. Other reasons have long since been lost to the one they wish to believe."

Bak strode through the south gate, bidding good night to the sentry posted there. As the heavy wooden doors thudded shut behind him, he hurried along the sandy lane at the base of the outer wall. The air was still and cool. The moon was a sliver and the stars stingy with their light, making the night dark and uninviting. He wished he had thought to get a torch from the sentry. At least he had had the good sense to borrow a tunic and a long cloak that he had secured with a bronze pin and wrapped tightly around himself. With only his right arm bared below the elbow, he felt rather like a man wrapped for eternity.

The lane, well-traveled in the daytime, was deserted at so late an hour. Some creature of the night, a rat most likely, dashed across Bak's path, and he heard the flapping wings and eerie hoot of an owl. A cough high above marked the location of a sentry on the battlements, but when he looked up the high, towered wall, turned an ashy gray by the feeble light, he saw no one.

He hastened on, thinking of his talk with Woser and of how little he had gleaned of Baket-Amon. His reunion with the commander and the other officers who had peeked in to greet him had in part made up for the paucity of information.

Ahead, a patch of black marked the place where the cliff face fell away, forming the steep cut through the escarpment that would take him down to the lower city. If only he could find a satisfactory reason for the prince's death. Look to the woman, he had been told when first he had been assigned to stand at the head of the Medjay police, and Nefret was a most desirable woman. Yet he was not entirely satisfied that she was sufficient cause for murder. Perhaps, he admitted to himself, because accepting her as a reason made Amonked the most likely slayer.

He entered the cut and headed downward. Each step he took stole away more of the meager light, forcing him to slow his pace and concentrate on where he placed his feet. As the walls closed around him, the darkness was nearly complete, leaving smudges of black in a world of lesser black.

A few paces ahead, something dislodged a rock. Bak's senses sharpened, but his step did not falter. He had no reason to fear; Iken was as safe as Buhen. Few men knew him here, none who carried a grudge. And though he hated to admit it, no one in Amonked's party had reason to wish him injury. He was much too far from learning the truth about Baket-Amon's death. Nonetheless, he freed his right arm to the shoulder and patted his side, reassured by the feel of his dagger inside the cloak.

A stone clattered. A large, solid object, the body of a man, struck him hard from the side, tearing away his sense of well-being. He lost his balance. Struggling to loosen the cloak and free his left arm, fumbling for the pin that held the garment together, he went down, hitting the ground with a solid thump. The man fell on top of him, knocking the breath from him, and struck him hard in the side with a fist. Bak lay quite still, stunned by the blow and by the realization that he was under attack.

Collecting his wits, he flailed his legs and twisted his body, hoping to throw off his assailant. The man struck him again, the blow grazing his shoulder, and at the same time struggled to remain on top. The cloak, wrapped so close around him, hampered Bak's attempts to free himself, confining him to a few ineffectual blows, but also hindered the other man's efforts to hold on to him, to strike a telling blow.

They began to roll, the steep slope carrying them downward, with one man on top and then the other. While his assailant tried with limited success to pummel him and to stop their downward plunge, Bak fought the cloak, frantically trying to rid himself of the wretched thing. His dagger was within easy reach—he felt it each time he rolled over it—but he could not get to it.

They struck with a solid thud a boulder at the side of the path, knocking the air from Bak's lungs and releasing the man's grip on a fold of fabric. Bak tried to scramble up, but his ungainly wrap confined his legs. Frustrated, angry, he gave up on the cloak and swung his free fist at his assailant. Unable to see in the impenetrable darkness, the blow struck at an angle, losing its power. His attacker rose to his knees, indistinct, slightly less dark than the night. Bak fleetingly glimpsed a shard of light—metal, he thought, or glass—and rolled. He felt across the top of his left shoulder the sudden warmth of his own blood.

Startled, suddenly afraid, knowing he could not adequately defend himself while wrapped in the accursed cloak, he rolled downhill, all the while desperately trying to find the pin that held together what he feared would be his shroud. Try as he might, he could not locate it. The garment had shifted in the struggle, hiding the pin within its folds.

He heard a noise. Footsteps on sand. Slow. Cautious. The man coming after him, prepared no doubt to finish the task he had begun.

Bak stopped his downhill roll and sat up. He grabbed hold of the fabric close to his neck, felt the warm stickiness of blood, gritted his teeth, and jerked as hard as he could. The cloth ripped with a shriek that to him sounded loud enough to awaken the dead. The footsteps paused. He jerked the linen again, tearing a long slit that released his left arm. Patting himself frantically around the chest, the neck, he located the pin. Tearing it free and throwing it aside, he let the tunic fall, wrenched his dagger from its sheath, and scrambled to his feet. His assailant lunged toward him. As dark as it was, Bak somehow managed to parry the blow. He heard the clank of metal against metal, his dagger against a similar weapon. With a muffled curse, the man swung around and ran. A vague figure in the dark, an image with no face, no identity.

Snapping out an oath, Bak raced down the slope after him. His shoulder was beginning to ache, to burn, and he guessed it was still bleeding. He ignored the wound as insignificant.

The man ahead was fast, but Bak gradually closed the distance between them. He reached the bottom of the cut a dozen paces back. The man sped on, racing along the broad street that continued to the harbor, with lanes branching off on both sides. The light was better, but all Bak could see was the naked back of a man wearing a thigh-length kilt.

The figure darted left into an intersecting lane. Bak found himself following a dark, narrow path with many abrupt twists and turns, many adjoining lanes. This was a district of warehouses, places of business and workshops, dwellings, some of the buildings occupied and in good repair, others empty and crumbling. An earlier visit to Iken made it vaguely familiar, but not familiar enough. Within moments, the man he chased had vanished.

As Bak hurried through the dark, empty streets on his way to the caravan encampment, he puzzled over the identity of his assailant, a man he had barely glimpsed. Had he come from Hor-pen-Deshret, or was he the man who had slain Baket-Amon? Or was he a simple thief, a transient unable to resist the temptation offered by a lone man in the dark?

He had worn a kilt made of some light-colored fabric. White, Bak thought, probably linen. His arms and chest had been bare; he had worn no jewelry. White linen would most likely be worn by a man of Kemet—but not necessarily. A lack of jewelry could simply mean the man had feared losing or breaking something of value or trinkets he especially liked. Or had he worn no jewelry because he feared it would betray his identity?

Chapter Eleven

"Troop Captain!" Sennefer called. "Lieutenant!"

The tall nobleman strode toward Bak and Nebwa through the flurry of activity around the donkeys. The lead animals were already on their way, as were Nefret and Mesutu, Pawah, Merymose, and Thaneny, the last leading Amon-ked's dog. Pashenuro nodded a farewell to the two officers and urged his string toward the outer gate.

Sennefer stepped over an odoriferous pile of manure, slapped a donkey on the flank, making it squeal, and gave the pair an amused smile. "Amonked wishes the two of you to accompany him on this morning's inspection."

Bak had ceased to be surprised that they were allowed to go along, but he was amazed they were actually being invited.

"What prompted that?" Nebwa asked, grinning broadly. "All those backs turned his way as we entered the city? The silent greeting? Troubled him, did it?"

"Perhaps he wishes to surround himself today with men of good sense." Laughing, Sennefer swung around and walked away.

The two officers looked at each other, not quite sure what to think. Had the nobleman passed along some kind of message? Or had he been making a joke at their expense?

*　　*　　*

"I'd wager a month's rations that you were meant to die." Nebwa kept his voice low so the inspection party, walking down the lane ahead of them, would not hear.

"The attempt to stab me was halfhearted." Bak also spoke softly. "You saw the wound. The dagger barely sliced through the skin."

Nebwa eyed his friend's left shoulder with open skepticism. He could see nothing, for Bak was wearing a tunic to cover the bandage. Unfortunately the salve the physician had applied smelled of a musty-scented herb, which anyone who came close might notice.

"You've been asking too many questions. One of them must've struck its target."

"I wish I knew which it was. I lay awake last night trying to think of anything I might've said that would plant fear in a man's heart. I came up with nothing."

They turned into an intersecting lane, following Sennefer and Minkheper, who in turn were walking behind Horhotep. The military adviser was trying hard to interject himself between Amonked and Commander Woser, who led the way, but the lane was too narrow to allow for three abreast.

They were in the lower city not far from the harbor, in the area where Bak's assailant had vanished in the night. They had seen warehouses filled with grain for the garrison; with cowhides, good-quality stone, and rare woods bound for Kemet; and with locally made pottery, export-quality linen, and a wine of unexceptional vintage bound for the land of Kush. They had just left a well-guarded building filled with jars of aromatic oils and colorful stones that would, in a few months, enhance the prestige and appearance of those who dwelt or toiled in the royal house.

"I might simply have been the chance victim of a sneak thief," Bak said, "a local man who thought to steal my weapons and jewelry. If he'd known who I was, he'd've stayed well clear."

His friend raised an eyebrow. "Are you trying to convince me or yourself?"

"Nebwa! I haven't the vaguest idea who slew Baket-Amon. Why would anyone wish me dead?"

"All who live in Wawat know you've not once failed to snare any slayer you've sought. That alone would drive fear into the heart of the man you seek."

Bak rolled his eyes skyward. "The slayer came from Waset. He's a member of Amonked's party. I doubt he's heard of my so-called prowess as a hunter of men."

"Our illustrious inspector of fortresses mentioned while in Buhen your success in laying hands on those who were smuggling elephant tusks. And Commandant Thuty vowed to sing your praises in the letter he wrote Amonked before we left Buhen. You delivered that letter yourself."

Nebwa did not have to spell out the obvious: if Amonked knew of Bak's successes, so, no doubt, would everyone else in his party.

"You don't rely on hunting to supply the garrison with fowl?" Amonked asked.

"We do, yes. The river offers an abundance of birds. Especially when the seasons change and they fly north or south in vast numbers." Commander Woser walked out from beneath the portico, in actuality four connected lean-tos with palm-frond roofs, built around the high mudbrick walls of the poultry yard. "The ducks and geese you see here are held captive for their eggs and chicks."

Amonked eyed, in the shade of the portico, several dozen flattish, large-mouthed baked clay bowls filled with straw, many occupied by nesting ducks and geese. "I see."

"Would it not be more worthwhile to raid nests in the wild?" Horhotep asked irritably. He stood at the edge of the shallow square pool in the center of the yard, scraping the bottom of a sandal on the rim, removing the smelly, gooey waste he had stepped in. "Look at the number of men you need here. They must clean the yard and carry away the manure. They must constantly fill the pool with water, clip the birds' wings and feed them, and perform innumerable tasks I can but imagine."

"Less than half the population of Iken carries spear and shield," Woser said, speaking with forced patience, "and only half the remainder are fully occupied with trading. What would you have us do with the balance? Let them idle away each day, with nothing better to do than foment trouble?"

"You've only to send them on their way, back to their homeland."

"No man comes to Iken without good reason," Nebwa stated in a flat, hard voice, "and none remain unless they must. They'd not retain their traveling passes otherwise."

A brownish goose waddled toward Horhotep, wings flapping, hissing. He wasted no time rejoining the men under the portico. "How long can it possibly take to conduct the kind of business available to the impoverished wretches I've seen so far?"

Nebwa raked the adviser with cold eyes. "The most powerful of kings need not wear fine linen and jewelry, Lieutenant."

"Some people await a ship, and many ships are delayed," Woser hastened to explain. "Others place orders for objects that have yet to be produced. And others await caravans that come across the desert from distant oases, their day of arrival impossible to predict—if indeed they arrive at all. They oft times bring too few trade items to provide sustenance over an extended period of time. Especially when they bring along large families."

"Nonetheless, they must eat and sleep while they're here," Amonked said, nodding his understanding. "I applaud your good sense, Commander, in seeing that they earn what they consume."

Horhotep's mouth tightened in resentment, but he had the wit to hold his tongue. Bak was pleasantly surprised by the inspector's open approval, and he could see that Nebwa and Woser shared the feeling.

As in each warehouse they had visited, Woser began to rattle off exact numbers—in this case, of birds consumed within the garrison and the lower city, of eggs laid and distributed, of sheaves of straw spread out and cleared away each week, and so on.

Half listening, taking care where he trod, Bak walked to the edge of the pool, where steps descended into the water, easing the path of the large flock that dwelt in the yard. Six or eight ducks swam toward him and gathered around his feet, quacking loudly, clearly expecting to be fed.

Bak turned his back to the pool and studied the men of the inspection party, wondering which—if any—had leaped upon him in the night, dagger in hand. If one of them had, it would not be the first time the man he sought had assumed he knew more than he actually did.

Amonked, the individual with the most promising reason for slaying Baket-Amon, seemed a most unlikely assailant. Of medium height, a bit stout, an indoor man through and through. But he had once been a youth, and all healthy sons of the nobility were schooled in wrestling and in the use of weapons.

Horhotep had envied Baket-Amon, but envy alone seemed a small reason for murder. A trained officer, as he was purported to be, would know how to steal up behind a man and stab him. The most skilled of soldiers would have had trouble striking a death blow on so dark a night, especially with the victim bundled up and shapeless the way Bak had been.

Sennefer, who claimed to have liked and admired Baket-Amon, posed a puzzle. Would a man of wealth and position come to Wawat out of simple curiosity about the land and its people? He was a hunter and fisherman, presumably skilled in the use of weapons, but, if he was as fond of the prince as he said, he had had no reason for slaying him.

Another man with no clear reason for murder was Captain Minkheper—for the simple reason that he had not known Baket-Amon well. Or such was his claim. Bak had no doubt he could slay a man. Men who sailed merchant ships on the Great Green Sea had to be strong and tough, prepared to do battle with pirates and competitors alike.

What of the others who had come with Amonked from Waset? Like Sennefer, Lieutenant Merymose claimed to have admired the prince. He was moderately skilled in the use of weapons, thanks to Sergeant Dedu, and he was young and strong. But he was another who had no evident reason for murder.

Thaneny was crippled, but his upper torso was more muscular than most, better developed. Bak was convinced the scribe would never have slain Baket-Amon—or any other man—for himself, but if he firmly believed an individual's death would help Amonked or Nefret, he would not hesitate.

What of Nefret? Bak did not think all women frail and helpless. Far from it. Given the prince's weakness for women, the concubine could easily have drawn him close and stabbed him. Stuffing the large, heavy body into the closet would have been no mean feat, but not impossible. Especially if she had help. The same was true of the boy Pawah. He might have been able to stab the prince but would have had trouble hiding the body—without help.

Neither had attacked Bak, of that he was certain. Nor had his assailant been a man with a leg too deformed to run.

The inspection party walked from the poultry yard to the animal paddocks, which were much like those in Buhen, and thence to the huge outdoor market, a place Bak remembered well from his earlier journey to Iken. It was much larger than that of Buhen and far more colorful.

With Amonked and Woser in the lead and Horhotep pressing close, they walked aisles that separated a multitude of lean-to-like stalls, the products on display shaded by swaths of linen or palm fronds or woven reed mats. People crowded the aisles, some who lived along the Belly of

Stones, many who came from afar. Long wraps in bright
colors and patterns vied with the stark white kilts of the
land of Kemet. Ordinary seed beads competed with the
most opulent of inlaid jewelry. Languages that clicked and
hissed and purred kept translators running from stall to stall
to aid in transactions simple or complicated. Transitory
smells, tantalizing or repugnant, drifted through the air: perfume and sweat, incense and rotting vegetables, flowers and
animal waste.

They stopped often, sampling fruits and vegetables, tast-
ing herbs and spices, peeking into wide-mouthed jars of
dried beans and peas and grain. They examined lengths of
cloth, laughed at performing monkeys, delighted in toys
with movable parts, ate braised beef and fresh bread, tested
for sharpness the edges of spearpoints and daggers. Amonked let down his guard, openly delighted with all he saw.
Horhotep, so full of himself he failed to notice, abandoned
all pretense of restraint and sneered at the thriving market,
the exotic people, the wondrous products.

As they walked away from the market, Horhotep stopped
to study the massive fortified wall that protected the lower
city, then his eyes darted toward the busy stalls and colorful
crowd. A scowl of extreme distaste marred his features.
"Tell me, Commander Woser, why have you expended so
much time and effort renovating the peripheral wall when
you allow inside that wall every wretched two-legged creature from upriver and off the desert?"

"This is the largest market on the frontier, Lieutenant."
Woser, who had evidently had enough of the man's inso-
lence, accented the rank, making it sound not quite respectable. "It draws more people than any other along the river,
from the border of Kemet at Abu to the unknown reaches
of the south. Products of every type are exchanged, each
of value in its own way. Should we ask those who come
to display their wares in a place unprotected from those
who take what they want, giving nothing in return?"

"If the market is worth protecting—and I have my doubts—why have you not repaired the spur walls on the citadel? Do you wish the heart of the fortress to collapse while you struggle to preserve its skin?"

Bak leaned toward Nebwa and muttered, "Does he never listen to anyone other than himself?"

"Repairs are made when and where necessary." Woser's voice was taut, betraying the effort he made to give a civil answer. Swinging away, he led them down a lane between two warehouses. "Come, we've a skiff awaiting us at the harbor. If you're to rejoin your caravan before nightfall, we must hurry on to the island fortress."

"How can you say the market isn't worthy of protection?" Bak demanded of Horhotep.

Amonked gave his adviser a curious look. "Yes, Lieutenant, explain yourself. I, too, am puzzled."

Horhotep flung a self-important smile Bak's way. "From what I've seen, products exchange hands here with no toll ever being paid. If the same objects were carried across the frontier by respectable merchants, each ship or caravan would hand over a substantial amount, giving our sovereign her rightful share of the merchandise."

"Tolls are collected at the outer gate," Woser said. "True, our demands are modest. Their purpose is not to increase the wealth of the royal house but to remind all who enter of the debt of gratitude they owe our sovereign for allowing them to trade here."

"Why settle for a pittance when we could have far more?"

"Increasing the toll would reduce the number of people who bring goods here to trade," Bak said, "allowing no gain to our sovereign and a loss to this city and this land. They would move their business elsewhere, probably to an island south of Semna. What they'd lose in safety, they'd gain in profit, for they'd pay no tolls at all."

"Must I give you a history lesson, Lieutenant?" Nebwa, the son of a soldier, had grown to manhood in the fortress of Kubban several days' sail north of Buhen and knew the reasons behind many decisions obscured by the passage of time. "Iken has been a market city for many generations, from the time of Khakaure Senwosret. When our sovereign's father, Akheperkare Thutmose, marched up the river with his army and conquered the lands far to the south, he ordered that this market remain open. Not only does it lure products seldom offered to traders, but it brings people together in a way not possible for the more formal trading expeditions."

"To survive and thrive, the market must be kept safe," Bak added, thinking of Amonked's mission. "The renovated wall discourages raiders, the army holds them at arm's length."

"I must admit this city intrigues me." Amonked stepped over a skinny black dog sprawled across the lane. "Far more than Buhen or any other place I've seen so far, it emphasizes the importance of trade to this region."

Woser's fast pace and the heavily populated lanes forbade further discussion, allowing Horhotep time to marshal his rebuttal. As they walked out on the northernmost of two long, stone quays, he sidled up to Amonked. "I see no tactical reason for the army to continue its occupation of this garrison. The local people, as sullen as they are, pose no real threat, and I'm convinced the raiding tribesmen we've heard so much about are mere figments of the imagination."

"I can take no more of that pompous ass," Nebwa muttered. "I'll meet you here when you return from the island." He swung around and stalked off, giving Bak no time to plead that he remain.

Amonked watched him go. After bending so far as to request that Nebwa and Bak accompany the inspection party, he had to be displeased by the troop captain's abdication, but as usual his face gave no hint of his feelings.

*   *   *

"You call that structure a fortress. I call it four walls with no purpose." Horhotep climbed out of the skiff and stood on the quay, looking eastward toward the island from which they had come, impossible to see beyond a closer rocky prominence. "No man of good sense would station soldiers there."

"If I'm not mistaken," Amonked said, clambering out of the vessel, "it proved itself quite useful when King Amon-Psaro came to Iken some months ago." He glanced at Bak, who waited in the prow while Woser climbed out. "Did you not prevent at that time what could have been a most serious incident, Lieutenant?"

"Yes, sir."

As Nebwa had said, Thuty had sung their praises. But in such detail? Or had Amonked, before he left the capital, read all the reports sent to Waset by the viceroy? A burdensome task. Necessary if a man wished to make a wise decision. A decision that would affect the well-being of thousands of men and women. Would a man be that conscientious if his sole intent was to carry out his sovereign's wishes?

"The rapids here are fearsome." Minkheper leaped onto the quay with practiced ease. "Is this the upper limit of those we looked upon yesterday from the watch station?"

"As far as I know." Scrambling out of the skiff, Bak looked toward Woser for an answer, but the commander had hurried on up the quay to meet Nebwa, leaning against the mooring post closest to shore. "I've had no chance to travel farther south."

"Even with the floodwaters at their highest, I'd not enjoy taking a ship through those rocks."

After Sennefer climbed out of the boat, the three of them strode up the quay behind the inspector and his adviser. A stiff breeze had come up and the warmth of the early afternoon sun was filtered through a dusty haze blowing off the desert from the northwest. A faint smell of braised lamb roused Bak's hunger.

"How has the fortress held up?" Nebwa asked, his good humor restored. "Is it overgrown already with tamarisk and weeds?"

"It'd take some clearing," Bak admitted, "but Woser could still shelter a king there if need be."

Nebwa lowered his voice and nodded toward Horhotep. "What did the visiting swine have to say about it?"

"He . . ." A movement deep in the shadow of the warehouse closest to the quay caught Bak's eye. He spotted a bow and glimpsed an arrow taking flight. "Look out!"

The missile sped past Amonked, missing him by an arm's length. Bak raced toward the hidden archer with Nebwa at his side. A stream of arrows flew past, their course nowhere near, their target uncertain. Too many arrows for one man to fire, Bak thought, the wild shots of inexperienced men—or men firing in haste or desperation.

Three men armed with bows burst from the shadow and raced like frightened hares into the nearest lane. Bak and Nebwa sped after them. They turned to the right into an intersecting street and to the left at the next lane. Another turn carried them deeper into the lower city, closer to the escarpment. People leaped out of their way, dogs barked, a small child wailed when an archer kicked its ball far down a lane. Bak feared the trio would split up, but in their panic they ran on together. He feared they would lose themselves in the maze-like lanes, as his assailant had done the previous night, but that, too, proved an unnecessary worry. A final turn carried them into a lane that went nowhere.

Bak and Nebwa found them standing at the base of the escarpment, caught in a trap of their own making. Panting for breath, frightened, shamed by so gross a failure, they dropped their bows and quivers to the ground and held their hands at shoulder level, signaling defeat.

"All right," Nebwa said, "who are you and what, in the name of the lord Amon, did you think you were doing?"

They looked at each other, each man pleading silently with the others to speak up. To think of a tale, Bak suspected, that would make them look as innocent as newborn calves.

"I'm Lieutenant Bak, head of the Medjay police in Buhen." He stared at them, his expression stern. "I must know your names and how you earn your bread."

Each rattled off a name and an occupation. One was an armorer, another butchered meat for the garrison, the third made the heavy leather sandals worn by the troops. Men not of the army, but men whose livelihoods depended upon the army's continued occupation of the fortress. Bak glanced at Nebwa, who nodded his understanding of the reason behind their foolishness.

Hearing a noise in the lane behind them, Bak glanced back. He could hardly believe his eyes. Amonked and Sennefer stood in an intersecting lane, too deep in its mouth to be seen by the three bowmen. The inspector's face was flushed and he was gasping for breath, while Sennefer showed slight strain as a result of the chase.

"Who were you trying to slay?" Nebwa, unaware of the men behind hīm, looked as severe as Bak had, but his voice carried a suspicious note of humor. "From your lack of skill, the wild manner in which your arrows flew, it was hard to know."

"We didn't want to slay anyone," the butcher wailed. "We wanted to scare him, that's all. The inspector."

"What'll we do if he tears the army from Iken?" the sandal maker whined. "We all have wives whose families dwell here. Our children know nothing but this city, this land of Wawat."

"What good would I be with the army gone?" the armorer asked. "Merchants have no use for weapons."

Bak secretly blessed the trio. In a few highly emotional words, they had unknowingly told Amonked what he most needed to hear.

Nebwa eyed them long and hard. "What shall we do with them, Lieutenant?"

"We could turn them over to Horhotep." Bak looked

from one man to the next, making sure they understood the worst possible consequence of their actions. "Lieutenant Horhotep, the inspector's military adviser is a cold, unforgiving man who'll insist you be sent to the desert mines as punishment."

"No!" they chorused, horrified.

"What would happen to our families?" the sandal maker cried.

"My wife. How would she feed our children?" the armorer wailed.

Nebwa frowned, pretending to think over their fate. "I'd prefer we turn them over to Commander Woser. They're his men, his problem."

"Let them go." Amonked came up beside the two officers, his breathing not yet under control. "I'd guess their attempt at murder frightened them as much as me. I doubt they'll ever again repeat so foolhardy an action."

Bak did not know which was the more surprising: the fact that the inspector had managed to follow them or that he had given so generous a judgment. "Are you sure you want to do this, sir?"

"Set them free."

No men had ever before dropped to their knees in front of Bak and bowed so low their foreheads touched the ground. He was startled—and discomfited—by their extreme gratitude. Amonked looked unmoved.

Nebwa set a fast pace at the head of the desert patrol Woser had assigned to escort them south to the caravan. The ten spearmen who regularly patrolled the desert sands were hard-muscled, tough-thinking young men burned dark by the sun. The sleek, well-groomed men from the capital maintained the same fast pace, but with an effort. Assuming the attempt on Amonked's life had shown him how vulnerable he was, Bak thought it a good time to probe for information. He drew the inspector off to the side of the column, close enough to be safe, far enough so no one could hear.

They were on high ground, following a trail that would, later in the day, strike off across the desert to avoid a bend in the river, saving many hours' march over hard, rough terrain. To the east, islands large and small broke the surface of the glittering ribbon of water contained between tree-lined banks interrupted at times by the mouths of dry watercourses covered with black, fertile soil or by streams of sand spilling out from the desert. In spite of the obstacles, the river flowed more freely than at any time since they had left Kor.

Amonked studied the surrounding landscape, his face clouded by worry. "Do you think it wise to walk so far from the patrol?"

Since leaving Iken, Bak had seen no one standing along the riverbank, watching them pass. The trees were thick enough to shelter an army, but was not the purpose of the endless watch to be seen? To unnerve with a continuing presence? "I wish to speak of Nefret and Baket-Amon, sir. If you have no objection to others hearing, we can rejoin them."

"Our experience in Iken has made me too cautious," Amonked admitted, looking chagrined. "If anyone chose to attack us now, we'd see them in plenty of time."

Bak forced himself not to look again at the river, but the temptation was great. The absence of watchers puzzled him. Why were they not there as always before? Something must have happened to discourage them, but what? Surely not Amonked's kindness to those three witless bowmen. Something of far greater significance.

"I know you quarreled with Baket-Amon," he said.

"So Thaneny told me." Amonked expelled a humorless laugh. "It was naive of me to believe you'd not learn of the confrontation, but I don't like to think of myself as a man of no self-control, and to proclaim my irrationality to a stranger is repugnant."

"Baket-Amon's reputation with women neared mythical proportions, and your concubine is a very lovely and desirable woman. You surely know that fact alone places you high among those who might have wished him dead."

"We argued about her, yes. But would I slay a man for her? Never!"

"Then tell me of your quarrel."

"I can assure you that our words spoken in anger were quickly forgiven and forgotten. By me, for a fact. By him as well, if I'm the excellent judge of men Maatkare Hatshepsut believes me to be."

Did he mention his cousin, thinking to intimidate me? Bak wondered. "To keep the quarrel a secret multiplies my suspicions ten times over."

The inspector threw him an irritated look. "I've no desire to speak further of the matter."

"Do you want the prince's death to go unresolved? Do you wish the thought to fester forever in men's hearts that you slew him?"

Amonked stared, thin-lipped, at the pack of feral dogs ranging across the sandy waste to the west. The animals had abandoned the inspection party in Iken, joining their brethren who dwelt within the walls of the fortress. The caravan had gone on without them, but some ancient instinct had caused them to again form a band and follow the desert patrol and their lofty charges.

Amonked tore his gaze from the dogs and, with a distasteful look, began to speak. "Yes, Baket-Amon desired Nefret. I'm not certain how often he came to my dwelling in Waset—neither she nor my wife would tell me—but at some point he made a nuisance of himself and the two of them together told me of his visits. I doubt he loved Nefret. My wife believes that because she held herself aloof while other young women doted on him, she became a challenge he could not resist."

"I've never heard that he pursued a woman uninvited."

"Nor have I, but my wife assured me such was the case

with Nefret. And my wife is a truthful woman." Amonked looked hard at Bak, daring him to challenge the assertion. "I confronted the prince and told him he must go away and forget her."

"He agreed, I assume."

"He offered to buy her." Amonked's annoyance was plain. "As if she were a common servant, one who'd come into my home and my bed to pay off her father's debts. I set him straight on that score and refused his offer. We quarreled. Unaccustomed to having his wishes denied, he . . ." Raising his chin high, Amonked said indignantly, "He called me a selfish old man."

Selfish and old, Bak thought. Words designed to wound, words no man wishes to repeat when applied to himself. "Not the judicious response I'd have expected from a royal envoy."

"Indeed not."

Bak offered an understanding smile. "You were incensed, I assume, and rightly so."

"I ordered him out of my house. He refused to leave without hearing from Nefret that she wanted nothing to do with him. I finally threatened to speak to my cousin, Maatkare Hatshepsut, and he hurried away in a huff."

"Never to return?"

"Never." Amonked's eyes darted toward Bak and he added with a certain amount of bitterness, "Why would I slay a man when I have merely to mention my cousin's name and my least significant wish becomes a command?"

This was a side of the inspector Bak had never imagined, and he liked him better for the admission. He yearned to respond, but could think of nothing appropriate to say. So they walked along together, saying nothing, their silence strained at first but soon strangely comfortable.

Late in the afternoon they stopped at a watch station located on a rocky knob that rose above the surrounding landscape. While Amonked spoke with the sergeant in charge, Bak looked off to the south, where the caravan was making its slow way across the rolling, sandswept landscape, leaving behind the river and the wrath of the people who dwelt along its banks.

A soldier on duty pointed out, some distance to the west, a half-dozen ant-sized figures. "I thought at first they were nomads coming to the river for water, but instead they traveled a parallel course to the caravan. Now, with the sun at their backs, making it hard to see them, they're getting closer."

Bak shaded his eyes with his hand. "They're up to no good, we must assume, but what do they hope to gain? Our archers could decimate so small a group in no time at all."

The inspection party rejoined the caravan as the sun sank toward the western horizon. Bidding good-bye to the desert patrol, who hastened east toward the river, they walked forward along the line of donkeys. They found the men in the lead unloading their animals and setting up camp on a broad sweep of desert with a cluster of sandy hillocks off to the west. Seshu stood in the midst of the commotion, issuing orders with skill and authority. Leaving the others to go their own way, Bak and Nebwa walked to him.

As they spoke of the next day's march, the lord Re settled on the horizon, preparing to enter the netherworld. The yellow-gold feral dog to which the bundle of sandals had been tied crouched among the piles of supplies, waiting to steal any food it could grab. The creature raised its head and sniffed the air, drawing Bak's attention. It stood, trotted up the shallow slope to the west, and stopped to sniff again. The hair rose on the back of its neck and it began to bark. Other dogs raced up from all directions and they sped out across the desert, barking for all they were worth. Nebwa and Bak exchanged a silent query: a gazelle? Or the nomads they had seen from the watch station?

Before they could go see for themselves, a half-dozen men crested a hillock. The dogs stopped to watch from a safe distance. With the light behind the men, detail was lacking, but Bak could make out long spears and shields. The sun dipped below the horizon, lighting the sky in one last brilliant flash of color. The figures were for a short time fully visible. Six men of the desert, one standing out from the rest. A man clad in a red kilt, with a red feather rising above his hair.

Nebwa spat out an oath. "Hor-pen-Deshret."

"The swine has come," Seshu said with venom.

"He must be the reason we've seen no people along the river," Bak said.

"I'd not be surprised." Nebwa glared at the men across the sand. "He raided farms and hamlets all along the west bank, taking the animals and harvest for his people and impoverishing the farmers. After he became more daring, robbing caravans and gaining more booty in a single attack than he had during a dozen before, he continued to take what was theirs."

"He's come to look us over, to evaluate the risk and gain." Seshu's expression was bleak. "I feared something like this would happen. So rich a caravan draws raiders like ants to grease."

Nebwa was equally grim. "For every man we see, he'll have eight or ten behind him, camped out of sight somewhere on the desert."

"He's surely heard of Amonked's mission," Bak said. "Wouldn't he be wise to hold off, waiting until the army is torn from the Belly of Stones?"

"You don't know Hor-pen-Deshret," Nebwa growled. "Greed drives him, not good sense. If he concludes this caravan is worth attacking—and he will—he'll think of to-day's gain, not tomorrow's."

The men's concern was contagious, infecting Bak. "What of the people along the river? Will they stand with us if we're attacked? He's their foe as well as ours."

Nebwa shrugged. "They fear him greatly and they mistrust Amonked. To them, one evil may be no better than another."

Bak muttered a curse. This was the longest stretch between fortresses, a three-day march across the open desert to Askut. He and Nebwa, the two sergeants, and twenty archers could easily hold off fifty or so men attacking en masse. But random attacks along the length of a moving caravan or an attack by a large party would be impossible to fight off. Unless . . . "Go find Lieutenant Merymose and Sergeant Dedu. Those fifty guards must be trained to be soldiers immediately."

Chapter Twelve

"I don't see Hor-pen-Deshret among them." Bak stared off across the desert at the half-dozen tribesmen who had kept pace with the caravan since they had broken camp at first light.

"Nor do I." Nebwa, standing with him on a tall granite monolith that rose above the rolling sandhills, eyed the distant figures, his face grim. "He's close by, though. I can feel him."

"Strange that none of the desert patrols from Iken noticed any unusual movement over the last few days."

"I'll wager the swine came from straight out of the desert."

Bak turned around to look at the long line of donkeys plodding south along the trail. The gentle morning breeze, its chill banished by the sun, was too weak to account for the clear blue sky above the caravan. The sand here was coarse and heavy, almost free of dust. Isolated granite ridges and knobs rose out of a seemingly endless blanket of gold, with long dunes trailing off from their downwind side.

He was worried. By crossing this segment of desert, avoiding the long bend in the river, they were shaving almost two days off their journey. But they had to pay for the shorter passage. The river would be more than an hour's walk away for a man in a hurry, a march from dawn to dusk for the heavily burdened donkeys. Forced to carry water, each animal was laden with the maximum it could manage, slowing the caravan as a whole while at the same time saving thousands upon thousands of steps.

Taking a final, long look at the tribesmen, he said, "We must assume those men are an advanced guard, keeping an eye on our progress while Hor-pen-Deshret's fighting force comes from farther afield. Two questions arise: How large will that force be? How long will it take to reach us?"

"He must know we've no intention of traveling beyond Semna, and he'll want to attack well before we get there. Other than Buhen, it's the only garrison with a full complement of troops." Nebwa climbed down the side of the monolith, taking care where he placed his feet on the eroded stone. "As for how many men he's gathered, only the lord Set knows. He's never been known to risk an attack unprepared."

"This long stretch of open desert looks to me a good place to strike."

"I can think of no better." Nebwa eyed the distant men, his face dour. "I imagine he came yesterday to look us over, to see for himself the riches we're carrying and the number of men he'll have to face. If he liked what he saw . . . And how could he not? . . . he'll think the gain worth the risk." He ran his fingers through his hair, making it look more out of control than usual. "Let's hope he's decided he needs more men and won't strike until they arrive. He'll have seen fifty spearmen and twenty archers, but he'd have no way of knowing the spearmen lack training in the arts of war."

Bak followed him off the protuberance, and the pair set out across the sand, heading toward the caravan. "Last night's session went better than I expected. If enthusiasm is any measure of success, Merymose will one day be a general. The guards who report to him, as soft as their lives have been in the capital, surprised me with their willingness to learn."

"They'd better show enthusiasm. Their lives may depend on it." A sudden thought banished the severity from Nebwa's face and he grinned. "Do you remember what Horhotep said yesterday, before we left Iken, about desert raiders?"

Bak altered his voice slightly and quoted the adviser word for word: " 'I'm convinced the raiding tribesmen we've heard so much about are mere figments of the imagination.' "

"I wonder what he thinks now."

"He won't admit he's erred until he has to."

"Did you notice him standing in the shadows last night, watching us school the guards?"

"I feared for a while he'd order Merymose away, but he didn't say a word."

"I'll wager Amonked got an earful."

Bak's laugh was short and humorless. "I've no experience training spearmen, as you have, but after we finished last night, I went to my sleeping place satisfied. Another few hours of schooling may not give the men the skill of seasoned troops, but I felt they'd be able to hold their own against tribesmen untrained in the finer points of warfare."

"They'll do all right with the spear," Nebwa admitted, "but they need replacement weapons should they lose or break those they have—and they'll need weapons more suited to hand-to-hand combat: scimitars, maces, axes, slings."

Bak's expression turned dubious. "Not even the lord Amon could supply those. This is a civilian caravan, not one meant to support an army."

Nebwa scowled, taking the words to heart. "I must take an inventory, learn which of the drovers was once a soldier, who brought arms along and who didn't. Better to know the worst from the start than to be surprised too late."

The caravan moved on through the morning, with the tribesmen keeping pace off to the west. Bak walked the length of the long train of animals, speaking with drovers, archers, and Merymose's guards, taking their measure in the face of a possible attack. Morale was good, thanks to a blind faith in Nebwa's ability to see them trained and armed—and in Bak's ability to lay hands on Baket-Amon's slayer, thereby regaining at least partial goodwill of the people who dwelt along the river. And maybe their help, should help be needed.

Feeling like a man pinned against a wall, Bak thought long and hard about the prince's death. He had been certain someone in the inspector's party, someone who had been inside their quarters in Buhen, had slain Baket-Amon. Yet out here in the desert, living among them, asking questions that led nowhere, doubts plagued him. As no courier had come from Imsiba, the Medjay must also have come up empty-handed, contrary to Amonked's initial prediction. Small consolation, with the caravan being so barren of results.

Midday came and went and the animals plodded on.

"What do they do with the women they take?" Nefret stared at the small figures on the horizon, her eyes wide with fear. "Do they slay them outright? Or use them and throw them away? Or do they enslave them?"

Mesutu trudged behind her mistress's carrying chair, her eyes straight ahead. Now and again she stumbled, as if her thoughts had fled to some far away and safer place.

The four porters holding Nefret aloft exchanged a surreptitious look among themselves, its meaning betrayed when one man rolled his eyes skyward. Those walking a parallel course, carrying Thaneny's chair, exchanged bored looks. They had apparently grown weary of the beautiful Nefret and her many complaints. The third carrying chair, Sennefer had left at Iken along with his four porters and many of his personal items. He could not have foreseen the arrival of Hor-pen-Deshret, but he had realized the value of traveling light.

"You're taking the presence of those desert nomads far too seriously, mistress." Lieutenant Horhotep, walking beside the young woman, had to know Bak could hear. "I'd not be surprised if they sneaked up in the night to steal, but would six men attack a caravan as large as this?" He answered the question with a derisive laugh.

Pawah, walking with Sennefer between the two carrying chairs, eyed the adviser doubtfully. "The drover Pashenuro thinks these men have come to seek out weak spots for a greater force soon to attack."

Assuming his most sarcastic look, Horhotep said, "A drover? A frontier drover? Where did he train in the arts of war?"

Pawah's face flamed. Eyes flashing defiance, he opened his mouth to retort. Thaneny touched him on the shoulder, drawing his attention, and shook his head to signal silence.

Sennefer put an arm around the youth's shoulder and drew him off to the side of the caravan's path. As Bak passed them, he heard the nobleman say in a voice too subdued for the adviser to hear, "Not everyone is blessed with common sense, Pawah, and those who aren't seldom listen to those who are."

"Hor-pen-Deshret." Amonked, walking at Bak's side, gave no sign that he had heard the exchange. "Before we left the capital, I read a few reports from Buhen, several of which mentioned the name. As I recall, Troop Captain Nebwa fought alongside Commandant Nakht when the wretched man was defeated and when he and the remnants of his tribal army were chased far into the desert."

Bak was no longer surprised that the inspector knew of past activities in the Belly of Stones. He was surprised by the depth of that knowledge. Amonked had clearly read more than "a few reports." "Yes, sir. That's why Nebwa's worried, why he believes we must prepare to hold off a fighting force. He knows from experience what to expect."

"You agree with him, I see."

"Wholeheartedly."

Horhotep dropped back to Amonked's side and gave Bak
a cool look. "Aren't you raising an alarm when no alarm
is warranted, Lieutenant? Or are you using the presence of
a few pathetic nomads to sway our decision about the future
of the fortresses along this segment of river?"

"Sir!" Bak swung around to face Amonked; his voice
hardened. "If the army is torn from the Belly of Stones, no
man will be safe whether he be farmer, trader, drover, or
royal envoy. Hor-pen-Deshret is a criminal, plain and simple, and he and his followers will have free rein."

Amonked looked from Bak to Horhotep and back again,
as if uncertain in which of the two he could place the most
confidence.

"I suggest you speak with Nebwa, sir," Bak said, "and
with Seshu. He also has firsthand knowledge of the desert
raiders."

"Yes," the inspector said thoughtfully. "Yes, I shall. I
understand the troop captain is presently taking inventory
of men and equipment. I'll see him when he's finished and
has the time to speak freely."

Horhotep's mouth tightened, sealing inside whatever
comment he wished to make.

"Oh, Thaneny, stop patronizing me!" Nefret's words cut
through the air, sharp with impatience. "I can't help being
afraid! I don't care what you say or what Horhotep says or
Amonked or anyone else, those men frighten me!"

"First it was the men along the river, and now this!"
Amonked expelled a long, irritated sigh. "I can understand
her anxiety—I also am concerned—but will she never learn
to suffer in silence?"

You don't know how fortunate you are, Bak thought, that
Thaneny so often stands between you, taking the brunt of
her wrath.

"She'll not be content until we return to Kemet, that
she's made clear, but I suppose I must make an effort to
soothe her." Amonked looked at the concubine for a long

time, as if he dreaded going to her. "Do you share your life with a woman, Lieutenant?"

"No, sir."

"You're a most fortunate man."

Bak walked back along the caravan in search of Captain Minkheper. Horhotep had once made a passing comment he hoped the seaman could enlarge upon. He spotted the tall figure walking toward him about halfway along the line of donkeys.

"Captain Minkheper," he said, smiling. "For one who's supposed to be studying the river, you're a long way into the desert."

"Why I ever accepted this accursed mission, I'll never know." The seaman bent to shake the grit from a sandal. "I've just talked with a drover, a former sailor who plied the waters in this area. He said, and I quote: 'If our sovereign thinks to build a canal through the Belly of Stones, she's got more rocks in her head than the lord Hapi has deposited in the river between Semna and Buhen.' " He paused, letting a smile spread across his face. "Needless to say, she'll hear nothing of the sort from me."

Laughing, Bak fell in beside him. "I've heard she has a sense of humor, but I wouldn't want to test the fact with a statement like that."

Minkheper's good spirits faded and he gave Bak a frustrated look. "I don't doubt your drover, but I should be on the river, studying its flow firsthand."

"Would that you could. I'd be by your side, enjoying a cool breeze and a swim. But until I lay hands on Baket-Amon's slayer, I can't guarantee that any man in the inspection party, walking alone and unguarded, would be safe from some irate farmer."

"Can you guarantee our safety here, on this dry and barren trail?" Minkheper asked, looking pointedly toward the distant figures of the desert tribesmen.

"There are few absolutes in life, sir."

A hint of a smile touched the captain's lips. "From what I hear, Hor-pen-Deshret is more of a threat to the local farmers than Amonked is. I'd think they'd be grateful we're here, deflecting his attention from them."

"When we get closer to Askut and the river, I mean to speak with a man influential in this area. Perhaps I can convince him it would be to the people's advantage to help us. Until then, we must wait. I dare not leave the caravan now lest the tribesmen attack out here in the open desert. In that case, every man and weapon will be needed."

"Can I help?"

"Speak with Nebwa. He can best tell you what needs to be done." The captain nodded and swung around, but before he could get away, Bak said, "Someone suggested that Baket-Amon patronized the houses of pleasure near the waterfront in Waset. As you're a seaman, I assume you visited the same establishments."

Minkheper gave him an odd look, then chuckled. "I keep forgetting that I, along with everyone else in Amonked's party, am suspected of murder. Each time you come to me with questions, you set me back on my heels."

"If you're innocent, you'll take my queries in stride." Bak smiled, cutting the sting from the words.

"If?" Minkheper asked, raising an eyebrow. "You've surely no reason to believe I took his life."

Bak ignored the implied question. He disliked having men fish for information while he was seining. "If you also frequent the harbor-side houses of pleasure, you must've bumped into him in one or another."

"I've been happily wed for years, Lieutenant, and I have three concubines in various ports of call. I've no reason to look elsewhere for entertainment or pleasure."

Bak recalled his recent conversation with Amonked and had trouble holding back a smile. The inspector would be appalled to learn of the captain's many female attachments. "You never stop for a beer or a game of chance?"

Minkheper laughed. "I must admit I'm sometimes

tempted by a game of throwsticks or knucklebones, and at times I feel a need for masculine company. Not often, mind you. I get plenty of that aboard ship. But often enough that I've heard tales of the prince's exploits."

"You never met up with him during one of those . . ." Bak smiled. ". . . domestic lapses?"

The captain acknowledged the jest with a quick smile. "If so, I didn't know at the time who he was." He paused, added, "I moor my ship more often in Mennufer than in Waset. Its harbor is bigger, its facilities better, and its trading establishments more lucrative. My wife dwells there with my firstborn son and three daughters I adore."

To a man who sailed the Great Green Sea, a preference for the more northerly port made sense. "Did you ever hear of anything Baket-Amon did in Waset that could've brought about his death?"

"Jokes were made that he might one day run up against an enraged husband. Otherwise, I don't recall a thing."

An irate husband, Bak thought glumly. Once again, the only man who came close was Amonked. Why did all signs have to point to Maatkare Hatshepsut's cousin? Yet he seemed such an unlikely slayer, and Nefret as a reason for murder seemed more unlikely each time Bak saw them arguing.

"Other than Lieutenant Bak and me, only Sergeant Dedu and his twenty archers are well-armed," Nebwa reported, "and they have a limited supply of arrows."

His rigid stance and the edge to his voice betrayed his irritation. As the senior military officer in the caravan, he had begun to ready the men for a possible battle, giving no thought to Amonked. The inspector's summons had caught him off guard, and nothing Bak said could convince him that he was not being called to account. As soon as the pavilion had been erected for the night, while still the donkeys were being fed and watered and the men had begun to prepare their evening meal, an ill-humored Nebwa had accompanied Bak to the shelter.

"Lieutenant Merymose and his fifty guards have spears and shields," Nebwa continued, "but they have no replacements and no small arms, and not a man among them has had sufficient training. Of the twenty-eight drovers, sixteen are former army men, experienced with bow or spear, but only nine brought along a full complement of weapons. One porter who brought a basket of herbs, potions, and salves has volunteered to tend any wounded we might have, and Thaneny has offered to help. The other porters have agreed to carry injured men to safety."

Amonked, seated on his chair, his dog sprawled at his feet, gave Thaneny a look of surprised pleasure.

Bak stood with Nebwa, facing the inspector. Horhotep stood beside the chair, while the scribe, Sennefer, Minkheper, and Merymose stood off to the side. Nefret sat on a low stool in an opening in the hanging that divided the pavilion, with Pawah on the ground beside her, clasping his knees to his breast. Though the chill of night had not yet set in, a brazier burned fitfully, giving off the faint smell of dung not as thoroughly dry as it should be.

"You failed to mention Lieutenant Horhotep," Amonked pointed out.

Nebwa's eyes darted toward the adviser. His face remained impassive. "I've yet to learn whether the lieutenant brought arms to Wawat, and I've no idea how skilled he is. Until proven otherwise, I must assume he's no better trained in the arts of war than was Lieutenant Merymose."

"Are you implying I'm unfit?" Horhotep, an angry flush spreading up his neck and face, glared at the troop captain.

"I'll have no quarrel!" Amonked barely raised his voice, but his tone broached no argument.

Nebwa went on, unperturbed. "As I'm certain you've noticed, Lieutenant Bak, Sergeant Dedu, and I have begun to train Merymose and his men. Given time, they'll become worthy soldiers."

"I'd like to take part in that training, if I may," Sennefer said. "I'm a fair shot with a bow, but my skills with the spear have declined. Other than the wrestling I learned as a youth, I know nothing of hand-to-hand combat."

Amonked gave his brother-in-law a nod of approval. "I suggest you follow his example, Lieutenant Horhotep. No matter how skilled you are, the practice can do you no harm."

"Yes, sir." The vicious look the adviser shot Nebwa would have felled a lesser man.

Bak staved off an urge to applaud.

Nebwa blinked, betraying surprise, but kept his voice level, unemotional. "We can use our batons of office as clubs, as well as other lengths of wood too short to be used for spears, and we can make weapons from unlikely objects. For example, several drovers wear leather kilts, which can be cut up for use in slings and to make thongs needed for constructing maces and other small weapons. Spears can be made from poles such as the uprights that support the tents and this pavilion."

Nefret gasped, drawing Amonked's attention and a scowl that discouraged complaint. If the inspector himself was dismayed by the suggestion, he betrayed no hint of the feeling.

"Captain Minkheper," Nebwa went on, "has offered to show the men how to make these weapons and to see the work done in the best manner possible and at a rapid pace."

Amonked again nodded approval.

Nebwa said no more, signaling the end of his report.

The inspector broke the ensuing silence, asking the question uppermost in each and every heart. "Should Hor-pen-Deshret waylay us with a large force of men, could we hold them off?"

"If they were to attack tomorrow while we're on the move, I doubt we could. In a day or two, after we're better prepared, I believe so. We'll be close enough to Askut by then to summon help. The garrison there is small, but a few well-armed and trained men could make all the difference."

"What of the local people?" Nefret asked, drawing all eyes her way. "First they were visible day after day and now they've gone. Where are they? Lurking somewhere nearby so they, too, can set upon us?"

"I doubt we'll have to fight on two fronts," Nebwa said. "While the people who dwell here don't like what this inspection party stands for, they hate Hor-pen-Deshret and his ilk."

"They've been victimized by men like him each time the leaders of this land grew careless or weak," Bak said, making a point he wanted to be sure the inspector understood.

"They may even decide to help us," Nebwa said, "when Bak snares Baket-Amon's slayer."

"And I will snare him." The words, spoken firm and positive, were prompted, Bak felt sure, by some mischievous god recently given a fine offering by Commandant Thuty, who took his success for granted.

"Lieutenant Bak." A man, speaking softly but firmly in his ear, caught him by the shoulder and shook him. "Wake up, sir. Wake up."

Bak rolled over, struggled into a sitting position, and shook his head to clear away the sleep. The night was black, the sliver of moon low, the stars miserly with their light. He could barely make out the individual hovering over him, a drover, he remembered. "What's wrong?"

"The donkeys are uneasy, sir. Seshu thinks we've an intruder. He asked me to summon you."

Muttering a curse, Bak hauled himself to his feet, found a spear and shield, and looked down at Nebwa and the archers, bundled up in heavy linen to stave off the chill, sleeping soundly. He thought of the man who had slipped in among them to steal their sandals. This might well be a similar prank. If he needed help, he decided, he could summon them later. With the drover in the lead, they headed across the encampment. Stepping over sleeping men and around braziers containing fuel long burned to ash, they wove a hurried path through the darkness. The cool night air seeped beneath Bak's tunic, chilling him to the marrow.

He soon heard the donkeys' restless movement, their troubled snorts and blowing. The drover led him around the herd to where Seshu stood with Pashenuro and two drovers who had been assigned to keep watch overnight, scaring off predators, preventing the hobbled animals from straying, and keeping a wary eye open for desert marauders. With eyes growing more attuned to the feeble light, he saw that only the men on watch were armed.

"There's somebody in there, all right," Seshu growled.

"Have you spotted him?" Bak asked.

A drover shook his head. "Too dark. Can't see a thing."

"Are you sure it's a man and not a jackal? Or maybe dogs?"

"The pack that's been following us wouldn't bother the donkeys and they'd chase off any unfamiliar animals, making a racket you could hear all the way to Buhen."

Pashenuro nodded agreement. "I'd guess a man, sir, probably one of the nomads who've been keeping pace with us."

Bak was not as sure as the sergeant was. The dogs had barked when the tribesmen had first appeared and had since stayed well clear of them, indicating a distinct lack of trust. Probably because, when catching the big yellow cur for their vile prank, they had frightened the rest of the pack. "If he's not to run away in the dark, we'll need torches." As Pashenuro and a drover turned to go, he hastily added, "And, for the lord Amon's sake, bring back some weapons. And shields."

The pair hurried off to do his bidding. While Seshu and the others remained where they stood, Bak walked in among the nearest animals, speaking quietly, trying to calm them, wishing fervently that he could see better. He could not understand why the dogs were silent. True, they were not trained to protect the caravan, but they were feral, and feral dogs barked at the least provocation.

He turned to sidle between two donkeys, at the same time raising his shield so it would not get in his way. He heard a soft thunk and felt a faint vibration through the heavy cowhide. The donkey to his right snorted fear. Bak's heart shot into his mouth. The white tunic, he thought, a target in the dark. He ducked low and lunged forward, hiding among the animals. Turning the shield, he looked at its face, at the arrow impaling the leather.

"Get down!" he yelled. "The intruder's using a bow!"

"Lieutenant!" Pashenuro's voice and the flicker of light played across the backs of the donkeys.

A whisper of sound caught Bak's ear. The animal nearest to him screamed and fell to its knees, an arrow planted deep in its thick neck. Bak tried to catch the rope halter to quiet it, but it flung its head and thrashed its legs, trying to escape the pain and the stench of its own blood, and it brayed nonstop. The nearer animals panicked and tried to run in spite of their hobbles. Their wild lunges instilled fear into the rest of the herd. The dogs, so quiet before, began to bark, their excitement triggered by the donkeys' terror.

"Get some men to quiet these animals," Seshu yelled.

"Lieutenant, are you all right?" Pashenuro called.

Hating what he had to do, Bak jerked his dagger from its sheath and slit the throat of the wounded animal, silencing it forever. Keeping low, he grabbed the halter of a jenny who, in her panic, was bucking madly, threatening to crush her foal. He led her and her baby away from the dead donkey, caught another animal and quieted it, and another and another. By the time he and the drovers had subdued the most panicked of the creatures, by the time Pashenuro joined him, torch in hand, he was certain the intruder had gotten away.

Nebwa and the archers came running, awakened by the clamor. They went through the herd, searching for the interloper, while the drovers quieted the animals and checked their well-being. As soon as they finished, Bak led a thorough search of the encampment, soothing people who had awakened in alarm, but finding no one who did not belong. The dogs settled down among the stacks of equipment and supplies as if nothing of note had occurred.

Nebwa assigned more guards to patrol the perimeter of the camp, and he, Bak, and the others returned to their sleeping places. Bak's last thought before he slept was of the dogs, of their failure to respond, their silence, when what everyone believed was a desert nomad had crept up to the encampment and in among the donkeys.

A nomad, a stranger from outside the camp. He was not so sure.

Chapter Thirteen

"You're right about the dogs. They'd've reacted to a stranger." Nebwa rubbed his chin, bristly from a failure to shave the previous evening. The training session had taken precedence over personal care. "Maybe someone in Amon-ked's party feels cornered."

"Why must the lord Amon be so whimsical?" Bak scowled at the long train of donkeys plodding south, the older animals sedate and well-behaved, the younger made frisky by the early morning chill, the fear in the night forgotten by one and all. "Thanks to him, I raised that shield when I did, but why, after saving me, did he allow the donkey to be a target, causing panic throughout the herd so the intruder could get away?"

Yawning mightily, Nebwa stared off to the west, his eyes on the tribesmen standing on the crest of a long golden dune. The six men had come closer at daybreak, making them easier to see in the clear morning light. "No sign of Hor-pen-Deshret, but I'm troubled that those vile barbarians have come so near. What accounts for their newfound courage?"

Bak was equally troubled. He wanted to walk out to them, to demand answers. Not feasible, he knew, for the instant he headed their way, they would slip from sight. "We're in urgent need of news, Nebwa. I hesitate to leave the caravan today, but I must. By late afternoon, when the air is cooler and I can cover the distance quickly, I'll walk to the river and the village of Rona, the man of influence Woser mentioned. He'll surely know more of the tribesmen's intentions than we do. And who knows? I may even convince him to sway his people's thoughts in our favor."

"You can't go alone." Nebwa's tone brooked no argument.

"I'll take Pashenuro. Other than befriending Pawah, his pretense of being a drover has led nowhere." Bak looked at the men on the dune, his thoughts on the journey ahead. "We can take nothing with us that the tribesmen would covet, inviting attack, yet we must take a gift of value for the old man."

Nebwa snorted. "What, may I ask, would that be? We brought nothing from Buhen. If not for our weapons, we'd be impoverished."

"Perhaps Amonked can live without one of the many objects he brought along from Waset."

"How about mistress Nefret? I'll wager he'd be glad to get rid of her."

"Two men crossing the barren desert, with Amon alone knows how many human predators lurking about." Amonked, his face grave, shook his head. "The very thought appalls me."

"If anyone knows what Hor-pen-Deshret is plotting, the old man will," Bak insisted.

"Would that wretched bandit not hold his plans close within his heart, letting no one know his intent?"

"He would if he could, but secrecy is impossible. During normal times, news travels along the river faster than dust in a high wind. That's doubly true now, when the people's lives depend on their knowing where he is and what he means to do."

Amonked laid his hand on the brush-like mane of the donkey beside which they were walking, a white jenny carrying two jars of water and a large basket containing the twin foals she had birthed during the night, lying in a nest of pungent straw. Pawah had discovered the tiny newborns at dawn and prevailed upon Amonked to allow him to look after them until they grew strong enough to keep pace with their mother.

Bak had found Amonked walking with the boy and donkeys some distance behind the rest of the inspection party, well away from Nefret and her complaints. Horhotep was walking alongside the concubine's carrying chair, assuring her, most likely, that she had no reason to worry. As soon as Bak had appropriately praised the foals, Pawah had dropped back to talk with Pashenuro, seeking suggestions about caring for his new charges.

"Can you not wait until morning?" Amonked asked. "If we maintain a good pace today, according to Seshu, we'll camp tonight not far from the river. Your trek would be considerably shorter—and safer."

"By the time Pashenuro and I strike off on our own, we'll be less than an hour's walk from the next signal station and the river." Bak studied the undulating sands off to the left, burnished gold where struck by the sun, tarnished by the long morning shadows. "Seshu knows of several places where the sandhills rise taller than a man. With the help of the gods and a diversion Nebwa is planning, we should be able to leave the caravan unnoticed."

"You're determined to go, I see."

"Yes, sir."

Amonked let out a long, weary sigh. "All right, do so if you must." He noticed a patch of sand on his kilt, brushed it off. "What would you suggest we give the headman?"

Bak could think of several objects that might be appropriate under different circumstances. Amonked's armchair would please the old man beyond words, but it was too large and noticeable and best carried on the back of a donkey. The racing dog would do, but would not survive for long when faced with tougher, meaner village curs. The pavilion would provide a wonderful setting for a headman who wished to impress, but they needed the poles for weapons more than Rona needed status.

Keeping his thoughts to himself, he shrugged. "An object that won't attract attention should we be spotted by men of the desert, one that will appear normal and natural from a distance. Something a proud and no doubt stubborn old man can look upon with satisfaction and at the same time show off to those who look to him for leadership and guidance."

Amonked glanced at the donkey by his side, his expression speculative, as if she and her twins might be suitable, then glanced toward Pawah and shook his head. Turning his back, he climbed a gradual slope of sand off to the side, gaining a broader perspective of the long line of animals, many of which carried his belongings and those of his companions from Waset.

Bak, who had followed, looked at the passing caravan with a soldier's eye, not that of a man seeking to gladden the heart of a stranger. No general would approve, he knew, but considering what little they had started with, he was pleased. Nebwa had spread the archers along the length of the caravan, close in to the animals. The guards, less well-trained and therefore more dispensable, he had distributed along a wider path on both sides of the column. Thanks to the lord Amon and a boundless effort late into the night, Minkheper and his helpers had not only created at least one small weapon for each guard but had made enough spears to arm the drovers, with a few to spare. One tent, saved for Nefret, had survived their assault, and the pavilion would be the next to go. The young woman was upset. Very upset. Thus Amonked's escape.

He could not help but see the irony of the situation. An attack by desert tribesmen would go a long way toward convincing the inspector the army was needed along the Belly of Stones. However, if set upon by a large enough force, both man and mission might come to an abrupt— and fatal—end. The number of men they had to face would make a crucial difference. The more men, the less chance they would have of succeeding in spite of Nebwa's best efforts.

"This is sure to satisfy him," Amonked said, pulling a ring off the middle finger of his left hand and offering it to Bak. "My cousin gave it to me when first she attained the throne. I treasure it greatly, but I value more my life and the lives of all who travel with this caravan."

The solid gold ring felt heavy in Bak's palm. The band was broad, supporting a good-sized bezel shaped as a scarab, inscribed on the under side for use as a seal. An object of considerable value. "Are you sure you wish to part with this, sir?"

"I do. Whether or not the headman can read, he'll recognize the symbol of protection surrounding the royal name. He'll be suitably impressed, I'm sure."

Bak looked closer at the inscription. *Maatkare Hatshepsut*, it read, after which were the symbols for life, health, and prosperity. The beauty of the scarab, the superb craftsmanship, made the ring worthy of the most illustrious of noblemen. He was astonished. The queen would not be pleased to learn that her cousin had given such a fine gift to the elderly headman of a poor frontier village.

Could he be wrong about Amonked? This stout, rather nondescript man whom everyone believed to be a tool of his powerful cousin had begun to display a far greater depth than Bak had expected. He had prepared well for his task in Wawat, studying many documents. He seemed not to leap to conclusions about the fortresses he inspected. True, he was impressed with the objects he saw in the storage magazines, but taking pleasure in items of value and beauty did not necessarily mean he thought less of the men who kept them safe. Though he had uttered no words of condemnation or praise, he appeared to recognize Horhotep's limitations and to approve of Nebwa's efforts to train and equip the men in case of attack. And now the ring.

The inspector just might be a good man. A man he might

come to like, might even learn to respect. For the first time, Bak found himself hoping Amonked innocent of Baket-Amon's murder for a reason other than his kinship with Maatkare Hatshepsut.

"I'm surprised to find you alone, mistress." Bak looked up at Nefret, seated on a thick pillow on the carrying chair, her face and voluptuous body shadowed by the canopy above her. She had substituted perfume for a bath, and its too-sweet strength tainted the air. "Your most avid admirer is neglecting you."

He had seen Thaneny walking with Amonked. The scribe's absence had offered an ideal opportunity to probe deeper into the young woman's life—and the inspector's. If she was the key to Baket-Amon's death, her guilelessness might lead to the slayer.

"Horhotep?" Nefret laughed. "He only talks to me because he fears Amonked has ceased to listen to him and he hopes I'll use my influence to improve his position." She laughed again, this time with a strong touch of cynicism. "He doesn't seem to realize that I, too, have lost favor."

Poor Thaneny, Bak thought, the invisible man as far as she was concerned. "Has Amonked not told you he's troubled by your many complaints, your failure to accept this journey as fact and adapt as best you can?"

The porters exchanged a surprised look, unaccustomed to such blunt speech from anyone other than Amonked.

"I thought this trip would . . . Well . . ." Nefret fussed with her dress, smoothing it across her thigh. "I thought we'd be together more. From the day he took me into his household, he . . . He's seldom spent time with me. Only at night. And then we don't talk much."

"I see," Bak said, stealing the noncommittal demeanor and words from the inspector himself.

The porters exchanged another look, this one a smirk.

Amonked had, Bak realized, brought this beautiful young woman on this most arduous journey without really knowing her. A woman he had taken into his household . . . How many years ago? Four? Five? Possibly longer. It was one thing to enjoy the pleasures of the body and leave the bedchamber as the sun rose, quite another to share all the hours of every day and night out on the barren desert, with a minimum of comfort and a lurking threat of attack.

"I miss Waset! I long to return!" She flung a fearful look at a yellow dog trotting past. "To sleep in a house, with no insects or reptiles or animals to fear. To bathe each morning in a placid pool. To spend my days in the shade of a sycamore tree, breathing the sweet scent of flowers. To be waited upon by servants who leap to obey my slightest command. To gossip with Sithathor, Amonked's wife, and his sister and his mother."

"While you enjoy the pleasures of life, what does he do?" Bak asked, silently thanking her for opening the door into their lives.

"When he's home, you mean? What do noblemen usually do? He swims, plays board games, receives guests. Mostly, he fusses with the household accounts and manages his estate and that of Sithathor." She wrinkled her nose as if so common a task was distasteful to her. "She tells me he's multiplied her holdings three times over since the day he took her as his wife."

Bak was surprised. Few men could accomplish such a feat. He had learned long ago not to take people at face value, but he had allowed Amonked's commonplace appearance and Nofery's old and outdated recollection of the past to influence him into thinking the inspector a shadow of a man. He had erred.

"As storekeeper of the lord Amon, he must now and again toil in the service of the god."

She rolled her eyes skyward. "He spends hours upon hours in the warehouses, going through records, checking quantities, doing innumerable tasks I suspect could be done by lesser men. He comes home smelling of dusty documents and sometimes of onions or the granary or the animal paddocks."

Bak had assumed the task a sinecure, Amonked nothing more than a figurehead. Another error, it seemed. "As a favorite of our sovereign, she must often summon him to the royal house."

"Not so much anymore." Nefret looked thoughtful. "I don't know why. Probably because he has too many other tasks."

"Among them would be to provide masculine entertainment for lofty friends of the court, such as the hunting and fishing trips you told me about before."

She waved away a fly. "Also chariot races, wrestling matches, games of skill or chance. Activities all men enjoy, I've been told. Most of the time, anyway."

Bak asked further questions about these gatherings, but without success. The woman knew nothing about the manly pursuits, nor did she show any interest. Her life clearly revolved around the domestic. "I gather you get on well with Amonked's wife."

"Sithathor is wonderful." Nefret's face glowed. "She's kind and gentle and she bears no jealousy toward me, as other wives sometimes do for their husbands' concubines." Her features clouded over, banishing the smile. "My failure to give Amonked the children he wants has been a great disappointment to her."

"Is she not barren?"

"That's why he took me into his household." Nefret's eyes dropped to her hands; she bit her lip. "I've failed them both."

Bak's physician father would have suggested that with two women childless, the fault might lay with Amonked, but as no man wanted to think of himself as incomplete, the thought was better left unsaid.

"Sithathor isn't beautiful or youthful like I am," Nefret said, "but she has a presence that draws everyone to her. She's very well-connected also. Well, you know she's Sennefer's sister." The concubine paused, awaiting his nod. "She can talk to our sovereign with ease, I've been told, and is equally comfortable with all the nobility. She gives wonderful parties. She's . . ." The young woman stopped, laughed softly. "I guess you can see that I adore her."

A quick glance toward the sun told Bak he must draw this conversation to a close. Pashenuro would be awaiting him. "Amonked admitted he quarreled with Baket-Amon because of you."

"So he said." Nefret looked down at her dress, again smoothing it across her thigh. "Sithathor was angry with me then. She said, and I saw for myself, that the confrontation shamed him." Her chin shot up and she gave Bak a defiant look. "Baket-Amon was a man with two faces: charming and handsome, but self-indulgent. He wanted me but I didn't want him. I vowed to die rather than go with him, and Amonked knew I spoke the truth."

Bak did not believe for an instant that she would take her own life. She was much too fond of herself. "Would you have slain the prince rather than share his bed?"

"No. Only myself."

"That's the formation you must slip behind." Seshu looked toward a black flat-topped hill with steeply sloping sides that rose above the desert sands not far ahead. "The dune on the far side goes all the way to the river. Unless tribesmen have been posted behind it, they'll never know you've gone."

The lead donkeys were already walking along the base of the formation, as were the members of Amonked's party. Bak and Pashenuro, carrying long spears and shields, were fifty or so paces behind, two soldiers among many. A yell cut the silence, drawing every eye toward the rear of the caravan. A drover and a guard, spouting curses, exchanged blows. Men abandoned their positions and ran toward the confrontation. Some donkeys plodded on without their drovers, others stopped in their tracks, a confusion of animals, a further distraction.

"May the lord Amon go with you," Seshu said and hastened off to break up the sham fight. Nebwa sped past a short time later, giving them the briefest of glances and a wink.

Bak and Pashenuro strolled away from the caravan. Two of the feral dogs, one brindled and one gray, trotted after them. Soon men and dogs were hidden from the tribesmen by the formation and the high, seemingly endless dune that had formed on the hill's downwind side.

The trek across the desert was uneventful, allowing Bak and Pashenuro to reach the river long before dark. A farmer weeding a melon field told them where they would find the hamlet in which the headman Rona lived. The lengthy floodplain, with its heavy black soil squared off into fields and dotted with groves of date palms, was richer in resources than any other location between Buhen and Semna. Along much of the oasis and beyond the reach of all but the highest flood, an equally wide but more irregular strip provided enough natural vegetation to offer limited grazing. The area's greater wealth and population accounted in large part for the old man's influence.

As the lord Re slid toward the horizon, turning the sky a flame red shot through with gold, Bak and the Medjay crossed a series of small fields lush with vegetables, fodder, and grain on the brink of harvest. Beyond, they climbed a low bluff to Rona's village, twenty or so dry-stone and mudbrick houses set among a scattering of spiny acacias. A heavy blanket of sand crept over the surrounding hills, threatening to smother the dwellings. A serpentine wall, looking small and fragile against so enormous a peril, held back the encroaching desert.

The village dogs, spotting intruders on their territory, began to bark, drawing men, women, and children from their homes. The people stood in silence, watching the armed strangers with wary faces and mistrustful eyes.

"I'm Lieutenant Bak, head of the Medjay police in Buhen. I must speak with your headman, Rona." Amonked's ring hung heavy on a leather thong around his neck, a gift of mutual regard, not a bargaining tool.

A stooped old man, using a long staff to help him along, hobbled forward. "I am the man you seek."

Stopping at a mudbrick bench that overlooked the fields, he sat down with a stiffness that told of worn and aged joints. He pointed toward his feet, indicating Bak should sit on the ground in front of him. Bak preferred to stand, feeling that height gave him an advantage, but prudence dictated he accommodate the old man. Seated cross-legged, spear and shield beside him, Pashenuro kneeling behind with the two dogs, he began the customary ritual, asking about the state of Rona's health. Proceeding along a time-honored path, they discussed the past year's flood, the promise of an abundant harvest and the flood soon to envelop thirsty fields. The villagers slipped away a few at a time, only to reappear on the rooftops, preparing their evening meal while watching and, if close enough, listening.

Courtesies complete, Bak said, "I speak for Troop Captain Nebwa, who in turn speaks for Commandant Thuty of Buhen."

The old man's expression hardened. "Don't try to mislead me, young man. You speak for Amonked, inspector of the fortresses of Wawat, newly come from the land of Kemet."

"I don't." Bak thought of the ring hanging at his breast, which made a falsehood of the denial. "Perhaps I do, but not from choice. If I had my way, he'd have traveled no farther south than Ma'am, and there the viceroy would've convinced him he came on a fool's errand."

Rona looked long and hard at the man seated before him. "I've heard of you, Lieutenant Bak. Since you've come to the Belly of Stones, you've proven to be a friend of my people. A man of honor."

"Commander Woser told me of you. He called you not only honorable and wise but a man of influence."

The old man ignored the compliment—and the implication that he had the prestige to assist, should he so desire. "Tell me of this man Amonked. Will he see our need for the army? Or will he return to your capital and your sovereign with a message of destruction?"

"I don't know," Bak admitted. "At first I thought he'd say whatever she wishes to hear, giving no thought to the consequences. I've since come to know him better, and I think he'll recommend what he truly believes to be the best possible action." Noting a glimmer of hope on the old man's face, he raised a hand to still the thought. "What he thinks of as best may differ from what you and I believe to be best."

The old man nodded, slowly, thoughtfully. "I appreciate your candor. Now what do you want of me?"

Bak reached out to the brindle dog, which had inched forward to sit beside him, but it ducked away from his hand. "You know Hor-pen-Deshret has returned."

"A nightmare come true."

"His men have been watching the caravan. We believe he wants the rich trappings Amonked has brought south and the weapons we carry and our many donkeys. He's not yet interested in the farms and villages along the river."

"Not yet, for a fact." Rona leaned forward, the weight of his upper body supported by his staff. "If the army is torn from the Belly of Stones, he'll take what he wants and lay waste to the rest, destroying all we've built up during his absence."

Bak refused to go down the same path twice. "We've seen Hor-pen-Deshret once—two days ago—and he left behind six men to watch us. We feel certain he means to attack, but we don't know when or where or the size of the force he'll bring against us."

"You're a man of arms, Lieutenant, as is Troop Captain Nebwa. Why have you not sent out spies?"

Bak longed to stand up, to tower over the old man. "We've seen men march off into the desert and never return, and we've no desire to lose the few skilled fighting men we have." He flashed Rona his most disarming smile. "Besides, Commander Woser assured us that nothing occurs between Iken and Askut without your knowledge."

"I've been told you've begun to train men to fight, men who set out from Kor knowing nothing of combat."

Bak's smile broadened. "You are indeed a man of vast knowledge."

A hint of a smile touched Rona's face. He rocked back, glanced toward a nearby rooftop from which the scent of onions drifted, and raised a hand to make a signal Bak could not interpret. "You will share my evening meal, you and your Medjay." The smile waned and he stared out across the oasis, saying nothing, until Bak feared old age had stolen his thoughts. "Hor-pen-Deshret will slay every living creature in this village if he hears I've helped you. And he will hear, I have no doubt."

"If we slay him or send him to Kemet a prisoner, he can no longer take anyone's life or property."

Neither Bak nor Rona felt a need to mention the death and destruction that would result all along the frontier if the caravan was taken by the tribesmen and Hor-pen-Deshret deemed himself invincible.

"He's forming a coalition of desert tribes," Rona said.

A coalition? Bak prayed the reality was not as ominous as the word.

"While the women and children, the elderly and infirm, remain behind to tend their flocks, the fighting men are gathering in the desert south of Askut, not far from the old island fortress of Shelfak, presently unoccupied, as you know. When he deems he's amassed sufficient forces, they'll attack your caravan."

Rona raised a hand, holding off the many questions risen in Bak's throat. "He planned at first to strike today, when the caravan was far from the river and the animals spread out along the trail. He thought the men traveling with you to be poorly armed and with no talent to fight back. When word reached him of your training efforts and the new weapons you've acquired, he decided to postpone the attack until he has a larger force."

Bak had to laugh. He and Nebwa had underestimated the tribal chieftain, thinking he would plan his attack based on numbers alone. "How many men have gathered?"

"The last I heard, close to a hundred and sixty. Additional men come each day."

Bak tried not to show how staggered he was by the news. One and a half times the number of men the caravan contained and more on the way. "It would be to your advantage and to the advantage of all who dwell along the river if your young men came to our aid."

"We'll do nothing to help you until the death of Prince Baket-Amon is avenged." Rona's voice was firm and flat, a statement of unalterable fact. "You must snare his slayer and see that he's punished."

"Are you speaking for yourself, or has so rigid an order come from elsewhere? Ma'am, I'd wager."

Rona bowed his head in acknowledgment. "I speak for the mother of his firstborn son."

As we suspected, Bak thought. A woman dwelling in the safety of a distant fortress, deep in mourning and yearning for revenge, has issued an order that might well destroy the people who would one day look to her son as their leader in name if not in fact.

"Your people, though far from helpless, always suffer at the hands of rampaging tribesmen. Does she have no pity?"

Rona clamped his mouth tight, refusing to commit.

Bak rose to his feet, his face grim. "I'll lay hands on the man who slew Baket-Amon—if I survive the attack Horpen-Deshret plans."

The old man gripped his staff, preparing to stand. "You will stay here through the night." He gave Bak a humorless smile. "I'll not have you slain by those wretched tribesmen before the battle begins."

Bak pulled the leather thong from around his neck, untied the knot, and held out the ring. "When I told Amonked I wished to give you a gift, he offered this symbol of his esteem."

Rona took the ring, studied it, and for a moment Bak feared he had forgotten to breathe. "I've seen nothing so magnificent in all my many years. Nothing." His eyes narrowed. "Does he hope, with this ring, to make me indebted to him? To oblige me to tell my people they must fight for you and then smile at the loss of the army along the Belly of Stones?"

"The ring is a sign of his regard, that's all. He hoped you'd show him a mutual respect, and you have. You've warned us of the multitude we must face and you've told us where we can find them. I'd hoped for more, but the lord Dedun has conspired against me, it seems."

The lord Dedun and Baket-Amon's chief wife.

Chapter Fourteen

Bak and Pashenuro left the village at first light and hurried to the nearest watch station, a couple of meager mudbrick buildings built on a high knoll to shelter the half-dozen soldiers posted there. They had expected the station to offer a good vantage point from which to see the caravan approaching from the north, but its expansive view proved unnecessary. Men and animals were less than three hundred paces away, breaking camp and preparing to depart. Seshu had kept them marching until nightfall, not stopping until they neared the river and its precious water.

They went first to the station, where they found the men on duty speculating about the tribesmen watching from afar. The sergeant in charge was dismayed to learn of the much larger gathering near Shelfak. He produced the highly polished mirror he used to pass on messages to north and south and, at Bak's direction, signaled a warning to Askut.

When the inspection party climbed the knoll, Bak drew Amonked and Nebwa aside to make his report.

"So the local people won't help us," Amonked said.

Nebwa screwed up his face in disgust. "Not unless Bak snags Baket-Amon's slayer. No surprise there. Even then I'd not want to count their numbers before seeing them in the flesh. Rona can recommend whatever he likes, but if the people think they'd be better off with you dead, they'll simply close their ears and get on with what suits them."

The inspector pursed his lips, irritated by so blatant a truth. "Do you have any idea who the slayer might be?" he asked Bak.

"None." Another truth hard to take, one Bak could not gloss over.

Amonked's tone sharpened. "Then the wretched creature could as easily be in Buhen as here."

"Every instinct tells me you brought him with you from Waset and he's traveling with us now."

"I'd feel better, Lieutenant, if you spoke of reason, not instinct."

"My life has twice been imperiled. One time in Iken, where a man waylaid me in the dark with a dagger . . ." He spread wide the neck of his tunic, displaying the scabbed-over wound. ". . . and again the night the donkeys were disturbed, when a man with a bow sent arrows my way. I'd like to believe both attacks occurred because I was in the wrong place at the wrong time. Instinct, however, tells me that two assaults in two days are not coincidental. As Hor-pen-Deshret doesn't know me and would have no reason to wish me dead, the attempts must've been made by one who fears I'll lay hands on him."

"I had no idea. Why did you not tell me earlier?"

A third truth, Bak felt, needed to be aired. "Because you've the most obvious reason for slaying the prince."

"I see." The inspector stared at him, his face drained of feeling, as bland as the sculpted demeanor of his illustrious cousin. "I assume you wish me to plead with my fellow travelers to confess to murder."

Bak had an idea he was being needled. "I'd be satisfied with the truth, sir."

"Anything else you'd like, Lieutenant?"

Bak stifled a smile. Now he was sure the inspector was being facetious. "The caravan should reach Askut around midday. Rather than letting it go on while you inspect the fortress, as we've been doing, I suggest we make camp there, giving the donkeys a respite and the rest of us additional time to prepare for battle. With the tribesmen no more than a half day's march south of Askut, we'd be tempting the lord Set if we moved on."

The caravan turned off the desert trail to follow a branch path down a dry watercourse to the river valley. Hurrying on ahead, Bak, Seshu, and Nebwa selected a campsite on a modest grass- and weed-covered rise that looked out over a patchwork of fields almost ready for harvest. Beyond lay the river, where wide channels untroubled by rapids flowed to either side of several large islands.

The fortress of Askut crowned the summit of the island directly to the east. The towered structure was smaller than Buhen and triangular in shape to better fit the contours of the land, a long and narrow protuberance of rock and sand dotted with trees and what looked from a distance like garden plots. The walls were a mottled white, which spoke of a multitude of minor repairs or the need for a coat of fresh plaster.

The small garrison, one company of a hundred men plus officers and support personnel, told of a long period of peace, a relaxation of vigilance, and an assumption that infrequent punitive expeditions would be the extent of their soldiering.

Bak turned his back to the river to look at the campsite, where Seshu awaited the lead string of donkeys. The animals had just begun to file out of the wadi, ears cocked, pace quickened to a fast clip-clop, at the sight and scent of fresh, green vegetation on which they could graze.

"I'd offer a dozen fat geese to the lord Amon if I could face Hor-pen-Deshret here," Nebwa said, eyeing the campsite and surrounding terrain. "If only we could find a way to lure those swine off the desert."

The wadi mouth held Bak's attention. "The trail through that dry watercourse offers a possibility almost too good to be true."

"An ambush, you mean."

"I can think of no better way to narrow the odds—and
we must narrow them. According to Rona, we're already
outnumbered, with more men joining Hor-pen-Deshret each
day. Even with help from Askut, they'll surpass us in numbers."

The feral dogs raced out of the wadi. Barking at cousins
loping across the fields from the nearest village, they sped
toward the cluster of houses, which promised fresh pickings
if not a warm welcome.

"To form so large a coalition, the snake must've dangled
dreams of vast wealth before the eyes of every chieftain
within a week's walk of the river. I'm surprised at the response, though. They're usually more independent, not so
eager to share hard-won spoils."

"If we could toy with those dreams . . ." Bak's voice
tailed off. He tugged the dried seed head off a stalk of wild
grass, his thoughts racing. "I'm uncertain of details. But if
we could somehow convince them we've all along been
transporting greater wealth than they ever imagined, riches
that will be gone in a day or two . . ." Bak's eyes fell on
the first of the donkeys carrying Amonked's personal possessions and he recalled how wrong he had been in thinking
the inspector a man of wealth. A common mistake, he felt
sure. "If we could lead Hor-pen-Deshret to believe Amonked fears for his life and plans to travel from Askut to
Semna aboard a ship, where no one can lay hands on him
or the riches he carries, I'd wager that'd draw that wretched
bandit here, just where we want him."

"Yes!" An evil smile touched Nebwa's face. "Under ordinary circumstances, he'd never attack us in a spot so tact-
ically superior and with a garrison close to hand. But
tempted by an abundance of treasure and faced with losing
it if he doesn't act, he'll take the risk. I know he will." The
smile waned. "How'll we get the message to him without
scaring him off?"

"I'll send Pashenuro back to Rona. The local people
won't help us openly lest they disobey Baket-Amon's

widow, but they should have no aversion to spreading a rumor."

"Good. Very good." Nebwa swung around to study the island fortress. "I see no ships moored at Askut. We won't even have to think up a reason for Amonked to remain with us for the next day or two."

"When you go over to the island with the inspection party, you must ask Lieutenant Ahmose, who commands the garrison, not only for men and weapons, but for the use of his signalman. Then send a message to Semna, asking that a ship be sent north. If Hor-pen-Deshret hears a vessel is on its way, he'll be certain the rumor is true."

"You're not going with us?"

"I've a slayer to snare." Forming a humorless smile, Bak added, "Anyway, you've a loftier rank than I and enough authority to get your way. While you're overwhelming Ahmose with your importance, think now and again of me, down on my knees, pleading for information."

"Haven't you asked every question you can think of? What new stone do you hope to overturn?"

Bak's laugh was short, cynical. "Stone, Nebwa? I'd be happy if I could stub my toe on a pebble."

Bak watched Nebwa, Amonked, and Horhotep climb into the skiff the troop captain had commandeered for the short journey to Askut. Everyone else had remained behind to prepare for battle. He hated to see Nebwa go off alone with the pair from Waset, but surely by this time Amonked had come to realize that Horhotep deliberately baited the more senior officer with malicious intent.

He spun around and walked into the rectangular encampment Nebwa had organized within an incomplete fence of shields, the gaps to be filled later with shields borrowed from Askut. The donkeys, freed of their loads, were being led twenty or so at a time to the river for a bath and a drink. Their eager braying could be heard in the distance. Other drovers were organizing baskets and bundles and jars for quick loading, but also in piles strategically placed to serve as obstacles should the tribesmen attack. Archers and guards formed islands of activity around make-shift hearths. Sentries had taken up their posts, with two men hidden partway up the wadi, watching the tribesmen who were watching the caravan. Food and beer were being distributed, and the yeasty aroma of baking bread wafted through the air. The camp was like an anthill, with innumerable small tasks quickly done and gotten out of the way, each man anxious to go on with his training and to help make weapons. Only Nefret, her maid, and Amonked's racing dog had nothing to contribute.

After a much-belated midday meal of bread and dried fish, Bak walked, beer jar in hand, across a camp abuzz with activity. He found Sennefer seated on a low stool surrounded by stacks of Amonked's possessions, including the tent Thaneny had given Nefret when the pavilion had been dismantled. The nobleman was knapping flint for use as a cutting edge on some type of weapon. Nefret stood before him, looking annoyed. Probably because he went on with his task, striking the stone with hard, crisp taps all the while she spoke.

"They've destroyed the pavilion and what little privacy I had. I suppose next they'll want my tent poles." Seeing Bak approach, she tossed her head in high dudgeon and stalked off, Mesutu at her heels.

Sennefer stopped his task to watch her retreating figure. Amonked's dog, tied close to prevent it from running with the feral dogs, rested its muzzle on his knee and stared up at him, its great dark eyes pleading for affection.

"Nefret's a beautiful woman," Bak said, drawing another stool close and sitting down.

"She is that." Sennefer tore his gaze from her and quickly rearranged his features to hide a sadness Bak barely glimpsed. "She needs a good spanking—or a half-dozen children. Or both. Unfortunately, her father doted on her and Amonked wouldn't lift a hand against a mosquito. And she's unable to conceive."

Bak broke the plug out of the beer jar and took a drink of the thick, bitter liquid. "She loves you, you know." He disliked revealing personal secrets, but a desperate man must take desperate measures.

"And I love her."

Bak stared, taken aback not so much by the content of the admission as by the admission itself.

"Yes, it's true," the nobleman said with a mocking smile. "I've loved her for years. She doesn't know, of course, nor will she ever." He struck the hammerstone against the other, sending a flake flying. "My father urged me to marry a woman of royal blood, and I took too long in deciding I wanted Nefret instead." A sharp rap and another flake flashed through the air. "By then it was too late. Amonked had taken her as his concubine with my sister's blessing."

The dog ducked away from the flying stone and, tail tucked between its legs, came to Bak. Whimpering softly, it nudged his hand with its nose. He scratched its head. "Did you know of Baket-Amon's attempt to buy her?"

"I'm one of the few people in this world in whom my brother-in-law confides. As he doesn't know of my feelings for Nefret, he speaks freely about their relationship." Sennefer paused, struck off another flake, added ruefully, "Often to my regret."

Bak sympathized; such a position would be untenable. "Did you feel any animosity toward the prince for pursuing her to such an extent?"

"Why should I? He was unsuccessful. If he'd persisted . . ." Sennefer struck the flint hard, too hard, ruining the flake. ". . . I'd've felt different. But he didn't. He had no need. He had but to beckon and beautiful young women came running in numbers too plentiful to count."

"As when you allowed Amonked and other favorites of our sovereign to host hunting parties on your estate?"

"The prince had to show restraint there." Sennefer

flashed a quick smile. "He'd have risked bad feelings if he'd moved onto someone else's territory, and he was too intelligent a man to allow an enmity to develop between himself and some lofty bureaucrat or nobleman or military man."

"Was he as careful when he was your personal guest?"

"One of my servants seemed to satisfy him." Sennefer dropped onto his lap the stones he had been working and picked up a goatskin waterbag lying on the sand beside his stool. "He more than satisfied her. She'll feel his death acutely."

"If not during hunting parties, you saw him at his most . . . expansive, shall we say . . . Where?"

"I spent a few evenings with him in the capital, visiting various houses of pleasure." The nobleman drank from the waterbag, smiled. "I must admit, I couldn't begin to keep up with him. Women hanging all over him, desirous of his attention. At first I felt inadequate, as if I'd aged before my time, but I finally concluded I'd not like to be so driven."

"I know of what you speak. I saw him in a house of pleasure in Buhen two nights before his death." Bak looked back on that night with sadness, but had second thoughts. Baket-Amon had been happy, and what more could one ask than to end one's life glad of heart. "The proprietor said he was always greatly in demand because, and I'll quote her: 'He was a brilliant lover and not rough like some men are.' "

"That I can believe. For a man so absorbed by the pleasures offered by women, he was singularly prudish. He'd drawn a line beyond which he'd never go." Sennefer frowned, thinking back. "I can only guess from a few things he said . . . Nothing specific, but . . . Well, you once asked if I knew of anything in his past that might have come back to haunt him."

To taunt, Baket-Amon had said, but Bak feared a correction would break the nobleman's thought.

"In truth, I know nothing. I've no more than a feeling,

a conclusion based on a few insignificant words. I believe something happened in the past that badly upset him, causing him to fear the harsher excesses of the bedchamber. What the incident was, I've no idea."

Later, walking back through the encampment in search of Minkheper, Bak tried to tamp down a surge of excitement. The incident Sennefer had mentioned more likely than not had nothing to do with Baket-Amon's death. Yet instinct told him he had come at last to the path he sought.

Instinct. Amonked would disapprove.

"Hit him hard!" Minkheper yelled. "Don't addle his wits! Disable him!"

The young, heavy-muscled guard backed up a couple paces, raised his arm high, leaped at the thick post driven into the ground, and struck hard at the top with a short, stout length of wood cut from a pole that had supported Amonked's pavilion. If the post had been a man, the club would have crushed his skull.

"That's the way it's done!" Minkheper looked around the ring of men, twenty or so guards, Sergeant Roy, and Lieutenant Merymose. All had come to learn the rough-and-tumble fighting practiced by men of the sea. "Remember, each time you strike with too little force, you'll soon find your foe back on his feet, ready to fight again. Why not save yourself the added effort? Make each blow count."

The men looked at one another and nodded, seeing the sense in his words.

Spotting Bak, Minkheper raised a hand in greeting. "We're about through for the day, Lieutenant. Anything you wish to add?"

"How're they coming along?" Bak asked.

The captain clapped the young guard hard on the shoulder. "You saw for yourself how this strapping example of manhood held back his blow. I pray none will be so squeamish when faced with the enemy."

Merymose came forward, giving Bak a tentative smile.

"I saw you last night, showing the men Sergeant Dedu was training how to use the baton of office for crowd control. Can you show us, sir? Since the men of the desert have no training in warfare, they're more apt to attack like a mob than an army."

"The lieutenant showed us a couple of your tricks, sir," an older man said. "We'd like to know more."

The other guards echoed the plea. Bak, who had ceased to be surprised at their eagerness to learn, hastened to agree. Summoning Roy from among the rest, primarily because the burly sergeant's disinclination to exert himself made him as stiff and unwieldy as any recalcitrant drunk or rabble rouser, he scooped up a pole cut to the appropriate length and clasped one end in his right hand.

Using the makeshift baton as an extension of his arm, he demonstrated how it could be used to hold off a man attacking with a dagger or spear and to knock the weapon from his hand. He showed them how to strike a man down, to prod him forward, to lash him across the back or buttocks or legs with the aim of startling or pressing forward or tripping up.

Taking the ends of the baton in widespread hands, he showed them how to push men forward, forcing them deeper into a crowd, causing disarray. How to raise the horizontal weapon above a man's head and bring it forward and down, entrapping him. How to steal up behind a man, slip the baton over his head, and pull back hard to break his neck.

He taught them a multitude of other actions, other ways to turn the simple object into a deadly weapon. Roy proved a surprisingly apt pupil and at the end, when Bak turned the baton over to him, he repeated every move, every technique, proving he had learned well. When Bak suggested the sergeant help teach the evening lessons, Roy dropped altogether his indifference to soldiering.

*   *   *

Bak raised his empty beer jar in salute to Minkheper. "You're a valuable man to have around, Captain. Patient, versatile, and able. Not only do you know how to make the best use of available resources, but you know the ways men fight when not guided by reason or training."

"If I've learned nothing else during the years I've spent on the Great Green Sea, I've mastered the ability to take care of myself, my crew, and my ship."

Merymose, carrying three beer jars, wove a path through the dozen or so men seated on the ground, putting the finishing touches to newly made spears, scimitars, and slings. Sergeant Roy followed with a basket from which he passed out beer to the toiling men.

Handing a jar to Bak, the young officer said, "Roy is a changed man, sir. I feared his sense of self-importance would make him unbearable, but he's thoroughly enjoying this new respect you've given him."

"I gave him nothing. He earned it himself."

Minkheper accepted a jar and broke out the plug. "With a baton in your hand, Lieutenant, you make a formidable adversary."

"If only I could resolve Baket-Amon's death as easily as I use the stick." Bak rapped the plug on the jar too hard, a measure of his frustration. Instead of the clean break he had intended, the dried clay shattered. "My quest has led me to the houses of pleasure along Waset's waterfront, and there I've come to a dead end."

"Would that I could help you," Merymose said, his regret evident. "He was a good and kind man, one I admired without reservation."

"You never accompanied him on his carousing?"

"Never." The young officer's regret deepened. "After the one brief time I served as his aide, I hoped he'd summon me. I wanted again to assist him, to run his errands and write his letters, perhaps go with him when he played. But he never sent for me."

"You never ran into him in a house of pleasure?"

Merymose barked out a cynical laugh. "You must've come into this world a man of means, sir. Someone like me, one with nothing but the clothes on my back and the weapons in my hand, must satisfy himself with small and lowly places tucked into out-of-the-way corners of a city."

"My father was a physician," Bak grinned. "For lack of wealth, I, too, spent my early years haunting such low places, most likely many of the same establishments you frequented."

The young officer blushed. "I'm sorry, sir. I didn't mean . . ."

"I take no offense." Bak sipped from his beer jar. The brew was thick and warm, scarcely satisfying. "Anyway, from what I've learned so far, I suspect you're too young to help me."

"You've made some progress since last we spoke?" Minkheper asked.

"Not as much as I'd like." Bak's scowl turned to a wry smile. "Would that you were as noted a carouser as the prince was."

"As I believe I told you, I've a wife I'm fond of, other young women elsewhere, and . . ." Minkheper took a sip of beer, grimaced. ". . . and a cook who makes a far better brew than this. Better, in fact, than any I can get in a house of pleasure." Someone cursed, drawing the captain's attention. A drover who had cut himself on a sharp flake of flint he had been setting into the cutting edge of a scimitar. "My brother impoverished himself in a search for the good life, a lesson to all who might wish to follow in his footsteps. I, for one, have no desire to destroy my life so willfully."

The moment he spoke, regret swept across his face. A family sadness, Bak guessed, a disgrace.

He stood up to look over the wall of shields, out across the fields to the river. In the distance, he saw Nebwa dragging the commandeered skiff out of the water, while Amonked watched and Horhotep stood higher on the bank, too important to help, Bak suspected. He prayed his friend's mission over the past few hours had gone better than his own.

"Lieutenant Ahmose is a reasonable man." Nebwa splashed water over his shoulders, making them glisten. "He'll help us all he can with the resources available to him."

Bak knelt down in the river and dunked his head under, refreshing himself. "He has no other choice that I can see."

"He knows of Hor-pen-Deshret, knows what havoc he used to wreak along this stretch of the river. When I told him about the coalition . . ." A braying donkey drew Nebwa's glance downriver, where Pashenuro, Pawah, and a couple of drovers were frolicking in the water with a small herd. "Suffice it to say, he'd rather stand and fight now, with us by his side, than face the swine alone with only one meager company of spearmen."

"How did Horhotep behave?"

"He kept his mouth shut—for a change." Nebwa exuded satisfaction. "I think he's finally beginning to realize he might have to prove himself the warrior he pretends to be."

Bak thanked the lord Amon for small favors. "Did Amonked have time to inspect the fortress?"

"We had a war to plan. He didn't so much as suggest it."

Standing up, Bak ran his hands over his hair, squeezing out the water. His demeanor grew serious. "We can no longer make plans with blind eyes, Nebwa."

"I know. We need firsthand news of the enemy." Nebwa gave his friend a regretful look. "Sending a man south to spy on them will be risky, but we've no other option."

Bak knew what his friend was thinking: few men in the caravan were capable of performing the task with any chance of success. One was far superior to the rest. "I'll go speak with Pashenuro."

Nebwa's eyes darted toward the donkeys and the Medjay

in the water with them. "I neglected to ask how his mission went. Did Rona agree to help?"

"Haven't you heard the rumor, my friend?" With a quick smile, Bak waded farther out in the river, where the current tugged at his legs. "Amonked has brought with him from the royal house a plain wooden chest filled to the brim with valuable jewelry. Maatkare Hatshepsut herself placed it in his hands and assigned him the task of delivering it personally to the powerful Kushite king Amon-Psaro. As he fears for his life and the treasure, he's summoned a ship from Semna to carry him south from Askut."

Nebwa laughed heartily at the somewhat altered version of the tale he had heard earlier.

Bak slipped into the water and swam downstream. The river was cool and refreshing. The setting sun bestowed upon the sky a glorious golden glow. The early evening air banished the skimpy heat of the day. Too soon he reached his goal, where he drew Pashenuro aside to speak in private.

"I've been talking with Nebwa. We've a need to learn more of Hor-pen-Deshret's plans. We wish you to seek out his camp and spy on him and his army."

"I'd be glad to, sir, but the tongue of the western desert is different from that of my people. How am I to know what they're saying?"

Bak, who had expected the problem, was reluctant to air the sole solution he had to offer. "Pawah was spawned in the desert, but has dwelt in Waset for the past four or five years." He glanced toward the slender youth, standing in the shallows, trying to spear a fish. "How much does he remember of his native tongue?"

"We've not talked of such details."

"Let's ask him."

They waded past the donkeys, who were leaving the water one or two at a time to nibble on the wild grasses and brush that thrived along the shore. Thaneny and a drover sat naked on a boulder farther downstream, drying themselves and their clothing and at the same time keeping an eye on four crocodiles lying on the sunny beach some distance away.

Unwilling to spoil the boy's fishing, Bak stopped a half-dozen paces away, with Pashenuro by his side. "Pawah, can you still speak the language of the desert?"

The youth looked up, startled out of a total concentration. "I don't know, sir. I've had no need for a long time." He looked harder at Bak, puzzled. "Why do you want to know? What do you wish of me?"

"I thought to send you with Pashenuro to spy on the desert tribesmen, but you must be able to tell us what they're saying."

The boy's eyes widened, his face lit up. "Oh, please! Please let me go! The words will come back to me. I know they will."

"The journey through the night will be hard, to draw close enough to hear them speak will be dangerous. Shall I risk your life only to learn later that you were unable to do your part?"

"I'm not afraid!" the boy exclaimed. "I risked far worse when I toiled as a servant in a house of pleasure in Waset. I saw two people murdered! I'll do anything . . . Anything at all to help Amonked and Sennefer. I owe them my life. If they hadn't taken me in, I'd long ago have been food for the fish."

"Pawah . . ."

"Oh!" The boy clapped a hand over his mouth, horrified by what he had said, and glanced around to see if anyone else had heard. "I beg of you, sir! And you, Pashenuro. Please give me your word that you'll never tell anyone about the murders. No one knows I saw. I don't want anyone ever to know. Please!"

"I'll tell no one," Bak vowed. He doubted the boy had any reason for fear, but as he still lived in Waset, silence was wiser than loose talk.

The Medjay echoed the pledge.

"Let me go with Pashenuro, sir. I'll never get a better

chance to repay Amonked and Sennefer. Never!"

Bak studied him long and hard. He had no doubt the youth would do the best he could, but would he remember words he had learned at his mother's breast? Without him, the mission would fail.

With him, it might succeed.

"All right, you may go."

Chapter Fifteen

Bak awakened several times during the night. He was unsure of the exact reason: the bitter chill in the air or thoughts of Pashenuro and Pawah. He knew the Medjay was competent, skilled at creeping through the dark unseen and unheard, and he would not have agreed to take Pawah if he had not believed the boy quick to learn. Nonetheless, each time he awoke, he prayed to the lord Amon that they would return safely.

His thoughts would shift then to Baket-Amon and the slayer he sought. A man he spoke with each day, he felt sure, more likely than not one he liked. The names would follow one another in an endless circle, and he would fall again into a fitful slumber.

Cold drove away the last vestiges of sleep as the first vague fingers of light breached the eastern horizon. An archer had already brought to life the fire contained within the rough mudbrick hearth and was sitting beside it, absorbing its warmth. Lying close were the two dogs that had accompanied Bak and Pashenuro to Rona's village. Bak knelt with them and held his hands over the heat. How Nebwa and the others could dream on, he had no idea.

He was almost warm when the dogs looked up, ears erect and tails brushing arcs on the sand. He turned to see a smiling Pashenuro and Pawah weaving their way through the sleeping caravan. Both wore leather kilts and, over their shoulders for warmth, the woolly hides of sheep discolored with dirt so they would be less visible in the dark. Relief swept through him. He offered a silent prayer of thanks and stood to greet them.

While the archer brought a bowl of milk and food left over from the evening meal, Bak awakened Nebwa. Arranging themselves around the hearth, they shared hard flattish loaves of bread and cold boiled fish.

"The encampment was easy to find," Pashenuro said. "It's in the desert west of Shelfak, as Rona said, encircled by low sand hills. Everyone along the river knows its whereabouts. The campfires can be seen from any good-sized knoll. No one would dare attack so big a force, so they take few precautions."

"Don't they have sentries?" Nebwa asked, his voice gruff from sleep and the ill-humor of being awakened too fast.

"Yes, sir, but men too innocent to be wary. The one I spoke with was a good, honest soul drawn into a fight for which he has no enthusiasm."

Bak tried to look stern, an effort not entirely successful. "Did I not tell you to watch from afar, not infiltrate their ranks?"

"We practically stumbled over him, sir. I thought it safer not to run." The Medjay grinned at Pawah. "He thought me a man who couldn't speak and my son slow-witted and harmless."

Pawah, unable to contain himself, burst in, "I could understand him, sir. Not every word, but enough."

"You must thank the lord Amon," Bak said, winking at Nebwa. "The troop captain and I spent half the night on our knees before Amonked's personal shrine."

The boy's eyes widened. "Did you really?"

Nebwa laughed, making a lie of the tale. "You did well, I'll wager. Now what did you learn?"

Pashenuro tore apart a chunk of bread, dunked both pieces in the milk, and threw them at the dogs, who gobbled them up in a bite and looked to him for more. "We spoke first with the sentry, making him believe we had no special curiosity, no place in particular to go, nothing of note to do." The Medjay would not be rushed, as Bak had long ago learned. "After he let us go on our way, we sneaked around the encampment in the dark. Approaching from another direction, taking care not to be discovered a second time, we crept as close as we could. We wished to see them for ourselves, to hear their talk of the battle they face."

"Go on," Nebwa growled, picking bones from a chunk of fish.

"We couldn't see much," Pashenuro admitted. "The fires burned bright, but the men were shadows walking hither and yon with no special purpose. We couldn't begin to count their numbers. If the sentry is to be believed, they've a fighting force of over four hundred men."

Bak sat quite still, a piece of soggy bread poised halfway between the bowl of milk and his mouth. "That's twice the size of our force, including the soldiers from Askut."

The Medjay spread his hands wide and shrugged, a silent reminder that he was only repeating what he had been told. "He claimed he heard Hor-pen-Deshret utter the number with his own lips, speaking to a tribal chieftain of note."

"We'd best pray he was exaggerating," Bak said, his face grim.

"We mean to go back after midday, when we can see for ourselves." Pashenuro spoke as casually as if he and the boy were going down to the river to fish.

Bak could not reject the offer; knowing the size of the enemy force was crucial. "This time you'll tell Amonked," he told Pawah, his tone severe. "He was very annoyed last night when he learned you'd slipped away without a word."

"Could you tell how well they're armed?" Nebwa asked.

"We know only what the sentry told us." Pashenuro spat out a fish bone. "He claimed never to have seen so many spears, bows and arrows, shields, and small weapons, all in good condition."

"Humph."

"How do they feel about the upcoming clash?" Bak asked.

"They talk a lot to bolster their own courage." The Medjay glanced up as two archers came close for warmth and to listen. "Pawah heard a half-dozen dialects. My guess is they're a motley crowd, with nothing in common but the lure of wealth. I doubt any have thought of the small portion they'll get when divided among so many men, with Hor-pen-Deshret getting the greater share."

Bak swallowed a bite of fish and threw what was left to the dogs. "If they've been pulled together from many different locations and they've had no time for training, they'll not fight as an organized unit, as a true army must."

"Such is my feeling, sir."

"We've been talking around the real question," Nebwa said. "When do they plan to attack?"

"They meant at first to wait until the caravan neared Shelfak, striking when we were spread out along the desert trail." A smile flitted across Pashenuro's face. "However, a rumor has reached them about a treasure to be placed on a ship soon to reach Askut. Hor-pen-Deshret wants to march north today and set upon us here in the valley, while the older and wiser chieftains urge patience. They were arguing when we left. If they do come today—and I believe greed will win out—they'll strike an hour or two before sunset. They must, for they know we'd hear of their coming and they'd be open to attack if they camp nearby overnight."

"They'll be tired after a long day's march," Nebwa said, "and we've a trick or two we think will even the odds."

"So a clash is imminent." Amonked dropped onto a stool next to his disheveled sleeping pallet, located beside Nefret's tent. "I'd hoped it wouldn't come to this."

The young woman peered out from the shelter, her face pale and frightened. "We'll all die," she whimpered unheeded. "I know we will."

"I've known of Hor-pen-Deshret for a long time, sir."

Seshu, his face clouded with worry, stood before the inspector with Bak, Nebwa, and Pashenuro. "He doesn't give up easily, especially when he feels the goal to be of sufficient worth."

"I know, Seshu, I know." Amonked spoke with a sharp edge of impatience. "You warned me in Buhen that I should travel with fewer amenities, and I failed to listen."

Horhotep, standing beside the tent, scowled at the quartet from Buhen. "I simply can't believe a petty tribal chieftain would have the audacity to face off against the royal house of the land of Kemet."

"Believe it, Lieutenant!" Nebwa waved off three approaching drovers carrying flint chips, leather thongs, and other bits and pieces with which to continue their weapons-making effort. He pointed them toward Sennefer, who had moved his makeshift armory some distance away.

"We must take shelter within the walls of Askut," the adviser said, "taking with us the animals and all they carry, leaving nothing behind for those wretched tribesmen to steal."

"And let Hor-pen-Deshret besiege us?" Nebwa laughed, harsh and cynical. "I think not. The fortress has been undermanned and poorly equipped for many years. They store sufficient supplies for only their own men and animals, with barely enough extra to help out the rare caravan in need. We'd get exceedingly hungry awaiting relief, even if for merely a few days."

Horhotep's haughty smile would have quashed a lesser man. "Then we must hasten south to the safety of Semna."

"Do you have any idea how difficult it is to defend a caravan spread out across the desert?" Bak did not bother to hide his contempt. "We could probably hold off a hundred men, maybe two hundred. But twice that number? No!"

"We'd be offering ourselves up to slaughter," Pawah said. The boy had been very quiet after the tongue lashing his master had given him for going on his nighttime adventure without telling him of his mission.

The adviser shot the boy an angry look. "Then Mistress Nefret and Amonked must go to Askut. And Sennefer and Minkheper as well."

Nebwa snorted. "All the important people, you mean."

Horhotep's chin shot into the air, he feigned indignation. "Not at all. I mean those of us who came from Waset. Thaneny, Pawah, Mesutu. The porters. We've no reason to be dragged into a local squabble."

"Squabble?" Bak would have laughed if the situation had not been so perilous.

Amonked looked directly at his adviser, and his voice turned hard and decisive. "Nefret will go with Mesutu—and they'll take my dog with them. Thaneny and Pawah may go if they wish."

"I won't!" Pawah said, looking defiant.

"I, for one, intend to remain," Amonked went on, "and I believe any man trained as a soldier should welcome the opportunity to prove himself."

Color flooded Horhotep's cheeks. "Yes, sir."

Bak stifled an urge to clap the inspector on the back. He doubted Amonked knew the first thing about facing the enemy on the field of battle, but he certainly had the courage of his convictions. A courage that would allow a man of ordinary abilities to slay an individual he deemed unworthy. A man like Baket-Amon. Yet the more he saw of Amonked, the more difficult it was to imagine him taking a life for any reason whatsoever.

"You've no need to worry, Lieutenant. My wife will tend to her as if she were her own sister."

Bak smiled at Lieutenant Ahmose, commander of the fortress of Askut, a tall, thin, balding man of forty or so years. "I hope you're wed to a patient woman. Nefret has much to complain about."

"She lives in the household of a wealthy nobleman and

she's unhappy with her lot?" Ahmose laughed. "She should dwell in a godforsaken place like this."

Bak glanced around the room in which they sat, a good-sized white plastered space with a ceiling supported by a single red column, bright with fresh paint. Except for its smaller proportions, the audience hall beyond the door could easily compete with that of Buhen, with six newly painted octagonal wooden columns supporting the ceiling and walls enlivened by crisp multicolored decorations. If any smell remained in the fresh colors, it was overwhelmed by the odors of braised fowl and new-baked bread wafting from the upper floor. Officers and sergeants hurried back and forth, talking of weapons and battle. Four soldiers sat on the floor with scribes, dictating letters to their loved ones in far-off Kemet, while a dozen or more others awaited their turn. Letters prompted by the knowledge that they might soon be facing the enemy on the field of battle.

"Askut is remote, yes," Bak said, "but this building is impressive, and I presume your quarters are, too."

"I keep them so for my wife and her servants. I'd not enjoy spending the rest of my assignment here alone."

Bak smiled at what was clearly an understatement.

Ahmose settled back on his chair, a simple affair with a low, no doubt uncomfortable back and no arms, a definite step down from those of Commandant Thuty and Commander Woser. "To bring the woman today, you must believe a conflict imminent."

"We sent a man to spy on Hor-pen-Deshret's camp and . . ." Pushing his stool back to rest his spine against a column, Bak spoke of all they had learned and all they had accomplished since Nebwa's visit the previous day. The voices in the audience hall faded away, shoved aside by thoughts more imperative.

"As for the confrontation itself," he went on, "we've created a plan we believe will work. You know the terrain far better than we do, so I've come to share that plan, thinking you can spot potential problems and make suggestions for improvement."

"Anything I can do to help, I will." Clearly flattered, the officer leaned forward, elbow on knee, chin cradled in his hand.

"We're assuming," Bak said, "that at least half Hor-pen-Deshret's men will have passed through the wadi to attack the caravan by the time the last man enters at the upper, desert end."

Ahmose nodded. "The trek from Shelfak isn't difficult, but what begins as a tight and compact group will gradually spread out, with many stragglers. I doubt Hor-pen-Deshret or anyone else could hold a group that large together for long."

"So we thought." Bak rubbed the healing, itching scab on his shoulder. "While Nebwa and his forces defend the caravan, holding off the first wave of men to charge, I'll lead a surprise attack in the wadi, with the archers at first picking them off from a distance and the spearmen following at closer hand. Those able to stand and run—less than half, we hope—we'll chase into the valley, where they'll join the larger band attacking the caravan.

"If your troops come in from the north while mine are approaching from the south, and with Nebwa's men inside the barricade of shields, we'll have the enemy trapped within a triangle, which we can squeeze around them until they become our prisoners."

Ahmose sat back in the chair, nodded. "Simple and straightforward. A good plan."

"Now let's see if we can make it better."

"Can you eat another pigeon?" Ahmose's wife asked. She was close in age to her husband, short and plump, a woman whose very ordinary looks were greatly enhanced by her cheerful disposition and merry smile.

Bak, who could well understand why Ahmose wished to keep her by his side, patted his full stomach. "Another bite and I'd burst. I haven't had such a fine meal since I came south to Wawat."

She smiled, pleased at the compliment.

He adjusted the woven reed mat on which he sat and glanced around the second-story courtyard, alive with potted acacias and flowers, a white calf orphaned at birth, and hints of domesticity such as a grindstone and loom. The woman was the consummate homemaker, he was convinced. "How's mistress Nefret adapting?"

She glanced at her husband, a query on her face. His nod encouraged her to speak openly. Laughing softly, she said, "She's not yet recovered from the shock of seeing me elbow-to-elbow with my servants, preparing our food."

Bak smiled. "She knows nothing of the world as it actually is. You'd be doing Amonked a favor if you took her around Askut, introducing her to the other women, showing her how they live. Giving her an idea of how pampered she is, how lucky."

She looked doubtful. "My husband and I live much better than most on this island."

"I've seen that for myself and so should she." Bak emptied his beer jar, added, "You needn't dwell on the hard life here, simply introduce her to the women and chat with them as you normally do. Let her think for herself, reaching her own conclusions."

She left the courtyard, her face a picture of indecision.

"She'll do the right thing," Ahmose assured him, shifting his mat away from a wedge of sunlight.

Bak fervently hoped she would, not solely for Nefret but for all the women. With their husbands marching off to do battle, they needed a distraction. He glanced up at the sun. Not long past midday. He must soon return to the caravan, to last-minute preparations for battle. Ahmose also looked upward, equally concerned with the passage of time.

Bak said, "You know of Baket-Amon's death and my need to lay hands on the slayer."

"I do." The officer took a handful of dates from a bowl

and pushed it across the floor toward his guest. "You surely know that even if you were to snare him within the hour, we'd have to face Hor-pen-Deshret with no help from those who dwell along the river. Too few would arrive in time."

"I've accepted already that we must do battle without them, but that doesn't relieve me from my task." Using natron as a cleanser, Bak scrubbed the grease from his hands. "Did you know the prince?"

"He never came to Askut. He had no need. Rona looks after the people in this part of the valley as if they're his own children. I've always dealt with the old man. I respect him, and I like to think he respects me."

Ahmose's age told Bak he was a part of the old guard, men appointed for their noble heritage or out of patronage, men like Horhotep who fought their battles in the corridors of the royal house. His attitude, however, spoke of the younger, newly rebuilt army, made up of men highly trained in the arts of war, wary of other men's help in rising through the ranks, less inclined to feel themselves above all others.

"You must know of the prince's reputation."

Ahmose smiled. "Before I came to Askut, I dwelt in Waset, performing liaison duties between the royal house and the regiment of Amon. Gossip lightened my load on many a dull afternoon. His name came up among all the others, and I've since heard more."

Bak had been a part of that regiment, but he had no memory of Ahmose. Not surprising since, as a chariotry officer, he had spent much of his time in the stables and out on the practice field. "Did you know Amonked at that time?"

Ahmose's smile broadened. "I served in a tiny building behind the royal house, listening to the lions roar in our sovereign's zoo. I never reached those lofty heights."

Bak returned the smile. He had a feeling he would enjoy serving with this officer, a man of good sense, having no delusions and no pretensions. "Since I began this quest, I've heard many praises of Baket-Amon's talents in the bed-chamber and his skills as a sportsman. The two activities dominated his life. I suspect what I seek has something to do with one or the other, something that happened some time in the past."

"Hmmm." Ahmose rested his head against the wall and closed his eyes. "There was a tale going round . . ." His voice tailed off, his brow furrowed in thought. "What was it?"

Bak remained mute, waiting, praying to the lord Amon.

"Let's see. It was about three years ago. While still I dwelt in Waset." Ahmose's eyes popped open and he snapped his fingers. "Yes, I remember! It was only a rumor, mind you. I don't know how much truth there was to it."

"Believe me, the vaguest of rumors is better than what I have now."

Ahmose gave him an fleeting smile. "The way I recall the tale, Baket-Amon slew a man during a night of carousing. I'm not sure where this occurred. Probably in Waset, since that's where I heard, but it could've happened any-where. Maybe here in Wawat." He paused, frowned. "The incident might've been untrue. Or it could've been hushed up. As far as I know, nothing ever came of it."

If the prince killed a man . . . Yes, revenge would be more than enough reason to take his life. But why wait three years? Amonked and every individual in his party had known Baket-Amon in Waset. They would have had mul-tiple opportunities to slay him there, where the odds against being caught were far greater than in the much smaller fron-tier post of Buhen.

Another thought struck. Could this rumored murder be the same as the crime witnessed by Pawah? The odds were long, he knew, but it was just possible.

"I thank the lord Amon you've returned!" Bak laid one arm over Pashenuro's shoulders, another over Pawah's, and ushered them to the archers' hearth. The fire was out, the twenty men from Buhen nowhere to be seen. "I feared you'd been captured."

"We almost were!" Pawah practically danced with excitement. "Only Pashenuro's quick wits saved us."

"You exaggerate," the Medjay said, cuffing the boy on the back of his head.

"I don't!" Pawah looked at Bak and his words bubbled over. "Hor-pen-Deshret sent out a hunting party, and we were the game they sought. If we hadn't found a stand of reeds in the river, and if Pashenuro hadn't thought to cut two off to use as breathing tubes so we could stay underwater, they'd've caught us for sure."

Pashenuro shrugged. "The child enlarges my actions and my good sense; otherwise he tells the truth. They were awaiting us, and we came close to getting caught. If a couple of dogs hadn't gone with us, if they hadn't barked a warning, we'd've walked into their arms."

"How'd they know to expect you?"

"The sentry we talked to last night must've spoken of our presence." Pashenuro looked around the encampment, emptied of about half the men. Those who remained went about their usual business, but with speech and laughter too loud and raucous, betraying a heightened tension. "Where is everyone, sir?"

"Assuming the tribesmen would strike today, as you guessed they would, we thought it best to position the men in the wadi long before they come." Bak gave the Medjay a sharp look. "Are they on their way?"

"What of those wretched men who've been watching the caravan?" Pawah asked. "Won't they warn their friends of an ambush?"

Bak handed each of his spies a jar of beer. "They've not moved, nor will they."

"They met an early death?" the Medjay guessed.

"Very early. Soon after you came back this morning."

He spotted Amonked and Nebwa circling around a barrier built of water jars. The inspector's relief at seeing Pawah alive and unhurt was evident. Dropping to the ground to sit beside the boy, he gave him a look blending fondness and pride. Nebwa sat on the low circle of bricks that formed the hearth.

"While we hid underwater, we couldn't hear a thing." Pashenuro evidently saw no need to go back to the beginning and repeat himself. "When the tribesmen moved on along the river's edge, we sheltered behind a drifting log so we could raise our heads and listen." He glanced at Pawah, who continued:

"They were arguing over where and when the caravan should be attacked. About half thought they should await us on the open desert, but the rest swore Hor-pen-Deshret was close to a god and whatever he deemed right should never be questioned. It sounded as if the decision had been made, but I couldn't be sure."

"So they're quarreling among themselves," Nebwa said. "Good."

Thinking of all the men poised to do battle later in the day, Bak asked, "Where's their main force? Are they still camped near Shelfak? Or are they on their way north?"

"The instant we could safely do so, we left the river and sped out onto the desert. The decision had indeed been made." Pashenuro flashed a smile. "We could hardly miss that wretched army, a rag-tag bunch if I ever saw one, coming north across the barren sands. We were too far away to hear them speak and the landscape too flat and open to let us draw closer. But we had no doubt they were marching off to combat."

"They're coming to us, as we'd hoped," Bak said.

"So it seems."

"Rag-tag army," Nebwa said. "Do you mean their clothing is worn and ragged or that there's no order to their march?"

"Both." Pashenuro, who had been trained as a soldier before becoming a policeman, knew exactly what Nebwa was getting at. "I saw few signs of a cohesive force, sir.

Any man who falls behind is left to his own resources. In the hour we watched, more than two dozen men simply walked away, abandoning their fellows."

Nebwa eyed the Medjay speculatively. "Would it be fair to say the alliance is fragile?"

"I suspect only Hor-pen-Deshret is holding it together."

Nebwa and Amonked left, each going his own way depending on what he had to do before the call to arms. Bak held Pashenuro and Pawah back so he could give them fresh orders. The Medjay would serve as the forward lookout, located in a spot where he could warn of the enemy's approach; the youth would carry any messages too lengthy to signal with a mirror. Eager to get on with their new tasks, the pair stood up to leave.

Bak held Pawah back. "Did Prince Baket-Amon patronize the house of pleasure where you dwelt in Waset?" Without realizing he was doing so, he held his breath in anticipation.

Pawah glanced toward Pashenuro, standing off to the side, waiting. The look was a silent but obvious apology for the delay. "I doubt he was, sir. Would so lofty a man ever visit a place so low?"

Disappointed in spite of himself, Bak let the boy go. Could Pawah have erred? he wondered. Not likely. The prince had been a man not easily forgotten.

Chapter Sixteen

"Won't those foul nomads notice as soon as they come out of the wadi that the animals are no longer with the caravan?" Sennefer asked.

Bak, standing at the nobleman's side, watched the long line of donkeys trotting three and four abreast down the path toward the river. A half-dozen drovers were with them, keeping them out of the adjoining fields and hurrying them along. Each man carried a shield and a spear and smaller weapons of choice tied to his belt.

"They'll spot them on the island right away." Seeing the foremost donkeys plunge into the water, he turned away and strode toward the boulder on which they had left their weapons. "With luck and the will of the gods, a respectable number will imagine instant wealth in the oases animal markets, and they'll break away from the main body to go after them. Lieutenant Ahmose has already stationed archers among the rocks."

"Divide and conquer."

Bak threw a smile his way. "It's also important to keep the donkeys alive and unhurt."

"Pawah will be grateful. He's worried about them, especially the foals." The nobleman glanced toward the sun, not quite halfway between midday and dusk, tinting shreds of cloud a pale yellow. "Shouldn't we be on our way?"

233

"You don't have to come with me, you know. You could stand at Amonked's side."

Sennefer's voice turned wry. "Horhotep calls an ambush dirty fighting, not the stuff of real soldiers. I wish to judge for myself."

Laughing, each man took up a bow and a quiver filled to bursting, a long spear and shield, and lesser arms for close conflict. Bak also carried a staff the length and weight of his baton of office. Fully arrayed and sobered by the weaponry, rude reminders of the impending battle, they strode into the wadi.

Bak sat on a low, flat rock high up on a steep slope of broken stone that had fallen through the years from the face of the cliff behind him. Located midway along the northern side of the wadi, he was plainly visible to every member of his small force of archers and spearmen. Pashenuro was hidden across the dry watercourse, a hundred or so paces farther west on a high knob of rock atop the escarpment. From there, the Medjay could see the open desert beyond and Hor-pen-Deshret's army. Equipped with a polished mirror, he would signal a silent warning if the tribal leader posted lookouts above the cliff, or when the enemy marched in force into the wadi. Bak carried a second mirror to relay the message to the men positioned along the opposite slope, unable to see the Medjay. Pawah, out of sight in a shady cleft at the base of the cliff below Pashenuro, would relay longer and more complicated verbal messages.

Bak looked to right and left, checking his men for what must have been the hundredth time. The moment Pashenuro signaled, every man would vanish, but now most were visible, spread out along the facing slopes, standing or kneeling or sitting near whatever shelter they had chosen: fallen slabs of rock, holes dug into the scree, deeply shadowed fissures in the cliff face. The cover was not as good as he would have liked, but it would have to do.

Through Pawah, Pashenuro had reported that the tribesmen had spread out for many thousands of paces along the desert trail, but were slowly collecting at the head of the wadi. In spite of his own impatience to get on with the battle, Bak had to laugh. Hor-pen-Deshret must be furious at the need to wait while half his army straggled in.

He thought of Nebwa and his modest troop of spearmen and drovers. Unlike his own men, who had to speak quietly so their words would not carry to the enemy, Nebwa's men would be laughing and talking, making a pretense of normality behind their barricade of shields. Not until the tribesmen came streaming out of the wadi would the men within the encampment take up positions among the high piles of supplies and equipment carefully placed to impede their foe. He also imagined Lieutenant Ahmose's force, equally small but better trained, concealed in nearby fields, crushing some poor farmer's crops.

A stiff breeze ruffled Bak's hair and dried the sweat on his body. Swallows, their voices sharp and squeaky, darted back and forth overhead, carrying insects to nests in the cliff. He shaded his eyes with a hand and looked up the wadi to the west. The lord Re hovered some distance above the horizon, with at least two more hours' journey before entering the netherworld. The tribesmen must make their move shortly or night would fall before the battle was won.

Though outnumbered two to one, Bak felt confident the combined force of drovers, guards, and soldiers would win. The lord Amon most often smiled upon men who took steps beyond the usual and expected. As they certainly had over the past few days.

He was sorry the local people had refused to take up arms on their behalf. With Amonked threatening to disrupt their lives and Baket-Amon's widow seeking solace in vengeance, the respect he and Nebwa had gained through the years had proven of little value. At least the old headman Rona had helped even the odds. His tale of a treasure ripe to be plucked had drawn the enemy . . . Well, not yet into their arms, but close.

Bak wondered if he would ever lay hands on Baket-Amon's slayer. He felt he was on the right path, and if the two attempts on his life told true, the man he sought thought so, too. Yet he had no idea who the murderer might be. Of all the men who had come from Waset with the inspection party, none had let slip any hint of guilt. Were his instincts betraying him? Was the slayer someone else altogether, the assaults mere coincidence, the reason for the murder something he had never thought of?

Lieutenant Ahmose had mentioned rumors of a murder sometime in the past. Had Baket-Amon actually taken a life during a night of carousing? Or was the tale a figment of the imagination, grown out of proportion by the passage of time and many wagging tongues? If true, this might well be the incident that had made the prince so averse to cruelty. What words had Sennefer used? Yes, "the harsher excesses of the bedchamber."

The murder had not occurred in Wawat. The way rumors traveled along the river, a tale of that magnitude would be impossible to keep quiet. Nofery would certainly have heard and, thanks to her unbridled curiosity, would have sought out the truth. Nor did Bak think the incident happened on an official hunting trip. There again, word would spread like the wind, and Maatkare Hatshepsut would have banished Baket-Amon from the royal house. After all, he was a wretched foreigner, a prince of no note, not worthy of forgiveness of so heinous a crime.

The incident must have occurred in a place of business in the land of Kemet. It could have happened at any location along the river but, as the prince spent most of his time in Waset, the odds were good that it took place there. The capital held many houses of pleasure, no two alike, each offering an infinite variety of delights. Some far from wholesome.

Pawah had been traded to the proprietor of such an establishment, one who had subjected the boy to unspeakable cruelties, so Thaneny had said. Only the lord Amon knew what the child had suffered before Sennefer bought him.

Sennefer had bought Pawah! Bak shot to his feet, opened his hand so the small mirror he held could catch the sun, and signaled the boy to come.

"Can you tell me what Prince Baket-Amon looked like?" Bak kept his voice level, his hope tamped down, and spoke softly so the words would not carry.

Pawah struggled to catch his breath after his long dash across the wadi and up the steep incline. "No, sir. I never saw him." He, too, kept his voice low.

Bak could barely maintain a calm facade. "Never once, though he was a frequent visitor to Amonked's home in Waset?"

"I always accompany my master when he leaves the house, and when we're home, when I'm not running errands, I keep to my place with the other servants."

Bak gave a silent shout of joy and at the same time cursed himself for being so slow to see the truth. He had forgotten the child's true position in Amonked's household. "He was a tall man, Pawah. Heavy, impressive in appearance. He dressed as a man of wealth from the land of Kemet, but his dusky skin identified him as having come from Wawat. He often wore a gold pendant of the ram-headed lord Amon and he . . ."

The boy's eyes widened with recognition—and shock. And a dawning fear much more intense than when he had blurted out his secret of seeing two people slain. A fear close to panic. "I . . . I can't say, sir."

"You mean you won't say."

"Yes, sir. No! That is . . ." Pawah's eyes darted in the direction from which he had come, his desire to flee palpable. "Sir, I must get back to Pashenuro. The men of the desert could come down the wadi at any moment."

Bak caught the youth by his slick, sweaty shoulders. "He'll signal if he needs you. If not, you can await them here as easily as there."

Pawah twisted and squirmed, trying to get away. Bak dared not allow him to run, perhaps to vanish forever in the depths of the desert out of which he had originally come. The youth's reaction spoke of a knowledge that must be aired.

"I don't know what you fear, Pawah, but you have my word that no harm will come to you."

"I must go back to Pashenuro, sir. I must!"

"The more people who know what you hold in your heart, the safer you'll be. You must begin with me, here and now."

The youth's will crumpled, as did the strength in his legs. He dropped onto the flat rock and Bak sat down beside him, close enough to grab him should he try to run.

"Now tell me what you know of Baket-Amon."

"He . . . He came often to Thutnofer's house of pleasure." Pawah's voice trembled, he looked close to tears. "We didn't know his name. Thutnofer—whose place of business it was—always called him the ram of Wawat, and so the rest of us thought of him." His eyes flooded. He wiped tears away with the back of his hand, making streaks on his face. "I'm sorry he's dead. He . . ." The boy faltered, added lamely, "He was a good man."

Bak looked up the wadi, listening, waiting. The swallows shot back and forth, their grating notes as quick as their flight. He saw no sign of Pashenuro atop the opposing cliff, no warning signal. He laid a hand on the youth's back and allowed gentleness to enter his voice. "Was he involved in the murders you spoke of yesterday?"

The boy stared at his hands, clutched tight together in his lap. "Yes, sir."

"Tell me what happened, Pawah, what started the trouble."

"Meretre." A long pause, then, "The ram of . . . the prince could've bought her ten times over—and I prayed many times to the lady Hathor that he would—but my prayers went unanswered." He bit his lip, blinked hard.

"She was barely a woman, untouched by any man. A special treat of great value, Thutnofer liked to say. He held her back, tempting one and all with her youth and beauty." Tears spilled over. "She was my friend, as close as a sister to me. We were meant to share a like fate." The boy squeezed his eyes tight as if to rid himself of memory. "I shall miss her always."

Bak guessed a deeper secret, one he needed to know for a fact. "What fate was that, Pawah?"

"It's not important!"

A bright flash of light flitted across Bak's breast. His head snapped up, his eyes darted toward Pashenuro's hiding place. Another flash of light, this of longer duration, that was meant to be seen by all who were posted on the northern side of the wadi. The men vanished from sight as if abducted by the gods. Bak took up his own mirror and repeated the signal, alerting the men on the opposite incline. They, too, scurried out of sight.

"They're coming!" Pawah whispered.

Catching the boy by the arm, Bak hustled him up the slope and into the deep shadow beneath an overhanging segment of cliff, where they could not be seen from the wadi floor. His weapons and shield lay against the wall. The swallows wheeled through the air near the alcove, their squeaks loud and angry, scolding the intruders.

"Were you also being held back, Pawah, as Meretre was?"

Hope for a respite fled from the boy's eyes. He lowered his head, hiding his shame, and spoke so softly Bak could barely hear. "The two of us, she and I together, were displayed over and over again to whet the appetites of wealthy customers."

Bak muttered a curse. A girl of twelve or so years, a boy of eight or nine. A package to sell to the highest bidder. Could this be the child's secret, he wondered, the reason he's so afraid? No, he was a long way from Thutnofer's house of pleasure, safe from that particular degradation.

"Sennefer didn't buy the two of you, did he?" He doubted the nobleman that kind of man, but the question had to be asked.

"Oh, no, sir! He found me after I ran away."

So Thutnofer still owns the boy, Bak thought. Or perhaps Sennefer or Amonked went to the swine with an offer he could not refuse. "Did Meretre flee with you?"

Looking as miserable as a child could look, Pawah stared down at his hands, shook his head.

Bak's heart went out to him. Whatever had happened must have been horrendous indeed. "You must tell me, Pawah."

The tears began to roll in earnest; sobs broke the youth's words into phrases. "One night . . . Three years ago, it must've been. A man came into Thutnofer's establishment. It was fairly early, but business was good, the rooms filled with pleasure-seekers. Meretre and I were on display." He tried to stifle his sobs, failed. "The man was young and well-formed, his name Menu. He'd come in before, but never had he been so . . . So full of himself. So demanding. He drew Thutnofer aside. Seldom taking their eyes off Meretre, they sat in a quiet corner and talked. Sometimes their words grew heated. Sometimes they spoke as the closest of friends. In the end, a bargain was struck. Thutnofer raised his hand and beckoned her."

Sobs choked off the boy's words; his body shuddered with anguish. He slumped to the ground and clasped his legs close to his breast as if to still the spasms, the sound. Bak knelt beside him, considered pulling him close, hugging him. He could not. Pawah was nearly a man, old enough to take offense should anyone treat him as a child.

While the youth exhausted his tears, Bak peeked outside their shelter. Other than the swallows, which had returned to their feeding, not a creature stirred. Then he heard a sound, words as elusive as a puff of smoke carried on the air. Shading his eyes with a hand, he looked toward the upper end of the dry watercourse. He glimpsed, coming out of the sun's glare, one small figure, two, five, a dozen, striding down the path along the wadi floor.

The tribesmen were talking to one another—bragging, Bak suspected, reinforcing their courage with bravado. At the same time, they were cautious, looking to right and left, glancing back as if to make sure they were not alone, that other men were following. They may not have been told that the spies Hor-pen-Deshret had sent out were missing, but they had to assume all who traveled with the caravan were prepared to hold off an attack, with soldiers from the garrison to help.

Pawah, his eyes puffy and almost dry, scooted up beside Bak. "How long before we set upon them?" he whispered.

"Not until Pashenuro signals that the last man is within range. We've a while yet. They're spread out far too much for their own good." Keeping his eyes on the approaching men and others appearing behind, Bak said, "Menu purchased a few hours with Meretre, you told me. Did Baket-Amon arrive about that time and interfere?"

"Would that he had," the youth said fervently.

"What did happen?"

The boy tried to look defiant. "Can I not tell you later? After we face these miserable barbarians?"

Bak caught the boy's chin, pulled his head around, and looked him straight in the eye. "Pawah, if you hadn't gone out with Pashenuro to spy on the tribesmen, we'd not be here today, with a good chance of winning the battle. Nonetheless, I feel like turning you over my knee and spanking you."

Pawah's face flamed, he swallowed hard.

"I want no more evasion, do you hear me?" Bak said, releasing his chin.

The youth's eyes teared, but anger and pride kept them from overflowing. "Menu took her to the back of the building. Thutnofer bade me carry on, walking around the room, showing myself to best advantage. I did so, all the while trying not to think of Meretre, thinking of nothing else. And all the while Thutnofer bragged of the wealth Menu had exchanged for her. A house—not large, he kept saying, but of good value in a city as crowded as Waset." The boy's words resonated with fury. "I hated Thutnofer. I wanted to slay him with my own two hands. But I could do nothing."

The foremost group of tribesmen reached a point immediately below their shelter, giving Bak his first good look at Hor-pen-Deshret. The tribal leader walked at the head of his army, strutting like a high-bred stallion. He was tall and lean and glistened with oil recently rubbed onto his body. He wore a leather kilt painted red, studded with circles of metal. A broad multicolored beaded collar adorned his upper chest, he wore wide leather bracelets and anklets, and a bright red feather rose from his short dark curly hair. He carried a long spear and a shield decorated with a red chevron design.

His army followed, loose clumps of men, widespread in many cases, coming down the trail in no particular order. Where their leader was a show horse, they were donkeys. Men dressed in leather or linen or wool, simple garb, unadorned, often ragged and patched. Men dragged away from their wives and children and flocks, wearing on their backs all they had brought with them, in many cases all they owned.

Bak longed to attack then and there, to slay with his own hands the man who had lured these people off the desert with promises of glory and wealth. He spurned the urge. That rag-tag army had to be crushed, putting an end forever to dreams of a tribal coalition.

Pawah, his voice husky with raw emotion, said, "Time passed. How many hours, I don't know. One, maybe two, maybe longer. When only a few men remained, Thutnofer ordered me away, telling me to get on with my duties as a household servant." The boy's face took on a strained look. "As I walked toward the back of the building, I passed the sole room that had a wooden door. I heard beyond that door a terrible cry. A woman in desperate need." His voice broke, words merged with sobs. "I knew before I flung the door wide that it was Meretre."

Bak placed a gentle hand on the boy's shoulder. By this time, he had an idea of what must have happened.

Tears rolled down Pawah's cheeks. "There she was, lying on the sleeping pallet, beaten and bloody, her life flowing away. A filthy, bloody rag muffled her screams. That vile beast Menu was on his knees astraddle her, his fist red with her blood, the rest of him smeared with it." Gasping for air through his sobs, Pawah gave Bak a look wild with anger and pain. "I wanted to help her, but I couldn't bring myself to go to her. I ran away, screaming, to the front of the building."

"That's all you could've done," Bak said, trying to calm him. "You had to get help."

"The ram of . . . the prince had just come in," Pawah went on as if in a trance. "I don't know what I said—I don't remember—but he ran with me to the room where Meretre lay helpless. He saw the state she was in and he saw that repellent creature pulling himself off her. He caught him by the arm, flung him against the wall, stunning him, and went to Meretre. She breathed her last in his arms. Crying out that her ka had fled, he laid her on the sleeping pallet. As he turned away, his face filled with sorrow and fury, he saw Menu trying to slip out the door. He caught him, took him by the neck, and squeezed the life from him."

The tribesmen walked by below, a broken stream of men. A word here and there floated up, a language Bak did not understand. Although he had foreseen much of the truth, he had trouble taking in the story, the terrible reality.

"You saw it all?"

"I did," Pawah whispered.

"Is that when you fled Thutnofer's establishment?"

The youth nodded. "The . . . the prince told me to leave that low place, to run as far and as fast as I could." The boy wiped his wet, swollen eyes. "I raced to the harbor and hid on a traveling ship moored at the quay, thinking it would carry me to some far-off place. It did. We sailed downriver to Mennufer. Sennefer, whose ship it was, caught me there, hungry and afraid, sneaking off the deck. He took pity on me and took me to his home, where he told everyone he'd bought me."

"Did you tell him of the slayings you witnessed?"

"I told him of Meretre and I said another man whose name I didn't know avenged her death. That's all." The boy drew in a deep breath, tried to smile. "Prince Baket-Amon saved my life, sir. I know he did. If I'd stayed in that accursed house of pleasure, I'd've died, as Meretre did."

Of that, Bak had no doubt.

The clumps of men walking along the trail below were wider apart, the number of stragglers growing. Bak fretted. Surely half had come and gone, possibly more. Yet no signal from Pashenuro. Had something happened to the Medjay? Had he been spotted and caught? Would the rabble army walk by untouched, making the final confrontation in the valley difficult, maybe impossible to win?

Recognizing his penchant to worry too soon, he asked, "Why are you so afraid, Pawah? Do you know who slew Baket-Amon?"

"No, sir, but you said yourself that the man who took the prince's life is among those who came with us from Waset. Would he not think me a threat?"

"Do you know something you haven't told me?"

"No, sir."

Bak doubted Pawah was in danger, but he could understand the youth's fear, rational or not. "Tell me of Menu. Anything you can think of, no matter how insignificant."

"He must've been a man of wealth." The youth knelt beside Bak and stared at the men on the path below. "Each time he came to Thutnofer's place of business, he drank the best vintage wine from the northern vineyards; wagered far too much on games of chance, whether or not he played; and used the most desirable and costly of women."

"Did he hurt any women before Meretre?"

"They'd sometimes come away bruised, and none wanted to go with him a second time."

"Thutnofer has much to explain." And to answer for, Bak thought. "What more can you tell me of Menu?"

"He always wore fine clothing and jewelry. When he had nothing else to trade, he sometimes offered a bracelet or anklet or collar for a night of pleasure."

Bak's eyes darted toward the men on the trail and back to the boy at his side. "A man who barters away his personal possessions isn't always as wealthy as he appears. Could that be true here?"

Pawah cocked his head, thinking. "I never thought about it before, but . . ." His eyes suddenly widened. "Yes! The house he traded for Meretre cleared other debts to Thutnofer."

A fragment of a recent conversation came back to Bak, words spoken by chance and regretted at the next breath. He did not like what he was thinking, prayed he erred. "Do you recall what Menu looked like?"

"I shall never forget. I see him even in my sleep. A beast of the night who vied with the gods in appearance." Pawah glanced at Bak, realized something more specific was needed. "He was of medium height and slender, thirty or so years of age. His eyes were blue-green and his hair reddish, but it glowed with gold in the lamplight."

Sadness entered Bak's heart. "Was he a man of the north?"

Pawah looked startled. "How did you know?"

" 'My younger brother impoverished himself in a quest

for the good life,' " Bak said aloud, quoting Captain Min-kheper. He had found the man he sought.

Light flashed into the alcove, Pashenuro's signal that the last of the tribesmen had entered the wadi. It was time to strike.

Chapter Seventeen

"Go tell Sennefer what I've learned and where it's led me," Bak said to Pawah. He flashed a signal to the men on the opposing, southern slope, warning them to take up arms and ready themselves for battle. "Tell him the whole tale, leaving nothing out, then you and he together must carry the word to Nebwa and Amonked."

"But sir!" Pawah looked devastated. "I wish to stand beside you, to fight Hor-pen-Deshret's army."

Bak donned a leather wrist guard, scooped up his quiver and settled it on his shoulder, and picked up the bow. "The task I've given you is more important by far, Pawah." He spoke with an edge of impatience. "If you and I both were slain in the fighting, no one would ever know the name of the guilty man. The others must be told. With so many men aware of the truth, at least one will surely survive."

"You speak as if we'll lose the battle."

Picking up spear, shield, and staff, Bak plunged downhill to the flat rock, the boy close on his heels. "I believe we'll win, but this is no local skirmish. Men will die."

"Sir . . ."

Bak dropped everything but bow and quiver onto the rock. "I want no more argument. You must do as I say."

A tribesman spotted them, shouted to his mates, pointed. Others looked up the slope, not overly concerned about what they evidently believed to be a lone soldier and his servant, out on a hunting trip. Two or three raised their bows as if to strike. Bak knelt, making himself smaller, and pulled Pawah down beside him, thinking to project a pose of innocent curiosity. The tribesmen chose in the end to save their arrows for game more formidable.

"Tell Sennefer, Nebwa, and Amonked to say nothing to Minkheper. I myself will face him after the battle." Bak, keyed up and eager to get on with the contest, rubbed the mirror on his kilt, brightening its already shiny surface. "As you and Sennefer make your way to the caravan, stay at the top of the slope, close to the cliff face. Keep yourselves safe from the men of the desert. Now move!"

"But . . ."

"Pawah! Men who disobey on the field of battle are sent to the desert mines, a fate I'd not wish on anyone."

"Yes, sir." The youth swallowed hard, taking the threat seriously, but he could not conceal his pleasure at being treated as a man. Pivoting on a heel, he raced diagonally up the slope to the boulder behind which Sennefer hid.

As the boy ducked out of sight, Bak signaled the archers across the wadi. Pashenuro repeated the signal for the men on the north slope, where Bak stood. Archers rose to their feet, appearing as if from nowhere, and let fly their arrows. Several men fell on the trail below. A tribesman shouted an alarm.

Bak raised his weapon and sent an arrow speeding downward. A man's knees buckled and he dropped, the missile protruding from his back. The archers rearmed and arrows again rained down on the enemy, dropping a dozen or more men. Those slow to realize they were under attack yelled out in anger and dismay. They all scattered, too many men seeking shelter behind the too few boulders fallen from the cliffsides. A third wave of arrows flew and a fourth, dropping more men to the earth.

Bak glanced toward Sennefer's hiding place. The nobleman, peering out from behind the boulder, signaled that he understood what he must do. An instant later, he and Pawah darted up the rocky slope and vanished in the shadow of a crevice in the cliff.

Confident they would carry out their mission or die trying, Bak focused on the tribesmen below. He had never considered himself much of a bowman, but standing high above the wadi floor, he dropped one man and another and another. The archers, more expert than he, felled the enemy as if they were cutting down grain in a ripe field. With missiles flying from both sides of the wadi and a minimum of shelter, with their shields an inadequate defense, the tribesmen could not protect themselves. Fallen men moaned and whimpered and pleaded for help, some injured, some dying, and no one to aid them.

The enemy bowmen fought a losing but valiant battle, running, ducking, dodging, providing no firm target while firing off their weapons. Bak saw two of his archers struck, one in the side, another in the arm, neither wound serious enough to force them from the battle.

Someone below, a man with a red cloth braided into his hair, a tribal chief most likely, shouted an order in a tongue Bak did not understand. Twenty or more tribesmen grouped around to form a block. Some of the men encircled the group with shields; those safely inside the ring fired back at the men on the slopes.

One of Bak's archers fell, an enemy arrow protruding from his breast, and lay still and quiet. Another dropped to his knees, an arm hanging useless. A third felled man pulled himself behind a fallen rock, dragging a leg. Though he had to be in pain, he turned his bow horizontal to the ground and continued to fire until he emptied his quiver. He dropped two men, one who fell with a yelp of pain, the second in silence.

Three archers down out of twenty. Far too many in too short a time. The deadly barrage must be stopped. Bak raced across the slope to where his best archer stood, his quiver almost empty. "Slay the leader, Huy, the man with red showing in his hair."

Huy eyed the block of men, looking doubtful. "I'll try, sir."

Bak ran on, snatched up the quiver of the dead man, and sped toward the man with the shattered arm. Realizing his purpose, the wounded archer held up his quiver, offering missiles he could no longer use. Bak thanked him with a quick smile and raced back toward Huy, who had taken shelter in a waist-high gouge in the earth, cut by runoff water from the infrequent rainstorms in the area.

As Bak reached the cut, an arrow sped by, slicing the flesh of his left thigh. Dropping awkwardly into the ditch, he flung the two quivers at the archer. Blood gushed from his leg, but a quick check revealed a flesh wound too shallow to cause concern. As fast as he could, he tore the hem from his kilt, made a pad, and tied it over the wound to staunch the bleeding. Each movement of the leg irritated it, making it burn—a small price to pay, he decided, and thanked the lord Amon for sparing him from worse.

The number of arrows in the donated quiver dropped to a dozen, a half-dozen. As Huy robbed it of its contents, he spat out oaths in a slow and regular manner, an incantation of sorts that followed the rhythm of his effort.

Pashenuro flashed a signal, letting Bak know the last stragglers had come down off the desert. The time had come to close the gap behind them, cutting them off from the sandy wastes they knew so well. Bak relayed the message, this time whistling a signal so loud and clear it echoed the length of the watercourse.

As the sound died away, Huy armed his bow and held it steady, glaring at the block of men below. Suddenly he released the string, launching an arrow. It sped straight and true, striking a man who scarcely showed himself. The man stumbled, briefly splitting apart the barrier of shields. Snapping out a curse that may also have been a prayer, Huy let fly the last arrow his dead comrade had bequeathed him. One head vanished from among the others, a body crumpled to the ground. Red showed in the hair. The wall of shields wavered and the block broke apart, leaving each man to his own resources. They ran down the wadi, leaving behind their fallen chief.

Huy wiped his brow, vastly relieved. Bak clapped him on the shoulder and climbed out of the ditch. The tribesmen were retreating in earnest, he saw, heading toward the valley, trying to escape the deadly shower of arrows and reach the main body of the desert force where they could stand and fight with some chance of success. They fought as best they could, firing on the run at those who had ambushed them. Men who were injured but mobile staggered along with them. The more seriously hurt and the dead were left behind. Lying on the wadi floor, the wounded men moaned or cried out for help or struggled to get up and away so they would not be taken prisoner.

A trickling stream of tribesmen turned their backs on their fellows and headed up the wadi, seeking safety and freedom on the open desert. They promptly fell into the arms of Sergeant Dedu and the archers who had blocked the trail, ending all hope of escape.

Bak whistled again. His spearmen—about half of Amonked's guards—came out of hiding, joining the archers on the slopes, more than doubling the size of Bak's small army. Other than the few men who remained behind to round up enemy deserters and the walking wounded, they pressed the enemy hard, harrying them, rushing them into the valley.

Where, if all went well, they would charge in among Hor-pen-Deshret's forces, disrupting the fighting and causing consternation among the men attacking the caravan encampment.

Bak led his troops out of the wadi and onto the valley floor. Many of the men they chased were loping across the higher ground where animals normally grazed. Others ran through fields knee-deep in ripening vegetables and wheat, partly trampled by the raiders who had preceded them.

Grim-faced men were pouring out of the village and across the fields from nearby farms and hamlets. A large pack of dogs accompanied them, those from the village and the feral animals that had traveled so long with the caravan.

Each of the men carried a spear or scythe or some other tool that could be used as a weapon. Bak had no delusions. These men had not come to help the caravan. They had come to save as much of the year's crop as they could. Any tribesmen wishing to wade out to the island to steal the donkeys would have serious reservations about passing through that hostile gathering.

"Stay out of the fields," he shouted, praying his men, whose lust for battle had grown to major proportions with their success in the wadi, would choose to hear him.

A second shouted order sent his archers running, hunched low, toward a jagged finger of land that projected from the escarpment. Eight or ten enemy archers stood atop the rise, their backs to the approaching men, firing arrows into the caravan encampment.

Bak ran on across the trampled grass and weeds, leading his spearmen to battle. Though he tried to remain rational, he was as exhilarated as they.

Ahead, the tribesmen who had swarmed out of the wadi rushed full tilt in among Hor-pen-Deshret's main force, which appeared from a distance poised to charge the barricaded caravan. Excited and boastful shouts wavered and died. A wave of consternation and dismay rose, crested, waned. An angry voice speaking a tongue of the desert rose above all the rest, haranguing the men. Hor-pen-Deshret, Bak guessed, urging his army to look forward toward victory, not back to a partial defeat.

He had expected them to have long ago charged the caravan, to be in the heat of battle. They must have awaited the remainder of their force coming through the wadi. Or had they re-formed after being rebuffed?

He glanced quickly toward the elevation where the enemy archers had stood. None remained. His own archers were climbing the slope to replace them. They had dispatched the others while he looked elsewhere. Satisfied that that source of danger no longer threatened, he scanned the fields to the north, beyond the enemy force. A white cloth draped over an acacia branch told him Lieutenant Ahmose and his troops were in position and waiting.

To the west, the lord Re hovered above the horizon, leaving the caravan in the shadow of the escarpment. About an hour of daylight remained. The battle in the wadi had lasted less than an hour, yet had seemed as long as a day. The men of the desert must shortly make their move, before the light began to fail, forcing them to retreat.

Bak whistled, signaling his men to charge. Ready, waiting, eager for action, they raced along in his wake. To the north, a trumpet blasted, Ahmose ordering his troops to battle. Soldiers rose from a grain field as if lifted from the earth by the gods and dashed toward the enemy.

A harsh yell ahead and the desert warriors surged forward, screaming like wild men to make themselves seem fiercer. They were halted momentarily by the wall of shields, which bristled with spears, felling many among the first wave of men. Those behind pressed the leaders on, forcing them through the barrier. Shields fell or were swept aside, and Nebwa's small force pulled back to regroup, to face the enemy again among the high stacks of jars, sacks, bags, and baskets of foodstuffs and gear, Amonked's furniture, piles of sheaved hay, every object the donkeys had carried upriver.

With more than half the enemy among and beyond the fallen shields, with their blood-curdling savage yells sporadic and individual, many voices silenced by the fierce fighting, Bak and his men fell upon their rear left flank while the troops from Askut struck the right flank. Sounds of the melee filled the air. The thud of wood against wood. The grunting of struggling men. The thunk of weapons striking tough, tight-stretched cowhide. Growled oaths and loud, excited shouting. The clang of bronze spearpoints.

Screaming and moaning. The thump of something solid striking softer matter.

Stirred by the excitement, the action, the dogs ran in among the contestants, teeth bared, hackles raised. Bak feared at first they would mistake friend for foe, and sometimes they did, but the vast majority set upon the enemy, nipping heels and buttocks and hands. Harassment, not a bold confrontation.

Thin dust rose in puffs around the feet of the struggling men. The stench of blood and sweat was strong. Forgetting the stinging in his thigh, the blood seeping from beneath the makeshift bandage, Bak parried thrusts with spear and shield, downed one man, disarmed another.

He fought hard, sweat dripping in spite of the evening chill. His spearmen, spread out among the enemy with Ahmose's soldiers, were battling with a skill and enthusiasm none would have dreamed of a few days before. He was proud of them. They could return to the capital with Amonked, holding their heads high.

Bak heard something behind him, a man's harsh breathing. He pivoted, striking an enemy warrior at waist level with the long shaft of his spear, knocking him off balance, deflecting the blade of a dagger. The tribesman grabbed the shaft to steady himself and held on. Bak jerked one way and another, trying to wrest the weapon free. Abruptly the man released his hold and crumpled to the ground. Seshu, standing over him, raised his mace in a triumphant salute and swung away to face a fresh conflict.

Muttering a hasty prayer of thanks, Bak pressed forward. Inside the fallen wall of shields, he found his long spear ungainly, his thrusts hampered by the narrow, twisting aisles between the high stacks of equipment and supplies. Most of Nebwa's troops had already abandoned their spears to fight on with smaller weapons. The tribesmen had been forced to follow suit. The congestion had been Nebwa's idea, and a good one. What hampered the men of the caravan in a mild way was bound to confuse the men of the desert—and distract them with innumerable desirable objects.

Bak rammed his spearpoint into the ground beside a pile of fodder and drew the staff from his belt. He had always found a shield awkward to manage, but since he had no armor, he dared not give it up.

Using the staff as a club, he knocked an ax from the hand of one man, broke the arm of another, clouted a third on the head. As they fell back, others replaced them, men more wary of drawing close. One threw a dagger, whose flight Bak stopped with the shield. A yell—Horhotep's voice—swiveled him around and he knocked a mace from a warrior's hand. As he downed the man with a second blow, another leaped at Horhotep, meaning to lay him open with a scimitar. Bak lunged, knocked the scimitar away, breaking the man's hand, and hit him hard across the lower legs, felling him like a tree.

Horhotep raised a hand in thanks and an instant later sank his dagger into the side of a man raising his mace to brain a drover. Blood gushed. The adviser bent double, vomited, and dived back into the fray. Bak was surprised—and pleased. Under duress, Horhotep was proving himself a worthy officer.

He glanced quickly toward the sun. Close to a half-hour of daylight left. How could time pass so slowly? His arms and legs felt weighted with lead, his breathing was labored. Sweat poured.

A shout drew him to Sergeant Dedu and a drover reclaiming a half-dozen vats of newly made beer from tribesmen who had dropped their weapons so they could carry off the brew. An easy victory.

Among the shifting, struggling throng, he spotted Merymose, side-by-side with Sennefer and Thaneny. They were fending off a small but concentrated attack by a half-dozen tribesmen led by a painted and befeathered warrior intent on reaching—and most likely taking as personal trophies—Amonked's and Nefret's carrying chairs. He offered a quick

prayer of thanks to the lord Amon that the nobleman had
arrived unhurt, added a plea that he and the young officer
and the scribe would survive the battle. Thaneny was awkward in his movements, slower than he should be, but he
thrust the harpoon he carried with deadly accuracy.

A tribesman plunged through a tangle of men and rushed
Bak with a spear. He sidestepped the weapon, knocked it
from the man's hand, and shoved him toward Sergeant Roy,
who tapped the man on the head with his mace, gave Bak
a quick grin, and leaped aside to fend off a man with an
ax. Roy also was showing brave colors.

"Bak! Behind you!" Nebwa bellowed.

Bak pivoted, deflected a harpoon aimed at his midsec-
tion, and raised his staff to clout the tribesman. His foot
came down on something wet and slid out from under him.
He fell hard on his back, his shield half beneath him. The
force of the impact knocked the staff from his fingers. A
vicious smile spread across his attacker's face and he leaped
forward to finish the task he had begun. As he raised the
weapon above Bak's breast, his mouth and eyes opened
wide, the harpoon slipped from his fingers, and he toppled
forward, falling on Bak with such force he knocked the
breath from him. A long dagger protruded from his back.

Minkheper stepped close and jerked the weapon free.
"Are you all right, Lieutenant?"

Bak nodded. "I owe you a debt I doubt I can ever repay."

The captain rolled the body aside and offered his hand.
"No debts of honor, I pray. The very thought makes me
ill." He pulled Bak to his feet, wiped the sweat from his
brow, smiled grimly. "Will this battle never end? I'm bone-
weary."

"Even Nebwa looks tired," Bak said, nodding toward his
friend.

The troop captain, Amonked, and a guard were fighting
a motley group of tribesmen bent on taking all they could
carry from a stack of chairs, stools, and woven reed chests.
One sat on the ground clutching his bloody side among a

cascade of fine white linen spilling from one of Nefret's chests.

"Maybe I can break the impasse," Minkheper said and strode in their direction. Blood dripped from the long blade of his dagger, making him look like the murderer he was.

Bak picked up his staff and shield. His debt to Minkheper lay heavy in his heart. How could he take the captain before Commandant Thuty or, more likely, the viceroy, and charge him with the murder of Baket-Amon? How could he plead for the death of a man who had saved his life?

With the sun squashed hard against the horizon, the numbers of men fighting within the encampment had dwindled. The enemy who remained were more intent on looting than risking their lives for a war that looked to be lost. The heart of the battle had shifted to the open grazing land. The tribesmen still on their feet and well enough to retreat now found themselves facing not only the men of the caravan and Ahmose's troops, but the farmers Hor-pen-Deshret had terrorized for so many years.

Bak wove a path through the piles of supplies and equipment, stepping around the dead and wounded. A few of his own men lay among the enemy, who had fallen in large numbers during the battle. Both friend and foe watched him pass, the few he knew with pained smiles, the rest with looks pleading for help or wearing the blank expression of exhaustion. He summoned one of Amonked's porters, going among the wounded with poultices and bandages, and ordered him to help as best he could.

Thinking to rejoin the battle on the open plain, Bak laid aside his staff with some reluctance and picked up a spear leaning against a high pile of grain sacks, their contents dribbling out of holes pierced during the battle. He swung around—and found Hor-pen-Deshret blocking the narrow aisle. They both stared, equally shocked by the unexpected encounter. The tribal leader was no longer the proud, strutting warrior. Sweat stained his leather kilt, armlets, and anklets; his broad collar hung askew; the bright feather drooped from his hair. Bak had no doubt he looked equally worn and tattered.

Shaking off his surprise, Bak bounded toward the enemy chief, thrusting his spear. Hor-pen-Deshret parried the attack with his own spear and lunged forward. Bak took a quick step back and raised his shield to deflect the deadly bronze point. His opponent, assuming the backward step a sign of retreat, bared his teeth in a triumphant smile and inched forward, moving in for an easy kill. Or so he thought.

Both men lunged, giving their opponents no time to think. While the tribal chief thrust forward, Bak swung his weapon sideways, using all the force he could muster, driving Hor-pen-Deshret's blade into a stack of water jars. With a loud crash, three of the tall, heavy cylindrical containers shattered, gushing water and unbalancing the stack. Thirty or more vessels tumbled to the ground and began to roll, striking Bak and his opponent in the ankles, unbalancing them. Both men lost weapons and shields in a futile struggle to remain upright.

They scrambled to their feet and waded through the still rolling jars to the edge of the encampment. Bak, like his opponent, searched frantically for an undamaged shield and spear among those that had fallen during the initial attack. Of the few remaining shields, most had been slashed or broken. Neither man could find an unbroken spear. As tired as he was, Bak dreaded close combat—but he had no choice. He jerked his dagger free of its sheath.

The tribal chief drew a similar weapon and bounded forward. Bak ducked away. The pair danced to left and right, out of arm's reach, feinting, testing each other's speed, strength, vigilance. More than once they clashed, each holding his opponent's weapon at a distance. Hor-pen-Deshret was the more muscular man but, thanks to the lord Amon and a hardy sense of survival, Bak drew on a strength and cunning he did not know he possessed.

When neither man could bear the tension any longer, they backed off to circle each other again, sweat pouring forth, gasping for air. Bak's legs grew heavy, his dance became a shuffle. Hor-pen-Deshret, the feather in his hair broken and bedraggled, looked equally tired, but his movements seemed lighter and quicker. Bak knew that if he did not soon conquer the tribesman, he would lose the battle. And his life.

Desperately in need of a spear, or any weapon that would place him at a distance from his opponent, he stepped back among the shields lying on the ground. Allowing his attention to stray for a mere instant, he spotted the shaft of a spear, its point broken off. As Hor-pen-Deshret lunged toward him, he scooped it up and slammed it against his arm, shattering the bone. The weapon fell from the tribal chief's hand. He gave Bak a look of utter incredulity.

And dropped to his knees in supplication.

Bak stood with Amonked and Nebwa, watching Ahmose and the troops from Askut rounding up what was left of the tribal army. The local people looked on, their eyes glittering with satisfaction. About a hundred men of the desert had survived unscathed, more than half were injured to a lesser or greater degree, and the remainder were dead, gathered together and laid out to be buried on the verge of the desert at daybreak.

"Such carnage," Amonked said, shaking his head sadly. "What will their families do?"

"Some will survive, the rest will starve," Nebwa said. "As always." He sounded cold, but a tightness in his voice betrayed his true feelings.

Amonked led them to the short line of fallen archers, guards, and drovers, fourteen men of the caravan who had died at the hands of the enemy. Pawah was on his knees at the end of the row, his head bent over the prone body of Thaneny. The scribe had fallen to an enemy spear toward the end of the fighting.

The youth looked up, unashamed of the tears rolling down his cheeks. "I loved Thaneny like a brother. I shall miss him always."

Amonked knelt beside the boy and placed an arm around his shoulders. "No man will ever take his place." He laid his free hand on the scribe's shoulder and his voice thickened with emotion. "He was my right hand, not my servant but my friend."

Bak turned away, unable to understand the whims of the gods. Thaneny had come so close to death in the past, overcoming unspeakable odds. Now here he was far from his home, his life taken in battle. One who had died because he refused to stand back and take refuge while men he knew fought to the death nearby. A man courageous to a fault. Where was the reward for a life lived so valiantly?

"You know, don't you?" Minkheper, standing at the river's edge, glanced at Bak, who had come up beside him.

"You slew Baket-Amon."

"Someone remembered my brother, I assume?"

Bak ignored the question. He had promised Pawah silence, and he would keep that vow. "Menu deserved to die. The prince did not."

"True." Minkheper stared at an irregular strip of torchlight falling across the faintly rippled surface of the water, golden reflections cast by a guard on the island where the donkeys had been left. "My brother, much younger than I and given all the advantages by our father, lived a life of utter depravity. He shamed my parents while they lived and he shamed me. Death by violence was inevitable."

Chilled by the cold night air and a lurking fury mixed with sadness in Minkheper's voice, Bak crossed his arms in front of his chest. "Did he always take pleasure in hurting others?"

Minkheper knelt and let the water flow around his hand, caressing his fingers like a lover about to lose its beloved.

"He always had a cruel tongue, which he used at first to pummel my mother and father and later his wife Iset. As far as I know, she was the first he struck with his fist. After that . . . Well, as the years rolled by, a fire seethed within him, making him less than human."

Bak tried to read the seaman's face, but the night was too dark. "You knew of his cruelty and did nothing to stop him?"

"I knew of the abusive way he spoke to our parents, and when Iset sought a divorce, I was told the reason. He made no secret that he wagered, drank himself witless, lay with innumerable women. As for the rest . . ." Minkheper tore his hand from the river, stood up, and expelled a bitter laugh. "My only excuse is that I was too far away for too long to learn the truth."

He paused, stared out toward the island. "When I came back to Waset to settle his affairs, I found nothing to settle. He'd lost everything our parents left behind, including property he and I held together. If Baket-Amon had not already taken his life, I'd have slain him myself."

"Were you ever told that the prince slew him because he found him with a young woman he'd just beaten to death?"

"So Thutnofer said."

Turning their backs to the river, they walked up the dark path toward the caravan encampment, which was ablaze with light. Bonfires reached for the sky, giving sight to the men tending the wounded. With so many in need of care, they had long since run out of poultices and bandages, but Nebwa and Ahmose had demanded from the nearby villagers additional lengths of cloth and medicinal herbs.

"Menu's death was justified in the eyes of men and the gods," Bak said, "yet you were driven to exact revenge. For the love of Amon, why?"

"As the eldest son, I was honor-bound to slay the man who took his life."

"No matter how just or unjust the cause." Bak's voice

was flat, uncritical, yet all the more censorious for its lack of reproach.

"Yes."

Sorrow flooded Bak's heart. Minkheper was as much a man of Kemet as Amonked or Nebwa or Commandant Thuty. Nonetheless, he had felt obliged to obey the deities of a far-off land, gods who demanded that a good man's life be taken in exchange for that of a brute. Unlike the lady Maat, who required that justice be done, never seeking a man's death for no good reason.

"Did Baket-Amon face you in Buhen, unaware of your purpose?"

"He knew what would happen should we meet." Minkheper took a deep, long breath. "The day after I learned the truth of my brother's death, I called upon the prince. I warned him of my duty, saying that the next time I laid eyes on him, I must slay him." Another deep breath that reeked of sadness. "We parted amiably, with the regret of men who could have been as close as brothers under other, better circumstances."

"He was fortunate you were a mariner who sailed distant seas much of the time."

Minkheper seemed not to hear. "We spent the intervening years far apart. In the rare instances when we inadvertently walked the streets of the same city, we went out of our way to avoid each other. Then fate, or perhaps it was the will of the gods—your gods or mine, I'll never know—placed us both in Buhen, both in that wretched house where Commandant Thuty quartered us. I was forced to avenge my brother, like it or not, and Baket-Amon did nothing to stop me."

Silence descended, accompanying them through the darkness to the edge of the encampment.

"You tried to slay me twice," Bak said.

"I'd heard of your reputation as a hunter of men. I had to make an effort to save myself."

"But you saved my life today."

Minkheper's wry smile was clearly visible in the light reaching out from the nearest fire. His bright hair glowed as if from an inner sun. "I thought I wanted to survive, to reach the lofty rank of admiral for which I've strived for so many long years. In the end, though, faced with a choice of holding my head high or bowing it in shame, I couldn't bring myself to slay a man I've come to like and respect."

Chapter Eighteen

"Look at them." Nebwa rested his hands on either side of the crenel and leaned forward, looking down at the prisoners collected at the base of the towered wall. "You'd think they'd've had enough of fighting, but there they are, squabbling among themselves already."

Bak, standing at the next crenel, eyed two men shouting insults at each other, each backed by allies, men from the same tribe, he guessed. He had long since ceased to be surprised at such behavior. "Hor-pen-Deshret must have a tongue of pure honey to've held his coalition together as long as he did."

"Even if he had the freedom to do so, he'd not form another very soon. The men of the desert still treat him with respect, so say the guards—in the heat of battle, he proved himself a more than able warrior—but now they listen to him with caution."

"They've learned a valuable lesson."

"Unfortunately, their memories are short."

The two friends stood in amiable silence, watching the confrontation below, well satisfied with the outcome of the previous day's battle. A cool northerly breeze eased the warmth of the morning sun. The smell of drying fish wafted up from the rooftop of a building block outside the wall.

The tribesmen, bedraggled and worn in defeat, squatted in the shade of the fortress wall or milled about on the patch of sand where they were being held, one of the few relatively level spots on the rocky prominence on which the fortress of Askut stood. They were ringed by guards to prevent escape, apprehensive about whatever punishment they might face, worried for their families far out in the desert, making tensions run high and feelings lie close to the surface. To add to their sense of defeat and unease, the walking wounded had been left among them, while the more seriously injured had been carried into the fortress, their fate unknown.

Voices drifted up from the passage within the massive twin-towered main gate, and presently Lieutenant Ahmose and Amonked climbed onto the battlements. The latter, unaccustomed to the long ladders used in exterior defenses for ease of removal in case of attack, stepped onto the rooftop with obvious relief. Ahmose followed with an agility that attested to his many years in the garrisons of Kemet. The pair strode along the broad walkway atop the wall to join Bak and Nebwa on the imposing tower that formed the sharpest corner of the roughly triangular stronghold.

Amonked raised his staff of office in greeting, scanned the panorama spread out before him, and smiled as if all was right with the world. "You may have to lower me down that wretched tower with a rope, but the view from up here is spectacular enough to make the humiliation worthwhile."

The genial smile faded, replaced by a gravity befitting the inspector. He studied the fortress's commanding position on the island, the immense expanse of landscape visible all around, and the water flowing on all sides, a moat provided by the gods. The island was little more than a gigantic rock on which pockets of earth supported trees, brush, and a few hard-won garden plots. A place easy to defend and difficult to assault. Yet, like Buhen and the other fortresses along the Belly of Stones, it had fallen more than once in the past, when official neglect had left it poorly manned, its too few troops abandoned.

Across the western channel, the caravan could be seen,

reduced in size by distance. The donkeys, returned from their island refuge, grazed on the trampled weeds and grass south of the encampment. The piles of foodstuffs and equipment which had proven such useful obstacles during the fighting had been redistributed in preparation for the next segment of the journey south, the long march to Semna.

"Have you and Lieutenant Horhotep finished your inspection, sir?" Nebwa asked.

Bak resisted a smile. Since fighting at Amonked's side, what had remained of the troop captain's resentment had melted away and his use of the word "sir" was a true sign of respect.

"We have, and I must admit I'm impressed. At least half the space inside these walls is unused, a veritable garbage dump, but the small force here has made the utmost use of the remainder."

"We do what we can, sir," Ahmose said pedantically.

Amonked looked down at the prisoners and his smile faded. "What shall we do with those men?"

Bak queried Nebwa with a glance. He was not sure if the question was rhetorical or genuine. The troop captain shrugged, as mystified as he.

"I believe all threat of a coalition has been banished for some time," Bak said, assuming the inspector truly wanted their counsel. "Hor-pen-Deshret has lost credibility. Thanks to him, there's not much likelihood that any other man who covets riches and power will be able to lure men from the desert in numbers anywhere near those we faced yesterday." Ever mindful of Ahmose's mission and their sovereign's wish to tear the army from the Belly of Stones, he added, "For how long we can lay down our guard, I make no prediction."

"Even if tempted, the tribesmen would refuse," Nebwa added. "At least, in the near future. Too many men are dead and injured, leaving too many families alone and hungry, women and children and the aged who must now be fed by the more fortunate among them."

Amonked walked to a crenel and looked at the men whose fate he held in his hands. "By rights, we should send to Waset all who are well enough to travel, offering them as servants to the royal house and the mansion of the lord Amon."

"We'd need extra men, at least a company of spearmen, to guard them on the journey north," Ahmose said, "and we can't keep them here while we await the arrival of troops from some distant garrison. We've no supplies to spare, and our next shipment of grain won't come until long after the harvest in Kemet. Without that, we've nothing to trade locally for the more perishable fruits and vegetables we'd need."

Eyeing the patchwork of fields along the river, Amonked asked, "Could not the captives help with the harvest, thereby earning their keep?"

Nebwa barked out a laugh. "The farmers would subject them to slavery—or, more likely, let them starve."

"What of Semna?" the inspector asked, untroubled by what came close to ridicule.

"It and its sister fortresses sit in a land devoid of life," Ahmose explained. "What food and supplies they don't receive from Kemet, they must get by barter from traveling merchants."

"We can't take them with us on the caravan." Bak said no more, the reasons too obvious to relate, too much like those given for Askut and Semna.

With much to think about and the choices limited, Amonked turned his back on his advisers to pace up and down the walkway, head lowered, hands clasped behind him. Bak rubbed the bandage on his thigh, a poor substitute for scratching the scabbed-over and itchy wound. He knew what he would do, but the decision was not his to make. Nebwa and Ahmose also remained mute, an ordeal if their faces told true.

Amonked soon rejoined the three officers. "I know men in the royal house who would order us to slay the tribesmen." Neither his face nor his voice betrayed what he thought of the idea. "They would say we fought a battle and won it fairly. We've earned the right to cut off their hands and count them."

Bak had heard grizzled veterans tell tales of hundreds upon hundreds of hands submitted to some lofty general in expectation of reward: the gold of valor, a portion of enemy wealth, captives who would make suitable servants. All very well in a major conflict, with king facing king on the field of battle, but here?

"We've fought no war," he said, "only a minor, local skirmish led by a man bent on theft. The taking of hands would be inappropriate, as would the death of all these men." What had he said to Pawah while awaiting the enemy? "This is no local skirmish; men will die." And they had. Many men on both sides.

Amonked flashed him a look of . . . relief? "Shall we set them free?"

Bak stifled a smile. "Other than slay them, sir, which would leave their women and children to walk the desert sands alone and fearful, many to die of starvation and want, I know not what else we can do with them."

"Turn them loose," Nebwa said in his usual blunt manner. "I see no need to wipe out whole families merely to boast that I won a small victory."

Ahmose hastened to second the suggestion. "I can spare enough food to see them on their way and sufficient men to escort them into the desert."

"So be it." Amonked, seemingly unaware of their relief, leaned into the crenel and his eyes settled on a dozen or so men seated in the shade slightly apart from the rest. The fallen head of the enemy coalition and the surviving members of his tribal unit. "What of Hor-pen-Deshret?"

"Now there's a man whose hand I'd gladly take," Nebwa growled, scowling at his longtime foe.

"He can't be set free," Ahmose stated. "He fled once into the desert, and here he is again. As certain as I am of the lord Re's return tomorrow, I know he'd come another day."

"I suggest you take him to Kemet," Bak said. "His presence in the royal house should pacify our sovereign for our failure to enslave or slay the rest." He had heard that Maatkare Hatshepsut enjoyed seeing powerful men kneeling low before her, their foreheads on the floor. A tale he deemed unwise to repeat to her cousin.

Amonked's eyes twinkled, as if he had read the thought. "Give him an hour alone, time enough to weigh his guilt with no friends or allies to offer support, then bring him before me in Lieutenant Ahmose's office."

"Hor-pen-Deshret. Horus of the Desert." Amonked sat stiff and straight on Ahmose's low-backed chair, which had been made as comfortable as possible, thanks to several thick pillows the lieutenant's wife had brought. As it had no arms, he rested one hand on a plump thigh and held his baton of office in the other. "Don't you think the name a bit presumptuous?"

"To you, perhaps." The captive chief tossed his head in a superior manner. "To you, a man who has no understanding of the desert and those of us who thrive in its barren wastes."

Rather than dropping to his knees as he should have, the tribesman stood tall and proud, unbowed by captivity, facing Maatkare Hatshepsut's cousin as if standing before an equal. He had been allowed to bathe and don clean clothing. One of his two guards, who stood a few paces behind him, had given him—in an instant of good humor or sarcasm—a brownish feather to replace the red one he had lost. His broken arm had been bound within the bark of a slender tree and bandaged to hold it close to his chest. It was a clean break, the garrison physician had said, and should heal straight and strong.

Nebwa snorted, drawing the prisoner's eyes to him, Ahmose, and Bak, standing at Amonked's right hand. With a cynical smile, the tribesman bowed his head to Bak, acknowledging the man who had laid him low and at the same time making light of the feat.

"I mean to release all those men you drew to your side with vain promises of wealth and glory." Amonked maintained a regal bearing, as if born a prince destined to sit upon the throne. "With you no longer among them, I doubt they'll form another coalition of tribes."

"Set me free and I'll see that they don't."

Amonked raised an eyebrow. "Are you pleading for mercy, Hor-pen-Deshret?"

"Never!" The tribesman raised his chin high. "I'm offering myself as an intermediary between my people and yours."

"You wish to serve as an envoy?" Amonked chuckled. "Have you not faced the fact that you're our prisoner?"

"I'm a true falcon of the desert. Captivity would not suit me."

Amonked wiped every trace of emotion from his face and stared at the proud tribesman standing before him. Not until Hor-pen-Deshret's haughty smile began to look forced did he speak. "I mean to take you to Waset to stand before our sovereign, Maatkare Hatshepsut. If she chooses to spare your life . . . Well, she can be whimsical at times, so I've no way of predicting her decision." Amonked stared again at the man standing before him, feigning contemplation. "This much I can tell you: if she's sufficiently impressed with your manly appearance and demeanor, she'll not merely allow you to live, but you'll be a pampered guest within the royal house."

Hope flared in Hor-pen-Deshret's face.

"Seeing your vast abundance of pride, she may even take you with her each day to the hall of appearances, showing you off as she would a favored pet."

The two guards snickered.

Hor-pen-Deshret exploded, fury suffusing his face. With

a growl of rage, he leaped toward Amonked. Bak lunged, shoving him aside. Nebwa grabbed his sound arm, jerked it high up behind him, and forced him to his knees. The guards came to life, hurrying forward to do their duty.

"I won't be made to look the fool!" the tribesman shouted. "Take my life. Hang me from the prow of your greatest warship. Treat me as the warrior I am."

"Our sovereign must be given something to show for the battle we fought," Nebwa said.

Amonked leaned forward, the better to make his point. "Do you wish her, in the depths of anger because I presumed to let you and all your men walk free, to send her armies into the desert to slay every man they come upon, take into captivity their women and children, and take their flocks to Kemet to be sacrificed to our gods?"

"You have that wretched sailor, Captain Minkheper, the man who slew Prince Baket-Amon. Will she not be content with him?" Through the defiance, an edge of sullenness crept into Hor-pen-Deshret's voice.

"Minkheper must be taken to Ma'am, where he'll stand before the viceroy. Baket-Amon's widow must see him charged with her husband's death and she must see him die for it. Only then will she willingly bend a knee to our sovereign."

"So I stand alone."

"You've done enough harm, Hor-pen-Deshret. You must pay."

"I'd rather die than play pet to your sovereign. To any woman."

"Either you submit to her or you'll be impaled, a long and agonizing death, I've been told."

The tribal chief stared at Amonked, made speechless by the force of his words. Seeing no hint of forgiveness on the inspector's face, no sign that he would relent, the tribesman's eyes slid away and his shoulders slumped. Bak sorrowed at the once-brave warrior's downfall, but he could not be allowed to rise again, to steal peace and tranquillity from the land of Wawat for many years to come.

"We'll stay another day before we move on to Semna." Amonked stopped midway along the sloping rock-strewn path that linked the main gate and the river. "The very thought of treading the desert trail so soon is abhorrent."

Bak and Nebwa, following in his wake, stopped with him. The trio looked across the narrow channel toward the west bank. Men and women toiled in the fields that had been trampled in the battle, salvaging what they could. Animals grazed on the wild grasses and brush along the irrigation ditches and on the higher reaches. A peaceful bucolic scene that made one forget that violence had reigned less than twenty-four hours earlier.

"If you're to complete your task, you must travel on sooner or later," Nebwa said.

"Sooner rather than later, I fear." Amonked sighed. "I've told Nefret that she must remain here. She, her maid, and my dog. I see no reason to drag any of them upriver. I plan to leave behind most of the furniture and other objects we brought along. With no pavilion for shelter and no amenities to speak of, Nefret would suffer intensely, feeling inordinately vulnerable and fearing every small sound in the night."

"A wise decision, sir." Bak glanced back at the high towered wall rising above them and the massive gate at the upper end of the path. "She seems to get on well with Ahmose's wife."

They walked on, descending the path to the river and the skiff Ahmose had loaned them for the duration of their stay. Amonked strode past the boat to stand at the water's edge. The smell of fresh-cut clover wafted across the gentle swells like a perfume of the gods. The inspector seemed not to know what to say, and his failure to speak stifled Bak's power of speech and Nebwa's.

Finally he turned to face the two officers. "I've sent a

complete report to Commandant Thuty, as you know, and another to the vizier. You saw the courier off yourself." Giving the pair before him a searching look, the inspector added carefully, "I see no immediate reason for you to return to Buhen—unless you choose to."

Bak threw him a surprised look. "Are you suggesting we remain with the caravan, sir?"

"I've talked with Lieutenant Horhotep and he agrees that the inspection party is sorely in need of your expertise and good sense."

Nebwa looked incredulous. "Horhotep agrees?"

Amonked's mouth twitched, betraying a smile. "I could issue an order that you travel on with us, but I'd rather not force you against your will."

"What of Captain Minkheper?" Bak asked. "We expected to escort him to Buhen."

"He can remain here, under guard."

"I suppose we could take him with us. His task remains undone. He has yet to see the river between here and Semna."

A far-off honking drew Amonked's eyes toward a formation of wild geese, dark spots flying north high above the river. "He's convinced, as I am, that the rapids below Iken run for too long a distance and are too mighty to be breached. He's preparing a report to explain the conclusion. Our sovereign will have to be satisfied with that."

Bak had heard many times of Maatkare Hatshepsut's insistence on having her way, whether or not the object or deed she desired was the best choice or even made sense. He himself had been the victim of her wrath. He had to admire Amonked, who seemed untroubled by the thought of facing her with news she did not wish to hear.

His thoughts leaped back to the inspector's suggestion that he and Nebwa remain with the caravan. As far as he was concerned the trip upriver would be no hardship. With Imsiba in charge of the Medjays at Buhen, they were in good hands. The journey would give him an opportunity to visit garrisons he had never had a chance to see, and he could make good use of the additional time to prepare for his appearance with Minkheper before the viceroy. His friend, on the other hand, was a man with responsibilities. He was second-in-command of Buhen, accountable for the well-being and training of the men in the garrison, and he was a devoted husband and father.

Nebwa must have guessed Bak's thoughts, for his eyes began to twinkle and he assumed a pose of exaggerated severity. "I haven't taken a look at the fortresses south of here for over two years. It's about time I did."

"So you see," Bak said, "you'll remain at Askut while we're gone. We'll stop by on our way north to pick you up. You, Hor-pen-Deshret, and Nefret."

Minkheper formed a crooked smile, one of forced humor. "I'd hoped to see the Belly of Stones in its entirety. Did you have to snare me before we reached Semna?"

Bak occupied a campstool beside the portable bed on which the captain sat. The room, given fresh air and light by two small, high windows, was located on the second floor of the commander's residence. Of a good size and opening onto a central courtyard, built to serve as a room for lofty guests in a fortress seldom visited by anyone of high status, it was used for storage by Ahmose's wife. She had provided the bed to acknowledge Minkheper's rank but at his urging, had shoved woven reed chests, tall wine jars and beer vats, and baskets filled with imperishable food-stuffs against the wall. The smell of spices mingled with onions and wine and grain, tickling Bak's nose.

"Would that you'd never offended the lady Maat, Min-kheper." He studied the prisoner, unable to understand and all the sadder for it. "I see you as a good and brave man, one who slew another good man to appease a god I know not, to follow a custom foreign to me. I'd set you free if I could, exile you to a distant land. But, like you, I must obey the will of my gods. The lady Maat. The lord Amon. All the deities of Kemet great and lesser."

Minkheper ran his fingers through his sunny hair, tried another smile. "Believe me, if I could repeat that wretched morning in Buhen, if I could once again glimpse Baket-Amon standing in the street, I'd close my eyes and turn away."

"I think you too upright and honest to ignore the demands of your god."

"Don't place me on a pedestal, Lieutenant. I'm a man and nothing more."

Bak eyed the captain, his thoughts tumbling. How best to ask the question that would give him an answer he was not sure he wanted to hear? "Before his death, I pleaded with Baket-Amon to go to Amonked, to tell him of the need for our army to remain in Wawat. He refused, saying his past had come back to taunt him. I assume he meant you."

"No doubt he did." Minkheper glanced toward the door, where a pretty young servant was sweeping the courtyard, all the while humming a merry tune. "He saw me at the harbor, so he said, when I made a last inspection to assure myself that our ships would have a secure mooring while we traveled upriver."

"You were in command of the fleet, but you were also a member of the inspection party. Did he guess you were staying at the house where they were quartered?"

"He wasn't surprised to find me there." The captain could not help but notice Bak's troubled expression, and quickly guessed the cause. "Did he come to see Amonked to plead your case? I can't say with certainty. I only know that I heard a commotion in the street and went to the door to learn the cause. While I stood there, listening to the young men of Buhen ridicule our sailors, I saw him standing at the far corner of the block, looking toward the house. Whether or not he meant to approach before I appeared, I know not."

"I've wondered time and time again if I brought about his death. Now I suppose I'll never know."

"Let me put it this way: Instead of walking away when he saw me, as most men would when under threat, he came forward."

Bak gave him a sharp look. "He was convinced you'd follow him, I'd guess, and thought it best to face you then and there."

"We were preparing to sail south to Kor. I hadn't the time."

That Bak could understand. As a man determined to attain the rank of admiral, Minkheper might well have set aside his personal mission. "He chose to come forward, but did he enter the building by choice?"

"He asked if I knew of a place of privacy." Minkheper stood up and walked to the door. Turning his back on the sunlit court, he stood in the portal, making his face hard to see. "I bade him go inside, into the room where you discovered his body."

"He invited death?"

"He walked into the room, looked around, and nodded his approval. Then he just stood there. Waiting." Minkheper's voice wavered. "I asked if he had come, intending to die. He said he could no longer tolerate the suspense, the uncertainty of never knowing which day would be his last. He said the death of the child in Thutnofer's house of pleasure, the slaying of my brother, and even the effort of living life to its fullest had stolen the heart from him." The captain paused, sucked in a tortured breath. "He'd lived his life to the utmost, he said, sired an heir he looked upon with pride, and had given his people prosperity and peace. What more could a man leave behind?"

"The prince took his own life, with you as his instrument of death," Bak said, appalled.

Minkheper left the doorway, an ironic smile on his face. "So I concluded, but too late."

Bak stared at the man standing before him. A man of

courage and kindness, honest and true. A man who, if allowed to reach the lofty rank of admiral, would serve the land of Kemet with honor and aptitude. Never before had he snared a slayer with so much regret. Yet he could not set him free. Justice must be done, order restored.

Bak returned to the commander's residence to prepare reports on his discovery of Baket-Amon's slayer and the defense of the caravan under Nebwa's command. The latter, a favor to the troop captain, whose stout-hearted effort to learn to read and write had borne small fruit, was the lengthier of the two and took more time. Many men had to be commended, their exploits described in the hope of appropriate reward.

He sat alone and undisturbed beneath a lean-to on the roof of the residence, shaded from the sun's heat, cooled by a breeze that stirred the air, sipping a local beer that smelled as harsh as it tasted. Ahmose had told him he would learn to like the brew. He was glad he would not remain at Askut long enough to develop a taste for it.

As the sun dipped below the western horizon, he scrawled the last symbol on the papyrus. Not long after, while cleaning his reed pen and scribal pallet, he heard Nebwa cross the triangular square between the house and the main gate. He quickly rolled the scroll, tied it with a cord, and impressed his symbol of office on the mud seal he affixed to the knot. Hurrying down the stairs, he met his friend and Amonked in the second-floor courtyard.

"Ah, there you are, Lieutenant." Amonked, his demeanor serious, purposeful, glanced into Ahmose's private reception room, which was smaller than that of Commandant Thuty's and considerably neater. "Where's Lieutenant Ahmose? I must speak with the three of you."

Noting the inspector's manner, his peremptory tone, Bak flung a querying glance at Nebwa. He got a shake of the head in return and a look that said he, too, was baffled.

Ahmose emerged from a rear door, rubbing his hands in

satisfaction. "You've come. Good. My wife's prepared a feast fit for our sovereign, but we've time for a bowl of wine before it's ready."

Without a word, Amonked walked into the reception room and sat down on the chair, which had been carried upstairs to the private quarters especially for his comfort. Ahmose gave the two officers from Buhen a startled look, got Nebwa's shrug in return, and led the way inside. When the three were seated on stools and a servant had handed out bowls of dark red wine that smelled of spices, the inspector said:

"You're puzzled by my attitude, as you've every right to be. We're here to celebrate our victory, yet I've come with a purpose of great and serious import."

Bak set his bowl on the floor by his feet, his taste for the wine momentarily lost. "Has something happened, sir, that makes our victory look small by comparison?"

"No." Amonked sipped from his bowl, nodded approval. "We will celebrate, but first things first." He sipped again as if reluctant to voice what he suspected his listeners might not wish to hear. "I've thought long and hard about Horpen-Deshret, about the fate of a man who places his own self-interest above that of all who look to him for leadership."

"His fate?" Nebwa demanded. "Have you not already decided to take him to Waset?"

"I fear we must allow the wretched criminal to escape."

Bak stared, his power of speech stolen by shock.

"What!" Nebwa roared.

Ahmose looked stricken. "You can't mean that, sir."

"I can and I do."

"But, sir," Ahmose said, "he'll come back, just as he did this time. He'll make the people's lives a misery, and we'll once again have to face him on the field of battle."

Amonked was unmoved. "He knows that no army he gathers, no matter how large, can defeat the might of Kemet. And he knows impalement will be the price he'll pay when he's caught."

"He'll have nothing to fear if the army is torn from this land," Bak pointed out.

Amonked formed an enigmatic little smile and bowed his head slightly in Bak's direction. "Shall I go to Maatkare Hatshepsut and tell her of the battle we fought, of the many enemy dead and their captured chieftain, of small groups of wandering nomads too downtrodden to do more than pilfer when they bring their flocks to the river? Or shall I tell her of our hard-won battle, of the wandering nomads who covet the riches traveling south to Kemet, and a powerful chieftain free to strike again?"

Bak began to understand. At least he thought he did. Nebwa and Ahmose stared at the inspector as if afraid their hearing had failed them.

Amonked wove his fingers together across his stomach and eyed the trio one after the other. "I cannot, in all good conscience, recommend to our sovereign that she leave the army on the Belly of Stones if the major threat to peace and security is no longer here."

"The local people will be incensed," Bak said.

"Which would they prefer? A distant threat of Hor-pen-Deshret far out on the desert, living among men weary of his vain promises? Or the very real possibility that the army might be torn from this land?"

Bak had come to like and trust Amonked, to see him as a far stronger man than Nofery had thought him to be, but would he maintain that strength in Waset, facing the all-powerful woman who sat on the throne? Bak saw indecision on Nebwa's face and Ahmose's. They had similar doubts. He looked again at Amonked, at the short, plump man with thinning hair he had seen fighting at Nebwa's side during the battle. He decided to take a chance on the man he had come to know.

"Hor-pen-Deshret can't escape until our caravan is well on its way to Semna," he said, "and he must free himself

at a time when the fortress of Askut is dangerously undermanned."

Ahmose looked relieved that the decision had been made
by someone other than him. "Half my troops are already
gone, escorting the tribesmen into the desert."

Nebwa, looking less certain, said nothing.

"You can work out the details later," Amonked said.
"But remember: whatever you do must seem normal and
natural. I want no blame to fall on any of us."

Bak noted the inspector's inclusion of himself as one
who might shoulder the blame.

"I see no reason to discuss this conversation with Commandant Thuty or anyone else," Amonked went on. "Even
Hor-pen-Deshret must be made to believe his escape is the
will of his gods."

"Yes, sir," the three officers chorused.

Bak thought of the tribal chieftain and Captain Minkheper, comparing their offenses, their fate. Hor-pen-
Deshret, whose vile crimes far exceeded that of the naval
officer, would be set free, while Minkheper would die. The
punishment in no way matched the crimes.

"Sir. Captain Minkheper helped teach the drovers and
guards to use their weapons to best advantage and he fought
valiantly throughout the battle. If not for him, I'd have died
at the hands of an enemy warrior. Must he be made to
suffer while Hor-pen-Deshret walks away alive and well?"

Amonked eyed him curiously. "What would you suggest,
Lieutenant? Baket-Amon's wife will demand justice."

Bak spoke carefully, thinking out his plea as he spoke.
A plea that would make sense when Amonked repeated it
to Maatkare Hatshepsut. "By insisting on Minkheper's
death, as she's sure to do, the prince's widow will be ex-
ercising her will over that of our sovereign, thereby bringing the land of Kemet to its knees. Maatkare Hatshepsut is
a proud woman. Is that the precedent she'll wish to set?"

"Go on," Amonked said, nodding. Whether in agreement
or merely understanding, Bak could not begin to guess.

"Though the captain obeyed the gods of his homeland, he's a true man of Kemet. He's lived in Waset and Mennufer most of his life and he loves our land as no other. To banish him, to tear him forever from the place he calls his home, to force him to die and be entombed elsewhere, would be to tear the heart from his soul."

Amonked sat unmoving, his eyes on Bak, his face empty of emotion. At last he said, "I'll speak with Viceroy Inebny and with Baket-Amon's wife. Then I'll take Captain Minkheper to our sovereign in Waset and plead for his exile."

Bak offered a silent prayer to the lord Amon, a prayer that Amonked would be strong enough to press his case and win, that justice would be served.

Epilogue

Four weeks later

"So they're sailing tomorrow," Nebwa said. "I shall miss them."

Bak, too, regretted the parting. "I never thought I'd count any of them as friends, but I've come to like them all."

With the troop captain in the lead, they hurried up the stone stairway to the second floor of the commandant's residence. Crossing the courtyard, they stepped over toys and around a baby nestled on a soft pillow in a large flattish bowl. From a rear room, they could hear Thuty's wife, her voice raised in anger, berating a servant. The odor of burned onions permeated the air, attesting to a mishap in the kitchen, where the women of the household were preparing a feast for the inspector and his party.

At the door of the commandant's private reception room, they saw that Amonked had arrived ahead of them. Seated with Thuty amid a clutter of toys, stools, and baskets filled with scrolls, he occupied an armless wooden chair that looked suspiciously like the one Nofery had acquired from Waset. Had the commandant, who would not give up his own chair for anyone of less importance than the viceroy, borrowed her treasure in recognition of his guest's lofty position?

"I must admit I'm looking forward to going home,"

Amonked said, smiling at the newcomers. "To seeing my wife again, to sleeping in my own bedchamber, to having at my beck and call servants and scribes who fill my days with ease and comfort."

"I regret our inability to provide such luxuries," Thuty said in a wry voice.

"I'm in no way being critical, Thuty. I understand the limitations of distance and difficult passage." Amonked gave the younger officers a satisfied smile. "I should. After all, I trod many miles through this land of Wawat along a desert trail unfit for any but the most hardy—man and beast alike."

"Frankly, sir, you surprised us all." Bak, pulling up a stool, tempered his words with a smile. "When first we saw you, we thought you'd never forsake your carrying chair. Instead, you seldom used it, allowing Thaneny to ride instead."

"Thaneny." Amonked's demeanor grew sorrowful. "He, like Sennefer, wanted to see the world beyond Waset. Should I feel glad I allowed him a few weeks of enjoyment, or should I regret for the rest of my life that I brought him along?"

Bak could think of no answer other than to point out that Thaneny had been spared a lifetime of yearning for a woman who treated him with disdain. Still, was not the world a better place to dwell than the netherworld? He kept the thought to himself.

Nebwa, clearing toys from a low bench and drawing it forward, cut through the uncomfortable silence. "I, for one, would never have guessed you'd one day stand at my side, dagger in hand, holding off a contingent of thieving tribesmen. You never once mentioned you knew how to use that or any other weapon—and with skill, too."

The inspector patted his stomach. "I wasn't always this plump, you know."

"I wish you were returning to Waset with more to show for your effort," Thuty said, frowning at Bak and Nebwa, clearly referring to the many men they had allowed to return to the desert and the escape of Hor-pen-Deshret.

Amonked raised a hand, halting the reproach. "I'll shoulder the blame if blame is to be had. It won't be the first time I've stood before our sovereign empty-handed, nor will it be the last."

"I pray she doesn't hold it against you when you recommend that our army continue to occupy the fortresses along the Belly of Stones. You will make that recommendation, won't you?" The commandant seemed never to hear often enough the reassurance he sought.

"With Hor-pen-Deshret free, I can do no less." Amonked's eyes met Thuty's with no hint of deceit.

Bak and Nebwa exchanged a conspiratorial glance. Thuty noticed, gave them a thoughtful, rather suspicious look. He had the good sense to remain silent.

Bak stood with Nebwa and Seshu atop the towered gate that opened onto the central quay, an ideal vantage point from which to watch the departing flotilla. Thuty, standing on the quay with the priests of the lord Horus of Buhen and the same local princes who had welcomed the inspector so long ago, waved a farewell. Amonked, on the deck of his ship, returned the salute as his sailors stowed away the gangplank. Imsiba stood behind the official party at the head of the guard of honor Thuty had deemed appropriate for the departing official. The day was bright and clear, the breeze sporadic and changeable in direction. The air smelled clean and fresh, unaccountably free of dust.

The terraces at the base of the fortress wall were jammed with people, every soldier in the garrison jostling for space with the civilians who dwelt within and with many dozens of people from the nearby villages. Rumors abounded all along the Belly of Stones that the inspector would recommend that the army remain. Amonked had boarded his ship amid cheers and whistles and clapping, an uproar of gratitude and good feeling.

"Amonked is a fine man," Nebwa said. "It's a pity he's not in a position to inherit the throne."

Bak watched the inspector's ship swing slowly away from the quay. The song of the oarsmen and the beat of the accompanying drum carried across the water. "Sometimes an adviser who stands behind the throne, whispering in a ruler's ear, has more power than the ruler herself."

"According to Nofery," Seshu reminded them, "he's a follower, not a leader."

Nebwa grinned. "So am I, but that's not prevented me from rising through the ranks."

"Whether he'd be a good ruler or a bad one is of no significance," Bak said. "Menkheperre Thutmose will one day sit on the throne, and he'll be a remarkable king."

Seshu laughed. "Do I detect a bias in his favor, Lieutenant?"

"Do you see what I see?" Nebwa chortled. "Amonked holding out his hand, inviting Nefret onto the deck with him. I was sure he'd have nothing more to do with her, that he was prepared to send her back to her father."

"Maybe he's forgiven her for all her complaints." Seshu eyed Sennefer's ship, following Amonked's out of the harbor, its colorful banners flapping in the breeze. "We didn't hear a word out of her all the way north from Askut."

Bak recalled the quiet, solemn-faced young woman who had kept very much to herself from the day she rejoined the caravan. If Amonked had talked with her, making peace, he had not done so until they arrived at Buhen. "She said nothing to me, but according to Sennefer, Thaneny's death distressed her greatly."

"And so it should," Seshu said with feeling.

"I'd wager Lieutenant Ahmose's wife taught her a thing or two," Nebwa said. "She and the other women stuck on that godforsaken island."

Bak's eyes shifted to the great cargo ship making a smooth exit from its mooring place—thanks to the captain of the vessel owned by Imsiba's wife. An experienced ship's master, he stood on the forecastle, shouting orders, easing the hull away from the quay. Sitamon had volunteered his services and Amonked had readily accepted, recalling the vessel's less than graceful and potentially dangerous arrival at Buhen.

Amonked's ship, he saw, had begun to swing northward for its downstream voyage. The drummer beat a quicker tattoo, the oarsmen followed with a louder, faster song that paced the swifter strokes of their oars. Pawah ran across the deck to stand with his master and the concubine. He waved farewell to Commandant Thuty and his party on the quay. Amonked pointed upward, toward the men on the battlements. The boy waved again, this time with the verve of one bidding good-bye to men he considered close friends. The inspector followed suit.

The trio stood at the railing for some time, looking back at Buhen as if reluctant to see the last of a place to which they would probably never return. When they finally turned away, tiny figures in the distance, Amonked placed one arm around Nefret's slender waist and another around Pawah's thin shoulders.

For all their sakes, Bak prayed the closeness would continue through eternity.

AN ARCHEOLOGIST DIGS UP MURDER IN THE ALAN GRAHAM MYSTERIES BY

MALCOLM SHUMAN

THE MERIWETHER MURDER
79424-1/$5.99 US/$7.99 Can

BURIAL GROUND
79423-3/$5.50 US/$7.50 Can

ASSASSIN'S BLOOD
80485-9/$5.99 US/$7.99 Can

And Coming Soon
PAST DYING
80486-7/$5.99 US/$7.99 Can